The Arab Renaissance:
A Bilingual Anthology of the Nahda

The Arab Renaissance:
A Bilingual Anthology
of the Nahda

EDITED BY

Tarek El-Ariss

ASSISTANT EDITORS

Anthony Edwards and
Anna Ziajka Stanton

The Modern Language Association of America
New York   2018

© 2018 by the Modern Language Association of America
All rights reserved
Printed in the United States of America

MLA and the MODERN LANGUAGE ASSOCIATION are trademarks
owned by the Modern Language Association of America.
For information about obtaining permission to reprint material from
MLA book publications, send your request by mail
(see address below) or e-mail (permissions@mla.org).

Library of Congress Cataloging-in-Publication Data

Names: El-Ariss, Tarek editor.
Title: The Arab Renaissance : a bilingual anthology of the Nahda / edited by
 Tarek El-Ariss ; assistant editors, Anthony Edwards and Anna Ziajka Stanton.
Description: New York : The Modern Language Association of America,
 2018. | Series: Texts and translations ; 30 | In English and Arabic. | Includes
 bibliographical references.
Identifiers: LCCN 2017054071 (print) | LCCN 2017055975 (ebook) |
 ISBN 9781603293082 (EPUB) | ISBN 9781603293099 (Kindle) |
 ISBN 9781603293037 (paperback)
Subjects: LCSH: Arabic literature—19th century—Translations into English. |
 Arabic literature—20th century—Translations into English. | Arabic
 literature—19th century. | Arabic literature—20th century. | BISAC:
 LITERARY COLLECTIONS / Middle Eastern. | POETRY / Anthologies
 (multiple authors). | FICTION / Anthologies (multiple authors).
Classification: LCC PJ7694.E1 (ebook) | LCC PJ7694.E1 A725 2018 (print) |
 DDC 892.7/08—dc23
LC record available at https://lccn.loc.gov/2017054071

ISSN 1079-252x
ISSN 1079-2538

Portions of the introduction to and translation of Hasan al-'Attar's "*Maqama*
of the French" and 'Ali Mubarak's "'Alam al-Din" are based on chapters 2
and 4 of Shaden M. Tageldin's *Disarming Words: Empire and the Seductions
of Translation in Egypt* (2011) and are reproduced with the permission of
the University of California Press.

Excerpts from and translations of *Seventy: A Life Story*, appearing in Mikhail
Naimi, *Sab'un: Hikayat 'Umr, 1889–1959*, vol. 1, are printed with the permission
of Nadeem Naimy.

Excerpts from and translations of *Al-Sufur wa-al-Hijab*, by Nazim Zeineddine,
are printed with the permission of Said Zeineddine.

Cover illustration: *The Reader*, by Silwan Ibrahim,
acrylic on canvas, 2013, Beirut, Lebanon.

Published by The Modern Language Association of America
85 Broad Street, suite 500, New York, New York 10004-2434
www.mla.org

CONTENTS

Contents

Part 2: Language and Civilization

Jirmanus Farhat (1670–1732)   71

Introduced by Kristen Brustad and translated by Anthony
Edwards
FROM *Issues Desired by Students Required*
بحث المطالب وحث الطالب

Ya'qub Sannu' (1839–1912)   83

Introduced and translated by Ziad Fahmy
FROM *The Egyptian Molière and What He Endures*
موليير مصر وما يقاسيه

'Abdallah al-Nadim (1845–96)   104

Introduced and translated by Benjamin Koerber
FROM *Raillery and Reproach*
التنكيت والتبكيت

Hasan al-'Attar (c. 1766–1835)   117

Introduced and translated by Shaden M. Tageldin
FROM *"Maqama* of the French"
مقامة الفرنسيس

'Ali Mubarak (c. 1823–93)   128

Introduced and translated by Shaden M. Tageldin
FROM *'Alam al-Din*
علم الدين

Part 3: Transnational Connections

Esther Moyal (1873–1948)   141

Introduced and translated by Lital Levy
"Is It Befitting of Women to Demand the Rights of Men?"
Introduction to *Biography of Émile Zola*
هل للنساء أن يطلبن كل حقوق الرجال
تاريخ حياة إميل زولا

Part 5: Novels and Novellas

Part 6: Poetic Expressions

ACKNOWLEDGMENTS

On 21 December 2009 I received from the MLA a message inviting me to undertake this project, and I am most grateful to Margit Longbrake, who sent that message. At the MLA I also thank James Hatch, who saw the project through to its completion, and Michael Kandel and the editorial team, who helped make this anthology a book to be proud of. Without my assistant editors, this project would never have been completed. Anthony Edwards came to my rescue like a knight in shining armor; Anna Ziajka Stanton stretched her arm to me as to a drowning man.

I thank all the contributors to this volume for their trust in me and their patience and willingness to introduce, translate, change, edit, and revise. I also thank Jens Hanssen, Max Weiss, Samah Selim, Michael Allan, Angela Giordani, Orit Bashkin, Suzanne Kassab, Amal Ghazal, Ilham Khuri-Makdisi, Dima Hamzeh, Hoda El Shakry, Eric Calderwood, Adam Mestyan, and Wail Hassan for their support and excitement about the project.

The support, encouragement, and generosity of my dear friends Aziz and Arwa Shaibani made this project possible. I thank Ussama Makdisi for his gracious engagement with my work and for inviting me to Rice University to discuss this project. I'm also grateful to Muhsin al-Musawi, Moneera al-Ghadeer, Roger Allen, William Granara, Abdel Razzaq Takriti, Samer Ali, Mohammad Salama, Jaroslav Stetkevych, Suzanne Stetkevych, and Frédéric Lagrange for all their help over the years.

In Austin, I thank Yoav Di-Capua, my interlocutor and friend, who read, commented, advised, and appreciated; my heroes Kristen Brustad and Mahmoud al-Batal; my students and colleagues who contributed ideas and feedback throughout; and Radwa al-Barouni, Ghayde Ghrawi, Laura Metzler, and Rawad Wehbe.

At the American University of Beirut, I'm grateful to Nadim Naimy, with whom I took my first *Nahda* class and who granted us permission to publish the selection from the great Mikhail. I'm also grateful to Nadia el-Cheikh, Mahmoud al-Batal, Bilal Orfali, Zeina Halabi, Sonja Mejcher-Atassi, Fawwaz Traboulsi, Rachid al-Daif, Rana Issa, and Hala Auji, who keep the *Nahda* mission alive. I also thank Abdelhalim Jabr and Christine Tohme for practicing the *Nahda* and sustaining it through their work and commitment.

Rana Issa and Helge Jordheim invited me to the Litteraturhuset in Oslo to prelaunch this anthology in the summer of 2017. Jana Traboulsi provided the beautiful brochure that we gave out. I'm also grateful to Gunvor Mejdell, Stephan Guth, Teresa Pepe, Ina Blom, and to all my friends and colleagues in Oslo.

At Central European University, I thank Nadia Al-Bagdadi and Aziz al-Azmeh for their support and engagement.

At Dartmouth College, my new home, I thank Susannah Heschel and Jonathan Smolin, with whom I will continue the *Nahda* project.

In Berlin, the capital of the new Arab renaissance, I'm grateful to Angelika Neuwirth, Georges Khalil, Friederike Pannewick, Barbara Winckler, and Christian Junge for their support and commitment to all things brilliant and Arabic.

For the cover image, I thank Silwan Ibrahim for sharing with us his thoughtful and beautiful *Reader* and Alain Tasso and Tania Haddad for help in obtaining this image.

I dedicate this anthology to two incredible women: Elham Kabbani, who raised me in the shadow of the *Nahda*, and Inaam Kabbani, who keeps the *Nahda* alive.

INTRODUCTION

In his widely circulated essay, *Being Arab*, published in 2004, Samir Kassir, a Lebanese journalist and public intellectual, laments the social and political malaise of the Arabs at the beginning of the twenty-first century. He explains how the term *Arab* became associated with a "negating culture," a "slump," and a "crisis" (xi–xiii). After a brief yet poignant review of different historical periods and political and religious movements, he elaborates on the collapse of the nineteenth-century project of cultural and political modernity, the *Nahda* (نهضة; "Renaissance" or "Awakening"), as a framework for the current crisis. Kassir exclaims, "Forgotten is Muhammad 'Ali's modernization, forgotten is the work of Tanzimat. . . . Forgotten is especially the *Nahda*, except perhaps for a small elite still holding on to the spirit of the Enlightenment" (41). All that is left of the *Nahda*, it would seem, is a fading trace and disappearing commitment to the idea of a universal and egalitarian Arab modern age.

The *Nahda* designates the project of Arab cultural and political modernity from the early nineteenth to the early twentieth century. Arab models of nationalism and secularism as well as Islamic revival are attributed to *Nahda* thought and institutions such as linguistic reform and the practice of translation; the emergence of new literary genres such as the novel; the periodical press, journalism, and a new publishing industry; professional associations and salons; a new education system; and, overall, an Enlightenment ideal of knowledge. As such, the *Nahda* ushered in innovative modes of reading and writing, and new social practices of knowledge transmission and transnational connections and political ideas, which, in turn, led to new aesthetics, models of community, and the inauguration of a so-called "modern Arab future." The term *nahda* is derived from the word *nahada* (نهض), which means to "rise" or "stand up vigorously." Starting in the 1850s, thinkers such as Butrus al-Bustani suggested that the Arabs were slowly emerging from their decadence (انحطاط; inhitat) and ushering in civilization (تمدّن; tamaddun)—see his "The Culture of the Arabs Today" in this volume. In this sense, the *Nahda* refers to an age of vitality that came after an age of torpor, sleep, or even death. This framework has contributed to the perception of the *Nahda* as that which put an end to a political and cultural slumber under an Ottoman rule that lasted four hundred years (from the sixteenth to the twentieth century). Ottoman rule is viewed from the perspective of the *Nahda* as a form of Arab Dark Ages; thought, culture, and social and political institutions were stunted or suppressed because of the primacy of the Turkish language and the corrupt and autocratic rule by the Turks over different ethnic and religious communities—Arabs, Greeks, Armenians, and Kurds, to name a few. Ushering in a revolution in the understanding of space and time, the *Nahda* foregrounded the advent of national consciousness, which took shape through people's awareness of their rights, aspirations, and place in history. Coupled with colonial interventions and the gradual erosion of Ottoman rule, the *Nahda* led to the emergence of a new regional map made up of nation-states such as Iraq and Syria.

Despite the chaotic unfolding of the uprisings against dictatorial regimes that have gripped the Arab world starting in 2010, in some cases degenerating into sectarian and tribal strife and challenging the very existence of Arab nation-states, these uprisings have reconstituted a stage for democratic practice, reinvigorating notions of rights, political participation, and youth power. What came to be known as the Arab Spring generated initially much hope for a new *Nahda* that would put an end to another age of decadence or torpor characterized by authoritarianism, corruption, and a culture of defeat that set in following the 1967 Arab defeat against Israel. The public debates and the circulation of texts, images, and ideas online and off, free from the overbearing oversight of the state, were very *Nahda*-like, a demonstration that the *Nahda* continues to haunt the Arab world and shape the interpretive models deployed to account for its transformation.[1] Though the *Nahda* is usually associated with the nineteenth century, its legacy persists, as if something in it has not yet been accomplished or settled. It is from this position of the never actualized but always becoming *Nahda* that we turn to Arabic literature and cultural writings from the nineteenth and early twentieth century in order to understand the place of the *Nahda* in the Arab imaginary by examining it in a comparative framework that goes beyond the Arab world.

The Prevalent *Nahda* Narrative

The general perception of the *Nahda* as an age of enlightenment and modernity meant to bring about progress and civilization in the Arab world resulted from the circulation of books and ideas, technological progress, and accelerated cultural exchange with or direct borrowing from Europe from the nineteenth century onward. The *Nahda* was compared early on with similar historical movements in Europe, such as the Renaissance, that witnessed the rise of nationalism and an artistic and cultural flourishing. Just as the advent of Gutenberg's printing press revolutionized book publication and exchange in the fifteenth century—and eventually undermined royal and Church authority to culminate in the eighteenth century with the French Revolution—the spread of printing presses especially in Egypt and the Levant in the nineteenth century spurred a renaissance, giving rise to new literature and new social and political models. The circulation of ideas, books, and newspapers across the region extended from Iraq and Syria to immigrant communities in North and South America. It contributed to the forging of a modern Arab subjectivity that would be expressed in various cultural forms and linguistic registers. What we call today Modern Standard Arabic, for instance, was in fact invented in the *Nahda*, as authors and thinkers sought to develop a new language that could successfully account for and contain the modern.

The scholarship in the field has generally attributed the *Nahda* to Napoleon's invasion of Egypt in 1798. While George Antonius coins the word "awakening" in 1938, defining the *Nahda* as a vigorous shedding of tradition and autocratic rule, Albert Hourani and Hisham Sharabi both point out that the *Nahda* was in fact a reaction to a European political onslaught, which exposed the cultural and technological retardation of the Ottoman Empire. The defeat of the much-feared Mamluks—decimated by Napoleon's cannons at the foot of the pyramids outside Cairo—best embodies this retardation. The defeat, with others, cast the *Nahda* as the outcome of violence that awoke Arabs from their cultural and historical slumber under Ottoman rule and forced them to forge new social, political, and cultural models in order to reenter world history. Through these new models, the story continues, the Arabs rose as a people with a common language and common past and reclaimed their present and future. Islamism as well as Arab nationalism in its various articulations (including Baathism) are ideological projects that could be traced to this moment of rude awakening.

The perception of the violent encounter with Europe as the *Nahda's* starting point or moment of origin has been complemented with other encounters through travel and cultural exchange known as the "Arab rediscovery of Europe."[2] Muhammad 'Ali Pasha, who seized power in Egypt in 1805 and established a dynasty that would be deposed by an army coup in 1952, initiated a series of exchanges by sending students to France in the 1820s. A key figure in this rediscovery project is Rifa'a Rafi' al-Tahtawi, whose career and writings embody the kinds of transformation that would sweep through the Arab provinces of the Ottoman Empire. Al-Tahtawi, who began his career as an imam at Cairo's center for Islamic learning, al-Azhar, ended up laying the foundations for some of the first modern educational institutions in Egypt after his return from a five-year stay in Paris. While abroad, he read Montesquieu and Voltaire and collaborated with the leading European scholars of language and culture at the time. He worked in translation, publishing key comparative works on European and Arabic cultures and treatises on modern education in Egypt. This Azhar imam turned state bureaucrat engaged in his work the main themes of the Arab encounter with Europe in the nineteenth century. He asserted the compatibility of Islam with progress by rereading the history of Arab-Islamic culture from the perspective of European modernity, reconciling Arab-Islamic conceptions of community with European models of nationalism and liberalism. The love for one's homeland or *watan* (وطن; "fatherland") emerges as a key theme in al-Tahtawi's work. He also translated "civilization" as *tamaddun* (from *madina* [مدينة; "city"]), which "consists in regulating economics, politics, social order, and technological and material development in accordance with an Islamic set of beliefs and ethical standards," leading to the elimination of war and poverty (El-Ariss 54). The concept of civilization or, more precisely, of becoming civilized[3] evolves and eventually incorporates the notion of *taraqqi* (ترقي), which involves processes of material progress and ethical and aesthetic refinement (أدب; adab), thereby framing the Renaissance as the end of barbarity, decadence, and the Arab Dark Ages. The convergence of civilization and patriotism (love for one's homeland) becomes the engine for *Nahda* thought and cultural production.

Rethinking the *Nahda*

The prevalent narrative of the *Nahda* summarized above was constructed and promoted by scholars and historians who ended up prioritizing political confrontation and borrowing from Europe as the path to Arab modernity. This narrative also contributed to the entrenchment of a clear binary between tradition and modernity, between East and West, that has shaped the way Arabs understood and continue to understand their relation to the world. The *Nahda*, then, was something that rose and fell, something that had clear starting and end points and was therefore confined to a historical span that could be studied. Finally, by emphasizing politics and history, this narrative dismissed the role of literature, imagination, and different cultural agents and geographic regions outside Western Europe as sites that have shaped and were shaped by the *Nahda*.

The *Nahda* narrative that this anthology offers, instead, is of a dynamic process, complex and multifaceted, crossing space and time, forged by great minds but also performed by daily and mundane practices, influenced by Arab exchanges and confrontations with Western Europe but never reduced to these exchanges and confrontations. Through a selection of novellas, plays, poems, letters, newspaper and journal ads, and linguistic and philosophical essays, all translated into English for the first time[4] and divided into seven distinct yet interconnected parts, this bilingual anthology focuses on narratives of progress, encounter, and a transnational mind-set linking Arabs to Western Europe but also to Russia, India, and beyond. The *Nahda* appears as a stage for negotiating religious and political authority, social norms, and linguistic and literary conventions, blurring the distinction between novel and travelogue, author and activist, and high art and popular culture. Crossing gender roles, economic divisions, and cultural boundaries, the translated texts in this volume include narratives about the body, technology, commerce, and travel. They align definitions of freedom of action and expression with sophisticated explorations of the nature of art and language, debates about gender equality with critiques of the representation of women in literature, and travel accounts of Europe and Russia with fictional encounters involving homesickness and seduction. Collectively, these texts dispel the perception of the *Nahda* as a homogeneous narrative and time period or a wholesale import of European social and political systems and conceptions of the individual. Rather, the *Nahda* emerges from processes of trial and institution building, fascination with and criticism of European modernity, and systematic incorporation and reassessment of older Arab models of learning and community.[5]

On close examination of *Nahda* texts, we recognize the discourse of progress but also realize its continuity with the Arab-Islamic past, as in al-Tahtawi's work or as in the reading by Muhammad 'Abduh of pre-Islamic poetry alongside European art as he tours Europe and discovers Arabic manuscripts in its great libraries, which is explored in part 3 of this volume. For these *Nahda* authors, there is a sense that civilization is in the air and that they are all taking part in it. Becoming civilized and loving the homeland become the constitutive practices of a trend linked to a belief or perhaps faith in strengthening communal bonds and advancing the nation. The belief or faith doesn't mean that this genre corresponds to the discourse on civilization and nationalism defined and practiced by European counterparts to justify colonial expansion. Rather, civilization and progress are on people's minds in the *Nahda*, and they are writing in the hope of forging an enlightened public and a better society. The translation of civilization as *tamaddun* or *taraqqi* doesn't merely render the French or English word into Arabic but opens it up as well to different meanings, interpretations, and practices that the texts in this anthology were chosen to showcase.

Nahda earnestness and faith in progress is complemented by cynicism and incredulity, by satire and parody of the notion of progress, especially because the discrepancy between *Nahda* discourse and Arab reality was great—as a result of economic, political, and aesthetic factors. Moreover, parody operated as a function of critique intrinsic to *Nahda* writing, which constantly presents yet undermines its borrowing from Europe to achieve progress. In the satirical text by 'Abdallah al-Nadim included in part 2 of this volume, describing how an Egyptian student returns to his parents after studying in France, the student mocks his parents' backward language and food while they mock his Europeanization. In this parody of the Arab rediscovery of Europe genre, the process of becoming civilized is both staged and mocked. But in mocking European progress, al-Nadim also chastises the young man for having forgotten his homeland and language. This ambivalence vis-à-vis the discourse on civilization fluctuates throughout the texts of this volume.

In addition to being the perfect arena for parody and critique, literature is discussed in the *Nahda* as the civilizing tool par excellence. The theories of literature presented in part 4 consider writing and reading novels as acts engaged with entertainment and fantasy but at the same time implicated in social and political projects that will either build the nation or precipitate its demise. Forging the modern subject through narratives of romantic love, *Nahda* literature became an important chapter in the history of emotions. But when reading *Nahda* novels and novellas, we get interpretations that go beyond the binaries of morality/immorality and barbarity/civilization. For instance, Zaynab Fawwaz's story in part 5 is about a love that transgresses social prohibitions and is punished by fate. What starts out as a tale with strong moral values becomes at the end less clear and more complex. In our approach to the *Nahda*, we must not only look at the discourse on morality and the intention of the author but allow ourselves as well to read these texts as we read any work of literature, which is open to interpretation beyond its stated objectives or narrow cultural context. Examining literature in this way enables us to understand how civilization and progress are practiced, tried out, but also critiqued and parodied. Literature does more than represent another culture or another people; it exposes, contests, and frames the way culture is imagined and idealized.

This anthology highlights the role of women in modern Arabic cultural development, integrating their work as constitutive of *Nahda* writing and thought rather than reducing it to a framework defined exclusively by issues of women and gender. Women contributed to a wide range of genres and topics— social justice, international politics, aesthetics, and cultural and linguistic debates. They appear as quintessential *Nahda* agents, discussing gender issues but also writing and reading literature comparatively. The texts chosen in this anthology emphasize their engagement with definitions of the individual but also with the development of the Arabic novel and poetry. In the selection from Mayy Ziyadah in part 7, for instance, a critique of patriarchy overlaps with a discussion of the relation between the Arabic and French languages, between literature and politics, and between eighteenth-century Europe and twentieth-century Egypt and the Levant.

Non-Muslim intellectuals and writers are presented in this volume also in an integrated fashion: they participate in debates

that go beyond the questions of nationalism and secularism
with which they have been traditionally associated. The philo-
sophical and literary works of Arabic-speaking Muslim, Chris-
tian, and Jewish thinkers share similar characteristics and take
up similar issues, which are both local and international. The
Dreyfus affair in France, which arose from anti-Semitic accu-
sations leveled against a French Jewish officer for spying for
Germany in 1887, reverberates throughout the Middle East,
preoccupying the Arab public across the religious and eth-
nic spectrum. While 'Abd al-Qadir al-Qabbani reports on the
affair by criticizing French nationalism and religious fanaticism
(in part 3), 'Abd al-Rahman al-Kawakibi refers to the affair as a
symptom of modern despotism (in part 7). The reception of
the Dreyfus affair presents the *Nahda* as a transnational stage on
which the debates that are unfolding on the global scale shape
local debates.

This anthology complicates the East/West binary that
has long governed discussions of Arab modernity. Russia, for
instance, figures prominently in the selected texts in part 3.
Muhammad 'Abduh, the grand mufti of al-Azhar, writes a let-
ter to Tolstoy, praising his enlightenment and social and polit-
ical stances. 'Abduh presents Tolstoy as a spiritual guide for all
human beings regardless of their faith and doctrine. Mikhail
Naimy becomes aware of his own poetic impulse by reading
Russian poets and authors while studying in Russia. Naimy's
and 'Abduh's texts, among others, serve to productively unsettle
the Arab-European literary and philosophical axis of compari-
son, which the prevalent reception and assessment of the *Nahda*
has centered on France and England. Introducing Russia, India,
and other locales and traditions in the selected texts creates the
possibility to make multiple comparisons and to consider the
multiple influences through which the *Nahda* took shape.

Including texts by both well-known and lesser-known
authors allows us to understand the *Nahda* debates concerning

language and education in dialogue with global culture, literary development and genres, and political, social, and economic transformations in the region. With texts from Tunisia, Syria, Lebanon, Egypt, and Iraq, ranging from the early eighteenth century (Jirmanus Farhat on the Arabic language) to the 1930s (Salama Musa's comparative definition of the Renaissance), this anthology counters the prevalent narrative of the *Nahda* as a break with tradition and presents it instead as a discovery not only of Europe but also of the Arab past and of Russia and India. This *Nahda* is no longer reduced to one cataclysmic, colonial event (i.e., Napoleon's invasion of Egypt) that shook—and continues to shake—the Arabs to the core, thus generating either resistance to or acceptance of European rules and standards. Rather, the *Nahda* presented through these selections relies on a complex negotiation that has multiple historical and geographic directions. The translated texts cast the Arab relation to the past and to Europe as an ongoing process of critique, redefinition, praise, and satire. The meaning of the *Nahda* arises from this dynamic movement that is never linear, simple, or complete. The literary approach adopted in the selection process for this anthology does not treat texts as representative of political positions and sociocultural realities but rather presents them as sites of imagination, artistic virtuosity, and contestation that could be connected to a literary and cultural modernity taking place elsewhere in the world around that time. The *Nahda*, as we discover, is constituted through a body of works that systematically raise key cultural and philosophical questions that continue to reverberate today.

Notes

[1]The Islamist party of Rashid al-Ghannushi in Tunisia, which came to power through democratic election after the fall of Ben Ali in 2010, is called *Nahda Islamiyya*, appropriating the idea of renaissance or revival in a new

political era. For another example, Lara Deeb claims that articulations of modernity can be identified in a set of contemporary social practices and forms of authority prevalent in Hizbullah-controlled areas of Lebanon.

[2] Abu-Lughod coined this phrase in his foundational work by the same title. See also El-Enany.

[3] Norbert Elias argues that to be civilized is tied to the development of civility as constitutive of European identity in relation to an untamed and savage other.

[4] The only three exceptions that I'm aware of are ʿAbdallah al-Nadim's "ʿArabi Tafarnag" ("An Arab-cum-European"), which previously appeared in volume 1 of Louis Awad's *The Literature of Ideas in Egypt* (Scholars Press, 1986); Khalil Gibran's "The Future of the Arabic Language," which was translated by Adnan Haydar and appeared during the course of the production of this anthology in Reza Aslan's *The Tablet and the Pen: Literary Landscapes of the Modern Middle East* (W. W. Norton, 2011); and Hasan al-ʿAttar's "*Maqama* of the French," translated by the historian Peter Gran and published as "Appendix 1: The *Maqāmat al-ʿAṭṭār*," in Gran's *Islamic Roots of Capitalism: Egypt, 1760–1840*, 2nd ed. (American U in Cairo P, 1999), pp. 189–91.

[5] On this topic, see Al-Musawi.

Works Cited

Abu-Lughod, Ibrahim. *The Arab Rediscovery of Europe: A Study in Cultural Encounter*. Princeton UP, 1963.

Al-Musawi, Muhsin. *The Medieval Islamic Republic of Letters: Arabic Knowledge Construction*. Notre Dame UP, 2015.

Al-Tahtawi, Rifaʿa Rafiʿ. *An Imam in Paris: Al-Tahtawi's Visit to France, 1826–1831*. Translated by Daniel Newman, Saqi Books, 2004.

Antonius, George. *The Arab Awakening: The Story of the Arab National Movement*. Hamish Hamilton, 1938.

Deeb, Lara. *An Enchanted Modern: Gender and Public Piety in Shiʿi Lebanon*. Princeton UP, 2006.

El-Ariss, Tarek. *Trials of Arab Modernity: Literary Affects and the New Political*. Fordham UP, 2013.

El-Enany, Rasheed. *Arab Representations of the Occident: East-West Encounters in Arabic Fiction*. Routledge, 2006.

Elias, Norbert. *The Civilizing Process: Sociogenetic and Psychogenetic Investigations*. Translated by Edmund Jephcott, edited by Eric Dunning et al., Blackwell, 2000.

Hourani, Albert. *Arabic Thought in the Liberal Age, 1798–1939.* Cambridge UP, 1983.

Kassir, Samir. *Being Arab.* Translated by Will Hobson, Verso, 2006.

Sharabi, Hisham. *Arab Intellectuals and the West: The Formative Years, 1875–1914.* Johns Hopkins UP, 1970.

NOTE ON TRANSLATION AND TRANSLITERATION

Many Arab authors read European thinkers from the eighteenth and nineteenth centuries, such as Montesquieu, Voltaire, and John Stuart Mill. They also read texts from ninth- and tenth-century Baghdad, comparing them with and contrasting them to texts by their contemporaries. These authors were coining new words but also resurrecting old ones and infusing them with new meanings in a modern age. One of the most important Arabic terms to be coined in the nineteenth century was *tamaddun* ("civilization," "becoming civilized"), a concept that would come to dominate *Nahda* writing and thought. The term *watan* ("homeland"), which one finds in classical Arabic poetry, invokes the French word *patrie* ("fatherland"), which had emerged from social and political transformations that gripped Europe at the end of the eighteenth century—especially after the French Revolution.[1] Similarly, the notion of *tanwir* (تنوير; "enlightenment"), which comes from *nur* (نور; "light"), went from having a religious connotation (of divine light) to a secular reference to the Age of Enlightenment in Europe. Coining new words and resignifying old ones, *Nahda* authors invented and practiced a language in transition, disciplining and refining it. This new language eventually gave rise to formal Arabic or what we call today Modern Standard Arabic.

The texts in this anthology illustrate this linguistic and stylistic transformation; they show Modern Standard Arabic in the making. A few of the selections are written in the colloquial Arabic spoken in Cairo or Beirut, but many blur the boundary between formal and colloquial, between classical and modern. Therefore the language of these texts, however modern we might consider it to be, is connected to the past as much as to the future. The translators met this challenge by adopting various approaches: some sought to maintain the foreign in the original text, believing in its power to generate a critical reading in the target language; others aimed for more idiomatic expression, making the translation more accessible to contemporary English readers. Thus there is variation in the tone, style, and language used in this volume. While the translations of the texts by Labiba Hashim and by Zaynab Fawwaz capture the language and the emerging literary genre of the nineteenth-century novella, the translation of 'Abdallah al-Nadim's piece attempts to bring its humor and sarcasm closer to the contemporary reader, on the principle that satire loses its meaning and effectiveness if not rendered in a more idiomatic fashion. In Salim Sarkis's essay, humor is an essential part of its relevance and literary context.

In the entry by Butrus al-Bustani, which is excerpted from a lecture he gave on Arabic culture in 1859, the translation not only addresses linguistic, historical, and cultural variations but also the genre of the text as such. Many expressions arise from the fact that al-Bustani is standing in front of a crowd describing the state of Arabic culture then. By pointing and gesturing, he encourages, invigorates, threatens, and warns. Because the lecture was a performance both physically and linguistically, it was important to convey that feature with "we are able to raise our heads up high given our current accomplishments" instead of with the more idiomatic "we take pride in our current accomplishments." Metaphors that embody movement needed to be translated literally: "If the bridle upon these publishing houses had been released so that they could operate at full capacity" and "releasing the mind from its reins and the will from its bridle." The image of horses running without inhibition is key in capturing the state (or desired state) of Arabic culture at the time. The printing presses running like horses bring together animal force and industrialization as necessary components of the *Nahda* in al-Bustani's lecture, to stress the importance of the freedom to publish, read, and learn for the *Nahda*.

The words used in Arabic in reference to the notion of civilization or being civilized are *tamaddun* for al-Bustani, *madaniyya* (مدنية) for Khalil Baydas, and *hadara* (حضارة) for Salama Musa. *Madaniyya*, which comes from the word *madina* ("city"), is more akin to the concept of urbanity or "becoming of the city." Though many of the Arab intellectuals thinking and representing the *Nahda* had an urban setting in mind, with the role of cities such as Beirut or Cairo as embodying the movement, the countryside was also important. Al-Bustani discusses the printing presses in various villages and small towns in modern-day Lebanon, Syria, and Egypt, describing how a remote convent was converted into a school to educate children from a particular region. In this sense, the urban is no longer the only characteristic of the *Nahda*, which relies more on a city-country interaction.

With Musa, who writes quite late in the *Nahda* (1930s), we move from civilization as the march toward the achievement of progress to an idea that is closer to the way we understand the word today: a historical continuity linking past, present, and future, providing a people with an identity and a role. By keeping the word "civilization" to translate *madaniyya* and *hadara*, we are able to observe how this word and concept evolved from the 1850s to the 1930s, how it moved from signifying an enlightenment project based on the founding of schools and the encouragement of learning and travel to involving a historical identity that would allow Arabs to compare their state to that of other nations undergoing revival and awakening in the nineteenth and through the twentieth century, especially in Asia.

The contributors to this volume had to think hard about the word *Nahda* itself, which has been criticized, contested, and reappropriated many times. Should it be translated as "awakening," "modernity," "enlightenment," or kept in transliteration as *Nahda*? We decided that it was important to connect this process, which begins to recognize itself as a renaissance movement in the nineteenth century, to the Renaissance with a capital R. This decision is based on the notion that what happened in Europe in the fifteenth and sixteenth centuries especially, what we call the European Renaissance, is linked to other processes in history and in the world, from Baghdad from the eighth to the tenth century to Harlem in the twentieth. Writing the Arab Renaissance with a capital R acknowledges the historical relation of the *Nahda* to what happened in Europe and thus engages the scholarship that went into thinking about European progress in the fifteenth and sixteenth centuries as a renaissance. *The Arab Renaissance* thus acknowledges a historical precedent but doesn't claim that the precedent is unique or that it is the origin and that all others renaissances (lowercased) are merely copies and imitations.

Another important term that is historically and politically tied to "civilization" and "renaissance" is "nation." In the texts we include, there are instances when the word *watan* was used to mean "nation" (أمة; umma), others when it meant "country," others when it meant "homeland," and still others when it meant "region," depending on what the author was referring to and at what moment in his or her text. *Watan* usually meant "nation" when used as an adjective, as in "the National School" (al-madrasa al-wataniyya), for instance. This was how

al-Bustani used it, because the idea of forging a national home-
land was fundamental to his writing and his educational proj-
ects. The same goes for a common expression like "sons of the
homeland" (abnaʾ al-watan), which we translated as "citizens"
(al-Qabbani) and "compatriots" (al-Bustani, al-Sayyid) because
it is meant to convey the notion of nation-state that is crystal-
lizing in the nineteenth century. These authors are thinking of
a collective movement involving writing and education that
will bring about the national good through unity. In this con-
text, "compatriots" (i.e., sons of our nation or homeland) and
"citizens" (i.e., sons of the nation) became clear choices in our
standardization of the translation in this volume.

Concerning the transliteration of Arabic words and names,
we decided to follow a simple model that allows them space in
English without the diacritical system that is often used in spe-
cialized transliterations. For instance, the reader will see words
that contain an ʿayn, like ʿAli, or a hamza, like Maʾmun. We tried
to use the most common transliteration of Arabic names in
English also to make it easier for English readers to conduct
searches on their own for critical material.

Note

¹On *watan*, see Noorani.

Work Cited

Noorani, Yaseen. "Estrangement and Selfhood in the Classical Concept
of *Watan." Journal of Arabic Literature*, vol. 47, nos. 1–2, 2016, pp. 16–42.

Part 1: What Is the Renaissance?

This part highlights how education and institution building become a major *Nahda* concern. The texts show that educational institutions and cultural policies engage and draw on European models and ideals yet are anchored in regional and historical specifics. In his famous speech on Arabic culture, Butrus al-Bustani discusses schools, presses, and the general state of learning in the Levant and Egypt that are contributing to the spread of civilization in the middle of the nineteenth century. Identifying problems and emphasizing success stories, al-Bustani, the founder of al-Madrasa al-Wataniyya (the National School) in Beirut, argues that cultural acquisition and learning are the only means to overcome sectarianism and achieve unity and enlightenment. This view is shared in Iraq by Fahmi al-Mudarris, founder of Al al-Bayt University in the 1920s, which was meant to forge the modern Iraqi subject beyond sectarian divisions. In the selection in this volume, al-Mudarris lists the different components of that university, discussing the importance of incorporating the arts, psychology, and sociology into the curriculum despite the resistance of colonial and conservative forces. From the articulation of al-Mudarris's national education project as the embodiment of the *Nahda*, we move to Salama Musa's reflections on the effects of *Nahda* language and education. Musa advocates the use of colloquial Arabic ('ammiyya) and sides with the moderns in the debate that consumed Europe throughout the eighteenth century.[1] In this respect, Musa illustrates that in the *Nahda* Arab and European thinkers faced and responded to similar problems. His comparative definition of the *Nahda* is followed by Khalil Gibran's discussion of the relation between Arabic and English. In the essay "The Future of the Arabic Language," Gibran engages the question of Arab modernity by identifying language as the dynamic site of cultural revival, thereby representing it as the manifestation of the modern. For him, the *Nahda* subject is one who sheds the cloak of imitation in order to invent and innovate in every field possible. He considers that blind imitation of the West would be fatal to Arabic culture and language.

Note

[1] In Europe, the moderns felt that they had surpassed their predecessors in progress and genius; the ancients still believed in the superiority of their predecessors.

Butrus al-Bustani
(1819–83)

Introduced and translated by Stephen Sheehi

Butrus al-Bustani was born to a family of notables and clergy-men in Dibbiyyeh, Lebanon, in 1819. He attended the presti-gious Maronite school 'Ayn Waraqa, where he studied Syriac, French, theology, and the traditional Arabic scholastic disci-plines: grammar, rhetoric, poetry, history, and mathematics. In 1840, he served as a tutor and translator for the American Protestant missionaries in Beirut, work that eventually resulted in his conversion to Christianity and his retranslation of the Bible into Arabic (1848–56).

During the sectarian violence of 1860 that resulted in the deaths of thousands of people, mostly Christians, al-Bustani wrote *Nafir Suriyya* ("Clarion of Syria"), a series of broadsheets extolling the virtues of fraternity among religious sects, patri-otism, civic-mindedness, and progress. Following the conflict, al-Bustani founded al-Madrasa al-Wataniyya in 1863, a school that served as a nationalist prototype. The first secular school in the Arab world, it maintained a multiconfessional student body and faculty. Al-Bustani founded the pioneering journal *al-Jinan* (1870; "Gardens") and the fortnightly newspapers *al-Janna* (1870; "The Garden") and *al-Junayna* (1871; "The Small Gar-den"). In addition to writing a comprehensive Arabic dictionary, *Muhit al-Muhit* (1869; "Encompassing the All-Encompassing"), al-Bustani set out to write a comprehensive and unprecedented encyclopedia, *Da'irat al-Ma'arif* ("The Scope of Knowledge"), in 1876.

Along with his missionary colleagues, al-Bustani founded the Syrian Society of Arts and Sciences in 1847. As secretary, he edited the publication of the society's proceedings, published in 1852. Before a similar learned society in 1859, he delivered "Lecture on the Culture of the Arabs," among the earliest critiques of Arab culture in the modern era. While the term is now understood as meaning both literature and manners, *adab* (the plural, *aadaab*, appears in the title) was a concept before the twentieth century that applied to more than humanistic and scientific knowledge and etiquette; it located all forms of personal and collective behavior, both material and spiritual, in a world organized by knowledge, self-awareness, morality, personal behavior, and social and political responsibility. Broader in its meaning than *belles lettres* or *the humanities* and more powerful than *etiquette* or *refinement*, *adab* remained a central organizing concept in the Arab intellectuals' formulas for reform that dominated the Ottoman world at the time. With this in mind, "Lecture on the Culture of the Arabs" should be read by students and scholars today not as a description of an empirical reality of Arab cultural decadence in the nineteenth century but as an engagement with modernity and an example of how Arab and Ottoman intellectuals, reformers, and literati were thinking about social, political, and economic reform in an era of European expansion.

Recommended Reading

Hanssen, Jens. *Fin de Siècle Beirut: The Making of an Ottoman Provincial Capital.* Oxford UP, 2005.

Makdisi, Ussama. *Artillery of Heaven.* Cornell UP, 2008.

Sheehi, Stephen. *Foundations of Modern Arab Identity.* UP of Florida, 2004.

Zachs, Fruma. *The Making of a Syrian Identity.* Brill, 2005.

"The Culture of the Arabs Today"

FROM "Lecture on the Culture of the Arabs"

Dear Gentlemen, if I were charged to stand before you thirty years ago and speak about this topic regarding the culture of the Arabs today, I—as a compatriot—would have been embarrassed to open a discussion that might expose the subject's inner workings. The topic might shame and disgrace my fellow countrymen in the eyes of foreigners, because at that time I was compelled to walk the city's souks (I will not even say the whole countryside, which in previous times was a wet nurse to culture and a cradle to civilization) and search with utmost effort for anyone who was able to read something written or, even as they say, "decipher his own name."

But now one finds many matters to strengthen our faith in the future. Although we are indebted to foreigners for most of these matters, we are able to raise our heads up high given our current accomplishments. . . . We can look at [the culture of the Arabs] from several perspectives, which can be condensed into the four following categories: the condition of Arabs in regard to culture, the state of culture itself among the Arabs, the condition of the means to acquire culture, and our hope for the future.

First, Arabs today are content with the state of culture. . . . They themselves think that they have reached the highest levels of learning even though they have not even begun to scratch the surface. Whoever among them has learned the Book of Psalms and the Qur'an is said to have completed his learning. If one has learned a modicum of basic Arabic syntax and grammar, it is said that he has become the scholar of his time. And if one composes some poetry, there is not an honorary title that is not bestowed upon him. This is only possible because a small ray of intellect is enough to blind the eyes of the ignorant individual.

Until now, people have not stood on Oceania's shore of knowledge to see its grandeur and expanse. Although we consider the Arabs today as the progeny of the ancient Arabs, we do not see in them the same resolution and effort in the acquisition of knowledge that we see in those ancient innovators. We refuse to accept that this progeny have become corrupted. This is because the excellence of the Arab mind and its readiness to receive knowledge these days both prove the contrary.

This current state of culture, however, is due to many reasons, which if time permits, we wish to reveal in order to exonerate our own flesh and blood from the accusations laid on them by foreigners—who, we do not doubt, would have arrived at a condition equaling our own had fate subjected them to the same circumstances. No matter the reasons, it cannot be denied that the market for the goods of knowledge has stagnated among the Arabs and that they no longer circulate among the Arab masses, especially not among their leaders.

Second, culture among the Arabs these days is in a complete state of decay. In regard to the science of language, we seldom find any Arab to whom we can point our finger and say that he truly knows his language and its grammar. For the majority of Arabs, language learning is limited to the memorization of a few archaic Arabic words that they employ in their writings and their poetry with the intent of showing off their knowledge and fooling the public, as though they were but the pebbles that men trifle with in childhood. Indeed, he who uses linguistic corruptions like "terd" for "third," "hows" for "how," and "dat" for "that," or "from she" instead of "from her" and "in he" instead of "in him" is still considered a grammarian. . . .

Moreover, whoever retains from mathematics and engineering the basic rules of addition and subtraction, or even better, multiplication and division, and memorizes a few theorems that the ancient scholars produced, his name becomes renowned far and wide as if he were the exemplar of scholars. . . .

As long as the Arabs are content with imitation and borrowing, and are unwilling to subject themselves to testing and verification, then one has no hope for their progress in the arts and sciences.

O Arab blood, boil not! Do not be annoyed by what is right when you hear someone who shares in your own culture reveal to you the truth about your condition. He reveals it not to slander or defame but rather to apprise you of the truth, to inform you and fortify you for your pursuit of knowledge and the endurance it demands. . . .

Third, the means of acquiring culture are many. . . . Paramount among them are publishing houses. It is clear that this generation has witnessed the increase of publishing houses considerably in both number and influence, although many of them are sectarian and devoted only to publishing religious books; some of these have still not justified their existence to the public. In fact, in this very town there are five or six presses producing a diverse assortment of books and articles. Undoubtedly, if these publishing houses took their work seriously and concerned themselves with providing publications on culture and civilization that would benefit the public, they could have provided us in a short span of time with the opportunity to make Arabs rich in books and libraries.

One should not neglect the presence of that great power above our heads, which the American missionaries themselves employ in their press: steam. There is no denying the press's ability to spread knowledge and civilization in our lands in just a short period. Valuable works on mathematics and history have already come out of them, in addition to many books related to religious matters.

If the bridle upon these publishing houses had been released so that they could operate at full capacity producing works on the arts and sciences, they would have provided this country with beneficial works, just as the Syrian Press, which publishes the newspaper *Hadiqat al-Akhbar* ("The Garden of News"). Undoubtedly, when used well, journals are the best means of civilizing the public and increasing the number of readers among them. We hope that this young press, which is the first Arabic press to specialize in publishing journals, flourishes, and that the labors of its owner and beloved manager, Khalil Effendi al-Khuri, are crowned with success. He will be remembered forever among our compatriots as a conqueror of the most formidable fortress, of whose benefits the previous generations were ignorant. Khalil al-Khuri stands at the shore of the great sea separating the Old World from the New World, peering out momentarily toward the New, then momentarily glancing back toward the Old. In his collection that marks the new age, al-Khuri pours classical poetry into a new mold, clarifying its intended meaning.

Many other Arabic presses are found in Qozhayha, El-Choueir, Aleppo, Jerusalem, and the Maghreb. Yet the publishing house that most deserves mention is Bulaq Press in Cairo, which has enriched the Arab race with a diversity of books. This press's excellent organization and great usefulness are reflected in its many original Arabic works and translations. The press's translators and directors have begun to avoid as much as possible using foreign terms in what they translate from European languages, even though in the beginning of their venture—when the press was in its infancy—they would mix foreign expressions with Arabic words.

It is obvious that the Arabic publishing houses in Europe and America outnumber those in our lands. Had not these presses been concerned with Arabic, no trace would have remained of many precious Arabic literary works. Thus we often see our Arabic manuscripts returning to us after their long absence printed with beautiful lettering. However, I wish that we were able to say that these books are completely accurate and grammatically correct.

Another means of acquiring culture is through libraries. Even though one finds many private libraries in our lands, one wonders at the parsimony of their collectors and their curators, on the one hand, and at the lack of good faith on the part of those who borrow books from them, on the other. Both librarians and collectors lock the libraries' iron doors and leave the books to the mercy of worms and dust. What is the benefit of accumulating books if there is no one to read them?

This leads us to mention another means of acquiring culture, that is, schools. Indeed, it is obvious that during this century, the number of schools has increased for every religious community and sect. Some of them teach languages and some teach basic reading. However, are they equipped to help students achieve their educational goals? Indeed, a quick glance at these schools' organization, teachers, and most of their books and facilities provides a clear answer. Families disparage primary schools and instead entrust their children to unqualified teachers. As such, decay has prevailed in this generation's culture and education since its infancy. One finds primary schools in most cities and villages, owing to the endeavors of foreigners, because most of our compatriots have failed until this day to recognize the value of education and to fund it properly. Oh how little do parents and children value education, which can be acquired free of charge without any expense to the parents!

As for the secondary schools, they are few in number and are restricted to learning in accordance with one's religious sect, so that we cannot rightly say that there is a single school that focuses on learning for its own sake. Among Christian national secondary schools, the famous Madrasat ʿAyn Waraqa, which we can justifiably claim is the mother of national schools in our lands, was in fact established at the end of the previous century, during a time of great ignorance and lack of enlightenment.

Its praiseworthy founder, Bishop Yusuf Istifan, encountered much resistance when he decided to move the nuns from 'Ayn Waraqa's convent to other convents in order to convert it into a school for boys. The efforts of His Eminence Bishop Yusuf Rizq in supporting this school should not be forgotten. He improved its financial standing and heightened its splendor by devoting his energies to erecting new buildings and to renovating numerous old ones. One of Bishop Rizq's success stories stands in front of you, Gentlemen, as I spent ten years there learning and teaching at this school. I benefited greatly from the abundant attention of its principal, who nurtured me through his supervision and care.

Others have emulated Bishop Yusuf Istifan. The Sfair family removed the nuns from the Rumiyeh convent and the Assaf family removed them from the Mar Abda Harhariya convent. They replaced these nuns, who by the nature of their work did only what benefited themselves, because the children were eager to learn. This was in order to strengthen the pillars of the Maronite community through learning and refinement. The Maronites are thus pioneers in this domain. In addition, this community has other secondary schools and dioceses concerned solely with children's education.

The Greek Catholics founded two secondary schools during this century. One is in al-Moukhalles monastery . . . and the other is in 'Ain Traz. . . . The Greek Orthodox community has been mindful in this matter as well, and now they are hard at work establishing schools and expanding their influence, in sharp contrast to what we observed in the case of their predecessors. . . .

In this regard, we should also acknowledge the Syriac Catholic school in the al-Sharfah monastery, the Armenian schools, the school of the Lazarite monks in 'Aintoura, the American school in 'Abey, and the Jesuit school in Ghazir. Though their benefits cannot be denied, there remains room for reform among these schools, and it is necessary that this reform be introduced step by step with the progress of each generation.

As for Muslims, among their most renowned schools is the one in Bulaq, in Cairo, which was founded by the Ma'mun of the nineteenth century, Muhammad 'Ali Pasha.[1] We hope that Egypt's schools continue to benefit from the favors of the current ruler, Khedive Said Pasha. The school has graduated many esteemed students and diligent scholars, who have become famous due to their writings and numerous translations. . . .

The Muslims have too many schools to mention. Most of them emulate Ibn Sina's [Avicenna's] model for the acquisition of culture. . . . Perhaps many Muslim shrines and hermitages are being converted into schools, for this generation's achievements have demonstrated that the pen takes precedence over the sword, contrary to what al-Mutanabbi says:

If I return, my pens would tell me,
"Glory is for the sword and not for the pen.
Use us to write after you have written with it [the sword],
for we are to swords as servants."

With this, the purveyors of knowledge and science achieve progress before the purveyors of bravado and swords do, because the wheel of the world spins on the tip of the pen. There is no better saying on this topic than that of Imam 'Ali:

There is no admiration like that for the learned ones
and guidance to him who seeks righteousness.
Seek learning and find no replacement for it!
For [other] people are dead while the learned ones live.

O compatriots! O offspring of notables and grandchildren of Syriac and Greek kin, mounted on the camel's hump of the nineteenth century, the century of learning and enlightenment, the century of inventions and discoveries, the century of culture and knowledge, the century of manufacturing and arts! Rise! Get up! Be aware! Wake up! Roll your sleeve up your forearm of determination! Culture is standing at your doors from all sides, knocking, requesting entry into your majestic and radiant mountains, your valleys, your plains, and your deserts, which nature has decorated with lofty ornaments of beauty. Reject your sectarianism, partisanship, and personal prejudices and outstretch your hand to shake the hand of culture. Open the doors to this old friend who is coming back to you after a long absence. Welcome it and greet it with utmost happiness, so that it can fill your land with contentment and comfort, and dress it in splendor and pride.

Undoubtedly, the sustained progress that has occurred in this country over the past few years strengthens the resolve of all who are involved in it with desire and passion to raise the Arab race from its fallen state. The labors of those compatriots and foreigners who have spent many years bringing culture and civilization to the Arabs will be crowned with success.

His Sublime Highness the great Sultan ʿAbd al-Majid Khan is munificent toward ensuring happiness, comfort, safety, success, and progress in all the realms of his domain. His sound decrees granting freedom [to all of his subjects], establishing schools, and expanding the scope of these schools throughout his protected lands have inevitably stirred emotions among his subjects and moved them to love him and raise their calls to God Almighty to prolong his reign and reinforce the pillars of his state.

The importance of these things is clear, along with the importance of allowing sophisticated Arabs to intermingle widely with civilized peoples, increasing the number of presses and schools, organizing salons and gatherings, enlightening government officials, opening the door to cultural, religious, and political discussion, speech, and dialogue, releasing the mind from its reins and the will from its bridle, and paying more attention to the education of women. All of this should be done especially within this city of Beirut, which was the wet nurse to jurisprudence in times past and which we hope will become the wet nurse to culture in times to come. Our sincere hope is that knowledge will spread among the Arabs to fill their homes and restore them to their previous splendor; and that the slender crescent of culture that has been born in the mid–nineteenth century will grow to a full moon.

Note

[1] Al-Ma'mun (r. 813–33) is the paragon of an enlightened Abbasid caliph.

Source of Arabic Text on Which the Translation Is Based

Al-Bustani, Butrus. خطبة في آداب العرب [khutba fi adab al-ʿarab; Lecture on the Culture of the Arabs]. 1859. الجمعية السورية للعلوم والفنون [al-jamʿiyya al-suriyya lil-ʿulum wal-funun; The Syrian Society of Arts and Sciences, 1847–1852], edited by Yusuf Qizma Khuri, Dar al-Hamraʾ, 1990, pp. 101–17.

بطرس البستاني
(١٨١٩-١٨٨٣)

خطبة في آداب العرب

في آداب العرب في هذه الأيام

لو كلفت الوقوف أمام سيادتكم لأجل الكلام عن هذا الموضوع نحو ثلاثين سنة قبل الآن، لكنت أخجل نظير ابن وطن من فتح هذا البحث الذي كشف مكنوناته، يوجب عاراً وخزياً على أبناء بلادي عند الأجانب لأنني حينئذ كنت ألزم أن أجول في أسواق هذه المدينة (حتى لا أقول في كامل البلاد التي كانت في الأزمان السالفة مرضعة للآداب وسريراً للتمدن)، وأفتّش باجتهاد على من يقدر أن يقرأ مكتوباً أو كما يقال يفك الاسم. وأما الآن فإنه يوجد أمور كثيرة تقوي آمالنا في المستقبل. ومع أننا مديونون في أكثر هذه الأمور للغرباء، يمكننا أن نرفع رؤوسنا بما وجد منها عندنا. . . . .

إنه يمكننا النظر إلى البحث الذي أمامنا من أوجه عديدة تقتصر على أربعة منها، وهي حالة العرب بالنظر إلى الآداب وحالة الآداب نفسها عند العرب وحالة الوسائط لاكتساب الآداب وآمالنا في المستقبل فنقول:

أولاً: إن العرب في أيامنا هذه قنوعون جدا في أمر الآداب . . . يحسبون أنفسهم أنهم قد وصلوا إلى أعلى طبقات العلم مع أنهم لم يقرعوا بابه. ومن تعلم منهم كتاب الزبور والقرآن يقال إنه قد ختم علمه، وإذا تعلم شيئاً من أصول الصرف والنحو يقال فيه إنه قد صار علامة زمانه، وإذا نطق بالشعر فلا يبقى عندهم لقب يصفونه به. وما ذلك إلا لأن ظهور نور قليل في العاقل كافٍ لأن يغشي على عيني الجاهل، ولأنهم إلى الآن لم يقفوا على شاطئ أوقيانوس العلوم ويروا عظمته واتساعه. ومع أننا نعتقد بأن عرب هذه الأيام هم من نسل العرب القدماء، لا نرى فيهم ما رأيناه في أولئك المجاهدين من الثبات والجهاد في ميدان العلوم ولا نقدر أن نسلم بأن النسل قد فسد وذلك لأن جودة عقول العرب وحسن استعدادها في هذه الأيام لتحصيل العلوم يبرهنان النقيض.

ولكن ذلك ناتج من أحوال كثيرة وأسباب متنوعة نود لو سمحت لنا الأوقات لبيانها لكي نخفف عمن هو من لحمنا ودمنا اللوم الواقع عليهم من الأجانب، الذين لا نشك بأنهم كانوا وصلوا إلى حالة أردأ من حالتنا لو ألقاهم الدهر في ظروف كظروفنا. ولكن مهما كانت الأسباب فلا سبيل إنكار كساد بضاعة العلم عند العرب وعدم رواج سوقها بين جماهيرهم وعلى الخصوص أكابرهم.

ثانياً: إن الآداب عند العرب في هذه الأيام هي في حالة انحطاط كلي. أما العلوم اللغوية فإننا قلما نجد أحداً من أبناء العرب يمكن أن يشار إليه بالبنان بأنه يعرف لغته وقواعدها حق المعرفة. فإنهم في الأكثر يكتفون من علم اللغة بحفظ بعض كلمات عربية ميتة يدرجونها في كتاباتهم وأشعارهم بقصد إظهار معرفتهم والتمويه على الجمهور . . . ومن قال منهم سلاسة والزي وهزا ومنهي وفيهو (أي ثلاثة والذي وهذا ومنه وفيه) وما أشبه من إفساد اللغة فهو ناحٍ. . . . وأما . . . الحساب والهندسة ومتعلقاتها فهذه يكتفون منها بالجمع والطرح، ومن زاد عليهما الضرب والقسمة وحفظ بعض مسائل بأجوبتها مما أوجده لهم الأقدمون يذيع اسمه في الآفاق أنه من فحول العلماء. . . . وما دام العرب يكتفون بالتقليد والنقل ولا يريدون أن يتعبوا أنفسهم بالفحص والتحقيق، فلا يؤمل تقدمهم في العلوم والفنون. لا تهج أيها الدم العربي ولا تغتظ من الحق عندما تسمع واحداً مشتركاً فيك، يبين لك حقيقة حالك لا على سبيل التقريع والطعن، بل لأجل إيقافك على الحقيقة عسى أن يكون ذلك واسطة لانتباهك وتقويتك في طلب العلم والتجلد في ميدانه. . . . .

ثالثاً: إن الوسائط لاكتساب الآداب كثيرة . . . فمن الوسائط التي قصدنا ذكرها المطابع، ولا يخفى أن عدد المطابع وقوتها قد زاد كثيراً في هذا الجيل إلا أن كثيراً منها طائفي مشتغل في طبع كتب دينية. والبعض منها إلى الآن لم يعطِ الجمهور برهان وجوده. فإنه في نفس هذه البلدة توجد خمس أو ست مطابع يخرج منها كتب وأوراق متنوعة. ولا ريب أن هذه المطابع لو اشتغلت حق الشغل وأعتنت في طبع ما من شأنه أن يفيد الجمهور بوجه العموم آداباً وتمدناً لكانت في ظرف مدة قصيرة تغني أبناء العرب بالكتب والمكاتب. ولا ينبغي أن نغفل عن القوة العظيمة الموجودة فوق رؤوسنا التي استخدم لها المرسلون الأمركان البخار. ولا شك في أنها قادرة على نشر المعارف

والتمدن في هذه البلاد في برهة قصيرة. وقد خرج منها كتب نفيسة في العلوم الرياضية والتاريخية فضلاً عن الكتب الكثيرة المتعلقة بالمذهب. ولو أطلق لها العنان وجرت بكامل قوتها في ميدان الآداب والعلوم، لأغنت هذه البلاد في التصانيف المفيدة. ولا عن المطبعة السورية التي خُصِّصت بحديقة الأخبار. ومما لا يشوبه ريب أن الجرنالات من أكبر الوسائط لتمدن الجمهور وزيادة عدد القراء إذا استعملت على حقها. والأمل أن هذه الفتاة التي هي أول مطبعة عربية خُصِّصت بالجرنالات تتقوى، وأن أتعاب مالكها ومديرها العزيز خليل أفندي الخوري تكلل بالنجاح فيخلد ذكره عند أبناء الوطن، كفاتح لهذا الحصن الحصين الذي أغفل المتقدمون عن فوائده. وكأني به واقفاً على شاطئ البحر الكبير الفاصل بين العالم القديم والعالم الجديد، يستشرف تارة على الجديد ويلحظ أخرى إلى القديم ولدى ديوانه الموسوم بالعصر الجديد الذي أفرغ فيه الشعر القديم في قالب جديد يتضح المعنى المقصود. وتوجد مطابع أخرى كثيرة عربية في قزحيا والشوير وحلب والقدس وبلاد المغرب، ولكن المطبعة التي تستحق الذكر وقد أعنت الجنس العربي بالكتب المتفننة هي مطبعة بولاق. ونستدل على حسن نظام هذه المطبعة وعظم فائدتها من الكتب الكثيرة التي خرجت منها من أصلية ومترجمة. وقد ابتدأ مترجمو ونظار هذه المطبعة يتجنبون بقدر الإمكان استعمال ألفاظ أجنبية في ما يترجمونه من اللغات الإفرنجية، مع أنهم في ابتداء الأمر عندما كانت المطبعة في سن الطفولية كانوا يكثرون من الألفاظ العربية مع وجود ألفاظ في العربية تقابلها. ولا يخفى أن المطابع العربية في أوروبا وأمريكا أكثر منها في هذه البلاد وأنه لولا عناية هذه المطابع لما بقي عين ولا أثر لكثير من تصانيف العرب النفيسة. وهكذا نرى كثيراً من كتبنا العربية راجعاً إلينا بعد غربته الطويلة مطبوعاً بأحرف جميلة، ويا ليتنا نقدر أن نقول بالضبط التام والصحة الواجبة.

منها المكاتب. ومع أنه يوجد مكاتب كثيرة خصوصية في هذه البلاد، ترى بخل مقتنيها أو متوليها من الجهة الواحدة وعدم أمانة مستعيري الكتب من الجهة الأخرى يقفلان عليها أبواباً حديدية ويتركانها لرحمة العث ومأوى للغبار. ولكن ما الفائدة من تكثير الكتب إذا لم يكن من يقرأها؟ وهذا يقتادنا إلى ذكر واسطة أخرى من وسائط اكتساب الآداب وهي المدارس.

لا يخفى أن عدد المدارس قد زاد كثيراً في هذا الجيل. فإنه يوجد في هذه المدينة مدارس كثيرة لكل ملة ومذهب، منها لتعليم اللغات ومنها لتعليم

القراءة البسيطة. وهل هي في حالة مناسبة لنوال الغاية المقصودة منها. فإن من نظر إلى نظامها ومعلميها وأكثر كتبها وأماكنها لا يشكل عليه الجواب. واستخفاف الأهالي بالمدارس البسيطة وتسليم أولادهم لمعلمين غير مقتدرين على تعليمهم كما يجب هو مما يوجب فساداً في آداب الجيل ومعارفه منذ طفوليته. وتوجد مدارس بسيطة في أكثر المدن والقرى وكثير منها بسعي الأجانب، لأن أكثر أهالي بلادنا إلى الآن متغافلون عن اعتبار قيمة العلم، فلا يشاؤون أن يفتحوا له باباً في دفاتر مصاريفهم. وكم تكون قليلة عند الوالدين والأولاد قيمة العلم الذي يكتسب مجاناً من دون أن يكلف الوالدين شيئاً.

وأما المدارس العالية فهي قليلة العدد تقتصر في الغالب على علوم تتعلق بالمذهب، حتى أنه لا يمكننا أن نقول بالصحة أنه توجد مدرسة كلية يُنظر فيها إلى العلوم باعتبار ذاتها. ومن المدارس العالية الوطنية النصرانية مدرسة عين ورقة المشهورة التي يسوغ لنا أن نقول بحق أنها أم المدارس الوطنية في هذه البلاد، وقد أنشئت في أواخر الجيل الماضي. ومن أطلع على شدة غباوة الأزمان التي أنشئت فيها افتقار الأهالي قاطبة في تلك الأيام إلى العلوم يتبين له فضل المطران يوسف أسطفان منشئها ويزيد اعتبار فضله عند من يقف على المقاومات التي حصلت له عندما رفع الراهبات من دير عين ورقة ووزعهن على الأديرة ووضع مكانهن فتياناً يتعلمون بنية الإفادة والتعليم. ولا ينبغي أن ننسى فضل مساعي سيادة المطران يوسف رزق رئيس المدرسة المذكورة حالاً، فإنه قد زادها قوة بواسطة زيادته أوقافاً على أوقافها ورونقاً بواسطة الأبنية الجديدة والإصلاحات العديدة التي أحدثتها همته ونشاطه فيها، وقد امتد فضله إلى الواقف أمام سيادتكم، إذ قد صرفت عشر سنين في المدرسة المذكورة أتعلم وأعلم محفوفاً بمزيد غيرته الخصوصية عليَّ ومشمولاً بأنظاره وعنايته.

وقد اقتدى بالمطران يوسف أسطفان غيره، فأخلت عائلة بيت صفير دير الرومية وعائلة بيت آصاف دير مار عبدا هرهريا من الراهبات اللواتي من شأن طريقتهن أن يقتصرن على ما به إفادة أنفسهن، ووضعتا مكانهن أولاداً يتعلمون هناك ما من شأنه أن يقوي أركان الطائفة المارونية ويهذب شعبها. ولهذه الطائفة فضل الأسبقية في هذا الأمر. ولها غير المدارس الطائفية العمومية المذكورة مدارس أخرى عالية، أبرشية توجد في أكثر الأبرشيات لتعليم أولادها.

وكذلك الروم الكاثوليكيون قد أقاموا في هذا الجيل مدرستين عاليتين الواحدة في دير المخلص ... والأخرى في عين تراز ... وأما الروم

الأرثوذكسيون فقد انتبهوا في هذه السنين الأخيرة وهم الآن باذلون الهمة في تكثير المدارس وتوسيع دائرتها، خلافاً لما نعهده من سلفائهم. . . . .

ولا ينبغي أن نغفل عن مدرسة السريان الكاثوليكيين في دير الشرفة ومدارس الأرمن ومدرسة الرهبان العازارية في عين طورة ومدرسة الأمركان في عبيه ومدرسة الرهبان اليسوعية في غزير، فإن فوائدهم لا تنكر. ولكن في جميع المدارس المذكورة محل متسع للإصلاح، ولا بد أن الإصلاح سيدخل رويداً رويداً مع تقدم الجيل.

وأما الإسلام فمن مدارسهم الشهيرة المدرسة التي أنشأها مأمون الجيل التاسع عشر محمد علي باشا في بولاق من الإقليم المصري، ونرجو أنها تبقى محفوظة بعطايا الخديوي سعيد باشا والي مصر حالاً ومشمولة بأنظاره. وقد خرج منها تلاميذ معتبرون وجهابذة مدققون اشتهر فضلهم بواسطة التآليف والترجمات العديدة. . . . . ولهم مدارس أخرى لا يسعنا الوقت لذكرها غير أن الأكثرين منهم الآن يقتدون بابن سينا في طريقة اكتساب الآداب. . . . . وعسى أن يتحول كثير من المزارات والخلوات إلى مدارس، لأن أحوال هذا الجيل تعلن أن القلم قد تقدم على السيف خلافاً لقول المتنبي:

المجد للسيف ليس المجد للقلم	حتى رجعت وأقلامي قوائل لي
فإنما نحن للأسياف كالخدم	فاكتب بنا أبداً بعد الكتاب به

وبذلك حصل التقدم لأصحاب المعارف والعلوم على أصحاب الشجاعة والسيوف لأن دولاب العالم يدور على رأس القلم. وما أحسن ما قاله الإمام علي في هذا المعنى:

على الهدى لمن استهدى أدلاء	ما الفضل إلا لأهل العلم أنهم
فالناس موتى وأهل العلم أحياء	فقم بعلم ولا تبغي به بدلاً

فيا أبناء الوطن يا ذرية أولئك الأفاضل وحفدة معاشر السريان واليونان، الممتطين سنام الجيل التاسع عشر جيل المعرفة والنور جيل الاختراعات والاكتشافات جيل الآداب والمعارف جيل الصنائع والفنون، هبوا استفيقوا انتبهوا استيقظوا، شمروا عن ساعد العزم، ها الآداب واقفة من كل جهة على

أبوابكم تقرع طالبة الدخول إلى جبالكم الشامخة البهية وأوديتكم وسهولكم وصحاريكم التي زينتها الطبيعة بحلاها الفاخرة، وانبذوا عنكم تعصباتكم وتحزباتكم وأغراضكم النفسانية، وقدموا لها يداً واحدة لمصافحتها وافتحوا الأبواب لهذا الصديق القديم الآتي إليكم بعد غربة مستطيلة، وترحبوا به وأقبلوه بكل فرح وحبور فيملأ بلادكم راحة ورفاهية رونقاً وفخراً.

ولا ريب أن التقدم المتصل الذي حصل في هذه البلاد في السنين القليلة المتأخرة مما يقوي عزائم كل من له رغبة وغيرة على إنهاض الجنس العربي من حالته الساقطة، وأن أتعاب الذين صرفوا السنين الكثيرة في إدخال الآداب والتمدن بين العرب من أبناء الوطن والأجانب ستكلل بالنجاح.

وسامي همة حضرة الذات الشاهانية حضرة سلطاننا الأعظم السلطان عبد المجيد خان ذي النية الخيرية نحو راحة ورفاهية وأمنية النجاح وتقدم كامل أصناف تبعته، وإراداته الصالحة نحو إعطاء الحرية وإنشاء المدارس وتوسيع دائرتها في ممالكه المحروسة، مما يجب أن يحرك عواطف كامل رعاياه إلى محبته وإلى رفع الدعاء إلى الله سبحانه وتعالى أن يطيل بقائه ويوطد أركان دولته.

ولا يخفى أن ذلك، مع امتداد المتجربين العرب واختلاطهم بشعوب متمدنة وازدياد عدد المطابع والمدارس، وانتظام حالة المجالس والمحافل وتقدم رجال الدولة في المعارف، وفتح باب ميدان الإنشاء والخطب والمحاورات الأدبية والدينية والسياسية، وإطلاق زمام العقل وعنان الإرادة، والانتباه إلى تعليم النساء وعلى الخصوص في هذه المدينة التي كانت في الأزمان السالفة مرضعة للفقه، ويؤمل أنها ستكون في ما يأتي مرضعة للآداب، كل ذلك يقوي عزائمنا وأملنا بأن العلوم ستمتد بين أبناء العرب وتملأ ديارهم وترجع إلى رونقها القديم، وبأن هلال الآداب الذي ولد في أواسط الجيل التاسع عشر سيصير بدراً.

Fahmi al-Mudarris
(1873–1944)

Introduced by Muhsin al-Musawi and
translated by Anna Ziajka Stanton

One of the foremost Iraqi writers, Fahmi al-Mudarris was effectively involved in the creation of the *Nahda* intelligentsia in Iraq. He achieved such a feat not only through his speeches and contributions to newspapers and journals but also through direct involvement in the politics of the emerging nation-state. He was manager of the Government Press, editor of the official gazette *Al-Zawra'*, and a member of the Education Council, and he later became director general of education. He was appointed as the chief chamberlain for King Faisal in 1921 but was discharged in 1922 after being accused of inciting demonstrations against the British high commissioner in Iraq, Sir Percy Cox. Many of the participants in the demonstrations were prominent leaders of the Iraqi national movement. More important, al-Mudarris was behind the establishment of Al al-Bayt University (1922–28), an institution that aspired to cement national bonds among Iraqis, regardless of their ethnic or sectarian divisions. He worked hard to promote an understanding of higher education as a comprehensive means of enabling Iraqi youth to lead the emerging nation-state. His many articles on education convey not only a fervent desire for transformation but also a balanced perspective and a well-informed mind, and their arguments are addressed to many different forums and audiences, including the British. To develop his rigorous reasoning, he drew on the history of university-level education among Arab peoples as well as on his experience as a professor at Istanbul University. The British were displeased with his national aspirations and alignment with the opposition, which was firm in rejecting British occupation.

As a writer, Fahmi al-Mudarris pioneered the art of the modern essay, making use of a long epistolary tradition with an eye to the needs of contemporary audiences. Direct, persuasive, and informative, his style marks a tendency among Iraqi writers to reach out to a wider readership.

Recommended Reading

Al-Musawi, Muhsin. *Reading Iraq: Culture and Power in Conflict.* I. B. Tauris, 2006.

FROM *A Brief Statement about Al al-Bayt University*

The History of Al al-Bayt University

A Word on the Topic. I wish to say a few words about the history of this university and its relation to Iraq's most splendid past and glorious future, and about what is still needed for the university to achieve its full potential—for through it the Iraqi *Nahda* will also realize the potential of its history, despite the obstacles that have stood in its way and the setbacks that it has faced.

Universities and Their Effect on Life. If there are, among the accomplishments of the mighty and powerful, those that can outlast the passage of time, then the greatest of these are surely educational institutions. And the greatest of all these are the universities, without which a nation can have no life.

If we wished to illustrate the effect that universities have on nations, we could not find a more suitable example than the work of that skillful artist who demonstrates plainly a life that has realized its potential [through education]. In such a life, the sentiments of the soul and the ideas of the heart traverse a straight course, without crook or curve.

Nine Centuries Ago. Baghdad was the first cradle in the world where universities flourished nine hundred years ago, and therefore Al al-Bayt University is not the first institution of its kind. For historians have noted that there were once thirty-five schools in Baghdad, their edifices high and lofty, which were spared from the hands of misfortune and accident. These included the Nizamiyya School, from which many famous scholars graduated, among them Hujjat al-Islam al-Ghazali. The fires of war consumed the school twice, but each time it was restored to its former condition.

Nizam al-Mulk Qawwam al-Din al-Tusi built this school in the middle of the Tuesday Market, and he opened it on Saturday the tenth of the month of Dhu al-Qaʿda in the year 459 [AD 1067], before the universities at Cambridge and Oxford, and before the Sorbonne, and before the University of Bologna, and indeed before the University of Salerno in Italy, which is the oldest university in Europe.

The Greatness of al-Mustansiriyya. Immediately after this, the Abbasid ruler Abu Jaʿfar al-Mansur al-Mustansir bi-llah built his school, al-Mustansiriyya, over the course of nine years. He began its construction in 625 [1227 or 1228] and completed it in 633 [c. 1236], and he opened the school on Thursday the twentieth of the month of Rajab in 631 [1234], four years before all its facilities and subdivisions were finished.

On the day it opened, the school's courtyard was filled with men of state and high dignitaries, many chamberlains and walis, teachers, judges, shaykhs of the outlying regions, important Sufis and scholars of Hadith, Qurʾanic reciters, preachers, eminent men, merchants, and a number of foreigners. At this assembly, poets recited the finest odes hailing the opening of the great institution, and the caliph himself looked out upon them from the balcony.

Al al-Bayt University and the Ruins. Al al-Bayt University was established in 1340 [c. 1922] atop the ruins of an [older] institution. We have already discussed the conditions in which this occurred [in the previous section]. The establishment of the university in such difficult circumstances is a miracle none could have accomplished except these miracle workers, the reformers.

The Objective in Establishing Al al-Bayt University

Dependence on Istanbul. The Iraqi people used to depend for their education in liberal arts and politics on the schools of higher learning in Istanbul and on specialists at Dar al-Funun there. Their diligence helped them overcome any difficulty they faced in comprehending the lessons, and the elements of culture and refinement that were instilled in them enabled them to establish their present government.

On Self-Governance. When the Iraqi people began administering their own affairs, they first had to consider—before thinking about anything else of importance for the country—how to find positions for those men capable of self-governance: workers on whom certain roles have long depended, intellectuals who are raising up Iraq and spreading the spirit of civilization and progress within it, and competent specialists on whom the government relies for its internal organization and without whom reform cannot be achieved.

The situation did, and still does, require haste in finding these positions, because stagnation can interfere with the works commissioned by the government. As long as stagnation lasts, idleness will spread, and this delays our nation in ascending to the ranks of the free nations and makes it vulnerable to various dangers and to the risk of failure in what it hopes to achieve, which is to move away entirely from the system of joint administration under the Ottomans.

The Building Committee. Each building throughout the six colleges will be built to hold four hundred students and will contain rooms for classes and lectures, a large seminar room, and administrative offices. Each classroom will be big enough for forty students, and the seminar room will hold two hundred and fifty.

As for the style of the buildings, there is no doubt that this requires further research and thought. The design and style of a building have a substantial effect on the experience [of those within it] generally, and on [their] education specifically. In the past, Iraq was a land with a building style that influenced the rest of the countries of the civilized world. Present conditions, however, require a new style. The hope is that if this style draws upon the finest artistic modes and makes best use of the country's natural resources, it will herald an Arab Renaissance (*Nahda*) in the arts.

Psychology and Sociology. [The study of] psychology and sociology is necessary for courses in religion, literature, and philosophy. The culture that is formed from these three disciplines does not carry any benefit when it is not infused with the spirit emanating from the bosoms of these two [former] fields. For example, if someone who is researching one of the religions is not knowledgeable about the psychology of converts to that religion or about the influence of society on them before and after their conversion or about the evolution of that society, which affects the outward expressions of the religion, then it is impossible for his analysis to trace each factor to its origin or understand the revelations that are the source of every religion. Each religion has its own outward expressions, which persist or change according to the social influences that shape the psychology of its converts.

The Intellectual Struggle at Al al-Bayt University

Modern Arts and Sciences. The system prescribes the teaching of the modern arts and sciences—psychology, sociology, metaphysics, jurisprudence, and the history of religions—in order to create a culture that suits the spirit of the current age. And the system grants licensees [in these disciplines] the right to employment in religious endowments generally and in education specifically. Work in endowments requires a knowledge of the assets that they administer, be they scientific, administrative, or economic, and work in education requires a knowledge of pedagogy.

The committees that set the curricula [at the university] are determined to eliminate or reduce the teaching of these disciplines, and this has generated debates that have raged for six years. The university takes a stand on the question and wins, then loses, then wins, then loses, and the modern arts and sciences are still in a state of peril and obscurity.

Al al-Bayt University: Between Doubt and Certainty

No Excuse for the Iraqis. I can find no excuse for a people who let themselves sleep for seven centuries to walk, when awake, the path of one who is frightened and doubtful, who steps uncertainly, shrinking from one action and hesitating before another, weary at times and rushing headlong at others. The West spared us the trouble of putting everything to the test of time. Nothing now remains for us to do except to claim civilization for ourselves using the most expedient methods possible. From a great distance, we can seize hold of what has filled the annals of progress, as the Japanese did, and after them the Turks and the Persians, who followed in their tracks. The notion that we might catch up with the West gradually, by following the path it followed since the beginning of its Renaissance to reach its current level of civilization, keeps us permanently seven centuries behind it.

The Youth of Iraq. In any case, the level of civilization in Iraq does not merit despair and despondence, because the youth have begun to feel that it is their duty to rise up with the country. Their talents and dispositions enable them to surmount all obstacles and traverse all necessary stages, and they have in His Highness [King Faisal I] the best benefactor and supporter.

Note

The translation is taken from these pages in Fahmi al-Mudarris: 293, 301, 303–06, 309, 330, 335, and 387.

Source of Arabic Text on Which the Translation Is Based

Al- Mudarris, Fahmi. فهمي المدرّس: من رواد الفكر العربي الحديث [fahmi al-mudarris: min ruwwad al-fikr al-'arabi al-hadith; Fahmi al-Mudarris: A Pioneer of Modern Arab Thought]. Edited by Yusuf 'Izz al-Din, Ma'had al-Buhuth wal-Dirasat al-'Arabiyya, 1970.

فهمي المدرّس
(١٨٧٣-١٩٤٤)

بيان موجز عن جامعة آل البيت

«التاريخ وجامعة آل البيت»

<u>كلمة في الموضوع</u>: أريد أن أقول كلمة عن حياة هذه الجامعة، وارتباطها بماضي العراق الجميل، ومستقبله العتيد، وعما يلزم لتكامل نموها الذي سيتكامل به تاريخ النهضة العراقية، مهما اعتورتها العراقيل، وانتابتها الشدائد.

<u>الجامعات وأثرها في الحياة</u>: وإذا كان هناك من مناقب العظام ما يخلد على كر العصور، فالمؤسسات العلمية من أجلها، وأجل منها الجامعات التي لا حياة لأمة بدونها.

وإذا أردنا أن نصور أثرها في الأمم، فلا نجد مثالاً ينطبق عليها غير عمل ذلك الرسام الماهر الذي يضع للأبصار أمثلة الحياة المتكاملة، المالكة لمشاعر النفس وخطرات القلوب لتسير عليها سيراً قوماً بلا اعوجاج ولا التواء.

<u>قبل تسعة قرون</u>: كانت بغداد أول مهد في العالم ترعرعت فيه الجامعات قبل تسعمئة عام، ولذلك لم تكن جامعة آل البيت هي الأولى من نوعها. فقد ذكر المؤرخون أنه: كان في بغداد مما تركته أيدي النوائب والحادثات خمس وثلاثون مدرسة عالية شامخة الصروح، منها: المدرسة النظامية التي تخرج فيها جمهور من مشاهير العلماء، منهم حجة الإسلام الغزالي وقد التهمتها نيران الحروب مرتين، وأعيدت كما كانت.

بناها في وسط سوق الثلاثاء نظام الملك قوام الدين الطوسي، وفتحها يوم السبت عاشر ذي القعدة سنة تسع وخمسين وأربعمئة، قبل جامعة كيمبريج وأوكسفورد، والسوربون، وقبل جامعة بولونيا، بل وقبل جامعة سالرن الإيطالية التي هي أقدم جامعة في أوروبا.

المستنصرية وعظمتها: وبنى على متوالها أبو جعفر المنصور المستنصر بالله
العباسي مدرسته المستنصرية في تسع سنوات، بدأ في عمارتها سنة خمس
وعشرين وستمئة، وأتمها سنة ثلاث وثلاثين، وفتحها يوم الخميس العشرين
من رجب سنة إحدى وثلاثين وستمئة، قبل إتمام مرافقها وفروعها بأربع سنين.
وفي ذلك اليوم غصت رحابها برجال الدولة، وأصحاب المناصب والمساند،
وسائر الحجاب والولاة، والمدرسين، والقضاة، ومشايخ الأرباض، وكبار الصوفية
والمحدثين، والقراء، والوعاظ، والأعيان، وطائفة من التجار، وفريق من
الغرباء . . . ينشد عليهم الشعراء غرر القصائد تنويهاً بافتتاح ذلك المعهد
القويم، وقد أطل من الشرفة عليهم الخليفة.

جامعة آل البيت والأطلال: وتأسست جامعة آل البيت سنة ١٣٤٠ هـ على
أطلال معهد يكتنفه من الأحوال ما ذكرنا فتأسيس الجامعة في ظروف صعبة،
خارقة لا يتحدى بها إلا أصحاب الخوارق من المجددين.

«جامعة آل البيت والغاية في تأسيسها»

الاعتماد على إستانبول: كان الشعب العراقي يعتمد في تربيته الفنية والسياسية
على المدارس العالية في إستانبول وعلى شعب الاختصاص في دار الفنون وعلى
ما كان في الأمر من صعوبة التناول ساعده الجد على أن يتقوم فيه من عناصر
الثقافة والتهذيب ما مكنه من تأسيس حكومته الحاضرة.

بعد الانفراد: فلما انفرد بالإدارة وجب عليه أن يفكر—قبل أي عمل من
الأعمال الضرورية للبلاد—في إيجاد مخارج للرجال القادرين على القيام
بواجبات الحكم الذاتي من موظفين تستند إليهم المناصب، ومفكرين ينهضون
بالعراق، ويبثون فيه روح الحضارة والتمدن، ومتخصصين أكفاء لا يمكن
للحكومة أن تعتمد في تشكيلاتها إلا عليهم، ولا يتحقق الإصلاح إلا بهم.
والموقف كان ولا يزال يحتم الإسراع إلى إيجاد تلك المخارج، لأن التوقف
يحول دون الأعمال المكلفة بها الحكومة، وعلى قدر إمداده يزداد الفراغ
اتساعاً يؤخر الأمة عن المستوى الذي يرفعها إلى مصاف الأمم الحرة، ويجعلها

عرضة للأخطار، وللفشل فيما كانت تؤمله من الانفصال عن الإدارة المشتركة في عهد الدولة العثمانية.

<u>اللجنة التأسيسية</u>: وكل بناء من أبنية الكليات الست سيشاد باتساع يستوعب أربعمئة طالب ويحتوي على غرف للصفوف والخطب وندوة كبيرة وإدارات وتسع كل غرفة من غرف الصفوف أربعين طالباً والندوة مائتين وخمسين شخصاً.

أما طرز البناء فلا شك في أنه يقتضي زيادة البحث والتبصر لأن للفن وطرز البناء تأثيراً كبيراً على الحياة عامة والتعليم خاصة، ولقد كان العراق فيما مضى موطن طراز من البناء امتد تأثيره إلى سائر أقطار العالم المتمدن، وأما الأحوال الحاضرة وكيفية البنيان فتقتضي طرزاً جديداً والأمل أنه إذا اتخذ من الوسائط الفنية أفضلها وأحسن استخدام المواد الطبيعية في البلاد أن يكون هذا البناء طليعة نهضة عربية في الفنون.

<u>علم النفس وعلم الاجتماع</u>: وأما علم النفس وعلم الاجتماع فإنهما من العلوم التي تستلزمها مناهج الشعب الدينية، والآداب، والفلسفة، لأن الثقافة التي تتكون في هذه الشعب الثلاثة لا تأتي بفائدة ما لم تمتزج بالروح المنبعث من جوانح هذين العالمين فالباحث في دين من الأديان مثلاً، إذا لم يكن عالماً بنفسية معتنقي ذلك الدين، وبتأثير الحالة الاجتماعية قبل الاعتناق وبعده، وتطورها المؤثر في مظاهر الدين يستحيل عليه عند التحليل إرجاع كل عنصر إلى أصله ويتعذر عليه معرفة الانبعاثات التي هي الأساس لظهور كل دين بمظاهر خاصة تمتد أو تتغير تبعاً للمؤثرات الاجتماعية المتكونة منها نفسية المعتنقين.

«جامعة آل البيت والجهاد العلمي»

<u>العلوم والفنون الحديثة</u>: يحتم النظام تدريس العلوم والفنون الحديثة لتكوين ثقافة دينية تلائم روح العصر الحاضر من العلوم والفنون الحديثة بعلم النفس وعلم الاجتماع وعلم ما وراء الطبيعية وفلسفة التشريع وتاريخ

الأديان—ويمنح النظام المجازين حق التوظف في أعمال الأوقاف عامة والتعليم خاصة والأعمال الوقفية تتطلب معرفة بأصول إدارتها علمية كانت أو إدارية أو اقتصادية والتعليم يتوقف على المعرفة بعلم التربية.

واللجان التي تضع المناهج تلتزم حذف هذه العلوم أو بترها، فتدور حولها المناقشات ست سنوات والجامعة تعالج الأمر فتفوز ثم تخسر ثم تفوز ثم تخسر، ولا تزال العلوم والفنون الحديثة تحت الخطر والإبهام.

«جامعة آل البيت: بين الشك واليقين»

<u>لا عذر للعراقيين</u>: ولا أجد عذراً لشعب استنام سبعة قرون أن يسير في يقظته سير المتهيب المرتاب متلمساً مواقع القدم محجماً عن عمل، متردداً في آخر، يهرم تارة وينقض أخرى. والغرب كفانا مؤونة التمحيص على أيدي القرون. ولم يبقَ سوى التمثل بالحضارة بما أعدته الحضارة نفسها من الوسائط السريعة التي نستطيع بها أن نختطف ما تخلل صفحات التطور من بُعد سحيق، كما فعل اليابان واقتفى أثرهم الترك والفرس.

وأما القول بالتدرج على نحو ما سار عليه الغرب منذ بداية نهضته إلى أن بلغ منزلته هذه من التمدن، فذلك مما يجعلنا طول حياتنا بعيدين عن الغرب سبعة قرون.

<u>شباب العراق</u>: ومهما كان الأمر فالمستوى العراقي لا يدعو إلى اليأس والقنوط، لأن شباب العراق أخذوا يشعرون بواجبهم نحو النهوض. ولهم من المواهب والملكات ما يعينهم على اقتحام العقبات وطي المراحل، ولهم من صاحب الجلالة خير ناصر ومعين.

Salama Musa

(1887–1958)

Introduced and translated by John Baskerville

Salama Musa, a journalist and public intellectual, was a prolific contributor to the debate on how Egypt should orient itself in the early-twentieth-century Arab Renaissance. A Coptic Christian born in the Egyptian town of Zagazig, Musa was intrigued by the natural sciences and read in Egyptian journals and translations of European works about the latest scientific and social theories and trends. As a young adult studying in France and then in London (1908–11), he developed a fascination with George Bernard Shaw and H. G. Wells and their various conceptualizations of a scientific basis for social progress and a universal world order founded in culture.

Musa's collection of essays *What Is the Renaissance?* (1935) reflects his intellectual influences and relays to the reader what Musa contends are the key currents of the early twentieth century: a universal spirit of independence and freedom, progress and development based on scientific knowledge, and international collaboration. In the first excerpt, from the work's introduction, he defines the Renaissance in its European context as liberation from esoteric academic pursuits and the study of doctrine, opening the door to true scholarship and experimentation. The second excerpt is from his chapter "Language and the Renaissance," which is a plea to his compatriots—especially members of the Arabic Language Academy in Cairo—to let the Arabic language embrace the spirit of the times and assume its rightful role in the Arab Renaissance. He calls for the adoption of a universal lexicon of science and technology terms, unhindered by the machinations of an institution that attempts to preserve cultural authenticity by keeping this lexicon out of the language. To counter the argument that the current era's universal values—as exemplified by Europe—are incongruous with Egyptian cultural integrity, Musa lists Arabic terms of European etymological origin that demonstrate a shared Greek-Roman-Egyptian heritage predating Egypt's Arab-Islamic heritage by centuries.

Recommended Reading

Al-Sayyid-Marsot, Afaf Lutfi. *Egypt's Liberal Experiment: 1922–1936*. U of California P, 1977.

Egger, Vernon. *A Fabian in Egypt: Salamah Musa and the Rise of the Professional Classes in Egypt, 1909–1939*. UP of America, 1986.

Ibrahim, Ibrahim A. "Salama Musa: An Essay on Cultural Alienation." *Middle Eastern Studies*, vol. 15, 1979, pp. 346–57.

Musa, Salama. *The Education of Salama Musa*. Translated by L. O. Schuman, E. J. Brill, 1961.

Suleiman, Yasir. *The Arabic Language and National Identity*. Georgetown UP, 2003.

FROM *What Is the Renaissance?*

Introduction

We are in a Renaissance, and we must understand the meanings of *Renaissance*. We must not adopt the position of distant observers but work within it, cooperate with it, and experience its movement toward the future.

The Renaissance is wealth, power, culture, health, and youth. However, wealth could comprise counterfeit currency, just as power, culture, health, and youth could be misleading and false. . . .

Psamtik was an Egyptian pharaoh who ruled between 712 and 666 BC. He was the founder of the twenty-sixth dynasty. The word *founder* means that he conquered enemies, set goals, and achieved them through much planning.

However, his good intentions in serving his homeland outweighed his shrewdness and foresight. Egypt's enemies surrounded the nation. They invaded it from the west and the south. And in the east, the Egyptians suffered defeats. The future looked bleak, with the nation fragmented and the allegiance of the people split between the men of religion and the ruling elite. The intrigues and plots were unceasing.

With pure devotion and iron will, the man [Psamtik] thought about what had happened to Egypt. He recalled those first centuries when [the pharaoh] Khufu said, "Erect a pyramid for me," and in a matter of years it was built and could be seen touching the sky. Psamtik saw the pyramids as we see them today. He read history and lamented his country's condition and weakness.

He thought. Then he thought some more. Finally he concluded that Egypt could not regain its past glory except through a return to the customs of its predecessors. So the ancient religious ceremonies were revived, as was the study of the ancient religious texts. Ancient styles of art were reinvigorated. In addition to these changes, he returned to Saqqara, where the pyramids housed the graves of the ancient pharaohs, and he called for burying the pharaohs in them once more.

Psamtik considered this a renaissance, despite the fact that many years separated him and Khufu, just as they separate Psamtik himself and us.

"Return to the ancients" was his slogan. It was a bankrupt slogan, though, as Egypt was more magnificent [in Psamtik's time] than it had been in the days of Khufu. We know this from the accomplishments of his successor, Nikau, who prepared ships to circumnavigate Africa. How does building pyramids compare with achieving such a great feat?

New conditions arose in the world around Egypt. They required new ingenuity, not returning approximately 2500 years into the past.

Barely one hundred years later, Egypt's Assyrian and Persian enemies overran and destroyed Egypt. The slogan "Return to the ancients" had done the nation no good.

Between the years AD 500 and 1000, darkness reigned over Europe.

It was a pitch-black darkness, because culture depended on monks, who were debating the geography of heaven rather than the geography of this world. The monks taught people how to die rather than how to live. They became embroiled in "intellectual" debates worthy of children (and even children should have scoffed at them), such as the value of the number 7 in the world and the hereafter, the number of angels that can stand on the tip of a needle, the location of the soul in the body, and so on.

They were debating doctrine and not facts.

However, little by little the Europeans realized that they were ignorant. They looked around them and found that the Islamic nation in Spain and in the East lived a life of power and intelligence. So they also began to pursue this life, studying and translating the works of Ibn Rushd [Averroes], Ibn Sina [Avicenna], Ibn Tufayl, Ibn Hazm, and others.

Then, when they were no longer content with what the Muslims had written, they translated into Latin the works of the ancient Greek that the Arabs had translated into Arabic. So they came to know Plato and Aristotle through the Arabic language.

When the Greeks migrated from Constantinople to western Europe, the Europeans learned even more. They corrected translation errors that the Muslim translators had committed when they translated Aristotle, Plato, and others into Arabic. The Renaissance men went on daring and thinking.

But little by little they realized that they had escaped from and rid themselves of the ancients of the church only to replace them with the ancient Greeks.

The Arabs did not disagree with the ancients. They relied upon them to the point that Ibn Rushd, just like Aristotle, did not believe in the creation of man.

But those European Renaissance men began to wonder: Is sound, true knowledge taken from the books of the ancient scholars or from nature?

They studied medicine, for example, in the books of Jalinus and Ibn Sina, but they did not know how to dissect the human body.

Here we may identify a Swiss man of German origin, born in 1493. He studied the ancient scholars but cursed them instead of blessing them. He is Paracelsus.

The name is a bit odd. It means "above Celsus," and it is a name that Paracelsus chose for himself and for which he discarded his birth name. Celsus, whom he announced that he was above, was a Roman scholar who had authored an encyclopedia that was studied in the universities in the Middle Ages and beyond.

Paracelsus said, "I am above the ancient scholars. I am above your respected scholar Celsus."

And he did not stop there.

He gave lectures in the city of Basel in the German language. Here, stop and consider that the language of education in European universities during that time and after was Latin. However, he refused to lecture in this "ancient" language.

He was a popular man—that is, a man of the people.

He dared to teach in the spoken language of the common people: German. In all of Europe, he was the first to do so.

His lectures focused on medicine and healing.

One morning, after searching, worrying, wondering, and not being able to rest, he decided to take the most definitive stance in the history of Europe and, as a matter of fact, in the history of humankind.

He did not go to the school to deliver his lecture, as was the custom.

Rather, he gathered the works of Ibn Sina and Jalinus and carried them on his back until he reached the city square. There, he laid them on the ground and began to speak:

"The ancient scholars were no better than we are; they did not know the scope of what we know.

"Studying the ancient scholars is beneficial, but studying nature is more beneficial.

"The ancient books are full of errors, and their authors are not infallible.

"Medicine relies on experiments, not on customs. We learn it from nature, not from books."

Throngs of students, professors, common people, and the elite gathered around him in the city market, the public square. When he finished his speech, he set fire to the works of Jalinus and Ibn Sina.

In our lands and in our time, a new spirit of vitality has burst forth, questioning anew the values and meaning of life, society, and progress. However, we are still mixed up, confused, indecisive. We do not know whether to adhere to the ancient values or the new ones.

What is the Renaissance?

Is it the ancient values?

What I fear most is that we will become victorious over the colonizers and manage to expel them, that we will defeat and subdue those who exploit us, but that we will fail to overcome the [influence of] the Middle Ages on our lives and that we will succumb to the slogan: "Return to the ancients."

Will we repeat Psamtik's tragedy? Does progress and civilization mean that we bury our dead in Saqqara?

Language and the Renaissance

In the Middle Ages, the Church dominated Europe. This domination was most intense in cultural matters. Aristotle was not read or studied except when it was in the interest of the Church. Books were not written and children were not taught in schools except for this purpose. The language of the Church [Latin] was not a language that the people spoke; it was only a language that they wrote.

But the spirit of independence that gained ground during the Renaissance allowed Machiavelli to take control of politics and separate it from the Church. It allowed Galileo to take control of astronomy and separate it from the Church. And it allowed Luther to separate religion itself from the Church.

European nationalisms originated with Luther. For, when he translated the Bible from Latin to German, he made the Christian religion a "national" religion. He elevated vernacular languages that had not been [previously] written or studied. Latin fell from its position of prominence, and the national languages began to flourish. Each of these languages became a language of religion, science, and literature and began to be studied, even as Latin faded into neglect and obscurity.

However, do not imagine that this battle between vernacular languages and the language of religion [Latin] was a minor struggle. The proof that Latin was a powerful force rests in the persistence of Latin in the European universities; the fact that high school students in France, Germany, and elsewhere are forced to learn it; and the persistence of its terms in legal

expressions and idioms. When the European nations modern-
ized the Church and its language, they were struggling through
the most difficult task of their social, religious, and intellectual
lives. Only a hundred years ago, Latin was the language of dis-
course in the Hungarian parliament.

One could surmise that Europe did not gain much by dis-
carding Latin (the language of writing among the educated
people) and having each nation adopt its own language. For
Latin brought people together as one nation, both religiously
and linguistically. However, reflection on the history of war
invalidates this assertion. For the English fought the Americans
despite the fact that they shared one language and one religion.
The wars of the Middle Ages, when Latin was universal, were
as numerous as the wars after the European Renaissance.

These days our minds have taken on a universal character,
and we have begun to look to our international organizations in
the hope of forging a universal language. Therefore we cannot
help feeling a bit sad about the loss of Latin or its relegation
to the realms of universities, convents, and churches. But the
spirit of the Renaissance is the spirit of independence itself.
The Renaissance scholars who called for science, literature, and
renewal in morals and politics also felt national pride, a feel-
ing that led them to hold vernacular languages in high esteem.
They looked toward the future, indifferent to what tied them
to the past. If the Europeans had put religion and the language
of religion above nationalism, then Europe would now be one
country with Rome as its capital.

European states faced great difficulties in order to achieve
independence. For more than a hundred years after the Renais-
sance, these nations continued to produce works in Latin and to
translate Arabic and Greek works into Latin until each nation
forged its own dignity, character, independence, and language.

Then, separation from the European Church—the Church
of Rome—became more widespread. As the humanist spirit of

independence took root, it led to the separation of church and state. Whereas the Church had dominated everything during the Middle Ages, it was now split from all affairs other than religion.

This split may trouble some readers. However, here we are trying to decipher the facts that appear to us as we read about the history of the European Renaissance.

Our Arabic European Words

Cultures mixed, made exchanges, and borrowed from one another. No nation separated itself from the world and lived in isolation, other than China. As China alone remained at a disadvantage, the rest of the world marched forward toward progress, such that when China opened its doors after its isolation, it trailed behind the rest of the world by about a thousand years.

Borrowing among cultures fertilizes them, as if a living body were breeding with a different living body—producing new breeds and then, through evolution, new species.

We describe the years between AD 500 and 1100 as the "Dark Ages" in Europe. Its main cause was Europe's isolation. Europe had lost contact with Asia and Africa and had become self-sufficient in its economic affairs. Rome no longer knew India, and Athens no longer knew China.

During this same era, the Arab nation avoided isolation and thus became civilized. It knew China, it knew Spain, and it knew everything in between. It engaged in cultural exchange with India, China, and Iran. It transported the practice of paper making from China to Europe and brought the numbering system from India to Europe as well.

If it were not for paper and numbers, Europe would not have reached this degree of knowledge and industry today.

About two thousand years before that, the Phoenicians (a Semitic nation like the Arabs) brought their letters that they had derived from Egyptian hieroglyphic script to Europe as well.

At present, we in Egypt are oppressed and exhausted by European colonization. This leads us to resent European culture.

We may be excused in this matter, for Europe imposes a brutal colonization on the Arab nation and on other nations. However, in European nations there are those who understand that colonization is a crime. One can read about the students in Paris who rejoiced on 21 February when Egyptian students, joined by Egyptian workers, demonstrated against colonization and demanded independence. And when they arrived at the Qasr al-Nil Square, English soldiers attacked them, killing some and injuring others.

This day became an international day of celebration, a symbol of the struggle for freedom and independence against the colonizing nations.

In Europe, there are decent people who denounce colonization. I am trying to make it clear to readers—especially to the members of the Egyptian Language Academy, who hate European words—that our Arabic language contains hundreds of European words, just as European languages contain hundreds of Arabic words. Together with the Europeans, we must find in this phenomenon grounds for cooperation, love, and the human unity for which every humane person strives.

Older nations preceded Europe in civilization. Therefore it is no wonder that the word *uruba* ["Europe"] is Semitic (from *urub* or *ghurub* ["sunset," from *al-gharb*, meaning "the West"]). This is because the Phoenicians described European territories as being west of their lands, on the other side of the Mediterranean.

If Hannibal the Carthaginian (his son-in-law was Hasdrubal) had not been defeated in his war with the Romans, Europe would now be linguistically linked to the Semitic nations.

As the Europeans borrowed from us, we borrowed from them.

For there was an Arab state near Damascus. It is the state of Palmyra or Zenobia. The Arabs call it al-Ziba'. It was a Greco-Arab state. Among the hundreds of words that entered our language before Islam, one may note that a lot of the Greek words point to the fact that the ruling class was Greco-Arab.

Consider, for example, the word *sayf* ["sword"]. It is a Greek word. I used to doubt this, given that the sword could be described as *muhannad* or *hindawani*, which means "from India" [*al-Hind*], a nation famous for its metal work. But, it became clear to me that *sayf* was a Greek word, in pronunciation and in meaning. . . .

I have also found a number of "cultural" words that could be traced back to Latin or Greek, such as *pen, paper, language, literature, dance, music, history, geography, philosophy, sophistry,* and *decoration.* . . .

All of this proves that cultures borrow from one another. In the end, this borrowing represents cross-pollination, fertilization, and an increase in mutual understanding and humanism.

Thus, there is no harm in our adopting European words for European inventions and discoveries.

Source of Arabic Text on Which the Translation Is Based

Musa, Salama. ‏ما هي النهضة؟‏ [ma hiya al-nahda; What Is the Renaissance?].
Al-Hay'a al-Misriyya al-'Amma lil-Kutub, 1993, pp. 3–8, 73–80.

سلامة موسى
(١٨٨٧-١٩٥٨)

ما هي النهضة؟

«المقدمة»

نحن في نهضة فيجب أن نفهم معاني النهضة.

ويجب أيضاً ألا نقف منها موقف المتفرجين، إذ علينا أن نعمل فيها ونعاونها ونعيش اتجاهاتها نحو المستقبل.

النهضة ثراء وقوة وثقافة وصحة وشباب. ولكن قد يكون الثراء مؤلفاً من نقود زائفة كما قد تكون القوة والثقافة والصحة والشباب خداعاً وليس حقيقة.

***

كان «ابساماتيك» فرعوناً على مصر. تولَّى الحكم فيما بين ٦٦٦ و٧١٢ قبل الميلاد، وهو مؤسِّس الأسرة السادسة والعشرين، وكلمة «مؤسِّس» تعني أنه كافح أعداء ونصب أهدافا ودرس وحقق.

ولكنه كان رجلاً خالص النية في خدمة وطنه أكثر مما كان ذكياً بصيراً بمستقبل بلاده. وكان أعداء مصر يحيطون بها. فمن الغرب غارات. ومن الجنوب غارات. وفي الشرق هزائم. والمستقبل مظلم والأمة مفككة وولاء الشعب موزع بين الكهنة والعرش. والدسائس لا تنقطع.

وفكر الرجل في نية خالصة وعزم حديد فيما أصاب مصر، وذكر تلك القرون الأولى حين كان «خوفو» يقول: شيِّدوا لي هرماً. فما هي إلا سنوات حتى يراه ينطح السماء. وكان ابساماتيك يرى الأهرام كما نراها نحن الآن. وكان يقرأ التاريخ. ويرثي لبلاده وضعفها.

وفكر. ثم فكر. وانتهى أخيراً إلى أن مصر لن يعود إليها مجدها الغابر إلا إذا رجعت إلى تقاليد هؤلاء الأسلاف، فأحيت الشعائر القديمة ودرست نصوص الديانة القديمة، ونهضت بالفنون على أساليبها القديمة. بل زاد على

ذلك بأن عاد إلى سقارة حيث الأهرام، أي حيث قبور الفراعنة من الدولة القديمة، فقال بوجوب العودة إلى دفن الفراعنة فيها.

وحسب إبساماتيك أن هذه نهضة، مع أنه كان يفصل بينه وبين خوفو من السنين مثلما يفصل بيننا نحن وبين إبساماتيك نفسه.

«عودوا إلى القدماء» كان هذا شعاره. وكان شعار الإفلاس لأن مصر كانت في عصره أسمى مما كانت أيام خوفو كما يمكن أن نعرف ذلك مما قام به خلفه «نيخاو» الذي هيأ سفناً تدور حول أفريقيا. أين بناء الأهرام من مثل هذا العمل العظيم؟

إن ظروفاً جديدة نشأت في الدنيا المحيطة بمصر. وكانت تحتاج إلى استنباط جديد.

ولم تكن تحتاج إلى الرجوع إلى الوراء نحو ٢٥٠٠ سنة تقريباً.

ولم تمض على مصر بعد ذلك مئة سنة حتى كان الأعداء من الأشوريين والفرس يكتسحونها ويغتالونها. ولم ينفعها شعار: «عودوا إلى القدماء.»

***

فيما بين سنة ٥٠٠ وسنة ١٠٠٠ استولى الظلام على أوروبا.

وكان ظلاماً حالكاً. لأن الثقافة كانت وقفاً على الرهبان، يبحثون جغرافية العالم الآخر وهم لا يردون جغرافية هذا العالم. ويشرحون للناس كيف يجب أن يموتوا بدلاً من أن يشرحوا لهم كيف يجب أن يعيشوا. ويشتبكون في مشكلات «ذهنية» أولى بها أن يبحثها الأطفال وأن يضحكوا منها، مثل قيمة الرقم ٧ في الدنيا والآخرة. ومثل عدد الملائكة الذين يمكنهم أن يقفوا على رأس إبرة. ومثل مكان الروح من الجسم إلخ.

كانوا يبحثون العقائد لا الحقائق.

ولكن رويداً رويداً تنبه الأوروبيون إلى أنهم جهلاء، ونظروا حولهم فوجدوا أن الأمم الإسلامية في إسبانيا وفي الشرق تحيا حياة القوة والذكاء. فقصدوا إليها يدرسون وينقلون مؤلفات ابن رشد وابن سينا وابن طفيل وابن حزم، وغيرهم. ثم لم يقنعوا بما ألفه المسلمون، إذ هم نقلوا أيضاً للغة اللاتينية مؤلفات الإغريق القدماء التي كان المسلمون قد ترجموها إلى اللغة العربية. فعرفوا أفلاطون وأرسطوطاليس عن طريق اللغة العربية.

واستطاعوا أن يعرفوهم أكثر عندما هاجر الإغريق من القسطنطينية إلى أوروبا الغربية. فأصلحوا أخطاء الترجمة التي كان المترجمون المسلمون قد وقعوا فيها عندما نقلوا أرسطوطاليس وأفلاطون وغيرهما إلى اللغة العربية.

ومضى الناهضون يجترئون ويفكرون.

ولكن رويداً رويداً اتضح لهم أنهم قد خرجوا وتخلصوا من قدماء الكنيسة إلى قدماء الإغريق.

***

وإن العرب لا يختلفون عن القدماء لأنهم اعتمدوا عليهم. أي على القدماء. حتى أن ابن رشد كان يعتقد أنه لم يُخلق في العالم إنسان مثل أرسطوطاليس. وعندئذ تساءل هؤلاء الناهضون:

«هل المعارف الحقة الصادقة تؤخذ من الكتب القديمة أو تؤخذ من الطبيعة؟»

فقد كانوا يدرسون الطب مثلاً في كتب جالينوس وابن سينا ولكنهم لم يكونوا يعرفون تشريح الجسم البشري.

وهنا نجد رجلاً ألماني الأصل سويسري الوطن، ولد في ١٤٩٣، يدرس القدماء ثم يلعنهم بدلاً من أن يبارك عليهم. هو «باراكيلسوس.»

والاسم عجيب. فإنه اختاره لنفسه وترك اسمه الميلادي. ومعنى هذا الاسم «فوق كيلسوس.»

وكيلسوس هذا الذي أعلن أنه فوقه هو عالم روماني كانت له موسوعة تُدرس في الجامعات أيام القرون الوسطى بل بعدها.

أي أن باراكيلسوس يقول: أنا فوق القدماء. أنا فوق عالمكم المحترم كيلسوس. ولم يكتفِ بهذا.

فإنه كان يلقي محاضراته في مدينة بازيل باللغة الألمانية. وهنا قف قليلاً: ذلك أن التعليم كان إلى وقته وبعد وقته باللغة اللاتينية في جميع جامعات أوروبا. ولكنه هو أبى أن يلقي محاضراته بهذه اللغة القديمة.

كان شعبياً. كان عامّياً. أي كان مع الشعب.

واجترأ على أن يعلّم بلغة العامة. اللغة الألمانية. وكان أول من أقدم على ذلك في أوروبا جميعها.

كانت محاضراته خاصة بالطب والعلاج.

وذات صباح بعد اختبار وقلق، وتساؤل وأرق، رأى أن يقف الموقف الحاسم في تاريخ أوروبا. بل في تاريخ الإنسان.

ولم يذهب إلى الكلية لإلقاء محاضراته كما كانت عادته.

ولكنه جمع مؤلفات ابن سينا ومؤلفات جالينوس وحملها على ظهره إلى أن وصل وهو يلهث إلى ميدان المدينة. وهناك وضعها أمامه على الأرض وشرح يخطب:

إن القدماء ليسوا أفضل وهم لا يعرفون مقدار ما نعرف.

إن دراسة القدماء نافعة ولكن دراسة الطبيعة أنفع منها.

إن الكتب القديمة تحفل بالأخطاء ولم يكن مؤلفوها معصومين.

إن الطب تجارب وليس تقاليد. إننا نتعلمه من الطبيعة وليس من الكتب.

واحتشد حوله، في سوق المدينة، أي الميدان العام، فئات من الطلبة والأساتذة والعامة والخاصة. فلما انتهى من خطبته أشعل النار في كتب جالينوس وابن سينا.

***

لقد انطلقت في أيامنا حيوية جديدة في بلادنا تجدد القيم والأوزان في معاني الحياة والاجتماع والرقي. ولكننا لا نزال في اختلاط وارتباك وتردد لا نعرف هل نأخذ بالقيم القديمة أم بالقيم الجديدة.

ما هي النهضة؟

هل هي القيم القديمة؟

إن أسوأ ما أخشاه أن ننتصر على المستعمرين ونطردهم. وأن ننتصر على المستغلين ونخضعهم. ثم نعجز عن أن نهزم القرون الوسطى في حياتنا ونعود إلى دعوة: عودوا إلى القدماء.

هل نعيد مأساة ابساماتيك؟ هل يعني الرقي والتقدم أن ندفن موتانا في سقارة؟

«اللغة والنهضة»

كانت أوروبا مدة القرون الوسطى تحت سيطرة الكنيسة. وكانت هذه السيطرة على أشدها في النواحي الثقافية. فلم يكن أرسطوطاليس يُقرأ أو

يُدرس إلا لخدمة الكنيسة، ولم تكن الكتب تؤلف، أو الأطفال يُعلّمون في المدارس، إلا لهذه الغاية. وكان للكنيسة لغة لم يكن يتكلم بها الناس وإنما يكتبونها فقط.

ولكن نزعة الاستقلال التي فشت في النهضة، وجعلت ميكافيلي يستقل بالسياسة ويفصلها من الكنيسة، وجعلت جاليل يستقل بالفلك، يفصله من الكنيسة، وجعلت لوثر يفصل الدين نفسه من الكنيسة.

ومن لوثر هذا نشأت القوميات الأوروبية. فإنه حين ترجم الكتاب المقدس من اللاتينية إلى الألمانية جعل الدين المسيحي «قومياً» ورفع بذلك من شأن اللغات القومية التي لم تكن تُكتب أو تُدرس. ونالت اللغة اللاتينية عن مكانتها وظهرت اللغات الوطنية. وأصبحت كل منهم لغة الدين والعلم والأدب، وهي الظاهرة المدروسة، حين صارت اللاتينية مغمورة مهملة.

ولا يظن القارئ أن هذه المعركة بين اللغات القومية وبين لغة الدين اللاتينية كانت من المعارك الخفيفة. فإن بقاء هذه اللغة في الجامعات الأوروبية وإلزام طلبة المدارس الثانوية على تعلمها في فرنسا وألمانيا وغيرهما، بل بقاء التعابير والمصطلحات القانونية بألفاظها القديمة، يدل على أنها كانت قوة كبيرة جداً. وأن الأمم الأوروبية عندما تُحدّث الكنيسة ولغتها كانت تكافح أوعر المشاق في حياتها الاجتماعية والدينية والثقافية. وإلى قبل مئة سنة كانت اللاتينية لغة التخاطب في البرلمان الهنغاري.

وقد يقال أن أوروبا لم تكسب بترك اللاتينية التي كانت لغة الكتابة عند جميع المثقفين واعتماد كل منها على نفسها واتخاذها لغتها بدلاً منها. فإن اللاتينية كانت تربط بينها وتجعلها أمة واحدة ديناً ولغة. ولكن المتأمل لتاريخ الحروب يجد أن هذا الاعتبار لا قيمة له. فإن الإنجليز حاربوا الأمريكيين وكلاهما ينتمي إلى لغة واحدة ودين واحد. ولم تكن الحروب في القرون الوسطى حين كانت اللغة اللاتينية عامة أقل مما كانت عقب النهضة.

ونحن في أيامنا قد اصطبغت أذهاننا بصبغة عالمية فصرنا ننظر نظرة الرجاء لمنظماتنا الدولية ونفكر في إيجاد لغة عالمية، ولذلك لا نستطيع إلا الأسف على ضياع اللاتينية أو انحدارها إلى زوايا الجامعات والديورة والكنائس.

ولكن الشعور بالنهضة هو نفس شعور بالاستقلال. والناهضون الذين دعوا إلى العلم والأدب والتجديد في الأخلاق والسياسة شعروا بكرامة قومية تبعثهم على الإكبار من شأن اللغة القومية. واتجه نظرهم إلى المستقبل دون المبالاة

للروابط التاريخية في الماضي. ولو أن الأوروبيين وضعوا الدين ولغة الدين فوق القومية لكانت أوروبا الآن دولة واحدة عاصمتها روما.

وقد لقيت أوروبا صعوبات كبيرة في كل دولة بلغتها استقلال، وبقيت أكثر من مئة سنة عقب النهضة وهي تؤلف مؤلفاتها باللاتينية وتنقل إليها المؤلفات العربية والإغريقية حتى أصبحت لكل أمة كرامتها وكيانها واستقلالها ولغتها.

ثم أخذ هذا الانفصال من الكنيسة الأوروبية، كنيسة روما، يتفشى. وأخذت النفس الإنسانية في الاستقلال حتى فصلت الدولة من الدين. وأصبح الدين بعد أن كان يسيطر مدة القرون الوسطى على كل شيء مفصولاً من كل شيء.

وقد يسوء هذا بعض القراء. ولكننا هنا نحاول أن نقرر الحقائق التي تبدو لنا كما نقرأها في تاريخ النهضة الأوروبية.

«كلماتنا العربية الأوروبية»

تقارضت الثقافات وتلاحقت وأخصبت ولم تنفصل أمة عن العالم وتحيا في عزلة قط إلا إذا كانت أمة الصين، وعاد الضرر عليها هي وحدها، وسار العالم في موكب الارتقاء حتى إذا فتحت أبوابها بعد عزلتها كانت قد تخلفت عن هذا العالم نحو ألف سنة.

وتقارض الثقافات يخصبها كما لو كانت جسما حيا يتلاقح مع جسم حي أجنبي. فتخرج منه السلالات الجديدة، ثم على مدى التطور، الأنوار الجديدة.

وهذا الذي نسمّيه «القرون المظلمة» الذي نصف به السنين التي عاشت فيها أوروبا بين سنة ٥٠٠ وسنة ١١٠٠ ميلادية إنما كان مرجعه انعزال أوروبا أيضاً حين انقطعت مواصلاتها مع العالم في آسيا وأفريقيا، وحين أصبحت القرية استكفائية في اقتصادياتها. فلم تعد روما تعرف الهند ولم تعد أثينا تسمع عن الصين.

وفي هذه القرون نفسها لم تكن الأمة العربية منعزلة. ولذلك كانت متمدنة. إذ كانت تعرف الصين وإسبانيا وما بينهما. وكانت تتقارض الثقافة مع الهند والصين وإيران. فنقلت صناعة الورق من الصين إلى أوروبا. ونقلت الأرقام من الهند إلى أوروبا أيضاً.

ولولا الورق والأرقام لما كانت أوروبا على علومها وصناعتها الحاضرة.

وعن قبل ذلك بنحو ألفي سنة أدخل الفينيقيون، هم أمة سامية مثل العرب، حروفهم، التي نقحوها من الخط الهيروغليفي المصري، إلى أوروبا أيضاً.

ونحن في مصر، في الوقت الحاضر، نحس أننا مظلومون مرهقون بالاستعمار الأوروبي. ولذلك ننفر من الثقافة الأوروبية.

وليس شك أننا نعذر في هذا الأساس. لأن أوروبا تمارس الاستعمار بكل ما فيه من وحشية مع الأمة العربية وغير العربية. ولكن في هذه الأمم الأوروبية طوائف تعرف ولا تنكر أن الاستعمار جريمة. وقد كتبت عن الطلبة الذين احتفلوا في باريس بيوم ٢١ فبراير، وهو يوم نهوض الطلبة المصريين وانضمام العمال المصريين إليهم حين هبوا في تظاهرة تستنكر الاستعمار وتطالب بالاستقلال إلى أن وصلوا إلى ميدان قصر النيل فخرج إليهم الجنود الإنجليز فقتلوا منهم وجرحوا.

وقد أصبح هذا اليوم عيداً عالمياً. هو رمز الكفاح من أجل الحرية والاستقلال ضد الأمم الاستعمارية.

إن في أوروبا أناساً طيبين يستنكرون الاستعمار. وأنا هنا أحاول أن أبيّن للقراء، وخاصة لأعضاء المجمع اللغوي المصري الذين يكرهون الكلمات الأوروبية، إن لغتنا العربية تحتوي مئات الكلمات الأوروبية. كما أن اللغات الأوروبية تحتوي كذلك مئات الكلمات العربية . وإننا نحن والأوروبيين يجب إن نجد في هذه الظاهرة مجالاً للتعاون والحب وميداناً للوحدة البشرية التي يهفو إليها كل إنسان إنساني.

***

لقد سبقت الأمم السابقة أوروبا في الحضارة. ولذلك لا تستغرب أن تكون كلمة أوروبا سامية (أروب أي غروب). لأن الفينيقيين كانوا يصفون الأقاليم الأوروبية بأنها غرب بلادهم على الجانب الآخر من البحر المتوسط.

ولولا أن انهزم هنى البال القرطجني، وصهره أسدر نيال، في محاربته للرومان لكانت أوروبا الآن في اشتراك لغوي مع الأمم السامية.

وكما اقترض الأوروبيون منا اقترضنا منها.

فقد كانت هناك دولة عربية حول دمشق أو بالقرب منها.

هي دولة تَدمُر أو دولة زينب وهي التي يسمّيها العرب الزباء. فقد كانت هذه الدولة عربية يونانية. ومن مئات الكلمات التي دخلت لغتنا قبل الإسلام. ومما يلاحظ أن كثيراً من هذه الكلمات اليونانية يدل على أن الطبقات السائدة، طبقة الحاكمين، كانت عربية يونانية.

اعتبر مثلاً كلمة السيف. فإنها يونانية. وقد كنت أشك في ذلك وخاصة لأن السيف كان يوصف بأنه مهند أو هنداواني، أي من الهند التي اشتهرت بصهر المعادن، ولكن اتضح لي أن السيف كلمة يونانية لفظاً ومعنى. . . . .

ثم وجدت أيضاً أن هناك كلمات ثقافية عديدة تعود إلى اللاتينية أو اليونانية. مثل القلم، والقرطاس، واللغة، والأدب، والرقص، والموسيقى، والتاريخ، والجغرافيا، والفلسفة، والسفسطة، والزخرفة. . . . .

وكل هذا يدل على أن الثقافات تتقارض بأخذ بعضها من بعض. وهذا التقارض هو، في النهاية، تلاقح وإخصاب وزيادة في التفاهم والإنسانية.

وليس علينا لذلك أي ضرر من الأخذ بالكلمات الأوروبية للمخترعات والمكتشفات الأوروبية.

Khalil Gibran

(1883–1931)

Introduced and translated by Angela Giordani

Philosopher-poet, doyen of Arab Romanticism, visual artist, and theorist of the literary *Nahda*, Khalil (or Kahlil) Gibran transcends all labels that his diverse legacy suggests we assign him, save for Renaissance man. His writings span a variety of linguistic and intellectual traditions, including American transcendentalism, Islamic mysticism, and Blakean Romanticism. The effectiveness with which Gibran forged a universal aesthetic and ethic from his eclectic background is evident in the wild success of *The Prophet* (1923). Translated into forty languages and outsold in twentieth-century America only by the Bible, this work of wisdom literature sings a humanist gospel in poetic aphorisms, drawing from Christian and Sufi mystical ideas of overcoming the self and achieving harmony with the world.

After receiving elementary education from a tutor in his native Bsharri, a Maronite Christian village in northern Lebanon, the twelve-year-old Gibran traveled to America and settled in Boston, where he attended school and cultivated his artistic talents. His drawings attracted patrons from the city's avant-garde elite, who mentored him and funded his studies and travels. After returning to Lebanon in 1897, where he studied classical Arab and Islamic thought and literature for two years, he moved to Paris to seek an education in art. There he met fellow Arab visionaries with whom he set out to devise a cultural *Nahda* to awaken the East from its so-called slumber. He continued this project in New York's Arab émigré intellectual circles, writing books in Arabic and English while also contributing to Arab literary journals such as the Cairo-based al-Hilal ("The Crescent"), which published "The Future of the Arabic Language" in 1920.

"The Future of the Arabic Language" presents Gibran's answer to one of the Nahda's defining questions: How can the Arabic language be reformed to absorb the knowledge systems of European modernity and thereby create a semantic-conceptual framework in which to build Arab modernity? In 1920, al-Hilal conducted a survey asking leading linguists and literati how Arabic should be renewed to accommodate and further the Nahda. While most who responded viewed this task as an institutional one, demanding that a centralized authority be founded to direct the modernization of Arabic, Gibran declared it the responsibility of the ingenious individual, whom he named "the poet." The vision outlined in his article of reviving the Arabic language by freeing the Easterner from both tradition and Western influence encapsulates Gibran's unique conception of the Nahda as first and foremost a personal renaissance, predicated on the liberation of the body, mind, and soul of the Arab subject.

Recommended Reading

Beshara, Adel. "A Rebel Syrian: Gibran Khalil Gibran." *The Origins of Syrian Nationhood: Histories, Pioneers and Identity*, edited by Adel Beshara, Routledge, 2011, pp. 143–62.

Bushrui, Suheil. *Khalil Gibran: Man and Poet: A New Biography*. Oneworld, 1998.

Gibran, Khalil. "From 'The Future of the Arabic Language.'" Translated by Adnan Haydar. *Words without Borders*, Nov. 2010, www.wordswithoutborders.org/article/from-the-future-of-the-arabic-language.

Karam, Antoine G. "Gibran's Concept of Modernity." *Tradition and Modernity in Arabic Literature*, edited by Issa J. Boullata and T. DeYoung, U of Arkansas P, 1997, pp. 29–42.

Naimy, Nadeem. "Gibran and the Arabic Literary Movement in America." *Al-Abhath*, vol. 47, 1999, pp. 5–21.

Waterfield, R. *Prophet: The Life and Times of Khalil Gibran.* Allen Lane, 1998.
————. *The Voice of Khalil Gibran: An Anthology.* Arkana, 1995.

"The Future of the Arabic Language"

1. What is the future of the Arabic language?

A nation's language is a manifestation of its collective ingenuity; for if a nation's power of ingenuity were to subside, its language would halt in its progress. In such a halt lies regression, and in regression lies death and extinction.

The future of the Arabic language thus hinges on the future of innovative thought—formed or unformed—in all Arabic-speaking nations. If that thought exists, then the language's future will be as great as its past. If that thought does not exist, then its future will be like that of its sister languages, Syriac and Hebrew.

What is this power that we have called the power of ingenuity?

It is a driving force pushing the nation forward. In its heart lie hunger, thirst, and a desire for the unknown. In its soul lies a series of dreams that it seeks to fulfill, day and night, but no sooner does it fulfill one segment on one of its ends than life adds another segment on the other.

It is genius in individuals and zeal in the collective. Individual genius is nothing other than the ability to express the people's hidden inclinations in clear and perceptible forms. The poet of the *jahiliyya* geared up for battle because the Arabs were preparing for war. In the subsequent era—that of the *mukhadra-mun*—the poet grew and expanded because the Arabs were in a state of growth and expansion. He then branched out creatively in the era of the *muwallidun*, mirroring the Islamic nation as it branched out into other nations.[1] The poet continued progressing, ascending, and changing—appearing sometimes as a philosopher, other times as a doctor, and still others as an astronomer—until a lassitude overcame the power of ingenuity in the Arabic language, and the language fell asleep. During its slumber, the poets turned into rhymesters, the philosophers transformed into theologians, the doctors became quacks, and the astronomers turned into soothsayers.

If the foregoing is true, then it is also true that the future of the Arabic language depends on the power of ingenuity in all Arabic-speaking nations. If these nations do indeed possess a unique self or unity of spirit, and if the power of ingenuity in that self awakens after its long sleep, then the future of the Arabic language will be as great as its past; and if not, then it will not be so.

2. What might be the influence of European civilization and the Western spirit in it?

Influence is a form of food that language takes in from the outside. It chews and swallows it, transforming the good in it into the language's living body just as a tree transforms light, air, and earth into its branches, leaves, flowers, and fruits. If, however, a language lacks molars for chomping and a stomach for digesting, then the food does not merely pass through it uselessly but is transposed into lethal poison. Furthermore, how many trees can outsmart life in the shade? If not moved into sunlight, a tree wilts and dies. Thus has it come down to us: "For whosoever hath, to him shall be given, and he shall have more abundance: but whosoever hath not, from him shall be taken away even that he hath" [Matthew 13:12, King James Version].

The Western spirit is only one phase of many for humanity and one chapter among the many in human life, an extraordinary parade continuously proceeding. Languages, governments, and faiths are formed from the golden dust that rises from the procession's flanks. The nations marching on its front line are ingenious, and thus influential, while those walking at the procession's end are imitative, and thus influenced. Because Easterners used to lead while Westerners followed, our civilization had great influence on their language. Now they have become the leaders and we the followers. Their civilization, therefore, has naturally become a source of great influence on our language, ideas, and morals.

In the past, Westerners ate what we cooked for them, chewing and swallowing it, transforming and absorbing the good in it into their Western being. As for present-day Easterners, they eat what Westerners cook for them and swallow it, but it is not transformed and absorbed into their own being. Rather, it transforms them into quasi-Westerners. This condition frightens and grieves me, because it shows me that the East is at times like an old man who has lost his molars and at other times like a child who has not yet grown any at all!

The spirit of the West is both our friend and enemy: a friend if we subdue it, and an enemy if it subdues us. A friend if we open our hearts to it, and an enemy if we surrender our hearts to it. A friend if we take from it what agrees with us, and an enemy if we put ourselves in a position to agree with it.

3. What will be the impact of the political developments currently under way in Arab countries?

Thinkers and writers from the West and East have reached the consensus that Arab countries are in a state of political, administrative, and psychological disarray. The majority agree that this disarray is contributing to ruin and decline in those countries.

As for me, I wonder: Is it disarray or boredom?

In the case that it is boredom: Boredom spells the end for every nation and the doom of every people. Boredom is demise in the guise of fatigue and death in the semblance of sleep.

In the case that it is truly disarray: Disarray, as I see it, is always beneficial, because it brings to light what was hidden in the nation's spirit, rousing it from a drunken stupor to a new vigilance. Disarray wakes the nation from its coma like a storm come to shake its trees, break their desiccated branches, and scatter their yellow leaves, but not to uproot the trees. The phenomenon of disarray in a nation that still possesses something of its innate, instinctual self is the clearest sign both of its individuals' ingenuity and of its collective's potential. Indeed, a nebula is the first sign of life, not a sign of its end, and what is a nebula other than life in disarray?[2]

The impact of political developments in Arab countries will transform any disarray and obscurity contained therein into order and clarity. It does not and will not, however, replace boredom with passion or ennui with enthusiasm. Indeed, the potter can make a jar for wine or vinegar out of mud, but he cannot create anything out of sand and grit.

4. Will the Arabic language and the teaching of all disciplines in Arabic become commonplace in our schools and institutions of higher education?

Arabic will not spread to all schools and institutions of higher education until they come to have a categorically national character, and all disciplines will not be taught in the language until the management of educational institutions moves from the hands of charitable organizations, sectarian councils, and religious missions into the hands of local governments.

In Syria [the greater Levant], education came to us from the West in the form of charity. We were and still are devouring the bread of charity because we are not merely hungry but ravenous. There were times when that bread brought us back to life and, in reviving us, killed us. It revived us because it stirred our senses and stimulated our minds a little. It killed us because it divided our popular will, weakened our unity, severed our ties, and estranged our sects from one another. As a result, our country turned into a group of little colonies with different characters and clashing loyalties, each colony firmly settled on a mountain belonging to one of the Western nations while waving the patron nation's flag and singing its virtues. . . . The disparate opinions and diverging loyalties that exist in Syria today and that will continue into her political future are the most telling imprints of what those Western schools gave our society. Those of us whose education was conducted in English want America or England as a mandate power in their country, and those who studied in French call upon France to take care of their affairs. Meanwhile, those who have not studied either language want neither of these states but rather follow a politics nearer to their education and intellectual capacity.

It could be that our political loyalty to the particular Western nation that pays for our education is a sign of gratitude in Easterners' psyche. But what is this emotion . . . that plants a flower and uproots a forest? What is this emotion that revives us for a day and kills us for an era?

The truly generous benefactors in the West did not put barbs and thorns in the bread that they sent us. Naturally, they tried to benefit us, not harm us. How, then, did that thorn come to be there, and where did that barb come from? This is another issue that I leave for another time.

The Arabic language and the teaching of all disciplines in Arabic will in fact spread to all our schools and institutions of higher education. When that happens, our political loyalties will converge and our national dispositions will crystallize, because it is in schools where such loyalties and dispositions are formed. This will not happen, however, until we can educate the youth with national funds. This will not happen until the individual in our society becomes a son of one nation instead of two opposing nations, one for his body and one for his mind. This will not happen until we replace the bread of charity with bread made in our own homes, because the needy beggar cannot impose conditions on his wealthy benefactor. Whoever puts himself in the category of receiver cannot oppose the giver, for the receiver's destiny is always predetermined, whereas the giver's is his to choose.

5. Will formal Arabic language prevail over the different colloquial dialects and unify them?

The colloquial dialects are being altered and refined. Although they bend and soften, they do not and will not prevail, nor should they be prevailed over. . . . Like everything else, languages follow the law of survival of the fittest. There is plenty of that quality of "the fittest" in colloquial dialects, which will survive because they are closer to both the nation's way of thinking and the collective's goals. . . . They will fuse with the body of the language. . . .

The modern Italian language used to be a colloquial dialect in the Middle Ages, when the elite called it the language of "the rabble." . . . The dialects in Egypt, Syria, and Iraq are not further from the language of al-Ma'arri and al-Mutanabbi than the dialect of the Italian "rabble" was from the language of Ovid and Vergil. If a great man were to appear in the Near East and compose an extraordinary written work in one of these dialects, that dialect would become a formal language.[3] Such an event, however, I view as distant in Arab countries, since Easterners incline toward the past rather than the present or future. Whether they know it or not, they are conservative. If a great man were to emerge from among them, he would first need to display his talent in the rhetorical and discursive devices of his predecessors, thereby following in their path, which is none other than the shortest path between the cradle and the grave.

6. *What is the best means of reviving the Arabic language?*

The best means, nay the only means, of reviving the language is in the poet's heart, on his lips, and between his fingers, because the poet is the mediator between humanity and the power of ingenuity. He is the wire that transmits the psychologist's discoveries to the scholar, and the luminary's ideas to the cataloger and scribe.

The poet is the father and mother of the language, which goes where he goes and rests where he rests. If he passes away, then the language sits on his grave, wailing in grief until another poet comes to take its hand.

If the poet is the language's father and mother, then the imitator is its shroud weaver and gravedigger.

By poet, I mean every inventor, major or minor, every discoverer, strong or weak, every creator, great or lowly, every lover of the pure life, priestly or wretched, and everyone who stands in awe before the days and nights, philosopher or vineyard keeper.

As for the imitator, he neither discovers nor contrives anything but rather copies his personal life from his contemporaries and sews his intellectual and moral raiment out of patches cut from his ancestors' clothes. . . .

By poet, I mean the sailor who raises a third sail for his two-sailed ship, the builder who builds a house with two doors and two windows among houses with one door and one window, and the dyer who mixes colors unmixed by anyone before to extract a new color. After this sailor, builder, and dyer, there will come those who call the fruits of their labor by new names and thereby add a sail to the language's ship, a window to its house, and a color to its clothing.

As for the imitator, he goes from place to place on the path taken by a thousand and one caravans without veering from it, fearful of going astray or getting lost. He takes the beaten path—marched over by a thousand and one generations—in his lifestyle, vocation, food, drink, and clothing. His life thus remains an echo, and his being an insignificant shadow of a far-away truth about which he knows nothing and wants to know nothing.

By poet, I mean the worshipper who enters the edifice of his selfhood and falls on his knees—crying in bliss, wailing and singing hallelujahs in passionate invocation of God—and then leaves it, his lips and tongue uttering new nouns, verbs, letters, and semantic derivations to describe the forms of his worship, which is renewed every day. . . . He thus adds through his work a silver string to the language's lyre. . . .

As for the imitator, he repeats the supplications of other worshippers without volition or emotion. He thus leaves the language where he found it. . . .

By poet, I mean he whose soul detaches from the ways of mankind when he loves a woman . . . and then returns to weave from its experiences a wreath for the language's brow.

As for the imitator, he is an imitator even in his love. . . .

I repeat that the life of the language, its unity, proliferation, and everything else related to it, has depended and will depend on the poet's imagination. So the question is, do we have poets?

Yes, we have them. Every Easterner can be a poet in his field and garden, before his loom, in his temple, on his pulpit, and in his library. Every Easterner can liberate himself from the prison of imitation, come out into the sunlight and march in the procession of life. Every Easterner can surrender to the power of ingenuity hidden in his spirit: that age-old, eternal power that created sons of God from stones.

To those of you devoting your talents to poetry and prose, I say: If you hope to thwart those of your contemporaries following in your predecessors' footsteps, it is better for you and for the Arabic language to build a lowly shack out of your innate self than to erect a towering mansion from your acquired self. If you take pride in your aversion to writing in traditional

poetic forms—like the praise poem, eulogy, and felicitation—
it is better for you and for the language to die shunned and
despised than to give up your hearts as burnt offerings to icons
and idols. If you have a nationalist passion for portraying East-
ern life in a way that reveals its marvels of pain and joy alike,
it is better for you and for the language to take as your subject
the simplest phenomenon in your native surroundings than to
Arabize the grandest and most magnificent of what Westerners
have written.

Notes

[1]Gibran refers to three eras of Arabic poetry: the pre-Islamic era or
jahiliyya (often translated as "age of ignorance"), followed by the era of
the mukhadramun (a term for the pagan poets who died after the coming
of Islam), who lived through the revelation of the Qur'an, and finally the
era of the *muwallidun* (literally, "creators" or "producers"), who lived
during the Abbasid period.

[2]In *The Prophet*, Gibran writes, "Vague and nebulous is the beginning of
all things, but not their end" (92).

[3]Here, Gibran refers to the formal register of Arabic that came to be
known in contemporary terminology as Modern Standard Arabic.

Work Cited

Gibran, Kahlil. *The Prophet.* Alfred A. Knopf, 1971.

Source of Arabic Text on Which the Translation Is Based

Gibran, Khalil. مستقبل اللغة العربية [mustaqbal al-lugha al-'arabiyya; The
Future of the Arabic Language]. المجموعة الكاملة لمؤلفات جبران خليل جبران
العربية [al-majmu'a al-kamila li-mu'allafat jibran khalil jibran al-'ara-
biyya; The Complete Collection of Arabic Writings by Gibran Khalil
Gibran], Dar al-Jil, 1994, pp. 626–34. Originally printed in the March
1920 issue (no. 6) of *al-Hilal*, pp. 489–98.

خليل جبران
(١٨٨٣-١٩٣١)

مستقبل اللغة العربية

١—ما هو مستقبل اللغة العربية؟

إنما اللغة مظهر من مظاهر الابتكار في مجموع الأمة، أو ذاتها العامة، إذا هجعت قوة الابتكار توقفت اللغة عن مسيرها، في الوقوف التقهقر وفي التقهقر الموت والاندثار.

إذاً فمستقبل اللغة العربية يتوقف على مستقبل الفكر المبدع الكائن أو غير الكائن في مجموع الأمم التي تتكلم اللغة العربية. فإن كان ذلك الفكر موجوداً كان مستقبل اللغة عظيماً كماضيها، وإن كان غير موجود فمستقبلها سيكون كحاضر شقيقتيها السريانية والعبرانية.

وما هذه القوة التي ندعوها بقوة الابتكار؟

هي في الأمة عزم دافع إلى الأمام. هي في قلبها جوع وعطش وشوق إلى غير المعروف، وفي روحها سلسلة أحلام تسعى إلى تحقيقها ليلاً ونهاراً ولكنها لا تحقق حلقة من أحد طرفيها إلا أضافت الحياة حلقة جديدة في الطرف الآخر. هي في الأفراد النبوغ وفي الجماعة الحماسة، وما النبوغ في الأفراد سوى المقدرة على وضع ميول الجماعة الخفية في أشكال ظاهرة محسوسة. ففي الجاهلية كان الشاعر يتأهب لأن العرب كانوا في حالة التأهب، وكان ينمو ويتمدد أيام المخضرمين لأن العرب كانوا في حالة النمو والتمدد، وكان يتشعب أيام المولدين لأن الأمة الإسلامية كانت في حالة التشعب. وظل الشاعر يتدرج ويتصاعد ويتلون فيظهر آناً كفيلسوف، وآونة كطبيب، وأخرى كفلكي، حتى راود النعاس قوة الابتكار في اللغة العربية فنامت وبنومها تحول الشعراء إلى ناظمين والفلاسفة إلى كلاميين والأطباء إلى دجالين والفلكيون إلى منجّمين.

إذا صح ما تقدم كان مستقبل اللغة العربية رهن قوة الابتكار في مجموع الأمم التي تتكلمها، فإن كان لتلك الأمم ذات خاصة أو وحدة معنوية وكانت

قوة الابتكار في تلك الذات قد استيقظت بعد نومها الطويل كان مستقبل اللغة العربية عظيماً كماضيها، وإلا فلا.

***

٢—وما عسى أن يكون تأثير التمدين الأوروبي والروح الغربية فيها؟

إنما التأثير شكل من الطعام تتناوله اللغة من خارجها فتمضغه وتبتلعه وتحوّل الصالح منه إلى كيانها الحي كما تحوّل الشجرة النور والهواء وعناصر التراب إلى أفنان فأوراق فأزهار فأثمار. ولكن إذا كانت اللغة بدون أضراس تقضم ولا معدة تهضم فالطعام يذهب سدى بل ينقلب سماً قاتلاً. وكم من شجرة تحتال على الحياة وهي في الظل فإذا ما نقلت إلى نور الشمس ذبلت وماتت. وقد جاء: من له يُعطى ويزاد ومن ليس له يؤخذ منه.

وأما الروح الغربية فهي دور من أدوار الإنسان وفصل من فصول حياته. وحياة الإنسان موكب هائل يسير دائماً إلى الأمام، ومن ذلك الغبار الذهبي المتصاعد من جوانب طريقه تتكون اللغات والحكومات والمذاهب. فالأمم التي تسير في مقدمة هذا الموكب هي المبتكرة، والمبتكر مؤثر؛ والأمم التي تمشي في مؤخرته هي المقلدة، والمقلد يتأثر، فلما كان الشرقيون سابقين والغربيون لاحقين كان لمدنيتنا التأثير العظيم في لغاتهم، وها قد أصبحوا هم السابقين وأمسينا نحن اللاحقين فصارت مدنيتهم بحكم الطبع ذات تأثير عظيم في لغتنا وأفكارنا وأخلاقنا.

بيد أن الغربيين كانوا في الماضي يتناولون ما نطبخه فيمضغون ويبتلعونه محوّلين الصالح منه إلى كيانهم الغربي، أما الشرقيون في الوقت الحاضر فيتناولون ما يطبخه الغربيون ويبتلعونه ولكن لا يتحوّل إلى كيانهم بل يحولهم إلى شبه غربيين، وهي حالة أخشاها وأتبرم منها لأنها تبين لي الشرق تارة كعجوز فقد أضراسه وطوراً كطفل بدون أضراس!

إن روح الغرب صديق وعدو لنا. صديق إذا تمكنّا منه وعدو إذا تمكن منا. صديق إذا فتحنا له قلوبنا وعدو إذا وهبنا له قلوبنا. صديق إذا أخذنا منه ما يوافقنا وعدو إذا وضعنا نفوسنا في الحالة التي توافقه.

***

٣—وما يكون تأثير التطور السياسي الحاضر في الأقطار العربية؟

قد أجمع الكتّاب والمفكرون في الغرب والشرق على أن الأقطار العربية في حالة التشويش السياسي والإداري والنفسي. ولقد اتفق أكثرهم على أن التشويش مجلبة الخراب والاضمحلال.

أما أنا فأسأل: هل هو تشويش أو ملل؟

إن كان مللاً فالملل نهاية كل أمة وخاتمة كل شعب، الملل هو الاحتضار في صورة النعاس، والموت في شكل النوم.

وإن كان بالحقيقة تشويشاً فالتشويش في شرعي ينفع دائماً لأنه يبين ما كان خافياً في روح الأمة ويبدل نشوتها بالصحو وغيبوبتها باليقظة ونظير عاصفة تهز بعزمها الأشجار لا تقلعها بل لتكسر أغصانها اليانسة وتبعثر أوراقها الصفراء. وإذا ما ظهر التشويش في أمة لم تزل على شيء من الفطرة فهو أوضح دليل على وجود قوة الابتكار في أفرادها والاستعداد في مجموعها. إنما السديم أول كلمة من كتاب الحياة وليس بآخر كلمة منها، وما السديم سوى حياة مشوشة.

إذاً فتأثير التطور السياسي سيحول ما في الأقطار العربية من التشويش إلى نظام، وما في داخلها من الغموض والإشكال إلى ترتيب وألفة، ولكنه لا ولن يبدل مللها بالوجد وضجرها بالحماسة. إن الخزاف يستطيع أن يصنع من الطين جرة للخمر أو للخل ولكنه لا يقدر ان يصنع شيئاً من الرمل والحصى.

***

٤—هل يعم انتشار اللغة العربية في المدارس العالية وغير العالية وتعلّم بها جميع العلوم؟

لا يعم انتشار اللغة في المدارس العالية وغير العالية حتى تصبح تلك المدارس ذات صبغة وطنية مجردة ولن تعلم بها جميع العلوم حتى تنتقل المدارس من أيدي الجمعيات الخيرية واللجان الطائفية والبعثات الدينية إلى أيدي الحكومات المحلية.

ففي سوريا مثلاً كان التعليم يأتينا من الغرب بشكل الصدقة، وقد كنا ولم نزل نلتهم خبز الصدقة لأننا جياع متضورون، ولقد أحيانا ذلك الخبز، ولما أحياناً أماتنا. أحياناً لأنه أيقظ جميع مداركنا ونبه عقولنا قليلاً، وأماتنا لأنه فرق كلمتنا

وأضعف وحدتنا وقطع روابطنا وأبعد ما بين طوائفنا حتى أصبحت بلادنا مجموعة مستعمرات صغيرة مختلفة الأذواق متضاربة المشارب كل مستعمرة منها تشد في حبل إحدى الأمم الغربية وترفع لواءها وتترنم بمحاسنها وأمجادها. . . . وأعظم دليل على ما تقدم اختلاف الآراء وتباين المنازع في الوقت الحاضر في مستقبل سوريا السياسي. فالذين درسوا بعض العلوم باللغة الإنجليزية يريدون أمريكا أو إنجلترا وصية على بلادهم؛ والذين درسوها باللغة الفرنسية يطلبون فرنسا أن تتولى أمرهم؛ والذين لم يدرسوا بهذه اللغة أو بتلك لا يريدون هذه الدولة ولا تلك بل يتبعون سياسة أدنى إلى معارفهم وأقرب إلى مداركهم.

وقد يكون ميلنا السياسي إلى الأمة التي نتعلم على نفقتها دليلاً على عاطفة عرفان في نفوس الشرقيين، ولكن ما هذه العاطفة . . . التي تستنبت زهرة وتقتلع غابة؟ ما هذه العاطفة التي تحيينا يوماً وتميتنا دهراً؟

إن المحسنين الحقيقيين وأصحاب الأريحية في الغرب لم يضعوا الشوك والحسك في الخبز الذي بعثوا به إلينا، فهم بالطبع قد حاولوا نفعنا لا الضرر بنا. ولكن كيف تولد ذلك الشوك ومن أين أتى ذلك الحسك؟ هذا بحث آخر أتركه إلى فرصة أخرى.

نعم سوف يعم انتشار اللغة العربية في المدارس العالية وغير العالية وتعلم بها جميع العلوم فتتوحد ميولنا السياسية وتتبلور منازعنا القومية لأن في المدرسة تتوحد الميول وفي المدرسة تتجوهر المنازع، ولكن لا يتم هذا حتى يصير بإمكاننا تعليم الناشئة على نفقة الأمة. لا يتم هذا حتى يصير الواحد منا ابناً لوطن واحد بدلاً من وطنين متناقضين أحدهما لجسده والآخر لروحه. لا يتم هذا حتى نستبدل خبز الصدقة بخبز معجون في بيتنا، لأن المتسول المحتاج لا يستطيع أن يشترط على المتصدق الأريحي. ومن يضع نفسه في منزلة الموهوب لا يستطيع معارضة الواهب، فالموهوب مسيَّر دائماً والواهب مخيَّر أبداً.

***

٥—وهل تتغلب (اللغة العربية الفصحى) على اللهجات العامية المختلفة وتوحدها؟

إن اللهجات العامية تتحور وتتهذب ويُدلك الخشن فيها فيلين ولكنها لا ولن تغلب ويجب ألا تُغلب. . . . إن اللغات تتبع مثل كل شيء آخر سنّة

بقاء الأنسب، و في اللهجات العامية الشيء الكثير من الأنسب الذي سيبقى لأنه أقرب إلى فكرة الأمة وأدنى إلى مرامي ذاتها العامة. . . . سيلتحم بجسم اللغة . . .

لقد كانت اللغة الإيطالية الحديثة لهجة عامية في القرون المتوسطة، وكان الخاصة يدعونها بلغة «الهمج». . . . وليست اللهجات العامية في مصر وسوريا والعراق أبعد عن لغة المعرّي والمتنبّي من لهجة «الهمج» الإيطالية عن لغة أوفيدي وفرجيل. فإذا ما ظهر في الشرق الأدنى عظيم ووضع كتاباً عظيماً في إحدى تلك اللهجات تحولت هذه إلى لغة فصحى. بيد أني أستبعد حدوث ذلك في الأقطار العربية لأن الشرقيين أشد ميلاً إلى الماضي منهم إلى الحاضر أو المستقبل، فهم المحافظون، على معرفة منهم أو على غير معرفة، فإن قام كبير بينهم لزم في إظهار مواهبه السبل البيانية التي سار عليها الأقدمون، وما سبل الأقدمين سوى أقصر الطرقات بين مهد الفكر ولحده.

***

٦—وما هي خير الوسائل لإحياء اللغة العربية؟

إن خير الوسائل، بل الوسيلة الوحيدة لإحياء اللغة هي في قلب الشاعر وعلى شفتيه وبين أصابعه، فالشاعر هو الوسيط بين قوة الابتكار والبشر. وهو السلك الذي ينقل ما يحدثه عالم النفس إلى عالم البحث، وما يقرره عالم الفكر إلى عالم الحفظ والتدوين.

الشاعر أبو اللغة وأمها، تسير حيثما يسير وتربض أينما يربض، وإذا ما قضى جلست على قبره باكية منتحبة حتى يمر بها شاعر آخر ويأخذ بيدها.

وإذا كان الشاعر أبا اللغة وأمها فالمقلد ناسج كفنها وحافر قبرها.

أعني بالشاعر كل مخترع كبيراً كان أو صغيراً، وكل مكتشف قوياً كان أو ضعيفاً، كل مختلق عظيماً كان أو حقيراً، وكل محبّ للحياة المجردة إماماً كان أو صعلوكاً، وكل من يقف متهيباً أمام الأيام والليالي فيلسوفاً كان أو ناطوراً للكروم.

أما المقلد فهو الذي لا يكتشف شيئاً ولا يختلق أمراً بل يستمد حياته النفسية من معاصريه ويصنع أثوابه المعنوية من رقع يجزها من أثواب من تقدمه. . . .

أعني بالشاعر الملاح الذي يرفع لسفينة ذات شراعين شراعاً ثالثاً، والبناء الذي يبني بيتاً ذا بابين ونافذتان بين بيوت كلها ذات باب واحد ونافذة واحدة، والصباغ الذي يمزج الألوان التي لم يمزجها أحد قبله فيستخرج لوناً جديداً، فيأتي بعد الملاح والبناء والصباغ من يدعو ثمار أعمالهم بأسماء جديدة فيضيف بذلك شراعاً إلى سفينة اللغة ونافذة إلى بيت اللغة ولوناً إلى ثوب اللغة.

أما المقلد فهو ذاك الذي يسير من مكان إلى مكان على الطريق التي سار عليها ألف قافلة وقافلة ولا يحيد عنها مخافة أن يتيه ويضيع، ذاك الذي يتبع بمعيشته وكسب رزقه ومأكله ومشربه وملبسه. تلك السبل المطروقة التي مشى عليها ألف جيل وجيل فتظل حياته كرجع الصدى ويبقى كيانه كظل ضئيل لحقيقة قصية لا يعرف عنها شيئاً ولا يريد أن يعرف.

أعني بالشاعر ذلك المتعبّد الذي يدخل هيكل نفسه فيجثو باكياً فرحاً نادباً مهلّلاً مصغياً مناجياً ثم يخرج وبين شفتيه ولسانه أسماء وأفعال وحروف واشتقاقات جديدة لأشكال عبادته التي تتجدد في كل يوم . . . فيضيف بعمله هذا وتراً فضياً إلى قيثارة اللغة . . .

أما المقلد فهو الذي يردد صلاة المصلين وابتهال المبتهلين بدون إرادة ولا عاطفة فيترك اللغة حيث يجدها. . . .

أعني بالشاعر ذلك الذي إن أحب امرأة انفردت روحه وتنحت عن سبل البشر . . . ثم عادت لتضفر من اختباراتها إكليلاً لرأس اللغة تصوغ من اقتناعها قلادة لعنق اللغة.

أما المقلد فمقلد حتى في حبه . . .

أقول ثانية إن حياة اللغة وتوحيدها وتعميمها وكل ما له علاقة بها قد كان وسيكون رهن خيال الشاعر. فهل عندنا شعراء؟

نعم عندنا شعراء وكل شرقي يستطيع أن يكون شاعراً في حقله وفي بستانه وأمام نوله وفي معبده وفوق منبره وبجانب مكتبته. كل شرقي يستطيع أن يعتق نفسه من سجن التقليد والتقاليد ويخرج إلى نور الشمس فيسير في موكب الحياة. كل شرقي يستطيع أن يستسلم إلى قوة الابتكار المختبئة في روحه، تلك القوة الأزلية الأبدية التي تقيم من الحجارة أبناء الله.

أما أولئك المنصرفون إلى نظم مواهبهم ونثرها فلهم أقول: ليكن لكم من مقاصدكم الخصوصية مانع عن اقتفاء أثر المتقدمين، فخير لكم وللغة العربية

أن تبنوا كوخاً حقيراً من ذاتكم الوضعية من أن تقيموا صرحاً شاهقاً من ذاتكم المقتبسة. ليكن لكم من عزة نفوسكم زاجر عن نظم قصائد المديح والرثاء والتهنئة، فخير لكم وللغة العربية أن تموتوا مهملين محتقرين من أن تحرقوا قلوبكم بخوراً أما الأنصاب والأصنام. ليكن لكم من حماستكم القومية دافع إلى تصوير الحياة الشرقية بما فيها من غرائب الألم وعجائب الفرح، فخير لكم وللغة العربية أن تتناولوا أبسط ما يتمثل لكم من الحوادث في محيطكم وتلبسوها حلة من خيالكم من أن تعربوا أجل وأجمل ما كتبه الغربيون.

Part 2: Language and Civilization

The texts selected for this part show how the Arabic language becomes a key element of the *Nahda* narrative, from the attempts to standardize and systematize its syntax and grammar to its fluctuation between the colloquial and what will become known as Modern Standard Arabic. Arabic is also presented here as an element of fascination that mediates European perceptions of the Arab world.

The section starts with a selection from Jirmanus Farhat, who seeks to transform Arabic into a *Nahda* language avant la lettre. Writing in the early eighteenth century, he argues for the need to reorganize Arabic grammar in order to empower readers and writers (especially Christian Arabs) and enhance cultural production. Butrus al-Bustani, who edits, prefaces, and comments on this work, situates Farhat's project as an integral component of the *Nahda*.

We then move to Ya'qub Sannu°'s parody of Molière, which deals with the tribulations of a playwright lacking the funds to produce his work in 1870s Alexandria. Written in colloquial Egyptian, Sannu°'s play allows us to understand the multiplicity of linguistic registers that constitute *Nahda* texts.

Sannu°'s piece is followed by 'Abdallah al-Nadim's story about the son of Egyptian peasants who pretends to have forgotten Arabic upon his return from his studies in France. Al-Nadim mocks the process of civilization as the outcome of travel and blind acquisition of European habits and language. His other stories depict a group of men who are unaware of the world outside as well as a homosexual encounter in Cairo gone awry.

The following selection, by Hasan al-'Attar, Egypt's grand mufti, describes how a French scholar seduces him through his mastery of Arabic. Set during the French occupation of Egypt (1798–1801), the story frames the colonial encounter through a narrative of learning and seduction based in language.

In 'Ali Mubarak's fictional travelogue *Sign of Religion*, an Azhar imam, visiting Paris years after the French occupation, contests the view that Egyptians shouldn't have opposed the French when the French came to Egypt. The imam claims that despite their good work, the French were invaders, and it was thus natural for Egyptians to resist them. In this encounter, the object of desire is the Egyptian imam, surrounded by eager and fascinated Europeans, listening to his conversation.

Jirmanus Farhat
(1670–1732)

*Introduced by Kristen Brustad and
translated by Anthony Edwards*

Jirmanus Farhat was a poet, monk, teacher, grammarian, lexicographer, archbishop, and prolific translator who, from a Maronite monastery, laid the foundation for the grammatical work of Butrus al-Bustani, a *Nahda* luminary. Farhat's life and work show us that the *Nahda* had roots in the Levant that predated the usual *Nahda* time line. Farhat came of age in seventeenth-century Aleppo, part of a new, wealthy, Catholic merchant class that enjoyed good relations with their Muslim counterparts in a booming economy. For the Maronite Church, the seventeenth and early eighteenth centuries were an era characterized by the Arabization of texts and liturgy from Syriac, the Latinization of doctrine and practice, the founding of schools and libraries, and a deepening and yet sometimes tense relation with Rome, marked with clashes between papal missionaries and local clergy (Farhat himself addressed this tension in a letter to the Vatican).

These circumstances helped give rise to an indigenous cultural movement: the development of a classical Arabic poetic tradition among the Christian upper classes. Well before Protestant missionaries founded schools in Beirut, the educated Christians of seventeenth-century Aleppo were both consumers and producers of poetry in the classical Arabic style, an activity that required a literary education usually associated with an Islamic framework. Christians acquired this knowledge through private tutoring or reading and through study groups that circulated books and poems, and they met to discuss them. Out of this experience, Farhat, possibly the first Christian to write an Arabic grammar, acquired the education that enabled him to write

Issues Desired by Students Required. As the translated excerpt shows, his motivation came not from the Europeans but from his own experiences in Aleppo and in the Maronite Church and community. His grammar was published with commentary at least five times during the late nineteenth century, including in al-Bustani's well-known edition.[1] For al-Bustani, not only the grammar book but also Farhat the scholar must have served as important models.

Recommended Reading

Allen, Roger, and D. S. Richards, editors. *Arabic Literature in the Post-classical Period.* Cambridge UP, 2006.

Brustad, Kristen. "Jirmanus Farhat." *Essays in Arabic Literary Biography: 1350–1850,* edited by Joseph Lowry and Devin Stewart, Harrassowitz Verlag, 2009, pp. 242–51.

Marcus, Abraham. *The Middle East on the Eve of Modernity: Aleppo in the Eighteenth Century.* Columbia UP, 1989.

FROM *Issues Desired by Students Required*

Commentator's Foreword [by Butrus al-Bustani]

Praise God the Most High, the Most Bountiful
He Who Taught [the Use of] the Pen
Taught Man That Which He Knew Not. [Qur'an 96.3–5][2]

I, Butrus b. Bulus b. 'Abdullah al-Bustani, the lowly servant known for his mortal shortcomings and sinful defects, assert that *Issues Desired by Students Required*—authored by the venerable master, the eminent active scholar, the late Maronite Archbishop Jirmanus Farhat of Aleppo—is one of the simplest to use, easiest to understand, most beneficial, and best organized of books on morphology and syntax. Unfortunately, its abandonment to the mercy of scribes just piling on corruptions and distortions has put it out of reach for many students who would otherwise benefit from it. Hence I decided that dedicating my efforts to publishing this book—after revising, correcting, and editing it—would be a noble aim and a good deed.

Many had informed me that copies [of *Issues Desired*] written by the author exist, so I searched high and low for one. When I realized that this ambition was impossible to achieve, I made do with the copies I had gathered already from those in public circulation that I believed to be accurate, and on the basis of them I compiled this manuscript and printed it in large type by itself, leaving the body of the text as it was and taking great pains to proofread the manuscript out of fear of errors.

Farhat's intent was to present the youth of his denomination with a comprehensive book on Arabic grammar so that they would not find the subject estranging and have a bad experience with it. However, the accumulation of other tasks and the limitations of time did not allow him to fully realize his objective, which was to rely solely on his knowledge of the principles of grammar and not on the books of others. His book was thus not free from complexity, padding, and verbosity in some places, as is obvious to the discerning reader with sound taste. For all these reasons, I saw the necessity of supplementing it with marginalia that gave the rules and exceptions that Farhat neglected, which are needed by anyone who seeks to immerse himself in sound Arabic books and wants to understand the language found in valuable works of poetry and prose, or to produce in this language something of sound expression and good style. In all this I relied on what the famous, leading scholars in the field have stipulated.

I also added to [Farhat's] book a treatise on prosody and rhyme written by the famous Shaykh Nasif al-Yaziji, due to the strong relation between these two fields in practice. I placed all these elements in an index arranged alphabetically in order to make it easy to use, and I pointed out the ambiguities that I had found, caused by the negligence of copyists and the indulgence of commentators—although I left out some of what I found because it was obvious or because it was analogous to what I had mentioned already. My intention was to enhance the benefits [of the book], especially for students. I made my comments in fine print separated from the body of the text by a vertical line, and in the body of the text and the marginalia I put Indic numerals that point to the places where I highlighted or supplemented something, as you will see.

With the help of the Almighty, Farhat produced a comprehensive book relieving the learner from having to study any other texts or lengthy treatises in this field. I named the book *Lanterns Burning for Students Discerning*. I did not comment on his errors in order to condemn him, as if he had made a mistake while I was correct, but rather to alert the reader that he should ponder both opinions and judge in favor of one of them. The reader might judge against me, and from this I would benefit, because it is not impossible that I have erred. Merit is not reserved for one person alone, and above every learned person is another more learned.

I recognize Farhat's merits in erudition and labor, and I bear witness that he is unrivaled among Christians in the science of the Arabic language. However, no utterance is free from delusion; we have seen many great scholars fall into many a delusion. He who faults them for this may be unable to reproduce even some of what they produced. I admit that I am unable to attain even one of [Farhat's] levels of achievement. He heard what I have not heard, saw what I have not seen, and learned what I have not learned. Still, neither he nor I invented anything in this field. The only knowledge that we possess is what the books of our predecessors taught us. And if I am correct, hidden things remain in every corner; and if I err, it is in the nature of those like me to err, while infallibility and perfection belong to God, praise be to Him alone, above all.

Who is he whose traits are all virtuous?

It is noble enough for one to have his shortcomings counted.[3]

Author's Preface [by Jirmanus Farhat]

Praise be to God who renders deficient souls whole with His word and gives expression to both sound and defective verbs with His almighty power. His created objects were derived from dissolved elements, after He made prominent the insolubility of reason. He added the elements each one to another, so they fit together perfectly and were not confused or awry. *Prostration* be to His only Son Jesus Christ, the incarnate of the holiest vestments, whom He sent out of mercy for all the world and for our deliverance from sins and offenses. *Glorification* be to the Holy Spirit, who guides living beings toward the best attribute. *Exaltation* be to the Most Holy Trinity, the Lord of one essence and invincible power.

I, the humble servant of our Lord and prisoner of his own guilty stain, Jirmanus b. Farhat—the lowly monk and Maronite minister of Aleppo, who follows the statutes of the Lebanese monks ensconced in the order of Saint Anthony the Great— observed the dedication of some Christian students striving to learn Arabic grammar and its syntactic principles. Their efforts, however, fell short of their objective because their hands were tied and their fists were clenched in defeat. At this I was seized with both brotherly love and fatherly compassion to transform the unintelligible and to eliminate the obscure. Willingly I obeyed it, following the command of the Almighty Master who must be obeyed and the request of Him whom

I must follow. [A helping hand] whose incapacity thwarted it, though the act of striving enabled it; whose response [to the task] gave it merit, though its aim fell short. I hastened to lift the mask that had veiled the countenance of the Arabic language for some time and for some unknown reason. I wrote a book consisting of an introduction, three sections, and a conclusion. In this work, I gathered the rules of grammar, syntax, and morphology, which had been scattered in various books. I set down what was necessary and I eliminated what is obscure to us. Therefore, do not believe the critical reader who scrutinizes this project of ours, but rather say to him, "Everyone receives the sustenance that he needs, and the master of the house knows this best." So I omitted boring explanations and unfounded oppositions. When I saw how Ibn al-Hajib veiled comprehension with his narratives, how Ibn al-Hisham crushed conjectures with his accounts, and how Ibn Malik ruled minds through his excesses, what is this [lack of restraint] except extreme preciseness and elaborate meticulousness? Or is it that their goals do not include ours and that their requirements do not dictate ours? To this [is said]: They are in one valley, and we are in another. Someone convenes every assembly, yet how can the summoned respond if there is no summons?

In summarizing everything that we have set forth, our intention in composing this work is trifold: first, to eliminate the difficulty that results from obscure expressions; second, to succinctly gather all indispensable knowledge from this field into a single composition; and third, to furnish examples from the Holy Bible whenever possible. I named this [composition] *Issues Desired by Students Required*, with the aim of benefiting Christian children so that they would not find the subject estranging and have a bad experience with it, so that they would not become tired and thus tiresome, and so that they would not spend endless time in futile verbosity and become jaded.

The hope is that students benefiting from this composition will learn from it wholeheartedly and will not deem it excessively long. This composition is a distillation that has been culled from pearls of wisdom with tiresome toil; and it is a flower that has been plucked from among the thorns of redundancy with ennobling effort. We ask God to bring its benefits to learners and to make it useful for their hearts and minds because He is the Most Merciful. Amen.

Conclusion

This is the end of what engrossed the [author's] pen from rough draft to writing, and then from revision to final draft. Praise God for the mercy He granted us in the beginning and for His seal at the end, for He is the First and the Last. He has no beginning and truly no end. The Maronite minister and monk Jirmanus b. Farhat of Aleppo said, "I finished writing this clean copy on 1 January 1708 at the monastery of the great prophet Saint Elisha, which stands at the foot of the sacred valley of the blessed Mount Lebanon, in the environs of Tripoli, Syria. Forget not the author in mercy and forgiveness [from God]."

Notes

[1] Butrus al-Bustani wrote a commentary to Farhat's grammar and retitled the work "Lanterns Burning for Students Discerning." The translation here consults al-Bustani's critical edition.

[2] The translation leans upon Yusuf 'Ali's.

[3] This line is by the Abbasid poet 'Ali b. al-Jahm (died 863).

Work Cited

Yusuf 'Ali, 'Abdullah, translator. *The Meaning of the Holy Qur'an.* 11th edition, Amana Publications, 2004.

Source of Arabic Text on Which the Translation Is Based

Al-Bustani, Butrus, editor. مصباح الطالب في بحث المطالب [misbah al-talib fi bahth al-matalib; Lanterns Burning for Students Discerning]. American Press, 1854, pp. i–iv, 416. Originally بحث المطالب وحث الطالب [bahth al-matalib wa-hathth al-talib; Issues Desired by Students Required].

جرمانوس فرحات
(١٦٧٠-١٧٣٢)

بحث المطالب وحث الطالب

«خطبة الشارح» [المعلم بطرس البستاني]

الحمد لله العليّ الأكرم الذي علم بالقلم علم الإنسان ما لم يعلم. أما بعد فيقول العبد الفقير المعترف بالعجز والتقصير الفاني الجاني بطرس بن بولس بن عبد الله البستاني إنه لما كان كتاب بحث المطالب وحث الطالب تأليف السيد الجليل الفاضل العالم العامل المطران جرمانوس فرحات الماروني الحلبي السعيد الذكر من أسهل ما ألّف من كتب الصرف والنحو مأخذاً وأقربها تناولاً وأعظمها نفعاً لكونه من أحسنها ترتيباً وكان تركه لرحمة النساخ لا يزيده إلا تحريفاً وتصحيفاً ويجعل امتلاكه دون أمد كثيرين من الطلاب المستفيدين. رأيت أن السعي في طبعه بعد تنقيحه وضبطه وتصحيحه من أفضل المآثر وأحسن المقاصد.

وكان قد بلغني من كثيرين أنه يوجد منه نسخ بخط المؤلف فأخذت في الفحص بتدقيق والتفتيش بتحقيق على نسخة منها ولما وجدت أن ذلك مقصد لا يُطمع في نواله بما جمعته عندي من النسخ المتداولة بين الجمهور التي أعتقد بصحتها وقابلت عليها هذه النسخة وطبعتها بحرف كبير على حدة تاركاً المتن على أصله وباذلاً الجهد في مناظرة طبعها خوفاً من الغلط.

ولما كان قصد المؤلف أن يتحف أبناء ملته بكتاب مستوفٍ في هذه الصناعة لئلا يتغربوا فيتجربوا ولكن تراكم الأشغال وقصر الوقت لم يسمحا له بنوال مرامه على أتم منوال بحيث يُستغنى بما جمعه من أصول هذه الصناعة عن كتب غيره وكان كتابه لا يخلو من التعقيد والحشو والتطويل في بعض المواضع كما لا يخفى عن صاحب الرأي الصائب والذوق السليم رأيت أن أذيّله في الحاشية بما أهمله من القواعد والشوارد التي يضطر إليها من طلب التعمق في الكتب العربية الصحيحة وأراد فهم ما يوجد في هذه اللغة

من الكتب النفيسة نثراً ونظماً أو يُنشئ فيها شيئاً يكون صحيح العبارة جيد الإشارة معتمداً في ذلك على ما نصته أكابر العلماء ومشاهيرهم في هذا الفن.

وأن أضم إليه رسالة في علم العروض والقوافي تأليف الشيخ ناصيف اليازجي المشهور. وذلك لشدة العلاقة بين هاتين الصناعتين في الاستعمال. وأن أجعل لجميع ذلك فهرساً على ترتيب القاموس تسهيلاً لطلبه. وأن أنبه على ما عثرت عليه فيه من الوهم الذي أحدثته غفلة النساخ أو تساهل الماتن تاركاً بعض ما تركته منه لظهور أمره أو لأنه يُقاس على ما ذكرته قاصداً في ذلك تعميم فائدته ونفع طلابه. وقد علقت ما علقته عليه بحرف صغير مفصولاً عن المتن بخط عرضي وجعلت في المتن والحاشية أرقاماً هندياً متماثلة ترشد إلى مواضع ما نبهت عليه أو زدته فيه كما سترى.

فجاء بحوله تعالى كتاباً مستوفياً يغني الطالبين عن درس ما سواه من متون هذه الصناعة ومطولاتها. وسمّيته مصباح الطالب في بحث المطالب. وأقول إني لم أتعقب عثاره على سبيل التنديد كأنه قد أخطأ وأصبت بل تنبيهاً للمطالع أن يتبصر في أحد القولين فيقضي لأحدهما. ولعله يقضي علي فأستفيد. لأنه لا يستحيل أن أكون قد ركبت في ذلك شططاً. فإن الفضل لا يسلم لأحد. وفوق كل ذي علم عليم.

وأنا أعترف بفضله علماً وعملاً وأشهد له بأنه منقطع النظير بين الملة المسيحية في علم العربية. على أن الكلام لا يتبرأ من الوهم. فقد رأينا كثيراً من أكابر العلماء قد سقطوا في كثير من الوهم. ولعل الذي يعيب ذلك عليهم يجد في كلامهم ما لا يستطيع الأتيان بمثله. وأقر بأني قاصر عن البلوغ إلى بعض طبقاته. فإنه قد سمع ما لم أسمع ونظر ما لم أنظر وعرف ما لم أعرف. غير أني وإياه لم نخترع شيئاً في هذه الصناعة ولا علم لنا إلا ما علمتنا إياه كتب الأوائل. فإن كنت قد أصبت ففي الزوايا خبايا وإن كنت قد أخطأت فلمثلي الخطأ ولله العصمة والكمال وله وحده الحمد أولاً وآخراً.

ومن ذا الذي ترضي سجاياه كلها   كفى المرء نبلا أن تعد معايبه

«خطبة المؤلف» [جرمانوس فرحات]

الحمد لله الذي أصلح بكلمته الأنفس المختلة، وأعرب بقدرته الفعالة عن الأفعال السالمة والمعتلة، واشتقت مفعولاته المحدثة بأمره من العناصر

المنحلة، بعد إبرازه تلك الجواهر العقلية الغير المضمحلة، وأضاف الاسطقسّات بعضاً إلى بعض إضافة متداخلة غير متبلبلة ولا مضلة، والسجود لابنه يسوع المسيح الوحيد المتجسد بأقدس حُلة، الذي أرسله رحمة للعالمين وخلاصاً من الجريرة والزلة، والتقديس للروح القدس الذي يدبر الكائنات لأحسن حُلة، والتعظيم للثالوث الأقدس رب الذات الواحدة والسلطة المذلة.

أما بعد فيقول العبد المفتقر إلى ربه، أسير وصمة ذنبه، جبريل بن فرحات القس الراهب الحلبي الماروني الحقير. والمنضوي تحت قانون الرهبان اللبنانيين المتوشحين بأشكيم القديس أنطونيوس الكبير، لما رأيت إقبال المستفيدين من المسيحيين منصبّاً نحو معرفة القواعد العربية، والأصول النحوية، لكن يدهم تقصر عن الوصول إلى غايتها لأسباب توجب الإضراب عن الانصباب، وتقرن الأكفاف بالانكفاف، جذبتني عند ذلك يد الغيرة الأخوية، جذب حنين الطبيعة الأبوية، إلى إحالة الحال المعجم، وإزالة الأمر المبهم، فأنقدتُ طائعاً نحوها بعد أمر الآمر المطاع، وسؤال من يحق له مني الاتباع، فمددت حينئذ يداً قد غلّها عجزها، وحلها رمزها، ومدها ردها، وردها مدها، فابتدرت كاشفاً عن مُحيّا العربية ذاك القناع الذي كان مسدولاً لأمر ما، حيناً ما، وأنشأت مؤلفاً ينطوي على مقدمة وثلاثة كتب وخاتمة، وجمعت فيه ما تفرق من القواعد تصريفاً ونحواً في كتب متعددة، وأثبت منها ما إثباته يلزمنا، ونبذت عنا ما هو غريب منا، فلهذا لا تصدقن المعترض الواقف على موضوعنا، والمختبر مشروعنا، بل قل له، كلٌّ يقتاتُ بما يكفيه، وصاحب البيت أدرى بالذي فيه، وأهملت التعليلات المملة، والاعتراضات المعلة.

لما رأيت ابن الحاجب قد حجب الأفهام برواياته، وابن هشام قد هشم الأوهام بإيراداته، وابن مالك قد ملك الأذهان بزياداته، فما هي إلا زيادة تدقيق، وتنميق تحقيق، أو أن لهم بذلك غرضاً لا يشملنا، ولازماً لا يلزمنا، ولهذا هم في وادٍ، ونحن في وادٍ، وكل منتدٍ يختص بنادٍ، وأنى يجيب المنادى بغير منادٍ. فتلخص إذاً مما لخصناه ونصصناه، أن المقصود من تأليف ما ألّفناه وألّفناه، ثلاثة أمور، الأول إزالة تعقيد العبارات المبهمة، الثاني ضم جميع ما تلزمنا معرفته من هذه الصناعة في مؤلَّف واحد بوجه الاختصار، الثالث إيراد شهاداته من الكتب المقدسة حسب الإمكان، وسمّيته بحث المطالب، وحث الطالب، والمقصود منه نفع أولاد المسيحيين لئلا يتغربوا فيتجربوا، ولئلا يتعبوا فيتعبوا، ولئلا يصرفوا الزمان بإسهاب باطل فينصبوا.

فالمأمول إذاً من الطلبة المستفيدين منه أن يتلقوه بوجه القبول، ولا يستكثروا المقول، لأنه خلاصة قد تنقت من بين قلائد الفوائد، بكد مل، ووردة قطفت من بين شوك الزوائد، بكدح يجل،

نسأل الله أن ينفع به طالبيه، ويفيد به أفئدة راغبيه، لأنه أرحم الراحمين، آمين.

«الخاتمة»

هذا نهاية ما جال القلم في ميدان تسويده وتقريره وتبييضه وتحريره. والحمد لله على ما أنعم به علينا في الابتداء وختمه في الانتهاء إذ هو الأول والآخر وليس له أول ولا آخر حقاً. قال مؤلفه جبريل بن فرحات القس الراهب الحلبي الماروني فرغت من بياض هذا التأليف في أول يوم من شهر كانون الثاني افتتاح سنة ألف وسبعمئة وثمان مسيحية في دير القديس اليشع النبي العظيم المشيد في سفح الوادي المقدس من جبل لبنان المبارك في جهات طرابلس سورية. ولا تنسوا المؤلف من الرحمة والغفران.

Ya'qub Sannu'
(1839–1912)

Introduced and translated by Ziad Fahmy

Ya'qub Rafa'il Sannu' was the eldest son of an Italian Jewish father and an Egyptian Jewish mother. Sannu', who was also known as James Sannu', became a part-time playwright in 1870, and with the financial support of Khedive Isma'il (r. 1863–1879) he established Egypt's first Arabic theater company. Sannu''s theatrical troupe performed primarily at a theater in the Azbakiyya Gardens in Cairo. After some of his plays were performed on the khedive's private stage at Qasr al-Nil, Sannu' was reportedly labeled the Egyptian Molière by Isma'il.

All Sannu''s plays were performed in colloquial Egyptian and contained subtle nationalistic themes and a significant amount of social criticism. For instance, *al-Darratayn* ("The Co-Wives") openly criticized polygamy. In *al-Amira al-Iskandaraniyya* ("The Alexandrian Princess"), Sannu' warned middle-class Egyptians against blindly imitating European customs and habits. In *al-'Alil* ("The Sick Man"), he championed modern medicine against traditional medicine. The subject matter of his plays became increasingly critical of Egyptian elite society, and his theatrical activities were banned in 1872. However, he soon found other outlets for his political expression, which in 1877 led to the advent of his journalistic career and the launch of his satirical newspaper *Abu Naddara Zarqa'* ("A Man with Blue Glasses"). Because of his continued criticism of the Egyptian government, Sannu' was exiled from Egypt in 1878. He eventually settled in Paris, where he continued to publish his newspaper and successfully smuggle it into Egypt until his retirement from journalism in 1910.

Muliyar Misr wa-ma Yuqasihi ("The Egyptian Molière and What He Endures") is a short, rhyming, autobiographical play reenacting some of Sannu''s recollections of his experience in Egypt as a writer, director, and producer between 1870 and 1872. All the main characters in the play are based on the actual actors and participants in his theater company. *The Egyptian Molière* reflects both the excitement and anxieties caused by the rapid changes taking place in Egypt in the 1860s and 1870s. In the play, Sannu' recounts a cautionary tale of the pitfalls and economic risks posed by the newly established Egyptian stock market and warns his audience about the unscrupulous practices of some stockbrokers. He also describes the controversy over his use of colloquial Egyptian in his plays and writings. He defends himself against his critics by explaining the importance of the vernacular in authentically expressing the cultural nuances and rhythms of the Egyptian street, while stressing the capacity of *'ammiyya* ("the colloquial") for reaching a wider audience.

Recommended Reading

Badawi, M. M. "The Father of the Modern Egyptian Theatre: Ya'qub Sannu'." *Journal of Arabic Literature*, vol. 16, 1985, pp. 132–45.

Fahmy, Ziad. "Francophone Egyptian Nationalists, Anti-British Discourse, and European Public Opinion, 1885–1910: The Case of Mustafa Kamil and Ya'qub Sannu'." *Comparative Studies of South Asia, Africa, and the Middle East*, vol. 28, 2008, pp. 170–83.

Gendzier, Irene. *The Practical Visions of Ya'qub Sanu'*. Harvard UP, 1966.

Mestyan, Adam. "Arabic Theater in Early Khedivial Culture, 1868–72: James Sanua Revisited." *International Journal of Middle East Studies*, vol. 46, 2014, pp. 117–37.

Moosa, Matti. "Ya'qub Sanu' and the Rise of Arab Drama in Egypt." *International Journal of Middle East Studies*, vol. 5, no. 4, 1974, pp. 401–33.

FROM *The Egyptian Molière and What He Endures*

ACT 1

Scene 1

Mitri's residence. Mitri and Hasan are in conversation.

MITRI: Hasan, I was waiting for you. Man, tell me your latest news! Did you hang up all of the advertisements? And did you distribute the flyers to the people and the notables?

HASAN: I have been on my feet since dawn, distributing the invites to all of the local stores and to all social circles. I did not neglect any of the districts in Cairo, from al-Hamzawi to Ghuraya and from Muski to al-Sarafiyya. I informed all, be they Jews, Christians, or Muslims, that tonight a new play will premiere, which will be attended by all the Pashas of the 'Abdeen district.

MITRI: You have become so garrulous, Hasan. You must have learned all of your cunning from Molière [Sannu'], our enchanting leader.

HASAN: Watch your mouth, "Mister" Mitri, when you speak of Molière; he is the consummate entertainer and a true invigorator of souls. By the Prophet you would not be worth an onion without him, and only the most despicable of us neglects his many virtues. By God, he is a kindhearted man who spends from his own pockets on the theater and has left to us all the profits from the ticket sales. He treats us all with kindness and respect whether we are young or old. The fact is that we are all rascals while he alone is kind.

MITRI: You speak the truth, Hasan, for James, who was dubbed the Egyptian Molière by our khedive, is a fine fellow. But he has no luck with these folks [i.e., the rest of the troupe]; the boys are all troublemakers and the girls are all spoiled. I swear there is no one like him in all the theaters of London and Paris, for he is the playwright, teacher, producer, and director.

HASAN: All of this is true and yet to no avail. Tomorrow the troupe may get a new director who will not be so kind. You see, Mitri, I know you are the wisest in the troupe, but it is noon already and the rest of the actors have yet to arrive! How are they supposed to act in this new play tonight if they don't rehearse?

MITRI: Yesterday night they promised me that they would be here before noon.

HASAN: Well, they have yet to arrive and poor Monsieur James is at the theater waiting for them. When I saw him there, he told me, "Rush over to Mitri's house and find them! Tell them that this is very unprofessional and that I'm not their servant. I've already been waiting for them for over two hours."

MITRI: Hold on, I hear someone knocking on the door. This must be Istifan. Go quickly and send for James, you drunkard.

HASAN: I am at your service, my dearest friend. *Leaves.*

Scene 2

Mitri and Istifan

MITRI: Bonjour, Monsieur Istifan! Come on in, my dear Don Juan, for everyone knows that you drive all the ladies crazy with your charm and good looks!

ISTIFAN: This indeed is a happy morning, especially after seeing your face, my dear friend. How are you doing?

MITRI: I feel alive and rejuvenated, *mon cher*. And how are you today, my brother? Are you still swimming in your many love affairs?

ISTIFAN: What love and what swimming are you talking about, pal? Listen to the important news I have, and enough of your joking around. These are serious times, for tomorrow we may all be in tears!

MITRI: God forbid, my dear Istifan!

ISTIFAN: Whatever happened was destined to happen!

MITRI: That's enough, man. Don't scare me like this! Are you serious or are you joking?

ISTIFAN: Here, take this newspaper and read it! It's a well-known Alexandrian newspaper, and it is attacking and insulting the Arabic theater [Sannu's] for performing all of its plays in colloquial Egyptian [and not in grammatically correct, high Arabic].

MITRI: And who wrote this article? Was it a native Egyptian or a European?

ISTIFAN: It's an Italian who wrote these words in his Italian newspaper.[1]

MITRI: I know now who you are talking about. That man is an imbecile. He is extremely jealous of our director. Every once in a while he passes by our theater and sees one of our plays, though he never greets us. He claims that our plays are scandalous and a waste of time and that no one young or old enjoys watching them. So we told him that he should show us if he could do any better and write his own play. He later brought us a play that he wrote, but it was so awful that we almost died laughing while reading it. The next day we met up with him and threw his play back in his face. We told him, "You wrote the dialogue in classical Arabic!" and we cited several examples.

ISTIFAN: He is a crazy man. No one heeds what he says, for we are successful and he is nobody!

MITRI: With just two words we can shut him up and make him run off to his mother's lap. Comedy consists in the things that happen among regular people.

ISTIFAN: Very true, Mitri. Your words are spot-on.

MITRI: And do people in the real world use classical Arabic or the colloquial?

ISTIFAN: Even the religious shaykhs and the intellectual elite never talk to each other in classical Arabic.

MITRI: This Italian critic of ours is indeed crazy, and he contin-
ues to attack our director's plays.

ISTIFAN: It is enough for James that newspapers in the East and
West sing his praises. Prominent men have already acknowl-
edged that he is a unique individual in this day and age, for he
was the first to establish an Egyptian Arabic theater. And our
effendi [Khedive Isma'il] has showered him with his blessings
and even dubbed him the Egyptian Molière. Just as Molière
established the theater in France, James was the first to estab-
lish the Arabic theater [in Egypt]. Since that time, *mon cher*,
from the palace in 'Abdeen to all other circles and institutions,
no one calls him James, but instead they call him Monsieur
Molière.

MITRI: By God, he deserves it, for he has endured a great deal
while establishing his great Arabic theater. He had to handle
the likes of Dranet Pasha, the president of the French Opera
House and Theater, who is truly the greatest enemy to the
establishment of an Arabic theater. But James can also be
clever and cunning, and he was able to stand up to him and
outwit him, making his blood boil with anger. Do you know
that back in the day, Dranet was a mere loud-mouthed phar-
macist who gave hypodermic injections to 'Abbas Pasha!

ISTIFAN: Khedive Isma'il laughed aplenty, when in Qasr al-Nil
we performed for him our plays *Ras Tur*, *Shaykh al-Balad*
["The Village Chief"], and *al-Qawwas* ["The Bowman"].
He [Isma'il] told Dranet, "James is not just fooling around.
He has succeeded in teaching young men and women who
have never seen theatrical plays before how to act on stage."

MITRI: And the night we performed *Hilwan*, *al-'Alil* ["The Sick
Man"], and *al-Amira al-Iskandaraniyya* ["The Alexandrian
Princess]" at the French Comedy Theater House, the khedive
and the notables were happy, and the women in the audience
laughed from the bottom of their hearts. That day the whole
world could hear the applause!

ISTIFAN: And Isma'il Pasha Sidiq, Khayri Pasha, and 'Amr Pasha al-Latif shouted, "Bravo, Molière, your writing is very amusing!"

MITRI: But our director epitomizes humbleness and modesty and dislikes it when people sing his praises. He always says to our distinguished audiences that writing comedy is not difficult; performing it is the real challenge. These words reached the khedive, and this is why he loves us so and allows us to use the Azbakiyya Theater free of charge. Now our theater is attended daily by notables from the district of 'Abdeen to Ismaïlia.

ISTIFAN: Oh Mitri, how I wish he had never allowed us to use this theater. This generosity will end up separating us and driving a wedge among us. For now the actors and actresses expect khedival sponsorship and want to be paid a monthly salary by the government, or else they threaten to go on strike. For you know that what they get from the theater revenues is not a great amount. I heard them talking about these things the other day.

MITRI: Be quiet, man, I hear people coming up the stairs. The rest of the actors are here!

ISTIFAN: You're right—it's them. Now you will hear all of their demands. Let's play the devil and have a little game with them to make sure our Molière, the director, wins out over their demands when all is said and done.

Scene 3

Hanin, 'Abd al-Khaliq, Ilyas, Butrus, and those previously mentioned

HANIN: Good morning, Mitri! Bonjour, Istifan!

MITRI: What morning? It's noon already, you wino!

'ABD AL-KHALIQ: And who cares, man! What difference does it make, even if it is dusk already?

ISTIFAN: It means that we don't have time to rehearse the new play!

ILYAS: Istifan, why don't you and Mitri act out the new play on your own? And then you can divide the profits between you?

BUTRUS: All of us, including the girls, have agreed to go on strike until we have monthly salaries. James is an idiot. If he were as crafty as Dranet Pasha, the president of the Opera House, then he would have convinced our effendi to give us salaries just like the actors in the opera and French theater.

HANIN: If we strike because we are not paid enough and our effendi hears about it, then he is sure to take action.

ILYAS: Now do you see the reality of the situation, Effendi Istifan?

'ABD AL-KHALIQ: And you, Mitri, do you understand where we are coming from, man?

ISTIFAN: You people don't have any mercy in your hearts. James has literally fed you meat after you were eating bisara [mashed fava beans] all your lives. And he who breaks bread with the merciless shall perish by the sword of the merciless. The honorable man will always be honorable and the dishonorable can go to hell.

'ABD AL-KHALIQ: Me? Eating bisara, my dear Istifan? Have you heard what he is saying about me, my friends?

ISTIFAN: Bisara was too expensive for you. Poor fellow, back then you probably survived on just bread and onions.

HANIN: Are you crazy? What about me? Was I also eating bisara every day?

ISTIFAN: Don't be a loudmouth! You probably survived on eating just olives and fisikh [fermented fish].

MITRI: Enough already about onions, fisikh, olives, and bisara. Bickering and shouting is inappropriate and unbecoming of all of you!

ILYAS: What's appropriate according to you, Mitri, is that we should forever side with your friend James and act in his troupe pro bono to make him famous and never forsake him.

MITRI: Pardon me, Mister Ilyas. All of you behave like cats: you eat and never acknowledge the kindness of those who feed you. James is not here, but truth be told, the man is sensitive to our needs and is always working to make things better for us. Here we are in our second year of acting for him, and we are well taken care of and enjoying the best that life has to offer.

ISTIFAN: And all James gets out of it is toil and drudgery, endless errands, sleepless nights, and wasted time.

BUTRUS: Guys, I told all of you that Mitri, Habib, and Istifan will stick together like brothers.

'ABD AL-KHALIQ: All this talk is meaningless. Let's be serious: in this world it's every man for himself. I couldn't care less if the Arabic theater ever succeeds—I will not act if I don't get paid a monthly salary.

BUTRUS: By God, you make perfect sense, 'Abd al-Khaliq! Ilyas, Hanin, and I are with you. Let us go, my friends, and look for real jobs. Enough of theater acting and all of these headaches.

ISTIFAN: You know, Mitri, these people think that they are the only actors in all of Egypt! The truth is that in recent days we've met twenty good actors who could take their places. We are not afraid of their empty threats. And James told me that a pasha who is a friend of his has advised him to hire two of his beautiful fair-skinned servants. These talented women can read, write, and learn the lines of the most difficult scripts. And then all of you will get what you deserve for your disloyalty and treachery. Time is up, Mitri. James is waiting for us. Let's go and tell him our good news.

'ABD AL-KHALIQ: So you have been conspiring against us and finding boys and girls to take our places?

ILYAS: We will perform tonight in spite of you, and we will not even take any money for it. And tomorrow you will see how real men behave.

HANIN: Do you think we are stupid? We are much more cunning than you, Mitri.

BUTRUS: Before arriving here, we sent the girls to the theater and told them to inform Monsieur James that we are on strike until we are paid a regular monthly salary.

HANIN: I have a feeling that with just two sweet words from Liza and Matilda, James will be convinced to ride out to 'Abdeen Palace and tell the khedive that the actors are on strike and won't act until they get a salary. The khedive is fond of James and he will certainly accommodate our salary requests.

MITRI: You are making an already difficult situation worse. You know full well that James has already worked night and day to make things better for all of us.

BUTRUS: Just be quiet, both of you, and let us do our business.

ILYAS: Why should they be quiet? Maybe they can help our cause.

BUTRUS: Let's head over to the theater. Time is running out.

'ABD AL-KHALIQ: If we are united and speak as one man, we can only succeed in our cause.

MITRI: So you guys are still going to rehearse with James?

ILYAS: Yes, and we will confront him about our cause just one hour before the play starts.

BUTRUS: And if he doesn't guarantee us a regular salary . . .

'ABD AL-KHALIQ: (*finishing Butrus's sentence*) . . . none of us will act in the play; no guys and no girls!

ISTIFAN: That's all fine and good, but today we have to perform several of our comedies, including *al-Hashshash* ["The Hashish Addict"], *al-Barbari* ["The Nubian"], and our wonderful new play, *al-Bursa al-Misriyya* ["The Egyptian Stock Market"].

'ABD AL-KHALIQ: I have the new play completely memorized, Istifan.

ILYAS: Fellows, I also learned all of my part.

BUTRUS: I have only two pages' worth of lines, guys, which I memorized in just fifteen minutes.

MITRI: It's true that in this play you all do not have much to say, as Istifan and I get most of the lines.

'ABD AL-KHALIQ: We all know how good you both are at memorizing your lines. I noticed, Mitri, that you in particular have a long soliloquy in *The Egyptian Stock Market*.

BUTRUS: Yes, it is quite a witty soliloquy, with beautiful rhymes.

ILYAS: Yes, only Mitri can memorize it because he's so cool and focused.

MITRI: I see you are making fun of me. The truth is that I am much better than any of you at memorizing and performing my lines.

ISTIFAN: Are we going to argue again?

'ABD AL-KHALIQ: God forbid, we just made up and reached an agreement.

ILYAS: By God, O Distinguished Mitri, why don't you perform your soliloquy and amaze us?

MITRI: Your wish is my command, my dear Ilyas, but under one condition, guys . . . that no one interrupts me. I play the role of a banker who has had only misfortune in his stock market dealings.

BUTRUS: Interrupt you to say what, Mitri? Come on, perform for us what is sure to be one of your classic performances, O Precious Star of the common people and comedian of the notables.

MITRI: After a long and powerful sigh, I declare: "May God curse the stock market along with the man who invented it! For a good man who invests in stocks will soon have only a list of endless troubles. I saved exactly ten thousand pounds from my work selling barley and cotton all over Egypt, from Asyut to al-Mahalla. Like they say, I was a happy-go-lucky man: secure, content, and always joking and laughing night and day. Every Sunday I would go on a joyful carriage ride with my wife and kids. We would go on a stroll along Shubra Road, enter the Azbakiyya Gardens, and in the 'Umar Agha Café we would listen to the sweetest music from the likes of Muhammad Salim, al-Shanturi, and Dawud. After dinner we would go to the Arabic Theater to be entertained by the performances of Mitri, Istifan, and Habib, and we clapped enthusiastically for 'Abd al-Khaliq, Butrus, Ilyas, and Hanin. Afterward we returned home to drink a delicious cup of coffee and smoke some wonderful shisha. But today, everything has changed, and our wonderful carefree world is no more. God damn this stock market and the cursed day when I decided to buy stocks! God will someday punish the stockbroker who blinded me with his cunning and tempted me to enter the stock market to buy and sell a bunch of paper and leave my real work behind! Everything I bought fell in value, and everything I sold rose in value after I sold it. I lost on both ends. In two years I made nothing. My 'friend' the stockbroker, on the other hand, is like a saw, moving up and down with the market and devouring profits either way. And there you have it: he is doing well, and I am consumed by my losses. You get what you ask for. I deserve it for picking such a wretched way to make a living! The stockbrokers would come in and out of my office with their stock advice. They would say hello to me and tell me how well business was going, and that we must buy more stocks to make up for all the losses. . . . They would guarantee that in just two weeks I could make 20,000 pounds. I believed what they told me. I bought and sold blindly, and in less than two years I lost everything, and became deeply in debt. . . . May God curse the stock market, which only led me to lose everything. Not only did I lose out financially, but the stock market destroyed my body, my reputation, my honor, and my name. Oh merciful God, I pray to you to protect me with your generosity and kindness, for death is better than such a wretched life."

ILYAS: Truly, tonight after your soliloquy all the stockbrokers will yell, whistle, and throw corncobs at you.

ISTIFAN: If the stockbrokers heckle you and throw corncobs on the stage, it will make you very famous, Mitri, because it will demonstrate the truthfulness of your performance and reinforce how much the people hate these stockbrokers.

HANIN: Hush everyone, Hasan has arrived. I hope he brings good news.

ISTIFAN: Well, Hanin, I truly believe that we will succeed, and that everything will work out for the best.

Note

[1] From the mid to late nineteenth century there were several European-language newspapers printed in Cairo and Alexandria, catering to the tens of thousands of southern Europeans and Levantines living in Egypt at the time.

Source of Arabic Text on Which the Translation Is Based

Yaʿqub Sannuʿ. موليير مصر وما يقاسيه: رواية تمثيلية هزلية. [muliyar misr wa-ma yuqasihi: riwaya tamthiliyya hazaliyya; The Egyptian Molière and What He Endures: A Satirical Play]. Al-Matbaʿa al-Adabiyya, 1912.

يعقوب صنّوع
(١٩١٢-١٨٣٩)

موليير مصر وما يقاسيه
الفصل الأول

«المنظر الأول»

دار متري

متري وحسن يتحادثان

متري: يا أبا الحسن انا كنت في انتظارك، اتحفني يا جدع باخبارك. هل علقت يا عم الاعلانات، وفرقت الاوراق على الاهالي والذوات؟

حسن: دانا صار لي من الفجر داير، افرق العزايم على الدواوين والدواير. وما خليت لا حمزاوي ولا غوريه، ولا موسكي ولا صرافيه. الا واخبرت يهود ونصارى ومسلمين، ان هذه الليلة رواية جديدة يحضرها باشوات عابدين.

متري: حقاً انت يا حسن اصبحت لهجاوي، وتعلمت المكر ده كله من موليير رئيسنا الحاوي.

حسن: يا خواجة متري بخّر فمك وتكلم في موليير ابو جموس، انس كل مكان محيي النفوس. والنبي ما تسوى بصله من غيره، وخسيس فينا اللي ما يكتّر خيره. دا رجل الشهاده لله قلبه رؤوف، تارك لنا ايراد التياترو وبيطلع من عبه المصروف. تراه يلاطف مزاجنا كبير وصغير، والحال اننا اشقياء وهو وحده الامير.

متري: والله يا حسن كلامك صحيح، عمنا جمس اللي سماه خديوينا بلقب موليير مصر دا رجل مليح. انما ما لوش بخت مع الجماعة، الاولاد بيسوقوا عليه الشيطنة والبنات بتسوق عليه الدلاعة. والله ما يوجد متله في تياترات لندرة وباريس، هو المؤلّف هو المدرس هو المبلغ هو الرئيس.

حسن: وداا كله ما بيتمرش فيكم، بكره يجيكم رئيس غيره يخفيكم. انظر يا بو متري يا اللي بالعقل مشهور، انت انصح الجماعة والا فالدواير علينا تدور. آدحنا بقينا الظهر وهم لسا ما جوش، فكيف يلعبوا الليلة قطعة جديدة اذا ما درسوش؟

متري: هم ليلة البارحة وعدوني انا، بان قبل الظهر يكونوا هنا.

حسن: اهم ما جوش والمسيو جمس المسكين، في التياترو منتظر اللعيبين. انا شفته وهو اللي قال لي اجري يا واد، رح بيت متري هناك تلاقي الاولاد. قل لهم دا ما يصحش انا مانيش خدامهم، صار لي هنا ساعتين في انتظارهم.

متري: هس سامع حد بيدق على الباب دا عمنا اسطفان، اخطف رجلك وهات لنا جمس يا خمران.

حسن: على العين والراس، يا سيد الناس . (يخرج)

«المنظر الثاني»

متري واسطفان

متري: بون جور يا موسيو اسطفان، تفضل يا سيد الغزلان. الله عليك يا مهيِّج المادامات، يا ساحر البلابل مصبب الحريمات.

اسطفان: ما اسعد هذا الصباح، بمشاهدة وجهك يا صاح. كيف حالك يا من للعين قره، وللقلب بهجة ومسرة؟ لعلك تكون بخير.

متري: دبّتي تخرق الارض يا مون شير. وانت يا اخ زيّك اليوم، برضك نازل في بحر المحبة عوم؟

اسطفان: محبة ايه وعوم ايه يا جندي؟ انت اسمع الاخبار المهمة اللي عندي. ده فرغ الهزار وبقي الجد، وغدا تسيل الدموع على الخد.

متري: الله لا يقدّر يا سي اسطفان.

اسطفان: آهو قدّر واللي كان كان.

متري: بس يا شيخ ما تصرعنيش، كلامك ده صحيح والا توشيش؟

اسطفان: خد واقرا ده جرنال شهير باسكندرية، يذم ويطعن ويلعن التياترات العربية. لكونها عن اصول النحو خارجه، ورواياتها مكتوبة باللغة الدارجة.

متري: واللي كتب الكلام دا هو مين، يا هل ترى من ابناء الوطن او من الاوروبيين؟

اسطفان: ايطالياني كاتب هذه الاقوال، كما وان ايطالياني ذات الجرنال.

متري: عرفته يا عم، دا رجل بالهمّ. دا من رئيسنا جمس بالغيرة بيموت، وكلما علينا بيفوت ويرانا في لعبة جديدة بنعيد، عوض ما يقول لنا نهاركم سعيد؛ يقول لنا لعب الروايات دي الهلس عار، ما ينبسطوا منها لا كبار ولا

صغار. فقلنا له ذات يوم ورينا رواياتك البديعة، فجاب لنا قطعة شنيعة.
متنا من الضحك لما قريناها، وتاني يوم في وجهه حدفناها. وقال انه كاتبها
بالنحوي بالقاف والنون، مثلاً نحن يدخلون، ويلبس البنطالون، وانتو
يشربون ويركسون ويظحكون وبعد ذلك كلنا ينطلقون.

اسطفان: دا رجل مجنون. فلا احد يعتبر كلامه، ونحن ننجح وهو ما ينول مرامه.

متري: احنا نقدر بكلمتين نجاوبه ونسد فمه، ونخليه يهرب ويستخبي في
حجر امه. الكوميدية تشتمل على ما يحصل ويتاتى بين الناس.

اسطفان: عفارم يا متري كلامك زي الالماس.

متري: فيا هل ترى العالم في مخاطباتها تستعمل اللغة النحوية، او اللغة
الاصطلاحية؟

اسطفان: المشايخ واصحاب المعارف والفنون، عمرهم ما بيكلموا بعضهم
بالقاف والنون.

متري: بقي رقيبنا الايطالياني دا رجل مجنون، هو والذي في تأليفات رئيسنا
جمس يطعنون.

اسطفان: من خصوص عمنا جمس يكفيه، مدح جرايد الشرق والغرب فيه.
دا رجل شهدت له العلماء بانه فريد العصر، ما احد قبله عمل تياترو عربي
في مصر. وافندينا انعم الله عليه بالعافية والخير، لما لعبنا امامه سمّاه موليير.
وموليير هو مؤسّس التياترات الفرنساوية، وعمنا جمس منشيء التياترات
العربية. فمن وقتها في سراية عابدين، وفي الدواير والدواوين. ما حدش
يسمّيه جمس يا مون شير، جميعهم يقولوا له يا موسيو موليير.

متري: والله يستاهل لانه قاسى عذاب اليم. في انشاء التياترو العربي العظيم،
ودرانيت باشا رئيس الاوبيرا والتياترو الفرنساوي، اللي كان اصله اجزخي
لهجاوي. وكان يضرب حقن لعباس باشا جنتمكان، كان لانشاء تياترو العربي
اكبر عدو ودشمان. اما جمس دا جدع مكار. طلّع عليه خامه وخلّى دمه فار.

اسطفان: ياما ضحك الخديوي اسماعيل، ليلة ما لعبنا في قصر النيل. على
لعبة راستور وشيخ البلد والقواص، وقال لدرانيت جمس ماهوش خباص.
آهو نجح وعلّم التشخيص لاولاد وبنات، اللي عمرهم ما رأوا التياترات.

متري: وليلة ما لعبنا في تياترو الكوميدية الفرنساوية، لعبة حلوان والعليل
والاميرة الاسكندرانية. انبسط هو والذوات، وضحكت من وسط قلبها
الحريمات. ومن سفر ساعة، العالم سمعت تصفيق الجماعة.

اسطفان: واسماعيل باشا صديق وخيري باشا وعمر باشا اللطيف، قالوا له براڤو يا مولير والله تأليفك ظريف.

متري: اما رئيسنا جمس ربة التواضع والاحتشام، ما يحبش احد يمدحه ودايماً يقول لذواتنا الكرام. كتابة الكوميديات ما هيش شطارة، الشطارة لعبها امامكم يا ابناء الامارة. والكلام دا وصلوه لافندينا، ودا سبب محبة الخديوي فينا. آهو اعطانا مجاناً تياترو الازبكية، اللي بيحضروه ليلاتي الذوات من عابدين والاسماعيلية.

اسطفان: يا ليته يا متري ما اعطاه لنا، الانعام دا رايح يفرّق بيننا. لان اللعيبين واللعيبات، بدهم من الميري تعيين ماهيات، والا ما يلعبش منهم لا كبير ولاصغير، لا اللي بيدخل لهم من التياترو ماهوش كتير. انا شفتهم في الصباح، فاسمعت منهم دا الكلام يا صاح.

متري: هس يا جندي انا سامع ناس في السلام طالعين، لا بد انهم اللعيبين.

اسطفان: نظرك في محله دول هما بذاتهم، دلوقت يا عم تسمع طلباتهم. انت شيطان وانا ابليس، ان كنا جدعان نغيظهم وننصر عليهم موليرنا الرئيس.

«المنظر الثالث»

حنين، وعبد الخالق، والياس، وبطرس، والمذكورين

حنين: صباح الخير يا متري بون جور يا اسطفان.

متري: صباح الخير ايه واحنا بقينا الظهر يا خمران؟

عبد الخالق: واذا بقينا المغرب رايح يجري ايه يا عم؟

اسطفان: ما تقدرش تدرس الرواية الجديدة ويبقا لعبنا بالهمّ.

الياس: العبها انت ومتري يا اسطفان. واقسموا بينكم المكسب يا جدعان.

بطرس: لان احنا والبنات، حلفنا ما نلعبش اذا لم تتعيّن لنا ماهيات. دا جمس اهبل لو كان زي دي درانيت بك رئيس لهجاوي، كان افندينا رتب لنا ماهيات مثل لعيبين الاوبرا والتياترو الفرنساوي.

حنين: بقا احنا نحرن ولما يسمع افندينا، اننا بطلنا اللعب لعدم الماهيات يبقى يكافينا.

الياس: رسيت على حقيقة الامر يا اسطفان افندي؟

عبد الخالق: وانت يا متري فهمت مرامنا يا جندي؟

اسطفان: انتم جماعة ما في قلبكمش رحمه، دا جمس بعد البيصارة صبحكم تاكلوا لحمه، واللي ياكل عيش الكافر يضرب بسيفه، الاصيل طول عمره اصيل الخسيس يعمل كيفه.

عبد الخالق: هو انا اللي كنت آكل بيصارة يا سي اسطفان؟ انتم يا خواني شاهدين.

اسطفان: البيصارة غالية. دي عيشتك كانت عيش وبصل يا مسكين.

حنين: امال انا اللي كانت عيشتي بيصارة يا زربون؟

اسطفان: ما تطولش لسانك انت عيشتك كانت فسيخ وزيتون.

متري: فضونا من البصل والفسيخ والزيتون والبيصارة، والزعيق والخناق دا ماهوش شطارة.

الياس: الحق بيد متري الشطارة نمثل لامر جمس حبيبه، ونلعب له بلاش ونشهره وعمرنا ما نسيبه.

متري: باردون يا سيد الناس، انت زي القطط تاكل وتنكر يا الياس. جمس غايب انما الحق يقال، الرجل بيراعي في مزاجنا وبيصلح لنا الاحوال. ادحنا صار لنا بنلعب تاني سنة. واكلنا وشربنا وشفنا العز والهنا.

اسطفان: وجمس ما نابه الا التعب والمقت، والجري والسهر وتضييق الوقت.

بطرس: ما قلت لكم يا جماعة ان متري وحبيب واسطفان، هم وجمس كأنهم اخوان.

عبد الخالق: كل دا كلام بوش احنا بدّنا في الجد، لان في الدنيا دي ما حدش لحد. ان شا لله ما فلحت التياترات العربية، انا ما العب اذا لم تتعيّن لي ماهية.

بطرس: والله يا عبد الخالق كلامك زين، واحنا كمان نتبعك انا والياس وحنين. يا الله بنا يا حنين يا الله بنا يا الياس، نشوف لنا شغله بلا لعب بلا كسر راس.

اسطفان: يا متري دول الجماعة فاكرين، ان في مصر ما فيش غيرهم لعيبين. متري وانا وحبيب وجدنا اليومين دول عشرين لعيب من اولاد البلد اللطاف، بقى من تهديدهم ده ما حدش فينا يخاف. والموسيو جمس بكلمتين لباشا من اصحابه يتحصل على جاريتين. جاريتين من البيض ايهم الجمالات، اللي يقروا ويكتبوا ويحفظوا اصعب الروايات. وانتم تطلعوا بوشكم، وهذا ما

ينوبكم من غشكم. والوقت راح يا متري ده جمس في انتظارنا. يا الله بنا
نسرّه باخبارنا.

عبد الخالق: بقى كنتم عاملين عصبه علينا يا خواجات، ووجدتم لجمس
اولاد وبنات؟

الياس: احنا نلعب الليلة ونغيظكم ولو بدون فلوس، وبكره نوريكم شغل
الرجال وايش تعمل النفوس.

حنين: هو احنا يا اسطفان نايمين، احنا اكتر منك يا متري مكارين.

بطرس: احنا قبلما جينا هنا ودينا التياترو البنات، وقلنا لهم اذا عصيتم على
اللعب تنعمل لكم ماهيات. وشفنا الموسيو جمس من بعيد، وسمعنا بنقول
له نهارك سعيد.

حنين: انا قلبي بيقول لي ان البنات ماتيلدة وليزة بكلمتين حلوين، يخلوا
جمس يركب يروح عابدين. ويقول للخديوي يا افندينا عاصيه عليّ
الكومبانيه، ولا راضية تلعب اذ لم تتعيّن لهم ماهيه. فالخديوي يحب جمس
وحالا نبلغ المراد. وتترتب لنا ماهيات يا اولاد.

متري: آه دا امر صعب، وجمس فيه ياما تعب.

بطرس: خلونا نعمل شغلنا ونقطونا بسكوتكم انتم الاتنين.

الياس: يسكتوا ليه؟ خليهم يساعدونا بكلمتين.

بطرس: يا الله بنا على التياترو لان الوقت راح.

عبد الخالق: والنبي اذا صرنا على قلب واحد ما قدامنا الا النجاح.

متري: بقى رايحين تعملوا الريبتيسيون قدام جمس يا جماعة؟

الياس: نعم وبعدها نقول له ان اذا قَبِل لعب الليلة بساعة.

بطرس: ما جاب لناش امر بترتيب ماهيات. . . .

عبد الخالق: . . . ما حدش منا يلعب لا اولاد ولا بنات.

اسطفان: كلام طيب اما الليلة عندنا احنا لعب كوميديات عديدة، لعبة
الحشاش ولعبة البربري واللعبة الجديدة. وهي كوميدية البورصة المصرية،
كوميدية صغيرة ومعانيها بهية.

عبد الخالق: انا حافظها على ظهر قلبي يا اسطفان.

الياس: وانا تعلمتها على الغيب يا اخوان.

بطرس: انا ماليش فيها الا صفحتين يا جماعة، اتعلمهم لكم في ربع ساعة.

متري: في اللعبة دي دخولكم قليل يا جدعان، والرك كله عليّ انا واسطفان.

عبد الخالق: عارفينكم ياخي ماهرين شطار، تحفظوا دروسكم زي النار. انت يا متري يا بو عين كحيله، لك في لعبة البورصة مقالة جليله.

بطرس: ودي مقالة كلها قوافي.

الياس: متري يحفظها لان فكرة رايق وذهنه صافي.

متري: يعني بتتمقلسوا عليّ طيب انا اخزيكم. لان ما حدش متلي يحفظ العابه فيكم.

اسطفان: احنا رايحين نرجع ثانياً للخناق.

عبد الخالق: الله لا يقدر احنا اصطلحنا وحصل بيننا الاتفاق.

الياس: بالله عليك يا متري يا نجيب، تسمّعنا المقالة ام كلام عجيب.

متري: يا سي الياس سمعاً وطاعة، بس ما تقاطعونيش في الكلام يا جماعة. بقى انا رايح اطلع في الكوميدية بصفة بانكير، اللي في لعب البورصة عمره ما شافشي خير.

بطرس: وتقول ايه يا متري؟ هات من تحايفك هات. يا قرة عين اولاد البلد يا مضحك الذوات.

متري: اقول بعد ما اتنهد لي تنهيده، تفلق الحجر وتتني الحديدة. لعنة الله يا بورصة على ما أنشاك، يدخل الانسان كافي شره ما يطلع منك إلا شاكي. عشرة آلاف جنيه مصري تمام، حوشتها بصداقة من ذواتنا الكرام. ومن شغل القطن والغلة، في اسيوط وفي المحلة.

وكنت زي ما يقولوا ألحس مسني، وابات مهني. وكنت دائماً اضحك ليل ونهار، واحب التنكيت والهزار. وكل يوم احد اطلع مع زوجتي واولادي بعربية، نتنزه في سكة شبرا وبعدها ندخل الازبكيه. نسمع في قهوة عمر آغا نغمة الاوتار، ومن محمد سالم والشنطوري وداود الطف الادوار. وبعد العشا نروح للتياترو العربي العجب، وننبسط في لعب متري واسطفان وحبيب. وعبد الخالق وبطرس والياس وحنين، ونصفق ونقول عفارم للبنين. ومن هناك نرجع بيتنا نشرب القهوة العظيمة، ونحبس بها نفس دخان شبقات اليسمينه. اما اليوم الاحوال تغيرت، وافكارنا الرايقة تحبرت. الله يلعن البورصة ويوم دخولي فيها، ارحم يا ربي عبادك واخفيها. الله يجازي السمسار اللي غواني، وادخلني البورصة ومكره عماني. وخلاني اشتري وابيع اوراق واترك اشغالي، والمشترى يصبح رخيص والمبيع يصير غالي. هكذا الخسارة من

الجهتين. عمري ما كسبت لي يوم في سنتين. اما صاحبي السمسار، بسلامته زي المنشار. ياكل نازل وطالع، وكدا صبح هو متحين وانا والع. والله استاهل، ما يصحش الا اعمل بورصجي، على شان ما تبقى السماسرة تروح عندي وتجي. والواحد منهم يقول لي نهارك سعيد، اليوم الاخبار عال بدّنا نعمل شغل جديد. نعوض الخسارة القديمة . . . تكسب فيهم بالقليل، عشرين الف جنيه يا بو خليل. آه وانا كنت اصدق كل الاقوال، وعلى العمياني اعمل الاشغال. فكدا في اقل من سنتين، ضعيت ما ورائي وما قدامي وصبح عليّ دين. . . . الله يلعن البورصة ما نابني منها الا الخسارة. يا ليت الخسارة بس الا كمان نحول الجسم. والهتيكة والفضيحة وكسر الاسم. اشملني بكرمك وحلمك يا رحمن، الموت افضل من دي العيشة اللي زي القطران.

الياس: حقاً الليلة جميع سماسرة البورصة يكفروا، ويحدفوك بقوالح دره ويصفّروا.

اسطفان: حدف قوالح الدرة والتصفير، من جهة السماسرة يجعلوا متري لعيب شهير. لان يتضح من ذلك ان المقالة غاظتهم، وفتحت قلوب العالم بكراهتهم.

حنين: هس. آدي حسن يا ربي تكون اخباره ملاح.

اسطفان: ايش يا حنين والله ما قدامنا الا النجاح.

'Abdallah al-Nadim
(1845–96)

Introduced and translated by Benjamin Koerber

'Abdallah al-Nadim was a man of many talents. Having begun his professional life as a telegraph operator and *udabati* (a clownish kind of colloquial poet), he later associated with Jamal al-Din al-Afghani, a fellow *Nahda* intellectual; served as an orator along-side the revolutionary general Ahmad 'Urabi; and eventually gained fame as writer and editor for several social and political reformist journals. The selections translated here come from the first of these journals, *Raillery and Reproach*, in which al-Nadim applied himself to what he called *tahdhib*, the "education" or "cultivation" of his fellow Egyptians. In the first selection, he clarifies the mode and method of his new journal in response to complaints from his readers: it is, he says, "a serious seed wrapped in a humorous shell," jest in the service of gravity. In the remaining selections, he treats, along with the recurring theme of education, one of the major tensions running through the reform project of the *Nahda*: relations with Europe. The exchanges, encounters, and conflicts between Egypt and its northern neighbors had generated a stock of new personality types, which the author profiles in scenes laced with an equal amount of mockery and disgust.

Recommended Reading

Awad, Louis. *The Literature of Ideas in Egypt*. Vol. 1., Scholars Press, 1986.

Fahmy, Ziad. *Ordinary Egyptians: Creating the Modern Nation through Popular Culture*. Stanford UP, 2011.

Gasper, Michael E. *The Power of Representation: Publics, Peasants, and Islam in Egypt*. Stanford UP, 2009.

Herrera, Linda. "'The Soul of a Nation': 'Abdallah Nadim and Educational Reform in Egypt, 1845–1896." *Mediterranean Journal of Educational Studies*, vol. 7, no. 1, 2002, pp. 1–24.

Selim, Samah. *The Novel and the Rural Imaginary in Egypt, 1880–1985*.
Routledge-Curzon, 2004.

FROM *Raillery and Reproach*

Objections against Raillery

[Objection:]
We had thought your journal was all for jest, only to find it
full of stories!
Response:
Suppose you were told to take heed of yourself, to become
aware of the feebleness and fragility of your position: such
would be a sufficient response to your objection.

Know that jest is best when cultured and refined, a serious seed
wrapped in a humorous shell. Let it be a test of your taste that you
apply what you read to what you see. The intent of this journal is
indeed Refinement and Edification: Take the lesson to heart!

An Arab-cum-European

Once there was a peasant to whom was born a son. The peasant
named him Zi'et and left him to play in the dirt and sleep in the
mud. When Zi'et became old enough to herd the she-buffalo,
he would be sent out to the pasture with the beasts to turn the
water wheel and irrigate the land. Each day, his father would
give him four cakes of corn bread and four bulbs of onion.
On holidays, Zi'et would get to enjoy a soup and to have meat
with his onions.

One day when he was out in the fields, a merchant came
passing by and said to his father, "Were you to send your son
to school, he would get educated and become a proper human
being." And so it was that Zi'et attended school, where he

completed his primary studies, after which the government sent him to Europe to acquire specialization in a field selected for him. Four years later, he returned via steamship to his homeland. Overcome with joy, his father set out to receive him in customs at the port of Alexandria. When Zïet landed and got off the boat, his father approached to embrace and kiss him—as any loving father would his son. But Zïet pushed him away, and they had the following exchange:

ZÏET: Dear Lord! You Muslims and your hugging, how vulgar!
MÏET: My son! How then are we supposed to greet each other?
ZÏET: Say *bon arrivée*, put your hand in mine, and there you have it!
MÏET: Preposterous! I am no country bumpkin, my dear son.
ZÏET: No country bumpkin, my old man? But you peasants live like animals!
MÏET: May God protect you, my dear Zïet. Get on now; get on home.

When Zïet reached the village, his mother gave him a meat-and-onion casserole fresh from the oven. And they had the following exchange:

[ZÏET:] Why did you make this with so much . . .
MAÏKA: With so much what, Zïet?
ZÏET: With the stuff, you know, the whatchamacallit . . .
MAÏKA: The stuff called pepper, you mean?
ZÏET: *Non, non!* The stuff, the whatsit, that you plant.
MAÏKA: The crops, my dear son!
ZÏET: *Non, non!* I mean that thing that has its head in the ground . . .
MAÏKA: By God, my dear son, there is not a hint of garlic in it!
ZÏET: I mean the whatchamacallit that waters your eyes, called *l'oignon.*

MA'IKA: By God, by dear son, this casserole has none of this "l'oignon," 'tis only meat with onions.

ZI'ET: *C'est ça!* Onions! Onions!

MA'IKA: My dear son Zi'et, have you forgotten your beloved onion, which was once the only thing you had to eat?

Soon after Zi'et's arrival, his father complained to one of the village elders, "My son traveled to Europe, only to return to curse his homeland and family. He has even forgotten his native language!"

The village elder responded, "Your son was not properly cultivated when he was young. He learned nothing of the glory of his nation or of the beauty of his native language. No appreciation did he ever have for the traditions of his folk or for the value of patriotism. Though he acquired knowledge, this did not benefit his homeland in the slightest. He neglects the company of his brethren and approves only of those who speak the foreign tongue. Yet he has become like the partridge that wishes to imitate the crow's manner of walking. He has failed to imitate properly, but he is incapable of returning to his original nature. Thus you find him hopping about wildly, transgressing the bounds of national identity and indeed the nature of his species. It takes a truly wretched fool, terribly aloof to his country, to commit the errors your son has.

"Take comfort, however, in those many youth who have gone to Europe to be educated and returned with respect for their native language and customs. These young men have used their learning for the benefit of their country, and are unstained by such a title as 'An Arab-cum-European.'"

Soiree of the Imbeciles

[One evening,] an Honest Gentleman came upon the house of a certain socialite known for his nightly indiscretions out on the town. [Upon entering,] he found nearly a dozen men sprawled limply across a number of couches, motionless and mum, not raising their eyes—one resting his head on his shoulder, one reclining on a pillow, one rolling about as if sleeping, one resting his head on his palm. The Honest Gentleman supposed that the Master of the House had been afflicted with some great calamity and that these men must be lounging about in a state of distress or mourning. So he went to sit down with them, and he asked the Master of the House, "I pray that my kind Sir is well, may God preserve him!" The man responded, "No worries, friend. This is our custom every night: a gathering for good fellowship and cheer!"

HONEST GENTLEMAN: I suppose you have been discussing the tremendous growth of Europe's industry and the spread of its products around the globe, such that its might is matched by none.

MASTER OF THE HOUSE: We have no knowledge of Europe or its people, as we have never left Egypt in our entire lives.

HONEST GENTLEMAN: Not having left one's country is no excuse for not knowing about certain facts and information. One has only to attend to the news of those who have traveled far. Indeed, histories and newspapers bring us reports of other nations when we are sitting at home.

MASTER OF THE HOUSE: Histories are read only by scholars, and newspapers concern only foreigners; they're just a bunch of stories that entertain the youth.

HONEST GENTLEMAN: Newspapers, my good man, are the Mouthpieces of Nations and the Interpreters of Kings. They report to you the statements of this or that president or premier from the far west, and how this or that prince or emir responded from the distant east. They inform you of political discussions, the affairs of kings, and the conditions of nations. They relate to you the state of commerce, the undertakings of wise men, the erudition of scholars, the speeches of honest men, and the

histories of great minds. They tell you what a certain nation
did to build itself up, to protect and preserve itself against the
reaches of others—as well as how a certain nation became a
victim of its own negligence, playing into the hands of for-
eigners who came to interfere in its affairs and rob its people
of their traditions and ways of life.

MASTER OF THE HOUSE: Such talk brings unneeded pain and dis-
tracts one from his thoughts. It occupies none but him who
is without occupation.

HONEST GENTLEMAN: Yet I suppose you discuss your own private
matters, in order to increase your fortunes. You thus seek
greater wealth so that your government may take pride in
you and reward you with higher salaries and honorary marks.

MASTER OF THE HOUSE: None of this concerns us. Whether the
country moves forward or backward, we would reap no more
benefits than we already do.

HONEST GENTLEMAN: And what sort of progress have you achieved,
my dear Sir?

MASTER OF THE HOUSE: Praise be to God, each of us has a mag-
nificent house with a spacious courtyard and pleasant guest
quarters. We have servants to take care of our chores, and
our parents have left us copious amounts of money. We live
with such blessings, looking with pity upon the one who must
work from dawn to dusk to earn his keep. We, on the other
hand, do not go out until the early afternoon, and we return
before nightfall for evenings of mirth and merrymaking.

HONEST GENTLEMAN: If this is your custom, what need have you
for such a soiree as this?

MASTER OF THE HOUSE: The "good stuff" [hashish] doesn't give
you pleasure unless you smoke it in the company of your
friends, with laughter and good cheer. We get together so
that each of us can have his dope, and we trade jokes. If one
of us gets drowsy or numb, he's free to fall asleep and spend
the night here, happy without a care in the world.

The Master of the House then turned to his companions and said, "Well, what do you all think, my good Sirs?"

To which the lot of them responded in a single voice: "Right on, good Sir! What more could we want? What have we got to do with commerce and histories and the world outside? Are we to become like the Europeans, who ask every single hour of the day about what's new in the world, what the newspapers have said, what the telegraphs have brought back—as if the whole world were theirs! Ha ha ha!"

HONEST GENTLEMAN: What a sorry lot you are! Such is the fate of one who was not properly cultivated in his youth. He becomes a prisoner of his desires, an ignorant coward, incapable of discerning the meanings of things. Yet your sun has dimmed, eclipsed by the light of the arts and sciences. Your government has committed itself seriously to these virtues, advancing men and raising them from the graves of ignorance to the gardens of knowledge. The nation searches incessantly for the reasons of its backwardness and for what it may do to progress. The nation and the government are now working hand in hand to revive the homeland, expand its commerce, and support its message. Before long we will see every house become an abode of the arts and every meeting place a bastion of learning and inquiry. We will see every child seek out the means for his own progress. Indeed, every child will gape with astonishment at the cowardice of his parents, ashamed at how they betrayed true knowledge for base pleasures and wallowed in folly, sloth, and moral corruption. Such errors and vices did they reap in the Soiree of the Imbeciles!

What I Have Seen Is More Than I Have Heard

[One day] at sunset I was passing by the Azbakiyya Gardens, when I ran into a young man dressed in a fine shirt and nice trousers. He greeted me, and so I thought that he must be one of the newspaper's subscribers. I said to him, "My good Sir, how do you do?," upon which he said, "I've got something special for you."

"Like what?" I asked.

"A pretty boy, gone out to have some fun this very night, content with little, easy to please!"

Utterly confused, I stood there, taking account of his appearance. At that moment, one of my friends came along, grabbed the boy, and cursed him quite fiercely. He went on to inform me that the "leaders" of these boys go out and buy European clothes for them to wear. Then they use their appearance as a ruse to ply their ugly trade. If you ask them about a certain boy, they will tell you that he is the son of so-and-so, a well-respected man in society, while in reality he is only a good-for-nothing idiot.

I was greatly astonished to hear that this ugly business has spread in our country to the extent that it has developed its own leaders and techniques. If only the police would take care to arrest these effeminates and pimps and exile them from our country, this would greatly purify the morals of men who have nothing to discipline them but flogging or the favor of the ruler. Otherwise, one can only expect this problem to spread further and corrupt morals and harm a great number of people who never knew of it before. Certainly we have enough officers and police to purge Azbakiyya, in Cairo, and Mansheya, in Alexandria, of this filth. Certainly we have enough crimes and forbidden deeds to deal with already besides this bestiality.

Source of Arabic Text on Which the Translation Is Based

Al-Nadim, 'Abdallah. التنكيت والتبكيت [al-tankit wal-tabkit; Raillery and Reproach]. Al-Hay'a al-Misriyya al-'Amma lil-Kitab, 1994, pp. 40-43, 69, 297. Originally published in June-Oct. 1881, nos. 1, 3, 16.

عبد الله النديم
(١٨٩٦-١٨٤٥)

التنكيت والتبكيت

«اعتراضات على التنكيت»

اعتراضات: كنا نظن أنها صحيفة تنكيت صحيح وإذا بها حكايات.

الجواب: لو قيل لك في وقفتك وقلت اشمعنه فقال لك عاجز وقليل الحيل لكان كفاية في هذا الباب فالأولى أن يكون التنكيت أدبياً وهو سياق الجد في معرض الهزل ولك ذوق تطبق ما تقرأه على ما تراه والقصد من الصحيفة التهذيب فتنبّه.

«عربيّ تفرنج»

وُلد لأحد الفلاحين ولد فسمّاه زعيط وتركه يلعب في التراب وينام في الوحل حتى صار يقدر على تسريح الجاموسة فسرحه مع البهائم إلى الغيط يسوق الساقية ويحوّل الماء وكان يعطيه كل يوم أربع حندويلات وأربعة أمخاخ بصل وفي العيد كان يقدم له اليخنى ليمتعه. يأكل اللحم بالبصل وبينما هو يسوق وأبوه جالس عنده مرّ بهما أحد التجار فقال لأبيه لو أرسلت ابنك إلى المدرسة لتعلم وصار إنساناً. فأخذه وسلمه إلى المدرسة فلما أتم العلوم الابتدائية أرسلته الحكومة إلى أوروبا لتعلم فن عيّنته له. فبعد أربع سنين ركب الوابور وجاء عائداً إلى بلاده فمن فرح أبيه حضر إلى [الـ]إسكندرية ووقف برصيف الجمرك ينتظره فلما خرج من الفلوكة قرب أبوه ليحتضنه ويقبله شأن الوالد المحب لولده فدفعه في صدره فجرت بينهما هذه العبارة:

زعيط: سبحان الله عندكم يا مسلمين مسألة الحضن دي قبيحة جداً.

معيط: امال يا بني نسلم على بعض ازّاي.

زعيط: قول بونَريفي وحط ايدك في ايدي مرة واحدة وخلاص.

معيط: لهو يا ابني انا باقول منيش ريفي.

زعيط: موش ريفي يا شيخ انتم يا ابناء العرب زي البهايم.

معيط: الله يسترك يا زعيط والله جا خبرك يا ابني فوت روح فوت.

فلما توصل به الكَفر قامت أمه وعملت له طاجناً في الفرن مملوءاً لحما ببصل فلما رآه قال لها:

[زعيط:] ليه كترتي من الـ

معيكة: من الـ ايه يا زعيط.

زعيط: من البتاع اللي اسمه ايه.

معيكة: اسمه ايه يا ابني الفلفل.

وعيط: نو نو الـ دي الـ البتاع اللي ينزرع.

معيكة: الغله يا ابني.

زعيط: نو نو دي اللي يبقى لو راس في الارض.

معيكة: والله يا ابني ما فيه ريحة الثوم.

زعيط: البتاع اللي يدمع العينين اسمو أُونيون.

معيكة: والله يا ابني ما فيه أونيون ولا دا لحم ببصل.

زعيط: سي سا بصل بصل.

معيكة: ويا زعيط يا ابني نسيت البصل وانت كان اكلك كله منه.

معيط شكاه لأحد النبهاء وقال ولدي توجه أوروبا وحضر يذم بلاده وأهله ونسي لغته فقال له النبيه ولدك لم يتهذب صغيراً ولا تعلم حقوق وطنه ولا عرف حق لغته ولا قدر شرف الأمة ولا ثمرة الحرص على عوائد الأهل ولا مزية الوطنية فهو وإن كان تعلم علوماً إلا أنها لا تفيد وطنه شيئاً فإنه لا ميل إلى إخوانه ولا يستحسن إلا من يعرف لغتهم على أنه أصبح كالحجل لما أراد أن يقلد الغراب في مشيته وعجز عن التقليد واستحال عليه عوده لطبيعته الأولى فأصبح يقفز قفزاً وقد خرج عن حد الجنسية وطباع النوعية ولا يفعل فعل ولدك إلا لئيم جاهل بوطنه فكم من شبان في أوروبا تعلمت وعادت محافظة على مذهبها وعوائدها ولغتها وصرفت علومها في تقدم بلادها وأبنائها ولم ينطبق عليهم عنوان عربيّ تفرنج.

«سهرة الأنطاع»

دخل أحد المهذبين بيتاً من بيوت رجال الملاهي فوجد عشرة من الرجال جالسين على الأسرة باهتين ساكنين لا يتكلمون ولا يتحركون ولا يرفعون

أبصارهم. هذا واضع عنقه على كتفه وذا مكفي على المخدة وذاك يتمايل
كالنائم وآخر واضع يده على خديه فظن المهذب أن رب الدار أصيب بمصيبة
وهؤلاء متكدرون مما أصابه مشفقون عليه فجلس في ناحية من المجلس
وسأل رب الدار قائلاً لعلكم بخير هل من أمر نزل بالسيد حفظه الله؟ قال لا
ولكن عادتنا أن نجتمع كل ليلة للأنس والمفاكهة.

المهذب: أظنكم لتذاكرون في تقدم صنائع أوروبا وانتشار تجارتها في سائر
الأقطار حتى عظمت أروتها وتقوّت شوكتها.
رب الدار: ما لنا علم بأوروبا ولا أهلها فإننا ما خرجنا من مصر مدة حياتنا.
المهذب: عدم الخروج من البلاد ليس شرطاً في وقوف الإنسان على حقائق
الأشياء وعليه بأخبار من بعد عنه فإن التواريخ وصحف الأخبار تقص علينا
أحاديث الأمم ونحن جلوس في بيوتنا.
رب الدار: التواريخ لا يقرأها إلا العلماء والصحف لا يسأل عنها إلا الخواجات
فانها عبارة عن حكاية يتسلى بها الشبان.
المهذب: الصحف يا سيدي ألسنة الأمم وترجمان الملوك تنقل لك ما قاله
هذا الرئيس وهو بأقصى الغرب وما أجاب هذا الأمير وهو في أطراف الشرق
وتخبرك بالمحاورات السياسية وأغراض الملوك وأحوال الأمم وسير التجارة
وأعمال العقلاء وصنائع العلماء وخطب النبهاء وتاريخ الأذكياء وما قامت به
هذه الأمة من عمار وطنها وحمايتها له وحفظه من امتداد أيدي الغير إليه
وما أهملت فيه تلك الأمة حتى خاذلها الغريب وتداخل في شأنها وحجر
على أهلها عوائدهم ومذاهبهم.
رب الدار: هذا شيء يوجب وجع الدماغ ويشتت الفكر ولا يشتغل به إلا من
ليس له شغل.
المهذب: أظنكم تتحدثون في شؤونكم وتتذاكرون في أشغالكم الخاصة بكم
لعلكم تهتدون لأمر يزيد في الثروة أكثر مما أنتم عليه لتفاخر بكم حكومتكم
وتكافئكم على أتعابكم واجتهادكم بالرتب العالية والعلامات الشريفة.
رب الدار: هذا أمر لا يهمنا فإن البلاد إذا تقدمت أو تأخرت لا تفيدنا شيئاً
أحسن مما نحن فيه.
المهذب: ما هو الذي وصلتم اليه يا سيدي من التقدم.

رب الدار: لله الحمد كل منا له بيت عظيم بحوش واسع ومضيفة لطيفة وعنده من الخدم ما يقوم بإدارة أشغاله وقد تركت لنا أباءنا أموالاً لا تفنيها الأيام فنحن في نعمة عظيمة ترى المسكين من الناس يقوم في الفجر لأشغاله ويبيت الليل يكتب ويحسب ونحن لا نخرج من البيوت إلا قبل الظهر بقليل ونعود إليها وقت العصر للمسامرة بالمضحكات والنكات اللطيفة.

المهذب: إذا كانت هذه عادتكم فلِمَ تجتمعون في مثل هذه السهرة؟

رب الدار: عادة الكيف أنه لا يفرح إلا إذا تعاطاه الإنسان في مجلس أنس يضحك ولعب فنحن نجتمع ليتعاطى كل منا منزوله ثم تدور النكتة بيننا فإذا وثّن الانسان وخدّر قام ودخل محل النوم حسب العادة فيبيت مبسوطاً لا يسأل عن الدنيا ولا من فيها.

ثم التفت إلى أقرانه وقال: رايكم ايه يا اسيادنا في هذه العبارة؟

فأجابه الجميع بصوت واحد: مفيش غير كده احنا مالنا ومال الدنيا والتجارة والتواريخ. احنا رايحين نبقى زي الافرنج يلي كل ساعة يقولوا الدنيا جرى فيها ايه والجرانيل قالت ايه والتلغرافات عادت ايه زي اللي الدنيا ملكهم. هأ هأ هاي.

المهذب: هكذا تكون حال من لم يتهذب صغيراً فإنه يخرج أسير شهواته بعيداً عن إدراك المعاني جباناً بليداً غبياً. ولكن قد كسفت شمسكم وظهرت أنوار المعارف والآداب وأصبحت الحكومة في جد واجتهاد تقدم بهما رجالها وتبعثكم من قبور الغفلة إلى جنات المعارف والأمة تبيت تبحث عن أسباب تأخيرها وما يوجب تقدمها فهي والحكومة يد واحدة في أحياء الوطن وتوسيع تجارته وتأييد كلمته ولا نلبث أن نرى البيوت والمجامع كلها محافل آداب ومجالس أبحاث وتصبح الأطفال تبحث في حال من تقدمها وتعجب من جبن أبائها وسعيهم في إعدام المعارف بما ألفوه من اللهو والبطالة وفساد الأخلاق وما كانوا يفعلونه من القبائح والرذائل في سهرة الأنطاع.

«رأيت فوق ما سمعت»

مررت بالأزبكية بعد الغروب فقابلني شاب عليه سترة وبنطلون وسلم عليّ فظننتُه أحد المستخدمين الذين له اشتراك في جريدتي وقلت له كيف

حال سيدي فقال عندي حاجة عظيمة جداً فقلت له مثل ماذا فقال غلام جميل لم يخرج ليتسالي إلا هذه الليلة ويرضى بالقليل فحرت في أمري وبقيت أنظر لهيئته وأتأمل في صفته وبينما أنا واقف معه حضر بعض أحبابي وانتهره وشتمه شتماً قبيحاً وقال لي إن قادة الغلمان يشترون الملابس الإفرنكة ثم يلبسونها ويُلبسون الأولاد منها ثم يتوسلون بالهيئة لرواج صناعتهم القبيحة وإذا سألتهم عن الغلام قالوا لك هو ابن فلان ويسمون واحداً ربما كان من العظماء وهو (الولد) في الحقيقة حمار أو ضايع لا صنعه له. فعجبت كل العجب من انتشار هذا الأمر القبيح في بلادنا حتى صار له قادة ووسائل فلو اعتنت الضبطية بالقبض على هؤلاء المخنثين والقواد وأبعدتهم من البلاد لطهرت كثيراً من أخلاق الرجال الذين لا يهذبهم إلا سوط الحاكم أو صنعه وإلا فإن الأمر يزداد انتشاراً فيفسد الأخلاق ويضر بكثير من الناس الذين لم يعرفوا هذا الأمر ولنا في همة المأمورين والبوليس ما نرجو به تطهير الأزبكية بمصر والمنشية بالإسكندرية من هذه القاذورات وعندنا من المصائب والمحرمات غير هذا الفعل الحيواني وفي البقية الكفاية.

Hasan al-ʿAttar
(c. 1766–1835)

Introduced and translated by Shaden M. Tageldin

Penned during the French occupation of Egypt, Hasan al-ʿAttar's "Maqamat al-Faransis" (1799; *"Maqama* of the French") throws the contradictory psychodynamics of the colonial encounter—its terrors and its seductions—into sharp relief. A major intellectual of late-eighteenth- and early-nineteenth-century Egypt, al-ʿAttar was born in Cairo and studied at al-Azhar, Cairo's millennium-old Islamic institution of higher learning. When Napoleon Bonaparte invaded Egypt in 1798, al-ʿAttar fled Cairo for Upper Egypt; he returned in 1799 to befriend those he had formerly feared, teaching Arabic to the French scholars who had accompanied Napoleon's armies. This association compromised his reputation in Egypt after the occupation ended, driving him to embark in 1803 for Istanbul, Damascus, and other Ottoman imperial centers. He returned to Cairo in 1814, and he won renown for his erudite teaching within and beyond al-Azhar. In 1828, Muhammad ʿAli Pasha, the quasi-independent Ottoman governor of Egypt, appointed him Arabic editor of *al-Waqaʾiʿ al-Misriyya* ("Egyptian Events"), the new Arabic-Turkish official state gazette, and, in 1831, rector of al-Azhar. By his death in 1835, al-ʿAttar had written over fifty works of grammar, rhetoric, and literature; history and geography; theology, philosophy, and logic; and natural science, medicine, and technology.

Al-ʿAttar registered the French occupation's impact in imaginative fiction. The *maqama*—a genre of narrative fiction often composed in rhymed prose and usually also containing lines of poetry—permitted him to explore taboo relations that defied dominant historical narratives. Traditionally, the *maqama* features a trickster figure who extracts money from his audience by rhetorical guile. Al-ʿAttar's *maqama* posits the French orientalist as a colonial trickster: one who, like Napoleon in his first Egyptian proclamation of 2 July 1798, deploys Arabic to seduce the colonized Egyptian into ceding self and country.[1] Here, an Egyptian narrator exchanges fear for love when a French orientalist addresses him in Arabic, quoting *al-Burda* ("The Mantle"), a thirteenth-century panegyric to the Prophet Muhammad by the poet Sharaf al-Din al-Busiri. As the colonizer speaks with the tongue of Arab-Islamic Egypt, the colonized narrator fancies the French "conquered" by Arabic and Islam and himself sovereign; he hallucinates the French occupiers as the feminine love objects of his erotic gaze and refers to them (largely) in the grammatical feminine.

Note

[1]Napoleon's first proclamation to the people of Egypt, delivered on 2 July 1798 as his forces landed at Alexandria, circulated entirely in Arabic (save for the words "République Française," which encircled its seal) and invoked Islamic doctrine. Strategically aligning the interests of the Muslim majority in Egypt with those of the French, the proclamation argued that the French were "sincere Muslims" and adduced as proofs the fact that Napoleon's forces had invaded Rome and destroyed the Papal See, had ousted the anti-Islamic Knights of Saint John from Malta, and had come to liberate Egyptians from the foreign-born Mamluks.

Recommended Reading

Abu-Manneh, Butrus. "Four Letters of [Sh]ay[kh] Hasan al-ʿAttar to [Sh]ay[kh] Tahir al-Husayni of Jerusalem." *Arabica*, vol. 50, no. 1, 2003, pp. 79–95.

Al-Jabarti, Abd al-Rahman. *Chronicle of the First Seven Months of the French Occupation of Egypt, 15 June–December 1798, Muharram–Rajab 1213*. Edited and translated by S[hmuel] Moreh, E. J. Brill, 1975.

Colla, Elliott. "'Non, Non! Si, Si!': Commemorating the French Occupation of Egypt, 1798–1801." *MLN*, vol. 118, no. 4, 2003, pp. 1043–69.

De Jong, F[red]. "The Itinerary of Hasan al-ʿAttar, 1766–1835: A Reconsideration and Its Implications." *Journal of Semitic Studies*, vol. 28, no. 1, 1983, pp. 99–128.

De Jong, F[red], and P[eter] Gran. "On Peter Gran, Islamic Roots of Capitalism: Egypt, 1760–1840: A Review Article with Author's Reply." *International Journal of Middle East Studies*, vol. 14, no. 3, 1982, pp. 381–99.

Gran, Peter. *Islamic Roots of Capitalism: Egypt, 1760–1840.* 2nd ed., American U in Cairo P, 1999.

Tageldin, Shaden M. *Disarming Words: Empire and the Seductions of Translation in Egypt.* U of California P, 2011. FlashPoints 5.

FROM "*Maqama* of the French"

A brother from the ranks of the dissolute and the intoxicated told me:

"Tuesday, when the French alarmed the people and forced most of them into the streets afraid and gasping for air, I left my house wandering. I had no idea where I would end up, so I plied the streets and byways. Anticipating imminent annihilation, I was terrified, unable to settle anywhere; I didn't turn toward anyone['s house] until inexorable fate drove me to Azbakiyya, which is the dwelling place of [the French] people. Delusion intermingled with my thoughts until I realized that I was making a risky move, for I had fallen back into that which I had just escaped. So I steeled my heart and fortified my resolve and I readied my mind for this assault. Thus my reason yielded the answer: I will reach security and safety because the people of this quarter are at peace with the French and mingle with many of them; no struggle or evil has befallen them, and there has been no attack or retreat [here]. Indeed, I used to hear from knowledgeable people and from those who had toured many regions and lands that these people [the French] were not apt to be cruel to any except those who made war with them, nor did they terrorize any but those who battled and resisted them, and that some of them aspired to understand the obscure mysteries of knowledge. . . . In fact, their hearts had been imbued with a love of all the philosophical sciences. They aspired to possess books in these sciences and to study them rigorously and deliberately, seeking out whoever knew about them and engaging that person in conversation.

"Once I came to rest in Azbakiyya and rid myself of this fear, I went to the house of a friend of mine, the sight of whom cheers me and whose company puts us both in a good mood—[a man who] had become one of the leading authorities on these branches of knowledge in our Egypt. Thus I chanced upon, in the neighborhood where his place lies and next to the house in which he resides, a group of youths, among them those who rose like suns, swaying with the lilt of a bride, with faces on which Beauty had dropped her loose flowing robe. Indeed, Beauty had turned the lances of [their] bodies into flags when she unfurled on them her locks of hair; they [the bodies] are a banner that legions of lovers follow, swaying with it in passionate love wherever [those bodies] sway—and I looked at them as one in love, mystified, looks at roses. I began to gaze at those bodies' bending gait; they grasped what I wished and they knew what I meant. So all turned toward me and began to greet me. One youth among them showed me a book and began a conversation with me. Lo and behold! His Arabic was free of any accent and his expressions free of any archaism. He had become acquainted with some books by great notables, and he mentioned the books and manuscripts that he owned. He went on to enumerate and explain them, going so far as to mention [Nasir al-Din] al-Tusi's *Memoir* [*on the Science of Astronomy*] and [al-Qadi ʿIyad ibn Musa's] *Healing* [*by Defining the Rights of the Chosen One*], calling it the honorable book of healing. At this, wonder flooded my senses and the intoxication of literature sent me reeling toward him. My admiration for him intensified when I said to him, 'Indeed, I am a guest who has dropped by to visit your neighbor.' He instantly recited to me [the line] 'From [sheer] remembrance of neighbors in Dhu Salam . . . ?'[1] And he informed me that he had translated it from Arabic into his language, and it was but a portion of the poetic corpus he had committed to memory. When conversation carried me as far as it could, and the devil of love had overpowered and mastered me, I resolved to depart, though my astonishment over him had penetrated the very lining of my heart. He asked me to come by his house early the next morning so I could see the books he had collected. Thus I went to the place where I had arranged to spend the night, and I knew that I had been smitten with his beauty. A youthful passion that belonged to the past stirred in me, and a literary intoxication—whose strength had previously subsided—intensified in me. I remained sleepless all night; daybreak found me passionately in love. Sleeplessness and restlessness drove me to compose verses about him. I said:

Among the French is a gazelle, the magic of whose eye lodged in
     the lover's heart;
he broke like the dawn in black garments, so I turned into the
     daylight sheathed in drapes of dark night.
A garden of beauty no hand could touch, a prize guarded by the
     folds of the eyelids,
slender-bodied, he shook loose his leaves of hair as if he were a
     branch in a garden planted.
He saw the love in my eye, so he addressed me with a pearl of
     speech containing friendliness in feminine form;
when his speech came into perfect harmony with his mouth,
     a harmonious beauty played in his countenance.
He hunted my mind with glances—what a wonder! The French
     might pillage even reason itself.

"Then, when morning's sword shone brilliantly and night's tail recoiled bit by bit, my wishes to see him were fulfilled—time's face smiled on me when I met him. So I met him in the afternoon of that day; he was with a group of French youths, each of them toiling over the mysteries of knowledge [and] tracking their footprints, turning their minds to study the fine points of literature with great care. When I had sat down and settled myself, they took turns reciting poetry of conviviality to me, heady stuff, and they showed me books large and small, both unknown to me and renowned—all of them in mathematical and literary studies—and astronomical and engineering instruments. They conversed with me about issues in these disciplines and recorded some of my opinions of them. They asked me to unravel verses of *al-Burda* (it was in their possession, written in Arabic in multiple copies), then showed me snatches of poetry and asked me about their subtleties. One of them informed me that in their country was a collection of the seven *Mu'allaqat* and that they have collections of poetry in their own language whose meanings delight the ear. Each time they asked me to clarify an utterance, they would look it up in a precious tome on language, written in Arabic in the style of *al-Jamhara* and translated into French.[2] I wrote verses for them in their dictionaries, and I explicated for them some of the words. Among these were two lines [of poetry] I had composed before, when I was in the bloom of beauty and passionately enamored, and these were:

> Draw security for me from your glances, which fill my heart
>   with arrows and spears
> that have shed my blood even though its shedding is forbidden;
>   for by what sin [of mine] have they transformed it into some-
>   thing lawfully shed?

"Then I reinforced the couplet with an impromptu ode that included a few words of their language. This was among what they suggested to me in their desire to test what I knew:

Among the French is a supple branch who appeared in all the
beauty of [his] creation, a little moon:
He has a face like a full moon [peering from] under a night of
clothing;
He showed me pearls in a smile flowing with the wine of vessels;
His black eyes acted on my innermost soul with the effect of wine.
O heart, patience in [your] love of him; for in love lies the resur-
rection of souls.
Union with him is now impossible, for he has no pity for an
insignificant thing:
I say, "Union!"; he says, "Non, non!"—I say, "Breakup?"; he says,
"Si, si!"

"Rapturous delight transported them, and they marveled over
me with such wonder; they kept singing my praises and compli-
menting me effusively, and they insisted that I stay with them.
I equivocated in my reply and resolved secretly not to oblige,
knowing that this was a matter for which the barb of blame
would target me, on account of which all humanity would heap
hostility and contempt upon me. Thus I returned to my senses,
and I sought pardon from God."

Notes

[1]The French scholar quotes only the opening hemistich of al-Busiri's
al-Burda.

[2]Al-Mu'allaqat ("The Suspended Ones") refers to at least seven famous pre-
Islamic odes widely memorized and recited by literati even today. By al-
Jamhara, al-'Attar may mean Ibn Durayd's Jamharat al-Lugha ("Collection of
Language") or Abu Zayd al-Qurashi's Jamharat Ash'ar al-'Arab ("Anthology
of Arab Poems"), both works of the late ninth to early tenth century.

Source of Arabic Text on Which the Translation Is Based

Al-'Attar, Hasan ibn Muhammad. وهذه مقامة الأديب الرئيس الشيخ حسن العطّار
في الفرنسيس [wa-hadhihi maqamat al-adib al-ra'is al-shaykh hasan al-'attar

fil-faransis; This Is the *Maqama* of the Foremost Belletrist Shaykh Hasan al-'Attar on the French]. هذه المقامات السيوطية للإمام الحافظ جلال الدين سيدي عبد الرحمن السيوطي [hadhihi al-maqamat al-suyutiyya lil-imam al-hafiz jalal al-din sayyidi 'abd al-rahman al-suyuti; These Suyuti *Maqamat* Are by the Trusted Master Jalal al-Din 'Abd al-Rahman al-Suyuti], edited by Salih al-Yafi, [Cairo] AH 1275 [1858–59], pp. 91–96.

حسن العطّار

(نحو ١٧٦٦-١٨٣٥)

مقامة الفرنسيس

حدثني بعض الإخوة من أهل الخلاعة والنشوة أنه لما أزعج الفرنسيس
الناس يوم الثلاث وجفل أكثرهم في الشوارع مهرولاً لهّاث خرجت هائماً من
داري لا أدري أين يكون قراري فقطعت السكك والشوارع وأنا مِن ترقُّب
الهلاك فازع لا أستقر بمكان ولا ألوي على أحد عنان حتى ساقني القدر
المحتوم إلى الأزبكية التي هي مسكن القوم فخالط الوهم مني الخاطر وأراني
أني بهذه الحركة مخاطر لأني قد وقعت فيما منه فررت. ثم ثبّت جناني وقوّيت
أركاني وأعملت الفكرة في هذه الكَرّة فأنتج لي البرهان بلوغ الأمن والأمان.

لأن أهل هذه الجهة لهم مسالمون ولكثير منهم مخالطون لم يقع منهم
نزاع ولا شر ولا كر في مقاتلتهم ولا فر وكنت أسمع من أهل العرفان وممن
جال في الأقطار والبلدان أن القوم لا يشددون الوطأة إلا على من حاربهم
ولا يعاملون بالرهبة إلا من نابذهم وغالبهم وأن للبعض منهم إلى غوامض
المعارف تطلُّع . . . قد أشربوا في قلوبهم حب العلوم الفلسفية وأحرصوا على
اقتناء كتبها وأعمال الفكرة فيها والروِيّة يبحثون عمن له بها إلمام ويتجاذبون
معه بأطراف الكلام ثم لما استقرّيت بالأزبكية وتخلصت من هذه البليّة
ذهبت إلى دار صاحب لي تسرني رؤيته وتنشرح لمخالطته له رؤيتي وروِيّته
قد أحرز قصب السبق في ميدان هذه العلوم وصار هو المشار إليه في مصرنا
بين أرباب هذه الفهوم.

فصادفت بالحارة التي فيها مثواه وبجانب داره التي بها مأواه فتية منهم
برزن كالشموس وهن يتمايلن تمايل العروس بوجوه سدل الحسن عليها
جلبابه وقد صيّر رماح القدود أعلاماً حين أرخى عليها ذؤابه فهي راية تتبعها
من العشاق أجناد وتميل معها حيث مالت مع الهوى في كل واد فتطلعت
إليهن تطلع الهائم إلى الورود ووقفت أنظر إلى حسن شتى هاتيك القدود
ففطنّ مني ما رمته وعرفن المعنى الذي قصدته فمال الجميع إليَّ وابتدأن
بالتحية عليّ وأراني فتى منهم كتاباً وجدد معي كلاماً وخطاباً فإذا عربيته

خالصة من اللكنة وألفاظه معراة عن وصمة الهجنة وأخذ يتعرف ببعض كتب
للأفاضل الأكابر وذكر ما تحويه يده من الكتب والدفاتر وشرع في التعداد
والتعريف حتى ذكر تذكرة الطوسي والشفاء والشفاء معبّراً عنه بالشفاء الشريف
فخالطني من ذلك العجب ورنحتني إليه نشوة الأدب وزاد إعجابي به أني حين
قلت له إني ضيف بجاركم ألم أنشدَني على الفور أمن تذكر جيران بذي سلم
وأخبرني أنه نقلها من العربية إلى لغته وهي من جملة ما استقر بمحفوظته
ثم لما أخذ الحديث مني ما أخذ وغلب شيطان المحبة عليّ واستحوذ عوّلت
على الانصراف وقد خالط تعجبي منه الشغاف سألني في البكور إلى داره لأرى
ما اجتمع عنده من كتبه وأسفاره فذهبت للمكان الذي أعددته للمبيت
وعلمت أني بحسنه دُهيت فتحركت مني صبوة تقادم عهدها وتقوت عندي
نشوة أدب كان قد ضعف أودها وطفقت طول ليلي سهران وأنا لرؤية الصباح
كالولهان وحملني عدم النوم والثبات على أن أنظم فيه أبيات فقلت:

عند المحبّ له في القلب تأسيس	من الفرنسيس ظبي سحر مقلته
صبح عليه من الأستار حنديس	قد لاح في حلل سود فحلت سنا
ومطلب بظبا الألحاظ محروس	روض من الحسن لا تدنو إليه يد
كأنه غصن وفي الروض مغروس	مهفهف القد قد أرخى ذوائبه
بدرّ لفظ به لطف وتأنيث	رأى المحبة من عيني فخاطبني
بين الكلام وبين الثغر تجنيس	تجانس الحسن في مرآهُ حين غدا
حتى على العقل قد تسطو الفرنسيس	وصاد عقلي بلفتات فوا عجبا

ثم لما سطع صارم الصبح وتقلّص ذيل الليل جنحاً بعد جنح أسفرت الأماني
عن مرآه وتبسم وجه الزمان لي بلقاه فاجتمعت معه في عصر ذلك اليوم وهو
مع فتية من هؤلاء القوم كل يعاني غوامض المعارف ويقتفيها ويجيل ذهنه
في تحصيل دقائق الأدب ويعتنيها. فلما استقر بي الجلوس أخذن يدرن من
المنادمة على سمعي حُمَيَّا الكؤوس وأرينني من الكتب الصغير والكبير والنكير
عندي والشهير وكلها في العلوم الرياضية والأدبية. وأطلعوني على آلات فلكية
وهندسية وتحادثن معي في مسائل من تلك العلوم وكتبن عني بعض هاتيك
الفهوم.

وسألنني عن حل بعض أبيات البردة وهي بأيديهن مكتوبة بالعربي في
نسخ عدة ثم أرينني من أبيات الشعر نتفاً وسألنني عما دق منها وخفا

وأخبرني بعضهم أن ببلادهم ديوان المعلقات السبع وأن عندهم من دواوين الشعر بلغتهم ما يُطرب معناه السمع وكانوا كلما سألوني عن تفسير كلمة لغوية راجعوها في سفر نفيس أُلّف في اللغة على طريق الجمهرة باللفظ العربي وتُرجم بالفرنسيس وكتبت لهم ببعض المجاميع أبيات وفسّرت لهم منها بعض كلمات فمن ذلك بيتان كنت نظمتهما سابقاً زمن أن كنت في أحاسن الملاح شائقاً وهما:

خُذ لي أماناً من لواحظك التي ملأت فؤادي أسهماً ونبالا

سفكت دمي وهو الحرام إراقةً فبأيّ ذنب صيّرته حلالا

ثم عززتهما بقصيدة بها البديهة سمحت وعلى بعض لغتهم اشتملت وهي مما اقترحوه عليّ لإرادة اختبار ما لديّ وهي:

من الفرنسيس غصن بان قد لاح بالحسن في جنوس

له مُحَيًّا كبدر تمّ من تحت ليل من اللبوس

أراني الدر في ابتسام تجري به خمرة الكؤوس

ألحاظه السود فاعلات بمهجتي فعل خندريس

يا قلب صبراً على هواه فالحب فيه رد النفوس

الوصل منه غداً محالاً إذ ليس يرثى إلى رسيس

أقول وصلاً يقول نو نو أقول هجراً يقول سي سي

فأخذهم من ذلك الطرب وتعجبن مني غاية العجب وطفقن في بث المديح لديّ والإفراط في الثناء عليّ وحثثني على الملازمة عندهم وأروني أن هذا طلبتهم وقصدهم فسوفت في الإجابة وأضمرت على عدم الإنابة علماً مني بأن هذا أمر تفوّق عليّ منه سهام الملام وترمقني بالعداوة والاحتقار لأجله كافة الأنام فرجعتُ لرشدي أقتفيه واستغفرت الله مما كنت فيه.

'Ali Mubarak
(c. 1823–93)

Introduced and translated by Shaden M. Tageldin

'Alam al-Din, a fictional travelogue of nearly 1,500 pages and arguably also the first Egyptian novel, was published in Alexandria in 1882, just before the British invasion of Egypt. Its author, 'Ali Mubarak, began his education in a village Qur'anic school yet soon entered the new secular system instituted by Muhammad 'Ali Pasha, ultimately enrolling in the military and polytechnic schools of Cairo and Bulaq. Between 1844 and 1849, Mubarak studied military engineering in France. In his positions as minister of education, public works, and religious endowments under the khedives Isma'il and Tawfiq, he founded Dar al-'Ulum, a teacher-training institution that bridged the modern (Western) disciplines and the traditional (Arabic and Islamic) sciences, and the Khedival Library, forerunner of today's Egyptian National Library (Dar al-Kutub).

Mubarak began writing *'Alam al-Din* around 1867. The text narrates the European voyage of an Egyptian Azharite shaykh named 'Alam al-Din ("Sign or Banner of Religion") and his son, Burhan al-Din ("Proof of Religion"), in which they are accompanied by an English traveler said to be among those "celebrated Englishmen occupied, in their country, with learning the Arabic tongue and reading its disciplines" (vol. 1, p. 70). Along the way, Burhan al-Din befriends a young English sailor, Ya'qub. Both Egyptians' friendships with the English emanate from the purported "love" of the latter people for Arabic, Arabs, and Muslims. The English traveler even carries a manuscript copy of *Lisan al-'Arab* ("The Arab Tongue"), a famous Arabic dictionary compiled by the thirteenth-century scholar Ibn Manzur. Later, in Egypt, this English orientalist employs 'Alam al-Din to correct his copy for print and wider dissemination to (European) students of Arabic. Although bound for England, the group never gets there; the narrative is set largely in France. The two excerpts translated here reflect the complexity of nineteenth-century Egyptian receptions of European orientalism. While Mubarak's Egyptians return the affections of an English orientalism not yet entangled with military invasion, they ultimately spurn those of a French orientalism haunted by the Napoleonic occupation. When a former member of Napoleon's military-academic complex attempts to convince 'Alam al-Din of the benefits that the French occupiers brought to his country, the Egyptian resists.

Recommended Reading

Al-Qadi, Wadad. "East and West in 'Ali Mubarak's 'Alamuddin.'" *Intellectual Life in the Arab East, 1890–1939*, edited by Marwan R. Buheiry, American U of Beirut, 1981, pp. 21–37.

Mitchell, Timothy. *Colonising Egypt.* U of California P, 1991.

Ouyang, Wen-chin. "Fictive Mode, 'Journey to the West,' and Transformation of Space: 'Ali Mubarak's Discourses of Modernization." *Comparative Critical Studies*, vol. 4, no. 3, 2007, pp. 331–58.

Powell, Eve M. Troutt. *A Different Shade of Colonialism: Egypt, Great Britain, and the Mastery of the Sudan.* U of California P, 2003.

Reimer, Michael J. "Contradiction and Consciousness in 'Ali Mubarak's Description of al-Azhar." *International Journal of Middle East Studies*, vol. 29, no. 1, 1997, pp. 53–69.

Tageldin, Shaden M. *Disarming Words: Empire and the Seductions of Translation in Egypt.* U of California P, 2011. FlashPoints 5.

FROM 'Alam al-Din

The Ninety-Second Evening Entertainment:
The Oriental Society

The two [Burhan al-Din and Ya'qub] were [deep] in conversation, aware of nothing else until they entered the city. They continued until they reached the shaykh's ['Alam al-Din's] house; they alighted from the carriage and entered to find his friend the Englishman with him. First the shaykh's son kissed his father's hand; then he turned to the Englishman, shook his hand, and sat by his side. The time had come for them to go to the home of the [Oriental] Society's president. The Englishman said to the shaykh's son, "Get ready. We are heading [there] within the hour." The shaykh's son said, "If my father permits, I hear and I obey." Then they all rose and got in the carriage, which conveyed them to the home of the society's president. The president received them with the utmost respect and greeted them with the salute of the honored. At the gathering was a group of renowned scholars, men of the Oriental Society, and notable princes. The society's president took the shaykh's hand, seated him, and sat by his side and kept him company. And at the gathering, with the lady of the house, were many women. All [the men] sat conversing until mealtime came, when they all rose, and each took the hand of a woman. The lady of the house approached the shaykh and took his hand, so he followed her lead and walked with her to the dining room. She sat down, with the shaykh to her right and his friend the Englishman to her left, and the man of the house sat in the second row, with the shaykh's son to his left. The rest sat in their designated places; they ate and then returned to the sitting room. All the while they encircled the shaykh as the halo does the moon, celebrating him as they would a king whose every order is obeyed. Whenever a point related to the discipline of Arabic occurred to anyone, he or she courteously expressed it, and the shaykh would answer with an irrefutable reply. They marveled at the eloquence of his expression, the pleasing quality of his articulation, and the excellence of his memory.

The Ninety-Third Evening Entertainment: The French in Egypt

At the gathering was a Frenchman who was among those who had gone to Egypt with Napoleon and witnessed his battle with its people and the diffusion of his men throughout its provinces. He knew firsthand what some of [Egypt's] rulers had done before the arrival of the French. Between the lines of this man's speech, his love for Egyptians and his inclination toward the Muhammadan family became apparent to the shaykh.[1] So he asked him, "Were you in Egypt during the events with the French?" Said the latter, "[Yes], and before that time as well." The shaykh said, "I cannot verify this [history of the French occupation], given my young age at that time; I can imagine it only to the extent that I used to see my father in those days, each time he entered or left the house, saying to my mother, 'What do you think of these dire straits we are in? The Bedouin Arabs are pillaging in the desert, the Mamluks are corrupting and destroying, and the French are in the streets killing and looting, so that he who flees one group falls into the hands of others,' and such talk of the sort that would terrify heroes and alarm women and children. Although among our countrymen, I know the deceased to have been hardy and tough by nature. Nothing could have driven him to air these complaints save the horror of what he saw."

Then this man said to him: "If you had investigated the origin of your problems, you would have found that it lay entirely in the presence of the Mamluks, who made Egypt loot for themselves and divided its land and its villages among them.

They turned the people and the Bedouin Arabs against us and warned them against us, saying, 'The French have no motive in your country except to plunder your wealth, defile your honor, and divert you from your religion,' and such odious talk, even though the French were innocent of all this, having no goal but to reform [the Egyptian] condition and to rescue the people from the curse of those [Mamluk] ignoramuses. So if fate had permitted us to stay in the land of Egypt until now, it would have been better for the Egyptians. But unfortunately for the Egyptians, events in our region compelled our leader, Bonaparte, to return to our country, so we left [Egypt] after we had nourished it with our finest men and watered it with the blood of our children. In spite of that, we enacted for the people of Egypt great laws and [left behind] beautiful, broadly beneficial works, from which one hopes good will come and harm will be avoided, for example, the sea- and fresh-water canals, the barrages [regulators at the entrance of the Nile Delta near Cairo], the printing presses, and the division of Cairo into districts, with an overseer and night guards for each district, who tour it night and day, warding off evildoers and corrupt folk and prodding [people] to sweep and clean the byways and the streets. Among our finest innovations was the command to hang lanterns on the doors of houses, markets, and shops; the district overseers used to make their rounds by night, and if they found a house or shop without a lantern at its door, they would board it up to safeguard whatever was inside, summoning its owner at daybreak to penalize him as they saw fit.

"Also among [our innovations] was the establishment of a hospital for the treatment of the sick, for which doctors and medicines for every disease were marshaled, lying between Fustat and Cairo proper—you call it Qasr al-'Ayni. Also, quarantine sites were designated in every city, and other [public] works were undertaken that—were it not for the application of our ideas—would never have occurred to them [the people

of Egypt], for the tendency of Egyptians, like other peoples
of the Orient, is to rely on memorization of the Qur'an and
knowledge of some religious matters, stopping at these and
never crossing their limits. They do not delve deeper into the
meanings of books and their secrets, nor do their rulers. . . ."

The shaykh replied, "As for what you've recalled with respect
to what happened between the Egyptians and the French where
the Mamluks are concerned, it's an established fact that defense
of the homeland at that time was obligatory for all, there being
no difference between the master and the slave, the noble and
the outlaw. So suppose that the people rose up [against the
French] in obedience to the view of their rulers. Did they do
anything besides what they had to do?"

Interjected the Englishman: "What the shaykh says is true.
Indeed, a human being's inclination toward his own people and
his faith is instinctive. Don't you see that the people of Paris
did not open the gates of the city to King Henri IV until he
had renounced his Protestantism for their sect [i.e., Catholi-
cism], even though he was royalty, and everyone [involved] was
French, and the origin of the faith was one?"

"From this," said the shaykh, "one should infer that no one
can blame the Egyptians for refusing to bow to the French and
obey them, given [the Egyptians'] natural inclination to object
to the rule of those who differ from them in religion and race
and to leave [in power] those who share one faith with them
and whose habits and legal statutes are the same."

That man [the Frenchman] said to him, "All this is granted
and reasonable. Now the French, when they entered Egypt,
did not introduce a [heretical] innovation amid Muslims—one
contrary to the opinion of their rulers and religious scholars;
rather, they acted on the counsel of those rulers and scholars
and took their opinions into account, as is known from the
proclamations on which marks of their approval and appreci-
ation appear. Indeed, several of their greatest were appointed

[to councils]. . . . Thus Bonaparte, commander in chief of the armies—despite the loftiness of his position, the extent of his ability and his knowledge, and the excellence of his administration and his politics—did not act in Egypt on his opinions alone. . . ."

Note

[1]By "the Muhammadan family," it is not clear if Mubarak means the family of the Prophet Muhammad (which Islamic sources call *ahl al-bayt*) or the community of the Muslim faithful.

Source of Arabic Text on Which the Translation Is Based

Mubarak, 'Ali. علم الدين، لحضرة العالم الفاضل صاحب السعادة علي باشا مبارك، ناظر الأشغال العمومية المصرية سابقا ['alam al-din, li-hadrat al-'alim al-fadil sahib al-sa'ada 'ali basha mubarak, nazir al-ashghal al-'umumiyya al-misriyya sabiqan; 'Alam al-Din, by His Excellency the Esteemed Scholar 'Ali Pasha Mubarak, Former Egyptian Minister of Public Works]. Alexandria, Matba'at Jaridat al-Mahrusa, vol. 3, 1882, pp. 1077–83.

علي مبارك

(نحو ١٨٢٣–١٨٩٣)

علم الدين

«المسامرة الثانية والتسعون: الجمعية المشرقية»

وبينا هما في الحديث لم يشعرا إلا وهما داخل المدينة فسارا حتى وصلا
محل الشيخ فنزلا عن العربة ودخلا عليه فوجدا عنده صاحبه الإنكليزي فبدأ
ابن الشيخ بتقبيل يد والده ثم تحوّل للإنكليزي فصافحه وقعد بجانبه وكان
قد حان وقت ذهابهم إلى منزل رئيس الجمعية فقال الإنكليزي لابن الشيخ
هيّئ نفسك فإنّا متوجهون هذه الساعة فقال ابن الشيخ إن أذن الوالد فسمعاً
وطاعة ثم أنهم قاموا جميعاً وركبوا العربة وسارت بهم حتى وصلوا منزل
رئيس الجمعية فقابلهم بغاية الاحترام وحيّاهم تحية الكرام وكان بالمجلس
جماعة من مشاهير العلماء ورجال الجمعية المشرقية ووجوه الأمراء فأخذ
رئيس الجمعية بيد الشيخ حتى أجلسه وقعد بجانبه وآنسه وكان بالمجلس
مع صاحبة المنزل نساء كثيرة فقعد الجميع يتجاذبون أطراف الحديث إلى
أن حان وقت الطعام فقاموا جميعاً وأخذ كل واحد منهم بيد امرأة وجاءت
صاحبة المنزل إلى الشيخ وأخذت بيده فتبعها ومشى معها حتى دخلت به
محل الطعام فجلست والشيخ عن يمينها وصاحبه الإنكليزي عن يسارها
وجلس صاحب المنزل في الصف الثاني وابن الشيخ عن يمينه وجلس الباقون في
مواضعهم التي رسمت لهم فأكلوا ثم رجعوا إلى محل الجلوس كل ذلك وهم
محتفون بالشيخ احتفاف الهالة بالقمر ومحتفلون به احتفالهم بملك مطاع
فيما أمر وكان كلّ مَن خطر بباله شيء يتعلق بفن العربية تلطف في إبدائه
فيجيبه الشيخ بجواب لا يحوم حوله من عداه فيعجبون من بلاغة عبارته
وعذوبة لفظه وجود حفظه.

«المسامرة الثالثة والتسعون: الفرنسيس في مصر»

وكان بالمجلس رجل فرنساوي ممن توجه مع نابوليون إلى مصر وشهد وقعته بأهلها وانتشار رجاله في أعمالها واطّلع على ما كان من أمرائها قبل توجه الفرنسيس إليها فظهر للشيخ من أطراف كلام ذلك الرجل حبه للمصريين وميله للعائلة المحمدية فقال له أكنت بمصر أيام حوادثها مع الفرنسيس فقال وقبل ذلك أيضاً.

فقال الشيخ إني لا أتحقّق ذلك لصغر سني إذ ذاك وغاية ما أتخيله أني كنت أرى والدي في تلك الأيام كل ما دخل وخرج يقول لوالدتي ماذا ترين في هذا الحرج العرب في البادية تنهب والمماليك تفسد وتخرب والفرنج في الطرق تقتل وتسلب فمن فر من قوم وقع في يد آخرين ونحو ذلك من الكلام الذي يخيف الأبطال ويزعج النساء والأطفال مع أني أعلم طبع المرحوم في تجلده وتجمده بين أهل بلده فما اضطره إلى بث هذه الشكوى إلا فظاعة ما رآه من عموم البلوى.

فقال له ذلك الرجل لو بحثت عن أصل ذلك كله لوجدته من المماليك الذين جعلوا مصر غنيمة لهم قسّموا أرضها وقراها بينهم فإنهم كانوا يحزّبون الأهالي والعرب علينا ويحذرونهم منا بقولهم إنه لا غرض للفرنج من بلادكم إلا سلب أموالكم وهتك أعراضكم وصرفكم عن دينكم ونحو ذلك من المنفرات مع أن الفرنج كانوا بريئين من ذلك كله لا غرض لهم إلا إصلاح الحال وإنقاذ الناس من ورطة هؤلاء الجهال فلو قدّر وبقينا بأرض مصر إلى الآن لكان خيراً لهم ولكن من سوء حظ المصريين أنه حدث بقطرنا بعض حوادث ترتب عليها عود رئيسنا بونابرت إلى البلاد فخرجنا منها بعد أن غذيناها بفلذ أكبادنا ورشحناها بدم أولادنا ومع ذلك فقد رسمنا لهم بها قوانين جليلة وآثاراً عامة النفع جميلة يرجى منها الخير ويتقى بها الضير كالترعة المالحة والحلوة والقناطر الخيرية والمطابع وتقسيم مصر إلى أخطاط لكل حاكم وعسس يطوف فيه ليلاً ونهاراً بمنعون الشرور وأهل الفساد ويحثون على كنس الطرق والشوارع و تنظيفها ومن محاسن مبتدعاتنا الأمر بتعليق قناديل على أبواب البيوت والوكائل والخانات فكان حكام الأخطاط يطوفون بالليل فإذا وجدوا بيتاً أو خاناً ليس على بابه قنديل سمروه للمحافظة على ما فيه فإذا طلع النهار أتوا بصاحبه فيجازونه على حسب ما يرون.

ومنها إنشاء اسبتاليه لعلاج المرضى جمع لها من الأطباء والأدوية ما
يلزم لكل داء وهي فيما بين القاهرة ومصر تسمونها بالقصر العيني ومنها
الكورنتينات وتعيين محلاتها في كل مدينة وغير ذلك من الأعمال التي لو
لم تشتغل بها أفكارنا ما كانت خطرت لهم على بال لأن شأن المصريين بل
سائر المشرقيين الاقتصار على حفظ القرآن ومعرفة بعض أمور دينية يقفون
عندها ولا يتعدون حدودها ولا يغوصون في معاني الكتب وأسرارها وكذلك
حكامهم. . . .

فقال له الشيخ أما ما ذكرت من نسبة ما وقع بين المصريين والفرنسيس
للمماليك فمن المعلوم أن المدافعة عن الوطن في ذلك الوقت كانت واجبة
على العموم لا فرق فيها بين مالك ومملوك وشريف وصعلوك وعلى فرض
أن الأهالي إنما قاموا تبعاً لرأي حكامهم الذين هم أمراؤهم فهل فعلوا غيرما
يلزمهم.

فقال الإنكليزي إن ما يقول الشيخ حق فإن ميل الإنسان إلى أهل ملته
وديانته أمر فطري ألا ترى أن أهل باريز لم يفتحوا أبواب المدينة للملك هنري
الرابع إلا بعد أن رجع عن المذهب البروتستاني إلى مذهبهم مع أنه من بيت
الملك والجميع فرنساوي وأصل الدين واحد.

فقال الشيخ من هنا يعلم أن لا لوم على المصريين في امتناعهم من الخضوع
للفرنساوية والدخول تحت طاعتهم بحسب الميل الطبيعي من عدم الرضى
بحكم من خالفهم في الدين والجنس وترك من هم معهم على ملة واحدة
وعوائدهم وقوانينهم في الأحكام متحدة.

فقال له ذلك الرجل الشيخ كل ذلك معقول ومقبول إلا أن الفرنسيس
لما دخلوا مصر لم يحدثوا بين المسلمين بدعة على غير رأي أمرائهم وعلمائهم
بل ما فعلوا فعلاً إلا بمشورتهم وأخذ رأيهم كما يعلم ذلك من ذلك من
المنشورات التي عليها إمارات رضاهم واستحسانهم فكانوا معينين لذلك جملة
من أكابرهم . . . فبونابرت رئيس الجيوش مع علو همته وسعة باعه وإطلاعه
وحسن إدارته وسياسته لم يستقل في مصر بآرائه. . . .

Part 3: Transnational Connections

The encounter with Europe and with Russia led to a transnational sensitivity and was formative of *Nahda* thought and writing. The selected texts showcase how the emerging *Nahda* public engages with international affairs and thus begins to see itself as part of a global conversation that involves scandals, wars, and debates happening in Europe, America, Russia, and elsewhere. The texts highlight this transnational sensitivity, which moves us beyond the purely national or Arab concerns with which the *Nahda* has been associated.

Esther Moyal critiques the representation of women in European literature, citing the plays of Molière. She shows that the West is not the site of women's freedom and rights, as is often assumed, and no less complicit in their dismissal as cultural agents than the East. Writing about the struggle and persecution of Émile Zola, she praises his defense of Dreyfus against the charges of spying. As a Jewish female intellectual from Beirut writing in Arabic, Moyal incorporates the questions of gender and ethnicity into a rigorous critique of social and political injustice operating in a transnational context.

The global *Nahda* theme continues with selections from the newspaper *Thamarat al-Funun* ("Fruits of the Arts"), published by 'Abd al-Qadir al-Qabbani. Al-Qabbani gives us a sense of the common issues preoccupying the *Nahda* public in turn-of-the-century Beirut. Reporting on the Dreyfus affair as well, he challenges French pretense to secularism and universalism. Included are news items about the health hazards of microbes, municipal elections, the Spanish-American War, and a fire that broke out at a Chicago fair in which many Lebanese and Armenian traders lost their goods.

The selections from Muhammad 'Abduh contain a discussion of Arab history in Sicily, European painting, and a letter to Lev Tolstoy as well as Tolstoy's response. Examining cathedral frescoes, 'Abduh produces a theory of art that challenges the traditional understanding of Islamic iconoclasm. He activates a dialogue between the visual and the poetic, expressing his admiration for European arts, archives, and preservation skills.

The final selection in this section is from Mikhail Naimy's diary from when he was in Russia in 1908, in which he discusses the experience of studying abroad and describes how he recognizes his own poetic impulse while reading Russian authors.

Esther Moyal
(1873–1948)

Introduced and translated by Lital Levy

A remarkable woman of many talents, Esther Moyal, journalist, literary translator, author, and feminist, was born Esther Azhari in Beirut in 1873 to a Sephardi Jewish family of modest means. She was educated from a young age in classical Arabic, French, and English. In 1890 or 1891, she received an academic degree in Beirut, probably from the Beirut Female Seminary (later the American College for Girls), after which she taught at local Christian and Jewish schools. She was also active in the earliest associations for women in the Levant. In 1893, she was nominated to represent Syrian women at the women's congress at the World Columbian Exposition in Chicago. She would eventually publish in many of the mainstream Arabic-language newspapers and journals of the era. Esther Azhari married Simon Moyal, a Palestinian Jewish doctor and writer who was active in *Nahda* circles. The Moyals moved to Cairo, where in 1899 Esther founded a journal for women, *al-'A'ila* ("The Family"), which ran through 1902 and was briefly revived as a newspaper in 1904. During the same period, she became a prolific translator of European works into Arabic, with over a dozen published titles (most of them French novels) to her credit; she also published numerous short dramas for performance in Jewish schools. After the Young Turk Revolution in 1908, the Moyals returned to Jaffa, Simon's birthplace, where they supported political reform in the Ottoman Empire while advocating a shared homeland for Jews, Muslims, and Christians. Esther also directed a school for Muslim girls and remained active in women's causes. In 1914, the Moyals founded a short-lived Arabic newspaper based in Jaffa.

The two excerpts of her writing given here represent different stages of her career. In 1894, she contributed a letter to *al-Hilal* ("The Crescent"), the leading Arabic cultural journal of the time; it was the journal's first signed contribution by a woman. A spirited defense of women's intellect, the essay is bold in style and expresses an impassioned commitment to the cause of women. In 1903, she published an Arabic-language biography of Émile Zola inspired by the French novelist's famous defense of Alfred Dreyfus, the Jewish French army captain falsely accused of espionage. Note her apology at the end, in which she intimates that as a woman she lacked the time and resources that would have been available to her had she been a man.

Recommended Reading

Behar, Moshe, and Zvi Ben-Dor Benite, editors. *Modern Middle Eastern Jewish Thought: Writings on Identity, Politics, and Culture, 1893–1958.* Brandeis UP, 2013.

Levy, Lital. "Jewish Writers in the Arab East: Literature, History, and the Politics of Enlightenment, 1863–1914." U of California, Berkeley, 2007. PhD dissertation.

———. "Partitioned Pasts: Arab Jewish Intellectuals and the Case of Esther Azhari Moyal, 1873–1948." *The Making of the Arab Intellectual: Empire, Public Sphere, and the Colonial Coordinates of Selfhood*, edited by Dyala Hamzah, Routledge, 2012, pp. 128–63.

Moyal, Esther Azhari. "Address at the American College for Girls in Beirut." Behar and Benite, pp. 31–37.

———. "Our Renaissance." Behar and Benite, pp. 38–46.

"Is It Befitting of Women
to Demand the Rights of Men?"

I read the serial article included in your esteemed periodical . . . signed by Dr. Amin Effendi al-Khuri; on finishing it, I realized that it had been written in response to an earlier article on the same subject, and the proverb about the pot calling the kettle black came to mind.[1] This was because the esteemed doctor spared no expense in castigating his opponent and heaping invective upon him for his flimsy arguments and weak reasoning, even though his own arguments were, if anything, even weaker.

Before delving into this subject, I would like to point out to esteemed readers, and especially to the esteemed doctor, that I don't intend in my remarks to enter into the heart of the debate or to prove that women's rights are equal [to those of men]; rather, these are some observations that came to mind after reading the aforementioned article and that I felt compelled to put forth.

I don't know how it could be that the esteemed doctor places our gender on a par with horses, donkeys, and dogs. How much more appropriate it would have been had he placed the birds of his pen in the cages of nightingales, canaries, and parrots. In all truth, I am utterly flabbergasted and astonished. I dispute his claim that a woman's mind is confined within a narrow circle. I don't believe that a seamstress other than his own mother sewed him the festive garment he wore to celebrate his weaning from milk, on the day that this selfsame mother also prepared the first solid food he ever tasted.

However I turn my glance upon the distinguished ladies who have honored me with their affection, I don't see the respected doctor's judgment applying to them. How often I attended

their meetings and heard their versatility in speaking on sub-
jects ranging from the scientific to the religious and the phil-
osophical. And how often I witnessed two people debate each
other in an argument, one of them belonging to the gender
of the esteemed doctor and the other one to our weak gender,
which is incapable of earning the doctor's regard: proofs were
exchanged, the debaters moved from one topic to the other,
and the woman was the life of the debate, and we might even
say the winner. . . .

Furthermore, I remind the esteemed doctor that women
only recently entered the domain of writing and scholarship,
not because of any shortcomings on their part but rather
because of the stronger sex's disdain for them. The mockery
of educated women by the famous French poet Molière and
others attests to the fairness of my words and supports my
claims.

In closing, I say that the woman who spends some small
change on ink and paper, and who passes her free time in read-
ing and writing and does not waste it with laziness and idle chat-
ter, knows quite well how to manage her household and raise
her children with the economy and wisdom that will ensure
their happiness and guarantee her peace and fortune in the
hereafter.

Introduction to
Biography of Émile Zola

Zola has died, and his death reverberates through the souls
of his readers in all languages throughout the world. Zola
has died, and the hearts of those who loved him are broken.
The eyes of his admirers have gone blood red from weeping.

A group of people, rotten to the core, have set out to tear at that great lion's corpse now that they are safe from his roar. Demons of oppression and darkness who were harmed by his advocacy of truth and light, they rose blustering like cowards who stand up to fight in an empty arena. He was an eloquent man, yet they disparaged his words; he was a philosopher, yet they distorted his principles. He was a brave man who stood up to aid the oppressed without a second thought, yet they impugned his courage.

Zola has died, and when his death was announced to the people, they read his open letter that very morning.[2] Without a doubt, that letter was a guide for the judiciary and a light revealing truth and dispelling falsehood. That very morning, his open letter to the president of the French Republic was published, which decried the injustice of the judges in Dreyfus's trial and their unfair verdict against him as well as their bias in the trial of that wily traitor Esterhazy and how they trampled on the law to exonerate him. That very morning, Zola's pen struck a blow against the sword and nicked it, assailing the officers [who had framed Dreyfus] with a reed pen sharper than their blades and an eloquence that shattered their edifices. Indeed, Zola's words split France into two: one half that viewed justice as sacrosanct and rose to its defense, and the other half that preferred to let the innocent be trampled by army boots—and the rest is history.

Zola has died, and al-Mutanabbi's poem could be said to truthfully depict the dignity of his funeral:

> They carried him out, and every mourner behind him
>   swooned as did Moses when Sinai was crushed.
> The sun overhead was ailing
>   and the earth was trembling and swinging to and fro;
> The fluttering of the angels' wings all around him
>   and the eyes of that host all around, surrounded him like a wall

Until they reached the grave,
    dug inside the heart of all his companions.
In him were eloquence, generosity, piety,
    courage, intelligence, and charity.
Were praise enough to return him to life,
    rather than be buried, he'd be resurrected.

The writers were divided in their response to the news of Zola's death. The champions of freedom lavished praise on him, the brothers of justice gave him his due, and the league of writers and the collectivity of scholars both eulogized him as he deserved. The rabble of clerics rose and spit the venom they were accustomed to spitting at anyone who disagreed with them or who would not submit to their tyranny or take orders from their bishops. The clerics were followed by a group of people who took France backward, endeavoring to return it to the excesses of Louis XIV in the face of the hunger of the people, and to the depravity of Louis XV in the face of the nation's decline. But the deceased [Zola] placed an unassailable wall before their greedy ambitions, and, blocking their base acts and low aims, he turned those fearful cowards back by the force of his pen.

"They are wearing gowns made of shame and stumbling over their own trains."

When we saw that the majority of Arabic readers had not heard of Émile Zola, the revolutionary writer, momentous philosopher, and man of integrity and unrivaled courage, and when we saw that some readers were perusing disreputable newspapers (to which they were misled into subscribing by the Jesuits in their midst), we were roused to gather fragments of what has been said about this prodigy of his times, to publish some of his pertinent opinions, beneficial wisdom, eloquent verses, and miraculous sayings, and to translate his famous letter "J'accuse," which he directed to the president of the republic [of France] and which was responsible for saving Dreyfus from the talons of evil traitors.

And we were also moved to describe the great gathering at his funeral, at which a hundred thousand people marched, awestruck, and to give a brief glimpse of his biography and other material we have gathered from the most trustworthy sources and witnesses. Our book comes with a full heart, laden with lessons, embellished with imagery, and worthy of being held in the hands of our esteemed citizens.

And here we turn our esteemed readers' attention to the quantity of sources from which we compiled this biography, for we did so after perusing numerous newspapers. To this we added information about him from our own memory and what remained in our mind after reading his work. Therefore, we did not organize the book into chapters or break it into sections but rather took the life of the departed as the basis for our work and mentioned everything we could recall as to the course of it. We admit that we did not make an outline for the book before writing it but wrote each chapter without knowing, for the most part, what would be in the next one, given the quantity of documents we had at hand for reference. So if readers find any inconsistency or error in [the book's] organization, they should remember that this book is not translated from another language and that writing a biography about the life of a man like Zola and judging his works requires time, effort, and resources beyond what was available to us. May peace prevail.

Notes

I thank Michael Cooperson for his assistance with the translation "Is It Befitting of Women to Demand the Rights of Men?"

[1]The Arabic proverb used translates literally as "Guarded from others when he himself is a guard."

[2]This is a reference to "J'accuse" ("I accuse"), the open letter that Zola published on 13 January 1898 in the daily paper *L'aurore*, in which he

addressed President Félix Faure and accused the judiciary and the military
of anti-Semitism and miscarriage of justice in their prosecution of Drey-
fus. The letter was reprinted at various times and in various publications
outside France.

Sources of the Arabic Texts on Which
the Translation Is Based

Azhari, Esther. ‏هل للنساء أن يطلبن كل حقوق الرجال؟‏ [hal lil-nisa' an yatlubna
kull huquq al-rijal?; Is It Befitting of Women to Demand the Rights of
Men?]. *Al-Hilal*, vol. 2, no. 4, 1894, pp. 438–40.

Moyal, Esther. ‏تاريخ حياة إميل زولا‏ [tarikh hayat imil zula; Biography of
Émile Zola]. Matba'at al-Tawfiq, 1903.

استير مويال
(١٩٤٨-١٨٧٣)

هل للنساء أن يطلبن كل حقوق الرجال؟

أطلعت على مقالة مدرجة في جريدتكم الغراء . . . بإمضاء الدكتور أمين
أفندي الخوري ولما أتيت على آخرها ظهر لي أنها كتبت رداً على مقالة سلفت
في هذا الموضوع فخطر في بالي المثل العربي القائل ومحترس ومحترس من غيره وهو
حارس لأن حضرة الدكتور أفاض في لوم مناظره وشدّد النكير عليه لوهن
براهينه وضعف حجته على حين أنه لم بات هو نفسه إلا بأوهن البراهين.

وقبل الدخول في هذا الموضوع أنبه حضرات القراء وخصوصاً حضرة
الدكتور بأنني لا أقصد بكلامي الدخول في أساس المناظرة ولا إثبات مساواة
حقوق المرأة بل إنما هي ملاحظات جالت في خاطري بعد قراءتي المقالة المنوّه
عنها ورأيت الواجب عليّ إبداءها.

لا أدري كيف ساغ لحضرة الدكتور أن يجعل جنسنا بمنزلة الخيل والحمير
والكلاب وما كان أحراه لو أسكن طيور قلمه أقفاص البلابل والكنار والببغاء.
وإني وأيم الحق لذاهلة ومستغربة ومخطئة زعمهُ بتحديد عقل النساء ضمن
دائرة مقصورة. ولا أظن خياطة غير والدته خاطت له ثوب فطامه يوم أعدت
له تلك الوالدة أول طعام ذاقه بعد الفطام.

وكيفما حولت نظري إلى السيدات والسائدات اللواتي شرفنني بصداقتهن
لا أرى حكم حضرة الدكتور ينطق عليهن فكم حضرت اجتماعات وسمعت
منهن مفتناً في مواضيع تختلف بين علمية ودينية وفلسفية. وكم تبارى
للجدال أمامي متناظران أحدهما من جنس حضرة الدكتور والآخر من جنسنا
الضعيف القاصر عن نيل اعتبار حضرته فتبودلت البراهين وتنقلت المناظرات
من موضوع إلى آخر وكانت المرأة نعمة المناظرة إذا لم نقل «الفائزة.» . . . .

ومع ذلك فأني أذكّر حضرته بأن النساء لم يدخلن باب العلم والكتابة إلا
من عهد قريب لا لقصور منهن بل لاستخفاف الجنس الأقوى بهن وكفى
باستهزاء موليير الشاعر الفرنساوي الشهير وغيره بالنساء العالمات شاهد عدل
يعضد كلامي ويؤيده.

و في الختام أقول إن المرأة التي تنفق البارات القليلة في شراء الحبر والورق وتقضي وقت عطلتها في القراءة والكتابة ولا تقتله بالكسل والكلام عن هذه وتلك تعرف جيداً كيف تدبّر بيتها وتربّي أولادها باقتصاد وحكمة يتكفلان بسعادة أولادها وثروة آخرتها والسلام.

تاريخ حياة إميل زولا

«مقدمة»

مات زولا فكان لوفاته صدى في أفئدة كل القراء في كل اللغات في كافة أقطار المعمور.

مات زولا فانصدعت قلوب محبيه. ودمت محاجر المعجبين به. وقام نفر من الذين في قلوبهم مرض يحاول نهش شلو ذلك الأسد بعد أن آمنوا زئيره. قوم هم شياطين الظلم والظلام ساءتهم نصرة للحق وللنور فنهضوا نهضة الجبان الذي خلا له الميدان. فأخذوا يعيبون قول ذلك المقول ويفسقون مبادئ ذلك الفيلسوف ويخطئون شجاعة ذلك الشجاع الذي وقف لنصرة المظلوم دون أن يبالي.

مات زولا وكان الناس حين نُعي إليهم في غداة يوم قرأوا فيه كتابه. ذلك الكتاب لا ريب فيه هدى للقضاء ونور أظهر الحق فأزهق الباطل. غداة يوم انتشر فيه خطابه الموجّه لرئيس جمهورية فرنسا يشتكي فيه عسف قضاة دريفوس وحكمهم الجائر عليه وتعرُّض قضاة استرهازي الخائن اللئيم ودوسهم على القانون لتخليعه. غداة يوم صفع فيه بقلمه السيف فثلمه وصال على الضباط ببراع أحدّ من سنانهم وبيان كسر بنائهم فقسم فرنسا إلى شطرين شطرٌ رأى الإنصاف أقدس شيء فعضده وشطرٌ فضّل أن يداس البريء بنعال الحربية فكان ما كان.

مات زولا وقد صدق في وصف مشهده ومهابة جنازته المتنبي حين قال:

صعقات موسى حين دُكّ الطور	خرجوا به ولكل باك خلفه
والأرض واجنة تكاد تمور	والشمس في كبد السماء مريضة
وعيون ذاك الجمع حوله سور	وحفيف أجنحة الملائك حوله

في قلب كل رفاقه محفور	حتى أتوا جدثاً كأن ضريحهُ
والبأس أجمع والحجا والخير	فيه الفصاحة والسماحة والتقى
لما انطوى فكأنه منشور	كفل الثناء له بردّ حياته

وقد اختلف الكتّاب في نعيه فأطراه بنو الحرية ووفاه حقه إخوان العدل
وأتته لفيف الكتباء وجموع العلام مما هو أهل له وقام رعاع الإكليريكيين
ينفثون من السمّ ما تعوّدوا على نفثه ضد كل من لم يقل قولهم ويذعن لجائر
حكمهم. ويأتمر بأوامر أخبارهم وتبعهم قومٌ من الذين ساروا بفرنسة القهقرى
واجتهدوا أن يعيدوا إليها إسراف لويس الرابع عشر إزاء جوع الأمة وفسق
لويس الخامس عشر إزاء اضمحلال الوطن. فوقف الفقيد دون مطامعهم
سوراً منيعاً وسدّ ما بين دنيء أعمالهم وسافل غاياتهم وأعادهم بقوة قلمه
خاسئين خاسئين.

«يتعثرون بأذيال من الخجل»

ولما رأينا الأكثرية في قراء العربية يجهلون من إميل زولا الكاتب النحرير.
والفيلسوف الخطير. والرجل المستقيم الذي لا يُبارى. والشجاع الكريم الذي لا
يُجارى. ورأينا أن البعض من القراء يطالعون الصحائف السوداء التي يغويهم
على الاشتراك بها من هم بين ظهرانيهم من الجزويت استفزتنا الحمية لجمع
شتات ما قيل في نابغة زمانه. وأعجوبة أوانه. ونشر ما طواه في مؤلفاته من
الآراء السديدة والحكم المفيدة والآيات البينات والأقوال المعجزات وترجمة
كتابه الشهير «أشكو» الذي وجّهه لرئيس الجمهورية فانبغى عليه نجاة
دريفوس من بين مخالب الخونة الأشرار.

ووُصف الاحتفال المُقام بتشييعه الذي مشى فيه مئة ألف من الخلق
وكأنهم على رؤوسهم الطير ولمعة من تاريخ حياته إلى غير ذلك مما اقتبسناه
من أصدق الموارد وأوثق الشواهد فجاء مؤلفنا عامراً بالفوائد مشحوناً بالعبر
مزيناً بالصُوَر خليقاً بأن يحفظ بين أيدي مواطنينا الكرام.

وهنا نستلفت أفكار قرائنا الكرام إلى تعدد المصادر التي جمعنا منها هذا
التاريخ فقد ألفناه بعد مطالعة الجرائد العديدة وأضفنا إلى ما تحصلناه منها
من المعلومات ما كان محفوظاً في مخيلتنا عنه وما بقي في نفسنا بعد مطالعة
تأليفه ولذلك لم نبوّب الكتاب ولم نقسم مباحثه بل اتخذنا حياة الفقيد قاعدة
للعمل وذكرنا كلما خطر لنا عنه في أثناء سردها. ونحن نعترف أننا لم نرسم

خطة لكتابنا هذا قبل الشروع فيه بل كنا في أثناء كتابة فصل لا ندري على الغالب ما هو الفصل الذي سيليه لكثرة ما بين يدينا من المستندات التي لجأنا إليها فإذا وجد القراء بعض خلل في الترتيب فليتذكروا أن الكتاب غير منقول عن لغة أخرى وأن كتابة تاريخ حياة رجل كزولا والحكم على مؤلفاته وأعماله يقتضي له من الوقت والمهارة والتطويل والشفقة ما ليس بين يدينا والسلام.

Thamarat al-Funun
(1898)

Introduced and translated by Tarek El-Ariss

Published by 'Abd al-Qadir al-Qabbani (also Kabbani) in Beirut, *Thamarat al-Funun* ("Fruits of the Arts") was a weekly newspaper that ran from 1875 to 1910. It included news from around the world, along with cultural and political articles by leading thinkers of the time, including Muhammad 'Abduh, Egypt's reformist grand mufti who resided in Beirut from 1885 to 1888 and with whom al-Qabbani closely collaborated. The news items selected here provide a glimpse of the changing times that transformed Beirut from a sleepy Ottoman province to a thriving cultural and political center in the second half of the nineteenth century. The encounters, connections, and different activities of al-Qabbani represent a new relation between the local and the global in Beirut during that time. These articles from his newspaper provide a sense of this relation, which is key to understanding the *Nahda*, the role of print media, and the emergence of Beirut as a cultural center.

Recommended Reading

Ayalon, Ami. *The Press in the Arab Middle East: A History.* Oxford UP, 1995.
Sheehi, Stephen. "Arabic Literary-Scientific Journals: Precedence for Globalization and the Creation of Modernity." *Comparative Studies of South Asia, Africa, and the Middle East*, vol. 25, no. 2, 2005, pp. 438–48.

"On the Dreyfus Affair"
and Other News Items

On the Dreyfus Affair

We never would have thought that the Dreyfus affair would achieve the degree of notoriety and significance that it has today, exposing the French people's religious fanaticism despite their claim that they have erased all traces of it through a unifying sense of citizenship. The French are in fact drowning in the very bigotry of which they unjustly accuse others.

Readers have learned about this serious affair, which risks becoming a second Panama [affair], and about the French military council that exonerated Commandant Esterhazy without any consideration for the objections of Dreyfus's family and supporters. The council in fact confirmed the judgment against Dreyfus, that he was the author of those papers that were stolen from the German embassy in Paris, as we noted previously.

The *Paris Telegraph* has reported that Monsieur Zola, one of the most renowned French authors, has published in the daily *L'aurore* ["Dawn"] a letter addressed to the president of the republic, Félix Faure, in which he accused Colonel du Paty de Clam of responsibility for the judicial mishandling of the Dreyfus case. He also accused Generals Mercier, Billot, de Bois-deffre, and Gonse of being complicit in the colonel's misconduct, and he placed blame as well on the two military councils that prosecuted Dreyfus and Esterhazy.

Zola's open letter had an unsettling effect on the French public and especially on the parliament, leading Prime Minister Méline to call for the prosecution of Monsieur Zola. Méline's call for taking the necessary measures to confront Zola's libelous accusations against the French army earned him a parliamentary vote of confidence, with 313 votes cast, of which 132 were against.

These developments led the war minister, General Billot, to order the attorney general to prosecute Monsieur Zola. They also led students to riot in Paris, chanting, "Down with Zola! Down with the Jews!" It is no secret that the Jews have become an integral part of the French government and military establishment, with many serving as commanders and officers, among them Dreyfus himself. Riots broke out for a second day, with people chanting, "Death to Zola! Death to the Jews! Long live the army!" The rioters then broke the windows of a house that they thought belonged to Monsieur Zola, and fifteen of them were arrested.

It is also being confirmed that the army chief of staff, General Saussier, has stepped down; this led about one hundred civil society organizations to demonstrate in Place Vendôme as a tribute to this leader. . . .

The French people were not content to riot only in Paris but went on to riot against the Jews in Nancy, Bordeaux, Clermont, Lyon, Nantes, Marseilles, and other French cities, vandalizing Jewish stores and businesses.

Reuters reports that French outrage against the Jews is on the rise, provoking riots throughout the French states and territories.

The Health Hazards Involved in Laying Goods in Front of Stores

The publication *Tabib al-ʿAʾila* ("The Family Doctor") reported the following: "Shopkeepers have grown accustomed to displaying their goods on the sidewalk right outside their stores to entice passersby. However, displaying goods in such a manner not only irritates passersby but also causes potential health hazards. For what if someone suffering from tuberculosis or some

other disease should pass by and spit in front of the store—
when his spit, which is full of tuberculosis microbes, dries, these
microbes will fly through the air and land on the merchandise,
and when the merchandise is moved, the microbes will fly into
the lungs of those breathing nearby. We would have accepted
this hazard if it were restricted to the stores selling textiles, but
it also affects perfumeries and stores selling oil, groceries, fruits,
and meats, since each of them displays outside goods such as
butter, ghee, oil, cheeses, fruits, and other food items that are an
integral part of our diet. These food items could easily rot and
become contaminated by microbes that would then make their
way to our stomachs, causing us contagious diseases without
our knowing how we had contracted them."

It is also reported: "The government and the municipal
councils in all Ottoman provinces prohibit stores from display-
ing their goods on the street or sidewalk and [will] fine all those
who break the law. However, shopkeepers may choose to pay
the fine and continue displaying their goods in this way."

Tabib al-'A'ila is right in warning people of these health haz-
ards and in advising them against purchasing foods displayed
on the streets.

Fire Consumes the Chicago Exhibition

An American newspaper reported that a fire broke out in
an exhibition that opened its doors on the eighteenth of last
month and was meant to run for five months. Hardly had the
merchants finished setting up their stands when a fire began
raging from all four corners of the exhibition space. In less than
twenty minutes, the fire reduced everything to ashes, causing
the deaths of many inside and of those who rushed in to save
them and their goods.

Among the people at the exhibit were thirty-five Lebanese
and Armenians, who survived but lost their goods to the fire.

The Spanish-American War

The wires are reporting that tensions between America and Spain are rising and that war is about to break out. Fear of impending war caused an apparent panic at the New York Stock Exchange, when new reports surfaced indicating that an act of treason was behind the explosion of the USS *Maine*. For this reason, one now sees preparations for war in full swing in both countries.

The United States government has declared officially that it does not yet know the cause of the warship's explosion because it has not yet received the report on this matter. As for the Spanish, they are awaiting impatiently the report of their own inquiry committee, which attributes the explosion to an accident on board the American ship. Spain will strongly endorse this report, even if it contradicts the American one. The latest news is that the Spanish government has contacted the American government regarding this incident, saying that war would be a crime against the human race. Yet both sides continue active preparations for war. Whether there will be a war seems to depend on the results of the investigation into what caused the explosion. Only Spain's innocence could avert the flames of war now. God alone knows what the future holds.

Beirut's Municipal Elections

The municipal elections will take place tomorrow in accordance with the announcement included in this issue. The state newspaper, *al-Wilaya* ("The Province"), has expounded in its latest issue on the importance of the municipal council and its beneficial institutions. So we would like to call voters' attention to this long-sought-after development [the elections], asking them to respect due process, avoid any incidents, and elect only those who are qualified to perform this valuable public service. *Al-Wilaya* wrote:

Choosing carefully the members of the municipal council who are eligible to run will bring great benefit to the government and the people. Praise God, there are many who are qualified to serve, be they Muslim or non-Muslim. The governor has taken all necessary measures to ensure that the elections will be conducted in accordance with the law. He has also brought to the municipality members of the governing council and scribes who will work under the supervision of His Excellency Maktubi Bek Effendi to oversee the process and guarantee its smooth operation. Eligible voters should cast their ballots without favoritism or thought of personal connections and base their decisions exclusively on the qualifications of the candidate and his ability to fulfill his duty to serve the public good, regularly attend the council's meetings, and diligently perform all the tasks associated with this position.

Source of Arabic Text on Which the Translation Is Based

ثمرات الفنون [thamarat al-funun; Fruits of the Arts], no. 1165, 12 Jan. 1898.

ثمرات الفنون
(١٨٩٨)

«مسألة دريفوس»

ما كنا لنظن أن مسألة دريفوس ستبلغ ما بلغت إليه في الوقت الحاضر من الخطارة والأهمية حتى أدت إلى إظهار ما تكنّه الصدور من التعصب الديني الذي يزعم الفرنسيس أن لا أثر لديهم منه وأنهم يفاخرون الأمم بالجامعة الجنسية إلى غير ذلك مما يرمون به غيرهم ظلماً وعدواناً وهم فيه غريقون وفي لججه تائهون.

علم القراء ما كان من أمر هاته المسألة الخطيرة التي كادت تكون بناما الثانية وأن المجلس الحربي الفرنسي قد برأ القومندان استرهازي دون أن يعبأ باحتجاجات عائلة دريفوس وأنصاره بل أيد الحكم عليه بأنه هو كاتب تلك الأوراق التي سرقت من سفارة ألمانيا في باريز مما سبق لنا ذكره غير مرة.

وقد أفادت الآن أنباء باريز «البرقية» أن الموسيو زولا أحد مشاهير الكتاب بفرنسا قد نشر في جريدة «أورور» («الفجر») رسالة وجه الكلام فيها إلى الموسيو فليكس فور رئيس الجمهورية الفرنسوية اتهم فيها الكولونل باتي دي كلام بأنه هو سبب الخطأ القضائي الذي أصاب دريفوس متهماً أيضاً كلاً من الجنرال مرسيه والجنرال بيلو والجنرال ودي بواريفر والجنرال كونز بأنهم مشاركون لذلك الكولونل في هذا الخطأ موقعاً الذنب أيضاً على المجلسين الحربيين اللذين حاكما دريفوس واسترهازي.

مما كان له في نفوس رجال فرنسا أسوأ وقع سيما مجلس النواب الذي استطلع رأي الموسيو ميلين رئيس الوزارة بهذا الشأن فصرح بوجوب محاكمة الموسيو زولا الآنف الذكر. وأظهر المجلس إذ ذاك ثقته بالوزارة معتقداً بأنها تتخذ التدابير اللازمة لحسم هذه المطاعن في الجيش الفرنسوي وذلك بأصوات قدرها ٣١٣ يضادها ١٣٢ صوتاً.

وعليه أصدر الجنرال بيلو وزير الحرب أمره إلى المدعي العمومي بمحاكمة الموسيو زولا وقامت طلبة باريز بمظاهرات في الشوارع صائحين: «ليسقط زولا! ليسقط اليهود!» ولا يخفى أن اليهود قد دخلوا في الحكومة الفرنسوية

مدخل الدم في العروق منهم العدد الوافر من القواد والضباط ومن جملتهم دريفوس. ثم تجددت المظاهرات في اليوم الثاني وكان الشعب الفرنسي يصيح: «ليمت زولا! ليمت اليهود! ليحيى الجيش!» وكسر المتظاهرون زجاج منزل كانوا يحسبونه للموسيو زولا فألقي القبض على ١٥ شخصاً.

ويؤكدون أن الجنرال سوسيه القائد العام للجيش الفرنساوي قد استقال من وظيفته هذه فقام نحو مئة جمعية من الجمعيات الوطنية بمظاهرة في ساحة «فندوم» إكراماً لهذا القائد العام. . . . .

ولم يكتفِ الفرنسيس ما تظاهروا به في باريز ضد اليهود بل تعدت هذه المظاهرات إلى نانسي وبوردو وكليرمون وليون ونانت ومرسيليا وغيرها من مدن فرنسا وكان المتظاهرون يكسرون واجهات مخازن اليهود وحوانيتهم.

وتقول «روتر» أخيراً أن الهياج في فرنسا ضد اليهود آخذ بالازدياد وأنه جرت مظاهرات ضدهم في جميع الولايات والمقاطعات الفرنساوية.

«ضرر وضع البضائع أمام المخازن»

جاء في «طبيب العائلة» ما نصه: أعتاد أصحاب المحلات التجارية وضع البضائع أمام أبواب مخازنهم ليظهروها للمارين ترغيباً لهم ولكن وضع البضائع على هذه الكيفية فضلاً عن أنه يضايق المارين على الرصيف فهو مضرّ بالصحة لأنه قد يتفق أن يمر أحد المصابين بالسل وغيره فيبصق أمام المخزن ومتى جف بصاقه المملوء من مكروب السل تتطاير هذه المكروبات في الهواء فتلتصق بالبضائع ومتى نقلت هذه البضائع تتطاير المكروبات وتدخل في رئات من يستنشق هواء ذلك المكان. ونحن كنا نكتفي بهذا الضرر لو اقتصرت هذه العادة على محلات تجارة الأقمشة فقط إلا أنها امتدت إلى الزياتين والعطارين والبقالين وباعة الفواكه واللحوم فترى كلاً منهم يعرض أمام محله الزبدة والسمن والزيت والجبن والفواكه وغيرها من المأكولات التي نستعملها يومياً ولا غنى لنا عنها وكل هذه الأشياء قابلة للعفونة وتلتصق عليها المكروبات بكل سهولة وعندما نأكلها تدخل المعدة وعليها هذه المكروبات فنصاب بالأمراض المعدية غير عالمين من أين أتتنا.

وقد ذكر البعض هذه الرواية فقال: إن الحكومة والمجالس البلدية في كافة الولايات الشاهانية تحظر على أصحاب الحوانيت والدكاكين بسط مواعينهم

وسلعهم في الطرقات وتغرم من يخالف ذلك بالجزاء النقدي. ومن العجيب أنهم يتحملون دفع هذا الجزاء ويداومون عملهم.

قال ولئن صح قول «الطبيب» وكان على الصحة الخطر من المأكولات المبسوطة في الطرق فليس على الأهلين إلا الابتعاد عن ابتياعها حرصاً على صحتهم.

«احتراق معرض شيكاغو»

ذكرت إحدى الجرائد الأمريكية أن النار قد شبت في المعرض الذي افتتحت أبوابه في اليوم الثامن عشر من الشهر الغابر وكان ميعاد انتهائه بعد خمسة أشهر غير أنه لم يكد يجهز التجار وغيرهم أماكنهم الداخلية حتى ثارت عواصف النيران من جهاته الأربع ولم تمض عشرون دقيقة حتى أصبح كل ما فيه رماداً ومات كثيرون ممن دخلوه حباً بإنقاذ من فيه من الرجال والمال.

وقد كان في المعرض خمسة وثلاثون نفساً بين لبنانيين وأرمن فنجوا بأنفسهم دون سلعهم التي ذهبت طعاماً للنيران.

«الحرب الإسبانية الأميريكية»

يستفاد من الأنباء البرقية أن الحالة ما برحت تزداد خطارة بين أميركا وإسبانيا حتى أوشكت نيران الحرب أن تستعر بينهما. وقد حدث في بورصة نيويورك ما يشبه الرعب الشديد بسبب الخوف من حدوث أزمة في علائق الدولتين إثر ورود تقارير جديدة مؤداها حدوث خيانة في مسألة انفجار الدارعة «مين» الأميركية ولهذا ترى الاستعدادات الحربية قائمة على قدم وساق في البلادين الأميركية والإسبانية.

على أن حكومة الولايات المتحدة قد أعلنت رسمياً أنها لا تعرف السبب في مصاب تلك البارجة إذ لم يردها بعد تقرير بهذا الشأن كما أن الإسبان ينتظرون بفارغ الصبر ورود تقرير اللجنة الإسبانية الذي يعزو فيه الانفجار إلى سبب داخلي وستؤيد إسبانيا هذا التقرير بعزم شديد وإن كان مخالفاً لتقرير اللجنة الأميركانية. وفي الأنباء الأخيرة أن حكومة إسبانيا خابرت أميركا بقصد المسألة قائلة إن الحرب في الحال الحاضرة تعد جنايةً على البشرية ومع

ذلك لا تنكف الدولتان عن إرصاد معدات القتال. والحرب الآن بين الحكومتين متوقف—على ما يظهر—على تقرير اللجنة المناط بها أمر التحقيق في سبب الانفجار فإن تبرأت ساحة إسبانيا منه اكتفت شر القتال وإلا اشتعلت نيران الحرب بينها وبين أميركا والله بالمستقبل عليم.

«انتخابات البلدية»

غداً (الأربعاء) يباشر بانتخابات البلدية على ما هو مبين في الإعلان المدرج في هذا العدد وقد قالت جريدة «الولاية» في عددها الأخير بعد أن أبانت أهمية المجلس البلدي ومؤسساته النافعة ما نستلفت إليه أنظار المنتخبين إذ هو لعمري الضالة التي طالما نشدناها وهي سلامة الانتخاب من كل شائبة ونبذ الأغراض ظهرياً وانتخاب من توفرت فيهم الصفات المطلوبة بهذه الخدمة الوطنية النافعة وإليك ما قالته جريدة «الولاية»:

ولما كان الاعتناء في انتقاء أعضاء للمجلس المذكور ممن توفرت فيهم الأوصاف القانونية هو مما يعود على الحكومة والأهلين بفوائد جمة وكان والحمد لله يوجد بين أهالي الثغر كثير ممن توفرت فيهم هذه الأوصاف من مسلمين وغير مسلمين وإذ كان حضرة ملاذ الولاية السامي قد أجرى بذاته ما يلزم من التدابير الكافلة بدوران الانتخاب على محور القانون وصونه من كل مداخلة كما أنه سيحضر في البلدية بعض من أعضاء مجلس الإدارة والكتبة تحت نظارة حضرة سعادتلو مكتوبي بك أفندي لإجراء المراقبة على جريان الانتخاب ودورانه على أحسن منوال فعلى من لهم حق بانتخاب أعضاء للبلدية أن لا يراعوا حين الانتخاب خاطر أحد بل ينبغي عليهم أن ينتخبوا من يرتجي النفع والفائدة من مساعيه بأن يكون ذا لياقة وكفاية وقادراً على حضور الجلسات في أوقاتها المعينة والقيام بأمور وظيفته بكل إقدام وبذلك يكونون قد حافظوا على خيرهم ومنافعهم وخدموا البلدة بما يعد لها من الفوائد والحسنات.

Muhammad 'Abduh
(1849–1905)

Introduced and translated by Tarek El-Ariss

Islamic jurist and reformer Muhammad 'Abduh was born in Egypt's Nile Delta in 1849. He studied at al-Azhar University in Cairo and eventually became Egypt's grand mufti in 1899, a position he held until his death in Alexandria in 1905. Offering a radical examination of Islamic law, tradition, and doctrine, 'Abduh embodies the Muslim reformer of the turn of the century. His association with Jamal al-Din al-Afghani, a revolutionary Muslim thinker residing in Cairo at the time, influenced 'Abduh's career path and shaped his interest in political and social issues. After being exiled from Egypt for his political views, 'Abduh lived in Paris and Beirut, traveling widely across Europe and the Ottoman Empire. In his writings, he addressed the state of the Muslim nation in the modern age, the relation between Islam and science, and the importance of education and rational thought for cultural and spiritual development. His ideas and reforms were part of the most comprehensive and earliest models to rigorously activate an intercultural and transnational dialogue and an introspective examination that continues to reverberate in Islamic social and political circles until this day.

These selections are taken from travel notes that 'Abduh made while in Sicily during his exile. In them, he discusses iconoclasm in Islam, methods of learning and preservation in Europe, and the current state of the Arabs in relation to their European counterparts. He critically engages exegetical tradition and religious practices, and he challenges simplistic explanations of religious dogma while exhorting the Arabs to emulate their predecessors who built a great civilization and

safeguarded that of others. Included are a letter addressed by
'Abduh to Lev Tolstoy, the Russian author and philosopher
who challenged religious obscurantism and social inequalities,
a stance that earned him the reproach of some and the praise
and admiration of others, and Tolstoy's response to that letter
in French.

Recommended Reading

Kerr, Malcolm. *Islamic Reform: The Political and Legal Theories of Muham-
mad 'Abduh and Rashid Rida*. U of California P, 1966.
Ramadan, Dina A. "'One of the Best Tools for Learning': Rethinking the
Role of 'Abduh's Fatwa in Egyptian Art History." *A Companion to Mod-
ern African Art*, edited by Gitti Salami and Monica Blackmun Visona,
Wiley Blackwell, 2013, pp. 137–53.

"Travels in Europe"

Sicily: Monreale Cathedral, the Tolerance of the Arabs, and the Current State of Affairs

Among the marvels I visited in Palermo is the Monreale Cathe-
dral. Its entire ceiling and most of its walls are covered with
mosaics whose colors and shapes delight the eye and give free
rein to the imagination. On one side of the cathedral is a domed
shrine known as the Chapel of the Cross, which contains stat-
ues and decorations of indescribable beauty. It is important to
mention that this cathedral was built in the sixth century of
the Christian calendar, so it is almost 1300 years old.[1] Its beau-
tiful and well-preserved icons date back to that period; thanks
to proper care and cleaning, no termite has dared to gnaw on
them. Some who are well versed in the habits of these tiny
insects say that the termites recognize the cross and its imple-
ments and thus show respect for the images and statues made

from this wood. Are these insects Catholic, if they are forbidden from gnawing on Christian wood and resist their appetite for food to fulfill this duty!? Of course I do not believe this to be true! It is said that King William II built the cathedral and is buried within it.

From which you can see that the Arabs, God rest their souls, did not damage this cathedral, despite their power and dominion over Sicily. It tells you that the Arabs, despite the fact that many of them went astray, upheld through their deeds the spirit of Islam, which prohibits the destruction of churches unless they present an imminent danger to the state. Unlike those who came after them, the Arabs preserved their subjects' churches and temples. They did not follow in the footsteps of their enemies, who used to demolish mosques and temples. So may God bless the reign of those Arabs.

Certainly Islam is Arabic, and the people who are most entitled to preserve Islam and uphold its values—once its truth is revealed—are the Arabs. But where are the Arabs [today]?! One could answer, "They are in the Arabian Peninsula, or in the Levant, Iraq, Egypt, Tunisia, Algeria, or Morocco. Aren't you satisfied with their spread over a thousand countries? So how then can you ask, 'Where are the Arabs [today]?!'" My answer is this: "Those people might be Arabs if the moral values and spiritual life of the Arabs are preserved in them. But if all that remains is the ghostly shadows of their spirits, then they are not Arabs, and so I have the right to ask, 'Where are the Arabs [today]?!'"

The Meaning and Significance of Images and Statues

These people [Europeans] pay unusual attention to preserving images drawn on paper and tapestries. One finds in the museums of great nations what is absent in smaller ones such as Sicily—namely, a process for determining the date that each work was created, and by whom. It is fascinating how nations compete to acquire paintings, so much so that one by Raphael might be worth hundreds of thousands to some museums, regardless of the actual value of the painting itself. What is important is this competition among nations to own these artworks, which are considered to be masterpieces left by the ancestors for their descendants. And such is the case for statues: the older they are, the more expensive they become, and the more the Europeans invest in preserving them. Do you [the reader] understand why this is?

If you can appreciate your [Arab] predecessors' keenness in memorizing and preserving their poetry, anthologizing and editing it—especially pre-Islamic poetry—and what care they took, God rest their souls, to collect and organize it, you can then understand why the Europeans preserve their paintings and sculptures. For drawing is a form of poetry that can be seen but not heard, just as poetry is a form of drawing that can be heard but not seen. These paintings and statues have recorded the state of the individual in different circumstances, and the state of groups in diverse places, and thus function as a register of the human condition, representing human beings and animals in states of happiness and contentment, peace and security. The meanings these terms contain are similar, and it is difficult to distinguish among them, but when you see them represented in drawings, the differences between them become stunningly clear. Drawings can represent conditions of anxiety [jaza'] and fright [faza'], fear and trepidation. Anxiety and fright have different meanings; I do not mention them together here because they sound alike but because they are genuinely different emotional states, although you might strain your mind trying to distinguish between them and to separate them. It is difficult to tell the difference between fright and anxiety and to recognize when a person is in fact experiencing one or the other. But if you look at a drawing—this silent poetry—then the truth will be revealed to you, offering enjoyment to your soul and pleasure to your emotions. If you wish to determine the meaning of the metaphor "I saw a lion," meaning a courageous man, then all you have to do is look at the image of the Sphinx by the Great Pyramid to see the lion as a man and the man as a lion. Preserving these monuments is thus like preserving knowledge, and it gives thanks to the artist for excelling in his craft.

If you understood anything of what I just explained here, then I have achieved my goal. But if you did not, then I don't have time to explain by elaborating further, and you must seek out one of those philologists or painters or poets so that he can explain to you whatever remains unclear, if it is in his power to do so.

You might wonder, as you read these lines, about the judgment of Islamic law regarding these images, and whether or not the law prohibits the visual representation of human beings in their various emotional states and physical shapes. Is this prohibited? Allowed? Frowned upon? Scorned? Or is it in fact a Muslim's duty [to represent such states and shapes]? My answer is this: The painter has painted something, and its benefit is indisputably clear, and any connotation of worshipping and glorifying statues or images is erased from the mind. So either you understand the judgment [of the law] by yourself after seeing the facts or you can raise this matter with the mufti, and he will answer you directly. If you mention to him the following Hadith [a saying of the Prophet], "Those who shall suffer most come judgment day are the painters [depicters]," or its general meaning as found in [the Hadith collection] *al-Sahih*, he will most likely tell you that this Hadith comes from pagan [pre-Islamic] times, when images were produced for two reasons. First, for entertainment; and second, for the blessing one might get from the image of the virtuous person depicted. While the first reason is frowned upon by religion, the second is completely prohibited by Islam, and in both cases the painter has forgotten God or undermined His oneness. If you paint for reasons other than these two, then depicting human beings is like depicting plants and trees for decoration, as we see in the margins of the Qur'an and on the first page of each sura [chapter]. Not a single religious scholar ever prohibited this practice. Although the benefit in decorating the Qur'an is disputed, the images used to decorate it were never themselves subject to debate given this line of reasoning. . . . So you cannot tell the mufti that images are always susceptible to being worshipped, for he will answer that the tongue is susceptible to lying, yet should one tie it up because it can lie at certain times and tell the truth at others?

Generally speaking, it is my conviction that Islamic law would never prohibit one of the most effective tools of learning once it verifies that this tool poses no threat to religion as such, neither doctrinally nor practically. Muslims should not question that which has an undeniable benefit to them, especially when they do not question their pilgrimages to the graves of those so-called holy men [saints] whose life stories and personal beliefs are often obscure. Muslims do not seek religious council for their acts of prostration and supplication at these graves or for their offerings of vows and money. Muslims fear these saints more than they fear God himself and ask them for favors they would not ask of God, thinking that they might be granted faster. Believers can never reconcile these practices with their belief in divine unity, but they can certainly reconcile their belief in God's oneness with images that represent human beings and animals and depict intellectual states for the purpose of learning.

That said, have you ever heard of us [Muslims] as a people managing to preserve anything from our predecessors, let alone images and paintings, despite our great need to do so? . . . Were you to examine what our religion has obliged us to preserve, you would realize that so much has been lost and ignored by one generation after another. Not once did we ask ourselves whether we were preserving the books and the knowledge that we needed to preserve; we lost our books and with them our precious knowledge. If you are looking for a rare book, a fine collection, a valuable reference, or a useful item from our tradition of learning, you will find it in the archives of European countries such as the one at Cambridge, in England. All that you can find here, in our countries, are but the works that the Europeans have left behind or ignored, such as the ones in the National Library in Egypt. If I were to give you the full narrative of what we have lost and what they have preserved of [our] books of learning, I would have to write a whole book on the subject—a book that would also be lost and then found in the hands of some European in France or elsewhere in Europe.

We are not concerned with preserving something that might be useful to those who will come after us. And if it occurred to one of us to do so, then the one who comes after him will surely squander this gift by failing to preserve it. The will to preserve is not a trait that is inherited among us. What is inherited instead are hatred and resentment, which pass from fathers to sons, corrupting our pious people and putting our land to waste, and their new owners will meet at the edge of hell when Judgment Day comes.

Letter to Tolstoy

18 April 1904

'Ayn Shams, Cairo suburb
Eminent man of wisdom, Monsieur Tolstoy,

We have never been fortunate enough to meet you, but we have not been deprived from encountering your spirit. The light of your ideas has shone upon us, and the suns of your opinions have lit our horizons, joining your mind with those of wise men. God revealed to you the secret of His design and showed you the path He set forth for His creatures. You have realized that human beings are in this world to cultivate knowledge and to reap the fruits of their labor, and that hard work comforts the human soul while the quest for knowledge elevates the human race. And you were grief-stricken when you saw human beings deviate from their natural course, misusing their power—with which they were endowed for the pursuit of their own happiness—in actions that disturbed their ease and shook their peace of mind.

Your examination of religion pierced through the veil of tradition; you arrived at the truth of God's oneness, and you raised your voice to show people what God had revealed to you. You led by example, encouraging people to work hard as you did, motivating them through your deeds as you guided them with your words. Your ideas were a light for those who had gone astray, while your deeds inspired them and showed them the right path. Your presence in this world is a sign of God's rebuke of the rich and compassion for the poor. You reached the highest glory and reaped the greatest reward for your guidance and enlightenment of the people when those so-called princes of religion decided to excommunicate you. Their banishment of you is but a recognition of the rightness of the path you are following; I thank God that they broke with you in words as you broke with them in deed and doctrine.

Our souls are ever eager for whatever new tracings your pen may produce, and we ask God to grant you strength and long life, and may He open people's hearts to your ideas and guide their souls to emulate you in your deeds.

Grand Mufti of Egypt
Muhammad 'Abduh

Should your eminence be so generous as to send a reply to this letter, let it be in French, for this is the only European language I have mastered.

Muhammad.[2]

Tolstoy's Response to 'Abduh

13 May 1904

Dear Friend,

I received your fine and laudatory letter and here I am hurrying to respond and to express the great pleasure it provided me, for it allowed me to communicate with an enlightened man. Though your faith is different from the one within which I was born and reared, we share the same religion. There are many different faiths but only one religion, true religion. I hope I'm not mistaken in assuming that, given your letter, the religion that I believe in is the same as yours, which consists in recognizing God and His law—to love our neighbor and treat others the way we wish to be treated. I believe that all true religious principles derive from this one and are the same for Jews as they are for Brahmans, Buddhists, Christians, and Mohammedans.

I believe that the more religions are saturated with dogma and talk of miracles, the more they split people and fill them with enmity toward one another. However, the more religions are simplified and refined, the more they are able to attain humanity's ideal—universal unity. This is why your letter has given me much pleasure and I would like us to continue to communicate.

What are your views on the Baha'i faith and its followers?

Please accept, my dear Grand Mufti Muhammad 'Abduh, all regard and respect.

Leon Tolstoy[3]

Notes

[1]In fact, King William II of Sicily built the cathedral in the twelfth century, that is, following Arab rule in Sicily.

[2]Imam Muhammad 'Abduh wrote this letter to the Russian philosopher and reformer when the Church rose against him, banning his teachings and excommunicating him. 'Abduh praises Tolstoy's position on social issues and the question of economic inequality. [This footnote is included in the Arabic edition.]

[3]Quoted in the French original in Kudelin 41–42.

Work Cited

Kudelin, A. "Presenting the Manuscript: Muhammad Abduh's Letter to Tolstoy (History of Russian-Arabic Cultural Dialogue in the Beginning of the Twentieth Century)." *Manuscripta Orientalia*, vol. 15, no. 1, 2009, pp. 41–49.

Source of Arabic Text on Which the Translation Is Based

'Abduh, Muhammad. الأعمال الكاملة [al-a'mal al-kamila; Complete Works]. Vol. 2, al-Mu'assasa al-'Arabiyya lil-Dirasat wal-Nashr, 1972, pp. 178–79, 204–08, 367–68.

محمد عبده

(١٩٠٥-١٨٤٩)

«السفر في أوروبا»

«كنيسة موريالي، وتساهل العرب، وأين هم اليوم»

مما رأيته في «بلرم» (صقلية) كنيسة «موريالي» وجميع سقفها والأغلب من جدرانها مغشى بالموزاياك ألواناً وأشكالاً من أبهى ما يبهج الناظر، وأجمل ما يسرح فيه الخاطر، وفي ناحية منها قبة تعرف بمعبد الصليب، فيها من التماثيل وضروب الزينة ما يقصر عنه الوصف، وأهم ما يذكر في شأنها أنها مبنية في القرن السادس من التاريخ المسيحي، فيكون لها نحو ألف وثلاثمئة سنة، والمصنوعات الخشبية الجميلة محفوظة من ذلك العهد، لم يجرأ السوس على قرض شيء منها ببركة العناية والاهتمام بالتنظيف، وأما ما يقول به بعض الحذّاق في معرفة طبائع هذه الهوام الدقيقة من أنها تعرف الصليب وما خصص له من الأدوات، وتشعر باحترام تلك الصور والتماثيل التي صورت في تلك الأخشاب، وأنها بذلك صارت مسيحية كاثوليكية، فلا يباح لها قرض الخشب المسيحي، ثم أن اعتقادها بحرمة القرض، حملها على العمل، فخالفت شهوة الأكل قياماً بالفرض؟!. فلا أظنه في غاية الصحة بل ولا في أولها كذلك!! ويقال أن الكنيسة من بناء الملك كيليومو الثاني وقبره فيها صندوق من حجر فيه جثته.

ومن ذلك تعرف أن العرب، رحمهم الله، لم يمسوا هذه الكنيسة بسوء، مع عظمة سطوتهم، وامتداد ملكهم في «سيسيليا،» وتلمح من هذا أن العرب—وأن فسق كثير منهم عن أمر ربهم—فروع الدين الإسلامي كانت تنوّس في كثير من أعمالهم، نهى الدين عن هدم الكنائس إذا لم تكن مربضاً لشر يخشى خطره على الدولة، فحفظوا لرعاياهم كنائسهم ومعابدهم، ولم يصنعوا بها ما صنع غيرهم ممن جاء بعدهم، ولم يريدوا أن يقتفوا أثر خصومهم ممن كان يهدم مساجدهم ويخرب معابدهم، وفحيا الله أيامهم.

لا جرم أن الإسلام عربي وأحق الناس برعايته والوقوف عند حدده—بعد فهم حقيقته—هم العرب، فأين هم؟! يمكن أن يقول قائل: إنهم في جزيرة

العرب، أو في الشام، أو في العراق، أو في مصر، أو في تونس والجزائر، أو في المغرب الأقصى، أفلم يكفك كل هذا العدد، في أكثر من ألف بلد، حتى تقول أين هم؟! ولكني أقول له: إنما يكون أولئك القوم إذا بقيت لهم أخلاقهم، وحياة أرواحهم، فإن كان لم يبقَ إلا أشباح تشبه أشباحهم، فليسوا بهم، فلي الحق أن أقول عن العرب: فأين هم؟!!.

«الصور والتماثيل، وفوائدها، وحكمها»

لهؤلاء القوم حرص غريب على حفظ الصور المرسومة على الورق والنسيج، ويوجد في دار الآثار عند الأمم الكبرى ما لا يوجد عند الأمم الصغرى كالصقليين ثلاً، يحققون تاريخ رسمها، واليد التي رسمتها، ولهم تنافس في اقتناء ذلك غريب، حتى أن القطعة الواحدة من رسم «روفائيل» مثلاً ربما تساوي مئتين من الآلاف في بعض المتاحف، ولا يهمك معرفة القيمة بالتحقيق، وإنما المهم هو التنافس في اقتناء الأمم لهذه النقوش وعدّ ما أتقن منها من أفضل ما ترك المتقدم للمتأخر، وكذلك الحال في التماثيل، وكلما قدم المتروك من ذلك كان أغلى قيمة، وكان القوم عليه أشد حرصاً، هل تدري لماذا؟

إذا كنت تدري السبب في حفظ سلفك للشعر، وضبطه في دواوينه، والمبالغة في تحريره، خصوصاً شعر الجاهلية، وما عني الأوائل، رحمهم الله، بجمعه وترتيبه، أمكنك أن تعرف السبب في محافظة القوم على هذه المصنوعات من الرسوم والتماثيل، فإن الرسم ضرب من الشعر الذي يُرى ولا يُسمع، والشعر ضرب من الرسم الذي يُسمع ولا يُرى. أن هذه الرسوم والتماثيل قد حفظت من أحوال الأشخاص في الشؤون المختلفة، ومن أحوال الجماعات في المواقع المتنوعة ما تستحق به أن تسمى ديوان الهيئات والأحوال البشرية، يصوّرون الإنسان أو الحيوان في حال الفرح والرضى، والطمأنينة والتسليم، وهذه المعاني المدرجة في هذه الألفاظ متقاربة لا يسهل عليك تمييز بعضها من بعض، ولكنك تنظر في رسوم مختلفة فتجد الفرق ظاهراً باهراً، يصوّرونه مثلاً في حالة الجزع والفزع، والخوف والخشية، والجزع والفزع مختلفان في المعنى، ولم أجمعهما ههنا طمعا في جمع عينين في سطر واحد بل لأنهما مختلفان حقيقة، ولكنك ربما تعتصر ذهنك لتحديد الفرق بينهما وبين الخوف والخشية، ولا يسهل عليك أن تعرف متى يكون الفزع ومتى يكون الجزع؟ وما الهيأة التي يكون عليها الشخص في هذه الحال أو تلك؟ وأما إذا نظرت إلى الرسم، وهو ذلك

الشعر الساكت، فإنك تجد الحقيقة بارزة لك، تتمتع بها نفسك، كما يتلذذ بالنظر فيها حسك. إذا نزعت نفسك إلى تحقيق الاستعارة المصرحة في قولك: رأيت أسداً: تريد رجلاً شجاعاً، فانظر إلى صورة أبي الهول بجانب الهرم الكبير تجد الأسد رجلاً أو الرجل أسداً، فحفظ هذه الآثار حفظ للعلم في الحقيقة، وشكر لصاحب الصنعة على الإبداع فيها.

إن كنت فهمت من هذا شيئاً فذلك بغيتي أما إذا لم تفهم فليس عندي وقت لتفهيمك بأطول من هذا، وعليك بأحد اللغويين أو الرسامين أو الشعراء المفلقين ليوضح لك ما غمض عليك إذا كان ذلك من ذرعه.

ربما تعرض لك مسألة عند قراءة هذا الكلام، وهي ما حكم هذه الصور في الشريعة الإسلامية، إذا كان القصد منها ما ذكر من تصوير هيئات البشر في انفعالاتهم النفسية، أو أوضاعهم الجسمانية، هل هذا حرام؟ أو جائز؟ أو مكروه؟ أو مندوب؟ أو واجب؟ فأقول لك: إن الراسم قد رسم، والفائدة محققة لا نزاع فيها، ومعنى العبادة وتعظيم التمثال أو الصورة قد مُحي من الأذهان، فإما أن تفهم الحكم من نفسك بعد ظهور الواقعة، وإما أن ترفع سؤالاً إلى المفتي وهو يجيبك مشافهة، فإذا أوردت عليه حديث: «إن أشد الناس عذاباً يوم القيامة المصوِّرون»، أو ما في معناه مما ورد في الصحيح، فالذي يغلب على ظني أنه سيقول لك أن الحديث جاء في أيام الوثنية، وكانت الصور تُتَّخذ في ذلك العهد لسببين: الأول: اللهو والثاني: التبرك بمثال من ترسم صورته من الصالحين، والأول مما يبغضه الدين، والثاني مما جاء الإسلام لمحوه، والمصوِّر في الحالين شاغل عن الله أو ممهد للإشراك به، فإذا زال هذان العارضان وقصدت الفائدة، كان تصوير الأشخاص بمنزلة تصوير النبات والشجر في المصنوعات، وقد صنع ذلك في حواشي المصاحف، وأوائل السور، ولم يمنعه أحد من العلماء، مع أن الفائدة في نقش المصاحف موضع النزاع، أما فائدة الصور فمما لا نزاع فيه على الوجه الذي ذكر . . . ولا يمكنك أن تجيب المفتي بأن الصورة على كل حال مظنة العبادة، فإني أظن أنه يقول لك إن لسانك أيضاً مظنة الكذب، فهل يجب ربطه مع أنه يجوز أن يصدق كما يجوز أن يكذب؟!

وبالجملة، أنه يغلب على ظني أن الشريعة الإسلامية أبعد من أن تحرم وسيلة من أفضل وسائل العلم، بعد تحقيق أنه لا خطر فيها على الدين، لا من جهة العقيدة ولا من جهة العمل. على أن المسلمين لا يتسائلون إلا فيما تظهر فائدته ليحرموا أنفسهم منها، وإلا فما بالهم لا يتساءلون عن زيارة قبور الأولياء، أو ما سمّاهم بعضهم بالأولياء، هم ممن لا تعرف لهم سيرة، ولم يطّلع

لهم أحد على سريرة، ولا يستفتون فيما يفعلون عندها من ضروب التوسل والضراعة، وما يعرضون عليها من الأموال والمتاع، وهم يخشونها كخشية الله أو أشد، ويطلبون منها ما يخشون أن لا يجيبهم الله فيه، ويظنون أنها أسرع إلى إجابتهم من عنايته سبحانه وتعالى، لا شك أنه لا يمكنهم الجمع بين هذه العقائد وعقيدة التوحيد، ولكن يمكنهم الجمع بين التوحيد ورسم صور الإنسان وحيوان لتحقيق المعاني العلمية، وتمثيل الصور الذهنية.

هل سمعت أننا حفظنا شيئاً حتى غير الصور والرسوم مع شدة حاجتنا إلى حفظ كثير مما كان عند أسلافنا؟ . . . لو نظرت إلى ما كان يوجب الدين عليها أن نحافظ عليه لوجدته كثيراً لا يُحصى عده، ولم نحفظ منه شيئا، فلنتركه كما تركه من كان قبلنا، ولكن ما نقول في الكتب وودائع العلم هل حفظناها كما كان ينبغي أن نحفظها؟ أو أضعناها كما لا ينبغي أن نضيعها؟!!! ضاعت كتب العلم وفارقت ديارنا نفائسه، فإذا أردت أن تبحث عن كتاب نادر أو مؤلف فاخر أو مصنف جليل أو أثر مفيد فاذهب إلى خزائن بلاد أوروبا تجد ذلك فيها. أما بلادنا فقلما تجد فيها إلا ما ترك الأوروبيون ولم يحفلوا به من نفائس الكتب التاريخية والأدبية والعلمية، وقد تجد بعض النسخ من الكتاب في دار الكتب المصرية مثلاً وبعضها الآخر في دار الكتب بمدينة «كبردج» من البلاد الإنجليزية. ولو أردت أن أسرد لك ما حفظوا وضيعنا من دفاتر العلم لكتبت لك في ذلك كتاباً يضيع كما ضاع غيره وتجده بعد مدة في يد أوروبي في فرنسا أو غيرها من بلاد أوروبا!!

نحن لا نُعنى بحفظ شيء نستبقي نفعه لمن يأتي بعدنا، ولو خطر ببال أحد منا أن يترك لمن بعده شيئاً جاء ذلك الذي بعده أشد الناس كفراً بتلك النعمة، وأخذ في إضاعة ما عنى من السابق بحفظه له، فليست ملكة الحفظ مما يتوارث عندنا، وإنما الذي يتوارث هو ملكات الضغائن والأحقاد تنتقل من الآباء إلى الأولاد حتى تفسد العباد، وتخرب البلاد، ويلتقي بها أربابها على شفير جهنم يوم المعاد.

«رسالة إلى تولستوي»[١]

عين شمس بضواحي القاهرة، في ١٨ أبريل سنة ١٩٠٤

أيها الحكيم الجليل، موسيو تولستوي،

لم نحظ بمعرفة شخصك، ولكنا لم نُحرم التعارف بروحك، سطع عليها نور من أفكارك، وأشرقت في آفاقنا شموس من آرائك، ألفت بين نفوس العقلاء

ونفسك. هداك الله إلى معرفة سر الفطرة التي فطر الناس عليها، ووفَّقك على الغاية التي هدى البشر إليها، فأدركت أن الإنسان جاء إلى هذا الوجود لينبت بالعلم، ويثمر بالعمل، ولأن تكون ثمرته تعبا ترتاح به نفسه، وسعياً يبقى به ويرقى به جنسه، وشعرت بالشقاء الذي نزل بالناس لما انحرفوا عن سنة الفطرة، واستعملوا قواهم—التي لم يمنحوها إلا ليسعدوا بها—فيما كدّر راحتهم، وزعزع طمأنينتهم.

نظرت نظرة في الدين مزّقت حجب التقاليد، ووصلت بها إلى حقيقة التوحيد، ورفعت صوتك تدعو الناس إلى ما هداك الله إليه، وتقدمت أمامهم بالعمل لتحمل نفوسهم عليه، فكما كنت بقولك هادياً للعقول، كنت بعملك حاثاً للعزائم والهمم، وكما كانت آراؤك ضياء يهتدي به الضالون، كان مثالك في العمل إماماً يقتدي به المسترشدون، وكما كان وجودك توبيخاً من الله للأغنياء، كان مدداً من عنايته للفقراء، وإنّ أرفع مجد بلغته، وأعظم جزاء نلته على متاعبك في النصح والإرشاد، هو هذا الذي سمّوه «بالحرمان» و«الإبعاد» فليس ما كان إليك من رؤساء الدين سوى اعتراف منهم أعلنوه للناس بأنك لست من القوم الضالين، فاحمد الله على أن فارقوك بأقوالهم، كما كنت فارقتهم في عقائدهم وأعمالهم.

هذا وأن نفوسنا لشيقة إلى ما يتجدد من آثار قلمك، فيما تستقبل من أيام عمرك، وإنا نسأل الله أن يمد في حياتك، ويحفظ عليه قواك، ويفتح أبواب القلوب لفهم ما تقول، ويسوق النفوس إلى الاقتداء بك فيما تعمل، والسلام.

مفتي الديار المصرية
محمد عبده

إذا تفضل الحكيم بالجواب فليكن باللغة الفرنسوية فإني لا أعرف من اللغات الأوروبية سواها. محمد

«رد تولستوي»

صديقي العزيز،

تلقيت خطابكم الكريم، وهأنذا أسارع في الرد عليه مؤكداً امتناني الكبير من هذا الخطاب الذي أتاح لي الاتصال برجل مستنير بالرغم من اختلاف عقيدته عن العقيدة التي نشأت عليها وتربيت. ولكن من الديانة نفسها،

حيث إن العقائد تختلف وتكثر، ولكن ليس هناك سوى دين واحد هو دين الحق. آمل إلا أكون قد أخطأت إذا افترضت من واقع خطابك أن الدين الذي أؤمن به هو دينك. الذي يرتكز على الاعتراف بالله وشريعته في حب الغير، وأن نتمنى للغير ما نتمناه لأنفسنا. وأعتقد أن جميع المبادئ الدينية تندرج من هذا المبدأ، كاليهودية، والبرهمية والبوذية والمسيحيين والمحمديين.

وأعتقد أنه كلما ازدادت العقائد في الأديان وامتلأت بالمعجزات، ساعدت على تفرقة البشر، وخلقت العداوات. وعلى العكس كلما كانت الأديان بسيطة، اقتربت من هدفها المثالي وهو وحدة الناس جميعاً، وهذا ما جعلني أقدر خطابك وأود استمرار اتصالي بك.

ما رأيك في عقيدة الباب ومذهب بهاء الله وأنصاره؟

وتقبل مني يا عزيزي المفتي محمد عبده كل التقدير والاحترام.

ليون تولستوي ١٢ مايو ١٩٠٤

---

١ كتبها الأستاذ الإمام من مصر إلى الفيلسوف والأديب والمصلح الروسي، عندما ثارت ضده وضد تعاليمه الكنيسة الروسية وحكمت عليه «بالحرمان» . . . والأستاذ الإمام يشير بالمدح والثناء، في الرسالة تلي الموقف «المثالي» لتولستوي من المشكلة الاجتماعية وعلاقة الأغنياء بالفقراء.

Mikhail Naimy
(1889–1988)

Introduced and translated by Margaret Litvin

Mikhail Naimy (or Nu'ayma) is a singular voice in the *Nahda* tradition. He played a major part in the early-twenteith-century Arabic literary revival; yet his work challenges most easy generalizations about the *Nahda* period. In publications spanning seven decades, three languages, and half a dozen genres (poem, short story, drama, critical essay, modern epic, biography, and autobiography), Naimy stands out as a modernizer willing to look to Eastern as well as Western traditions in search of techniques and wisdom. His poems and short stories in Arabic and English show an unpretentious pioneer impatient to concretize the language of prose and poetry.

Born into a Greek Orthodox family in the mountainside village of Baskinta, Mount Lebanon, Naimy enjoyed an upbringing both intensely local (travel to Beirut was a rare treat) and unexpectedly cosmopolitan. His brilliance at Baskinta's Imperial Orthodox Palestine School—that is, the "Muscovite" School—and Nazareth Teachers College helped him win a scholarship to the Diocesan Seminary in Poltava, in Russian Ukraine, where for five formative years he devoured contemporary Russian literature (Gorky, Lermontov, and above all Tolstoy) and saw firsthand the aftermath of the 1905 Russian Revolution. (Other pioneers of translation, criticism, and literary journalism, including Antun Ballan, Abdelmessih Haddad, and Khalil Baydas, were Russian-educated as well.)

In 1911, Naimy emigrated again, joining two older brothers in Walla Walla, Washington. After graduating from Washington State University (in law and literature), he moved to New York in 1916. There he plunged into the expatriate (*mahjar*) Arabic literary scene, publishing in his school friend Nasib Aridah's literary magazine *al-Funun* ("The Arts"). He worked briefly for the Russian arms-buying delegation at the Bethlehem Steel Factories, and near the end of World War I he served in the United States military in France.

In 1920, Naimy wrote the founding charter for *al-Rabita al-Qalamiyya* ("The Pen League"), an influential Arabic literary society whose most famous member was Gibran Khalil Gibran, who was also his friend. In 1932, after Gibran's death, Naimy retired to Lebanon, and his prose took on an increasingly mystical, even scriptural cast. His signature English-language work, *The Book of Mirdad* (1948), preaches man's spiritual ascent, through suffering, from material reality to higher truth. Naimy also wrote a controversial biography of Gibran; a travelogue, "Beyond Moscow and Washington"; and the 1959 memoir excerpted here, *Seventy: A Life Story.*

Naimy wrote his 1908 seminarian's diary in Russian and translated sections of it into Arabic for *Seventy.* These entries show his literary sensibility developing under the self-sought tutelage of Russian sources and models, which he does not perceive as simply European.

Recommended Reading

El-Enany, Rasheed. "An Early Arab Encounter with America: The Story of Mikha'il Nu'ayma." *Yale MacMillan Center*, opus.macmillan.yale.edu /workpaper/pdfs/MESV5-7.pdf. Yale University Council on Middle East Studies Working Paper.

Imangulieva, Aida. *Gibran, Rihani, and Naimy: East-West Interactions in Early-Twentieth-Century Arab Literature.* Translated by Robin Thomson, Inner Farne Press, 2009.

Naimy, Mikhail. *A New Year: Stories, Autobiography, and Poems.* E. J. Brill, 1974.

Naimy, Nadeem. *Mikhail Naimy: An Introduction.* AUB Faculty of Arts and Sciences, 1967.

FROM *Seventy: A Life Story*

23 March 1908

I've resolved, in the end, to act on the idea that has been pursuing and worrying me for some time: the idea of keeping a diary. I confess that what pushed me to act on it was reading Nikitin's diary, which had the deepest effect on my soul.[1] To the point that, after I finished reading it, for a whole week I could think of only one thing, which was: Why don't I take Nikitin's lead, at least in keeping a diary? Perhaps, by doing so, I might gain the power to express my thoughts spontaneously and freely, and my style might gain fluency and flexibility. . . .

What is it you thirst for, my soul, and what is it you strive for? What you thirst for is the writer's glory and the poet's luck. Who does not aspire to have a pen that can control people's thoughts, or play with their hearts, when it pours forth glittering poetry? . . .

These days I am reading "Demon" and other compositions by Lermontov. What poetry! What a noble soul! In his verse, the Caucasus Mountains seem more splendid than they are in nature. . . . If I were a poet, I would sing of your fascinating beauties, O Lebanon, cradle of my childhood and focus of my thoughts.

> [O Lebanon, O motherland of mine]
> I'd sing of your ancient tree trunks gleaming white
> Your caverns full of magic murky light,
> The place of my home and family.
> Where the wise cedars and the silvered brooks
> Enchant life with their pure simplicity,
> The world is full of new-created beauty,
> Unsullied and untouched by human hands.[2]

24 March

. . . A wondrous thing! In recent days, poetry has taken over my whole consciousness, and all my thoughts have focused on one point. My early efforts offer some hope of success. . . . More wondrous still is the outpouring of energy I have felt since I started keeping a diary. I run to write in it as a thirsty man in a wasteland runs to a spring of fresh water. I want to write and write without stopping; only a dangerous inflammation in my eye forces me to be brief. . . . I wake up early but not in order to do my homework, to which I no longer give much attention, unlike my schoolmates, whose schoolbooks never leave their hands. Once upon a time I cared for the honor of being first in my class. This was an honor I held in Nazareth and in my first year here. But today I don't envy anyone—only those whose eyes let them read all they wish to. . . . I want to find a writing topic in which I can immerse myself wholly and to which I can devote all my spare time, so as not to lose a single minute.

27 March

I returned Lermontov to the library two days ago. Oh God, what feelings this poet stirred inside me, and how he has influenced my thoughts and dreams! Not finding another volume of his verses in the library, I preferred to leave empty-handed rather than borrow anything else. But then I returned and borrowed a book by another great author, *War and Peace*, by Tolstoy, which I haven't started reading yet because of the bothersome irritation in my eye . . . since I read Lermontov, I've been seized by a relentless desire to compose poetry. . . . I will go where my soul calls me. I will walk the path that has tempted me ceaselessly since early boyhood . . . it is the path of literature. And I am for it, wholly. . . .

6 April

Today I left the hospital, carrying with me a mixture of impressions and thoughts. After today, I will no longer be woken by the voice of the kindhearted physician's assistant: "Good morning, gentlemen!" Instead, I will be jarred awake at seven o'clock each morning by the bell, followed by the warden's rough voice: "Time to get up! Out of bed right now!" . . .

. . . Yesterday, and not for the first time, one of the wardens remarked on my absence from church services. He has threatened to write a report about this—about Mikhail Iskandar and me—to the [Russian Imperial Orthodox] Palestine Society, which is sponsoring our studies. This could soil our names and moral characters, or even lead to our expulsion. Otherwise his threat wouldn't merit our notice. . . . May God forgive our administration! If it believes that good moral character consists in diligent church attendance, then, to make it happy, I'll attend diligently. And my comrade from Homs [Syria], for his part, has promised to attend as well.

Let me set aside these principles on which I rarely compromise. Clinging to them while at seminary means sacrificing both my education and my future. I am not alone in holding that true Christianity does not consist in standing in church for two or three hours on Sundays, Saturdays, and holy days, but in learning and following the teachings of the Gospel. . . .

What good is there in worship that severs the soul from the object of worship, and in a Christianity that makes you forget Christ? If you stand in a church, you can't help but compare it to a theater. In church, as in the theater, there are actors: the priest, the deacon, and others. They have rehearsed their roles and play them artfully. Sometimes they appear before the audience; sometimes they are hidden. And in church, as in the theater, they change their vestments and costumes. There might be no difference between the two except that the performers in the theater direct their words and gestures to the audience, whereas men of religion direct theirs to the Supreme Being—but only with their lips and not their hearts, and without their thoughts reaching Him. This takes away the desire for prayer even from those who have it. And how is a person who is praying supposed to raise his thoughts and his heart to God, while his eyes are distracted by the glittering stone on the bishop's crown, the candles lit by the sacristan, and the movements of the priest and the deacon, and while the sounds of the chanters fill his ears, and the scent of incense tickles his nostrils? . . .

11 April

I finished *War and Peace* a while ago. . . . I agree with the author's view of Napoleon, because I hate war and those who call for it and wage it. However, I can't help but see a contradiction in what he says about Napoleon and Kutuzov. In his view, Napoleon acted not of his own will but was pushed by circumstances and the will of the people; whereas he gives Kutuzov's wisdom, prudence, and will the main credit for his defeating Napoleon and driving him out of Russia. . . .

It makes me laugh to see myself challenging a great thinker of Tolstoy's caliber. Forgive me, Lev Nikolayevich [Tolstoy]! I am indebted to you for many ideas that have illuminated what had been dark in my spiritual world. In many of your recent works that I have read in the past year, I have found a light to guide my every step. . . . Indeed, you have come to be my teacher and guide without knowing it. . . .

26–29 April

. . . I received six issues of *al-Hilal* ["The Crescent"] all at once, from the first of the year. I had subscribed to it in order to stay connected to the Arabic language. We still lack a literature in the proper sense of the term. Our output does not include what could properly be called independent literature. But there is one phenomenon that delights me. Namely: the freethinking press in Egypt has begun, with one voice, to call on the people to seek freedom and demand Britain's withdrawal from Egypt. Even our Arab East [the Levant] has caught the freedom fever. . . . Whatever happens to me, O my country, I promise you that I will dedicate my youthful energy to your greater good and to the good of your children. . . .

3 May

I spent the evening in the seminary garden. What could be better than to sit by oneself in the evening savoring the company of the trees, the stars, and the memories of one's past! . . . These recollections rushed in on me until it was impossible to restrain my tears. So I shed them, hot and abundant. . . . I recently read the novel *The Black Fog*, by the writer [Pyotr] Gnedich. I also read a lengthy essay by Tolstoy titled "The Great Sin" [1905], in which he treats the problem of land and the injustices of its distribution. I could not help but agree with him.

14 May

At the seminary there is a feverish bustle. It's examination time. On the eighth of this month was the history exam. The competitive composition topic was: "The importance of the printing industry in the cultural advancement of the masses." I spent two hours on it. Three days later, the news reached me that the history teacher had said that my essay was the best essay submitted to him! . . . Anyone who has gone through exams knows how exhausting and draining they are, taking away the desire for any other work. I'm not even drawn to the work closest to my heart, by which I mean writing. . . . I got a letter from my maternal uncle. A few days earlier I had received one from my brothers in Walla Walla and with it a wire of 100 rubles. I had written to them of my plans to spend the summer in Russia.

All of them—my uncle, my family in Lebanon, and my two brothers in Walla Walla—place great hopes in me. And I, in my uncle's estimation, will be "the man of the future," "the pillar of the family," "the pride of Lebanon," and so on. I will gather all my strength, O dear ones, and try to make your hopes come true. But I wonder—will this be enough? . . .

12 June

I am reading the poet [Semyon] Nadson. He is a poet with a tender sensibility, whose life was extinguished in its springtime. And how the sufferings of his youth resemble mine! He was thinking of the same things that I do and building castles in the air just like me. And he worried, just as I do, about whether or not he was gifted enough to reach his goal. . . . What good is there in a life without glory? . . . I will never be satisfied to live in obscurity. If only I could lift the curtain of the future! . . . I will work. I will strive. I will struggle as hard as I can—and the rest is for God to determine, not me.

Notes

[1] Naimy's note: "[Ivan Savvich Nikitin (1824–61) was] a very delicate poet who died in the middle of the [nineteenth] century. He also studied in a seminary, and he published a book titled *A Seminarian's Diary* [Дневник семинариста]."

[2] The first line of this poetry is in the Russian version of Naimy's diaries but not in the Arabic. Naimy's note in the Arabic edition: "These lines are verse in the original; I have translated them as prose. They represent my first attempt to write poetry in Russian."

Source of Arabic Text on Which the Translation Is Based

Nuʿaymah, Mikhāʾil. ١٩٥٩–١٨٨٩ عمر حكاية :سبعون [sabʿun: hikayat ʿumr, 1889–1959; Seventy: A Life Story]. Vol. 1, Dar Sadir, 1959–60. I also consulted Mikhail Nuaime, Мои семьдесят лет [Moi semʾdesiat let], translated by S. M. Batsieva. Moscow, Nauka, 1980.

ميخائيل نعيمة

(١٩٨٨-١٨٨٩)

سبعون: حكاية عمر

من يومياتي

٢٣ آذار سنة ١٩٠٨

عزمت، في النهاية، أن أحقق الفكرة التي أخذت تلاحقني وتقلقني من زمان. وهي أن أدوّن يومياتي. وإني لأعترف بأن الذي عجّل في تحقيقها هو أنني طالعت يوميات «نيكيتن»[1] فكان لها أعمق الأثر في نفسي. حتى أنني بقيت أسبوعاً كاملاً بعد مطالعتها لا أفكر إلا في أمر واحد. وهو: لماذا لا أقتدي بنيكيتن ولو في كتابة اليوميات؟ لعلني، لو فعلت، لاكتسبت المقدرة على التعبير عن أفكاري بطلاقة وحرية، واكتسبت المرونة والسلاسة في الأسلوب.

. . . ما الذي تتعطشين إليه يا نفسي، والذي إليه تتوقين؟ إنك تتعطشين إلى مجد الكاتب وحظ الشاعر . . . وأي الناس لا يطمع في أن يكون له قلم يتحكم في أفكار الناس، أو يتلاعب بأفئدتهم إذا ما هو سال بالشعر الرقراق؟

. . . أطالع في هذه الأيام «الشيطان» وأشياء أخرى من نظم لرمونتوف. يا له من شعر! يا لها من نفس سامية! إن جبال القفقاز لتبدو في نظمه أكثر روعة مما هي في الطبيعة . . . لو كنت شاعراً لغنّيت فتنة محاسنك يا لبنان، يا مهد صباي وقبلة أفكاري. أجل.

لغنّيت شماريخك البيض
وأغوارك الساحرة
حيث لي بيت وأهل.
وحيث الأرز يخبر عما كان،
والجداول تتدفق ضفة
والعيش طيب في بساطته،
والجمال لم تشوّهه يد الإنسان.[2]

٢٤ آذار

. . . أمر عجب! إن الشعر في الأيام الأخيرة يستأثر بكل وعيي ويركز كل أفكاري على نقطة واحدة. ومحاولاتي الأولى تبعث الأمل بالنجاح . . . وإني لأعجب لهذا الدفق من النشاط الذي أخذت أحسه منذ أن باشرت تدوين يومياتي. فأنا أُقبل على كتابتها إقبال العطشان في القفر على نبعة من الماء. إني أريد أن أكتب وأكتب بغير انقطاع. إلا أن التهاباً خطراً في عيني يُكرهني على الاختصار.

. . . أنهض باكراً. ولكن لا بقصد الاستعداد للدروس التي بُثّ لا أعيرها كبير اهتمام، على نقيض رفاقي الذين لا يفارق كتاب الدرس أيديهم. كان زمان كان يهمّني فيه شرف الأولية في صفي. وكان لي ذلك الشرف في الناصرة وفي سنتي الأولى هنا . . . أما اليوم فإني لا أحسد أحداً إلا الذين عيونهم تمكنهم من المطالعة حتى الشبع . . . سأفتش عن موضوع للكتابة أستطيع أن أغرق فيه بكليتي وأن أكرّس له كل أوقات فراغي بحيث لا تضيع منها دقيقة واحدة.

٢٧ آذار

أعدت «لرمونتوف» إلى المكتبة منذ يومين. لله كم حرّك هذا الشاعر في داخلي من أحاسيس، وكم أثار من أفكار وأحلام! ولأنني لم أجد في المكتبة مجلداً آخر من منظوماته آثرت أن أخرج منها من غير أن أستعير أي كتاب. لكنني عدت فأخذت كتاباً لفنان آخر من كبار رجال القلم هو كتاب «الحرب والسلم» لتولستوي، ولم أباشر مطالعته بسبب الالتهاب المزعج في عيني . . . منذ أن قرأت «لرمونتوف» تولتني رغبة لا تُقهر في نظم الشعر . . . سأمضي حيث تدعوني نفسي. سأمشي في الطريق الذي ما برح يغريني منذ صباي الباكر . . . إنه طريق الأدب. وإني له بكليتي . . .

٦ نيسان

خرجت اليوم من المستشفى حاملاً معي خليطاً من المؤثرات والأفكار. لن يوقظني بعد اليوم صوت معاون الطبيب الطيب القلب: «صباح الخير أيها السادة!» وبدلاً منه سيزعجني في السابعة من كل صباح صوت الجرس ثم صوت الرقيب الخشن: «آن وقت النهوض. انهضوا في الحال!»

. . . أمس، وليس لأول مرة، سمعت ملاحظة من أحد الرقباء بشأن تغيُّبي عن الصلوات في الكنيسة. وقد هدد بأن يرفع تقريراً بذلك—عني وعن ميخائيل اسكندر—إلى الجمعية الفلسطينية التي ندرس على نفقتها. وذلك أمر قد ينتج عنه تسويد سمعتنا وسلوكنا، وحرماننا من الدرس. ولولا ذلك لما كان حرياً باهتمامنا . . . سامح الله إدارتها! إذا كانت ترى أن حسن السلوك ينحصر في المواظبة على الصلوات في الكنيسة فإني، إرضاء لها، سأواظب على الصلوات. ورفيقي الحمصي، من جانبه، قد وعد أن يواظب مثلي.

لأدع جانباً مبادئي التي قلما أتساهل فيها. فالتمسك بها في السمنار يعني التضحية بالثقافة وبالمستقبل. لست وحدي في ما أذهب إليه من أن المسيحية الحقة لا تقوم بالوقوف في الكنيسة ساعتين أو ثلاث ساعات في الآحاد والسبوت والأعياد، بل باتّباع تعليم الإنجيل وإرشاداته . . .

أي خير في عبادة تصرف القلب عن المعبود، وفي مسيحية تنسيك المسيح؟ فأنت إذ تقف في الكنيسة لا تستطيع إلا أن تقارن بينها وبين المسرح. ففي الكنيسة—كما على المسرح—ممثلون هم الكاهن والشماس وغيرهما. وهؤلاء قد حفظوا أدوارهم وأتقنوها. وهم يظهرون أحياناً للنظارة وأحياناً يختفون. وفي الكنيسة—كما على المسرح—تتغير الزينة والملابس. أما الفرق بين الإثنين فقد لا يكون إلا في أن الممثلين على المسرح يتوجهون بكلامهم وحركاتهم إلى الجمهور، في حين يتوجه رجال الدين إلى الكائن الأعلى، ولكن بشفاههم لا بقلوبهم، ومن غير أن تتصل به أفكارهم. وهكذا تضيع الرغبة في الصلاة حتى عند الذين يرغبون فيها. وكيف للمصلي أن يرفع فكره وقلبه إلى الله ما دامت الحجارة المتلألئة على تاج الأسقف، والشموع التي يضيئها القندلفت، والحركات التي يقوم بها الشماس والكاهن تشغل عينيه، وأصوات المرتلين تملأ أذنيه، ورائحة البخور تغزو منخريه؟ . . .

١١ نيسان

أنهيت «الحرب والسلم» من زمان . . . إني أوافق المؤلف في رأيه عن نابوليون، لأني أكره الحرب والذين يدعون لها ويقومون بها . . . ولا يسعني، مع ذلك، إلا أن أرى تناقضاً في ما يقوله عن نابوليون وعن كوتوزوف. فنابوليون في رأيه لم يكن مدفوعاً بإرادته، بل بحكم الظروف وإرادة الشعوب. في حين

أنه يجعل لحكمة كوتوزوف وحنكته وإرادته المقام الأول في قهر نابوليون وردّه على أعقابه من روسيا.

. . . إنه ليضحكني أن أراني أناقش مفكراً عظيماً من عيار تولستوي. عفواً يا «ليف نيكولايفتش.» فأنا مدين لك بأفكار كثيرة أنارت ما كان مظلماً في عالمي الروحي. ففي الكثير من منشوراتك الأخيرة التي طالعتها في العام الماضي قد وجدت نوراً أهتدي به في كل خطوة من خطواتي . . . أجل. فأنت، من هذا القبيل، قد أصبحت معلمي ومرشدي من حيث لا تدري. . . .

٢٦-٢٩ نيسان

. . . جاءني دفعة واحدة أعداد ستة من «الهلال»—ابتداء من أول سنته—وكنت قد اشتركت فيه لأبقى على اتصال باللغة العربية. إننا لا نزال نفتقر إلى أدب بالمعنى الصحيح. فليس لنا من نتاجنا ما يصح أن يدعي أدباً مستقلاً. لكن هناك ظاهرة أغتبط بها. وهي أن الصحافة الحرة في مصر أخذت—بلسان واحد—تدعو الشعب إلى الحرية وتطالب بجلاء الإنجليز عن مصر. إن عدوى الحرية تنتشر حتى في شرقنا العربي . . . مهما يكن شأني أيها الوطن، فإني أعاهدك على تكريس قواي الفتية لخيرك وخير أبنائك . . .

٣ أيار

أمضيت السهرة في حديقة المدرسة. ما أطيب أن يجلس الإنسان وحده يسامر الشجر والنجوم وذكريات ماضيه! . . . لقد تدفقت عليّ تلك الذكريات حتى لم يبقَ في إمكاني أن أحبس دموعي. فأطلقتها غزيرة، حارة . . . قرأت مؤخراً رواية «الضباب الأسود» للكاتب «غنيدتش.» وقرأت رسالة مطولة لتولستوي بعنوان «الخطيئة الكبرى.» وهو يعالج فيها قضية الأرض والإجحاف في توزيعها. فلم يكن في مستطاعي إلا موافقته في رأيه.

١٤ أيار

في المدرسة حركة محمومة. إنها الامتحانات . . . في الثامن من هذا الشهر كان الامتحان في التاريخ. وكان موضوع المسابقة: «أهمية الطباعة في تثقيف

الجماهير الشعبية.» وقد أنفقت عليها ساعتين. وبعد ثلاثة أيام نقلوا إليّ عن
لسان أستاذ التاريخ أن مسابقتي كانت أفضل مسابقة تقدمت له! . . . كل
من خبر الامتحانات يعرف الإرهاق الذي تسبّبه للطلاب، وكيف أنها تعطل
فيهم كل رغبة في أي عمل آخر. وها أنا لا أحس أي رغبة حتى في العمل
الأحب إلى قلبي. وأعني الكتابة . . . تسلمت رسالة من الخال، وقبلها بأيام
جاءتني رسالة من الأخوين في «والا والا» ومعها حوالة بمئة روبل، وكنت قد
كتبت إليهما أنني سأمضي الصيف في روسيا. إنهم جميعهم—الخال والأهل
في لبنان، والشقيقان في والا والا—يعقدون عليّ آمالاً كبيرة. فأنا—في نظر
الخال—سأكون «رجل المستقبل» و«عماد العائلة» و«مفخرة لبنان» وما
أشبه. سأجمع كل قواي، أيها الأعزاء، وأوجّهها إلى تحقيق آمالكم. ولكن—هل
تراها تكفي؟ . . .

١٢ حزيران

أطالع الشاعر «نادْسُن.» إنه شاعر لطيف الحسّ، انطفأت حياته في ربيعها.
وما أشبه ما عاناه في شبابه بالذي أعانيه. لقد كان يفكر في مثل ما أفكر.
وكان يبني قصوراً في الهواء مثلما أبني. وكان يقلقه، مثلما يقلقني، أن يتأكد من
أن له المؤهلات لبلوغ هدفه . . . أي خير في حياة لا مجد فيها؟ . . . إني لن
أرضى أبداً أن أعيش مغموراً. . . ليته كان لي أن أخترق سجف المستقبل . . .
سأعمل، سأجتهد، سأكافح على قدر طاقتي، وما تبقَّى فالحكم فيه لله لا لي.

١ شاعر رقيق جداً، توفي في أواسط القرن الماضي. وكان هو الآخر من طلاب إحدى السمنارات.
وقد أصدر كتاباً بعنوان «يوميات طالب في السمنار.»
٢ الأسطر السبعة الأخيرة وردت شعراً في الأصل. وقد ترجمتها نثراً. وهي أول محاولة شعرية
لي باللغة الروسية.

Part 4: Theories of Literature

In this part, the selections shed light on the function of literature as a civilizing tool and formulate a theory of the novel, which is often imagined as an exclusively European import and literary field. *Nahda* literary theorists reflect on the meaning of literary modernity in a comparative context, involving such diverse genres as the historical novel, American jazz, and Russian literature. These selections put *Nahda* literary debates in a comparative and world literature context.

This section begins with an excerpt from Farah Antun that pays close attention to the historical novel, arguing that art and literature are meant not only to provide the reader with pleasure but also to bring about the reader's ethical and political awareness. Antun's aesthetic model is rooted in the telling of history and the exposure of its different narratives. Echoing his literary theory and Naimy's dialogue with Russian novelists, Khalil Baydas distinguishes the good novel from the commercial one: he argues that whereas the former elevates the human soul, the latter demeans it. In his essay on Arabic literary modernity, Zin al-'Abdin al-Sanusi, a Tunisian critic and author, goes back and forth between medieval Andalusian songs and Afro-American jazz. He situates the classical Arabic tradition as an integral part of the *Nahda* revival.

Farah Antun

(1874–1922)

Introduced and translated by Ghenwa Hayek

Farah Antun was born in Tripoli, in what is now Lebanon, in 1874, and died in Cairo in 1922. He worked briefly in the family business—the lumber trade—before leaving it to become a teacher in Tripoli. He emigrated to Alexandria in 1897, having already published his work in some of the more widely read newspapers of the day, including *al-Muqtataf* ("The Chosen Selection"). In Egypt, he worked for the *al-Ahram* ("The Pyramids") newspaper and translated works from French to Arabic for the journal *al-Manar* ("The Lighthouse") His deep knowledge of French literature and culture, and in particular his love of Rousseau, Voltaire, Renan, and Montesquieu, influenced his writing.

Antun founded his own journal, *al-Jami'a* ("The Unifier"), in 1899 and continued to publish it intermittently until 1910. He moved to New York City in 1906. In addition to publishing *al-Jami'a*, he dabbled in fiction, writing plays as well as novels, including *Urushalim al-Jadida* ("The New Jerusalem"), which appeared serially in *al-Jami'a* in 1904. After he returned to Cairo in 1909, his dramatic and literary output increased.

Like many of his contemporaries, Antun in his writing during this period articulates tenets of Arab modernity—for example, his self-conscious and deliberate use of the term *Nahda* to situate his literary project and his commitment to socially progressive ideals, in particular secularism, which he considered to be the decaying, stultified East's best path toward attaining the same level of enlightenment and civilization that existed in Europe. He viewed modern—in the sense of Europeanized—forms and ideals of aesthetic production as vital tools in this struggle. Yet his writing also reflects some of the tensions and contradictions of his time—for example, his view of *adab* encompasses both traditional (as "moral edification") and modern (as "literature") understandings of the word. He concludes his preface by speaking of the value of local knowledge in producing historical fiction, perhaps implicitly criticizing what we now describe as orientalist forms of cultural knowledge production.

Recommended Reading

Farah, Cesar. "Nationalist Concerns for Syria: The Case of Farah Antun, Mayy Ziadah, and al-Kawakibi." *The Origins of Syrian Nationhood*, edited by Adel Beshara, Routledge, 2012, pp. 210–22.

Feini, David. "French Decadence, Arab Awakenings: Figures of Decay in the Arab *Nahda*." *Boundary 2*, vol. 39, no. 2, 2012, pp. 143–60.

Flores, Alexander. "Modernity, Romanticism and Religion: Contradictions in the Writings of Farah Antun." *Nationalism and Liberal Thought in the Arab East: Ideology and Practice*, edited by Christoph Schumann, Routledge, 2010, pp. 115–31.

Hourani, Albert. *Arabic Thought in the Liberal Age*. Cambridge UP, 1983.

Sheehi, Stephen. *The Foundations of Modern Arab Identity*. UP of Florida, 2004.

Preface to *The New Jerusalem*

There are three kinds of novels, in order of importance. First, there are social and moral novels. These are the best sort because they seek to reform the morals of a nation and its constitution and to point its attention toward what will benefit it. Second are historical novels, meaning those that aim to present the history of nations. These novels describe a nation's historic roots and origins, allowing readers to draw conclusions from them freely; they neither exaggerate nor show prejudice in describing the rise or fall of nations. Third are psychological novels, which include romantic novels that deal with the representation of emotions and the struggles and affairs of the heart.

But there is another type of novel that is better than all three kinds above, the novel that combines them. Such a novel is historical for those who admire history; social and philosophical for those who admire philosophy and social realism in writing; and literary and romantic for those who like reading about pure, lofty emotions and disdain descriptions of cold lust and lewdness. Some of the most celebrated and seminal novels belong to this genre, novels whose publication became a major event in their nation's history, since they upheld certain principles and downplayed others. Examples are Victor Hugo's *Les misérables* and Dante's *Inferno*.

This is the path that *al-Jami'a* has chosen to take with its new novel, *The New Jerusalem*, which combines philosophy, social matters, history, love, and moral edification [*adab*]. Moreover, it adds religion to the mix, because the era whose affairs we are exploring was a religiously significant one for Christians and Muslims alike. So any discussion of this era must of course touch on religion; otherwise, it will lack an important dimension.

I am well aware that those in the vanguard of our time, our era's loftiest writers, who aim to arouse the East from its slumber and cleanse it of the shame of having yielded to injurious forces, those who demand the truth wherever they can find it, will look kindly on this book, helping its writer to forget some of the trouble he endured to write it. If he had not been confident that such men would be pleased with and invigorated by the story's contents, then he would not have found in himself the strength necessary to write a book like this, given the state of education and culture in our lands and how freedom of thought and the integrity of the publishing process are notoriously crushed to win favor with the feebleminded and those with vested interests, particularly in issues pertaining to the nation and the affairs of the East.

In this preface, it behooves us to bring the esteemed reader's attention to two matters:

First, the formal method that we have adopted in this book. We were particularly attentive to what the Europeans call "aesthetics," since in this book it is left open for the writer to think and write as he wishes without hindrances to either process. This aesthetic sensibility is the primary component of all great books that have stirred people's souls on this earth, edifying them and instilling in them hope for goodness and perfection. Without aesthetic beauty, writing would have no effect on the soul, nor would it have the appeal to attract readers, nor create a thoughtful, critical audience that can distinguish the wheat of matters from their chaff and beauty from ugliness and can express this in popular opinion.

The language that we have adopted here depends on the existence of an aesthetic sensibility in a person's soul, that quality that most distinguishes him from animals; indeed, man is defined as "being the animal with a knowledge of and feeling for beauty."

Many scholars believe that it was the "beauty" of fine arts and crafts, and of writing in general, that initiated the European Renaissance. The rise of the fine arts in Italy was an outgrowth of the rise of an aesthetic sensibility there that refined people's tastes and raised their souls to lofty heights; from here emerged the inclination for freedom and progress that eventually spread across all of Europe. Because of the importance of this aesthetic sensibility, you see people buying paintings by Raphael, for example, for millions of francs. In buying them, they are buying the fruits of the most refined soul, because in these paintings aesthetic sensibility reached the highest level of refinement achievable on earth. If we compare this concern for "the beautiful" in civilized countries with the fact that some among us here [in the East] consider beauty in writing and other arts to be secondary, consisting merely of decorative fancies, embellishments, and flourishes, then we will feel justifiable regret. In the East, we have not yet realized what the essence of true refinement is; we continue to disparage the rose in the same manner as that Arab poet who described it with that famous simile.[1]

Fortunately, however, the innate aesthetic sensibility in people's souls is too strong to be strangled by those few who do not understand it. And for this reason, the belles lettres, the art of creating beautiful works with the pen, affects people in the East even if they are unaware of it. This explains the Renaissance [*Nahda*] of Easterners who have taken up writing and reading and are fond of these two things. As the aesthetic sensibility within them increases, that is, as their souls flourish, so too will their inclination toward this craft and to all the fine arts at once. The level of refinement in different nations can be measured by examining the sort of aesthetic sensibility that they are capable of producing. This sensibility is always coupled with its sibling, the sense of the good, "because true beauty can never be separated from goodness." Refinement can never be measured by what nations derive from or imitate in others.

Philosophers add to the aesthetic sensibility and the sense of good "the sense of truth," which aims to reveal the truth and which demands complete autonomy and the avoidance of cowardice and hesitation. They say that these three things are the highest goals of learning and the loftiest subjects of philosophy. This is indeed true. For this reason, we hope that these three sentiments will develop in our beloved countries, because they are the foundation of all refinement, honesty, and virtue and the source of all greatness. The nations that are not founded on this tripartite base strive and build in vain, since they are merely built on material, animal interests.

As for the second matter: We would like to note that historical novels are not meant merely to narrate the facts and figures of history. He who seeks such things should go search for them in history books, where they are easily attainable and not entangled with the imaginative threads of fiction, which will try the patience of those seeking unembellished historical fact. Historical novels (in addition to narrating events and dates and representing what is meant to be represented and showing the emotions and thoughts that preoccupied those who lived during those times) fill in the gaps of history and round off its rough edges.

What I mean by "filling in the gaps of history" is that the author of historical fiction puts himself in the place of historical figures about whom he then speaks and whose ideas and opinions he expresses in scenes that he invents for them—of which no historical trace can be found but in whose invention he is guided by what he knows about these people. This is what the famous Alexandre Dumas does in his novels. He brings back to life the heroes of whom he speaks, and he makes them feel things that are appropriate to their time and intentions, and he reveals the secrets buried in their souls. We have followed this course in this novel. However, we were wary of mixing history with the ahistorical, and we worried that less knowledgeable readers might get lost, so we have placed markers within the story to distinguish between what is historical and what is conjectural. The passage below explains them:

The marker (*)—the asterisk—indicates that this text is historical. And the marker (–) indicates the opposite, that it has been made up by the author and has nothing to do with history. Spoken text that is placed between brackets, such as « », ( ), or quotation marks " " and is accompanied by an asterisk * is historical material quoted verbatim. However, if there is text between brackets without an asterisk, or if there is dialogue without brackets or an asterisk, then this dialogue is not historical, particularly if it is conducted between fictional characters in the novel—unless there is a note about it in the margin.

We will follow these same conventions in all our historical novels, in order to broaden our scope for invention and historical inference in these matters. Without these conventions, the author would distort the history that he worked so hard to reveal, and in so doing he would be neglecting the most important aspect of historical fiction. Readers in the East in particular know that to write of Muslim and Christian affairs in these lands requires such precautions, because of the delicacy of the situation and the difficulty of such subject matter. We have used several sources for this novel, both Arabic and foreign. We consulted Arabic books on the Arab affairs and foreign books on the affairs of the Christians. This is how it must be, since each group is most knowledgeable of its own history. We have indeed noted these sources in the margins.

This is what we wanted to say in the preface. And now, we take the esteemed reader by the hand, and we begin our lengthy travels together, side by side.

Note

[1]Footnote in the Arabic original: "Anatole France, a member of the French Academy, spoke in the voice of the Greek goddess of wisdom, Athena, in a speech before the statue of Renan this year: 'The ingenuity of the Greeks lured me down to earth. And when it departed, I too left. Then the barbarians arrived and took over the world. They were afraid of "beauty," and considered it to be evil. When they saw that I was "beautiful," they doubted me and did not realize that I was wisdom itself. And they expelled me,' etc. (*al-Jami'a*, fourth year, p. 310). We quote this to show the link connecting the advancement of the Italians to that of the Greeks, which is why they claim that the latter is the origin of the former, as you can see in the above-mentioned speech and in Renan's speech that preceded it."

Source of Arabic Text on Which the Translation Is Based

Antun, Farah. أوروشليم الجديدة [urushalim al-jadida; The New Jerusalem]. *al-Jami'a*, 1904, pp. i–iii.

فرح أنطون
(١٨٧٤-١٩٢٢)

أوروشليم الجديدة

«المقدمة»

أهم أنواع الروايات ثلاثة (الأول) الروايات الاجتماعية والأخلاقية وهي أفضلها لأنها تبحث في إصلاح أخلاق الأمة وتكوينها وتنبيه نفسها إلى ما فيه منفعتها (والثاني) الروايات التاريخية وغرضها بسط تاريخ الأمم أي ذكر أسبابه ومسبباته لاستخلاص النتائج منها بحرية تامة وبلا تزلف ولا تحامل للوقوف على الفواعل في تقدم الأمم وتأخرها. (والثالث) الروايات البسيكولوجية وتدخل فيها الروايات الحبية التي يصور فيها احتكاك العواطف وتنازع القلوب والأهواء.

على أن هنالك نوعاً آخر من الروايات أفضل من هذه الأنواع الثلاثة وهو الذي جمع بينها في سياق واحد فيكون تاريخياً لمحبي التاريخ فلسفياً اجتماعياً لمحبي الفلسفة والاجتماع أدبياً حبياً لمحبي الأدب والعواطف الحبية الطاهرة المنزهة عن الخلاعة والغرام البارد. ومن هذا النوع أشهر الروايات الخطيرة التي كان ظهورها عبارة عن حادثة وطنية كبرى لأنها رفعت مبادئ وخفضت مبادئ كـ«ميزارابل» لفيكتور هيغو و«الجحيم» لداتني وغيرهما.

ولقد سلكت «الجامعة» هذا المسلك في روايتها الجديدة «أوروشليم الجديدة» فجمعت فيها بين الفلسفة والاجتماع والتاريخ والحب والأدب. وفوق ذلك ضمّت إليها «الدين» لأن العصر الذي تُبحث هنا في شؤونه عصر ديني محض سواء كان ذلك عند المسيحيين أو عند المسلمين. فالكلام عنه يشمل الدين بالطبع والضرورة وبدونه يكون الكلام ناقصاً أهم وجوهه.

وهي على يقين من أن من أبناء العصر وكتّابه الأفاضل الذين يرومون تنبيه الشرق من سباته وأن يمحوا عنه عار الاستسلام للسلطان المضرة ويطلبون الحقيقة أينما وجدوها سينظرون إلى هذا الكتاب نظراً يُنسي مؤلفه شيئاً من التعب الذي عاناه في تأليفه. لأنه لو لم يكن على ثقة من رضاهم وتنشيطهم

قياساً على ما مضى لما وجد في نفسه القوة اللازمة للإقدام على كتاب كهذا الكتاب مع ما هو معروف في بلادنا عن بضاعة العلم والأدب وما هو مشهور من تهشيم حرية الفكر ونزاهة النشر تزلّفاً للسذج وذوي المصالح خصوصاً في الشؤون الوطنية والمسائل الشرقية.

***

ويجدر بنا في هذه المقدمة أن ننبه القارئ الكريم إلى أمرين (الأول) الطريقة الإنشائية التي اعتمدنا عليها في هذا الكتاب. فإننا عنينا هنا بما يسمّيه الإفرنج «جمال التأليف» عناية خاصة لأن الجمال في هذا الكتاب واسع لفكر المؤلف وقلمه ولا قيد يقيدهما البتة. وهذا الذي يسمّونه جمال التأليف عليه المعوّل في كل الكتب الجليلة التي هزّت نفوس البشر في الأرض ورقتها وأمالتها نحو الخير والكمال. وبدونه لا يكون للكتابة أثر في النفوس ولا جاذبية تجتذب القراء للإقبال عليها وتأليف جمهور مفكر يميز غث الأمور من سمينها وجميلها من دميمها وهو ما يعبّرون عنه بالرأي العام. وهذا الأسلوب الذي اعتمدنا عليه هنا يعتمد على عاطفة الجمال التي في نفس الإنسان والتي بها يميّز عن الحيوان حتى عرّفوا الإنسان «بأنه حيوان يعرف الجمال ويشعر به.» ويقول كثيرون من علماء العمران أن «الجمال» في الفنون والصنائع الجميلة و«صناعة القلم في جملتها» هو أساس نهضة أوروبا. فإن ارتقاء هذه الفنون الجميلة في إيطاليا كان ناشئاً عن ارتقاء عاطفة «الجمال» فيها. وهذا الارتقاء لطّف الأذواق ورفع النفوس وكبرها ومن هنا نشأ الميل للحرية والارتقاء فسرى إلى أوروبا كلها. وبناء على أهمية عاطفة الجمال هذه ترى الناس يتباعون صورة من صور المصوّر رفائيل مثلاً بملايين فرنكات. فهم يباعون بابتياعها ثمار أرقى نفس لأن عاطفة الجمال بلغت فيها أقصى درجات الارتقاء الممكن في الأرض. فإذا قابلنا بين هذه العناية «بالجميل» في بلاد المتمدنين وبين اعتبار بعضهم عندنا الجمال في الكتابة وغيرها شيئاً ثانوياً بل تخيلات وتصورات وأدبيات جاز لنا أن نأسف لأننا في الشرق لم ندرك بعدُ ماهية الارتقاء الحقيقي لكوننا لا نزال نذم الورد على أسلوب ذلك الشاعر العربي الذي شبهه ذلك التشبيه المشهور.[١]

ولكن من حسن الحظ أن عاطفة الجمال الطبيعية الموجودة في نفوس الناس في الأرض أقوى من أن تُخنق إذا لم يفهمها بعض الناس. ولذلك ترى

«جمال صناعة القلم» يؤثر في الناس في الشرق من غير أن يدروا به. وهذا سبب نهضة الشرقيين إلى الكتابة والمطالعة وتعلقهم بهما. وكلما ارتقت فيهم عاطفة الجمال أي كلما ارتقت «نفسهم نفسها» ارتقى فيهم الميل إلى هذه الصناعة وجميع الصنائع الجميلة على نسبة واحدة. فمقياس ارتقاء الأمم إذا إنما يكون بالنظر إلى ما تقدر على إبرازه من عاطفة الجمال هذه مقرونة بشقيقتها عاطفة الخير «لأن الجمال الحقيقي لا ينفصل عن الخير مطلقاً» لا بالنظر إلى ما تقدر على تقليده من شؤون غيرها. والفلاسفة يضيفون إلى «عاطفتي الجمال والخير» «عاطفة الحق» التي مقتضاها الجهر بالحقيقة وطلبها باستقلال تام ونزاهة عن كل مواربة وجبن. ويقولون إن هذه الثلاثة هي أغراض العلم العليا ومواضيع الفلسفة السامية. وهو قول حق. ولذلك نتمنى أن يكثر في بلادنا العزيزة كل ما ينمّي هذه العواطف الثلاث لأنها أساس كل ارتقاء ونزاهة وفضيلة ومصدر كل شيء عظيم. والأمم التي لا تُؤسَّس على هذا الأساس المثلث تتعب وتبني عبثاً لأنها لا تبني إلا على المصالح المادية والقابلية الحيوانية.

***

(والأمر الثاني) الذي أحببنا التنبيه عليه أن الروايات التاريخية لا يُقصد بها سرد وقائع التاريخ وأرقامه. فإن طالب هذا الوقائع والأرقام يلتمسها في كتاب التاريخ حيث تكون قريبة المنال لتجردها عما ليس منها لا في الروايات المطولة التي تشتبك وقائعها الخيالية بها ولا يصبر طالب التاريخ البحث على مطالعتها. وإنما المقصود من الروايات التاريخية (فوق سرد الوقائع والأرقام وتصوير الوسط المراد تصويره وإبراز العواطف والأفكار التي كانت تختلج في هذا الوسط) بـ«تكميل التاريخ» في جوانبه الناقصة.

ونعني هنا بـ«تكميل التاريخ» أن يضع المؤلف نفسه موضع الأشخاص التاريخيين الذين يتكلم عنهم ويعبر عن أفكارهم وآرائهم في المواقف التي يصوّرها لهم والتي لا أثر لها في التاريخ مستدلاً على ذلك بما يعرفه عنهم. وهذا الأمر في روايات «دماس» المشهور كان أهم الأمور. فكأنه به يحيي الأبطال الذين يتكلم عنهم ويجعلهم يشعرون بالأمور التي كانت تنطبق على تاريخهم ومقاصدهم ويكشف لك خبايا كانت مدفونة في صدورهم. ولقد سلكنا هذا المسلك أيضاً في هذه الرواية. غير أننا خشينا أن يختلط التاريخ

بما ليس هو في شيء منه فيضل القارئ سيما القليل الاطلاع فوضعنا علامات للتفريق بين التاريخ وبين التنصيف والاستدلال. وإليك هذه العلامات.

هذه العلامة * (أي النجمة) تدل على أن ذلك القول وارد في التاريخ. والعلامة (-) تدل على عكسه أي أنه تصنيف أو استدلال من المؤلف لا أثر له في التاريخ. والكلام الموضوع بين قوسين هكذا « » أو ( ) أو ضمتين " " ومع نجمة هو نص تاريخي بحرفه. وأما إذا كان الكلام بين هذه الأقواس بلا نجمة أو كان بلا أقواس ولا نجمة فليس هو من التاريخ في شيء خصوصاً إذا كان بين أشخاص الرواية الخياليين—هذا إلا إذا نُبه عليه في الحاشية.

وسنتابع هذه الاصطلاحات في كل رواياتنا التاريخية ليتسع لنا مجال الاستنباط والاستدلال التاريخي في أمثال هذه المسائل. إذ بدون هذه الاصطلاحات يشوّه الكاتب التاريخ إذا حرص على الاستنباط والاستدلال ويهمل أهمّ ما في التاريخ الروائي إذا أهملهما. والقراء في الشرق على الخصوص يعرفون أن الكاتب في شؤون المسلمين والمسيحيين في بلادهم لا غنى له عن هذا الاحتياط لحرج الموقف وصعوبة الطريق.

أما المصادر التي اعتمدنا عليها في هذا الكتاب فهي عدة لمؤلفي العرب والإفرنج وقد رجعنا في شؤون العرب في كتب العرب وفي شؤون الروم إلى كتب الإفرنج كما يجب أن يكون ذلك لأن كل قوم أدرى بتاريخهم. ولقد أشرنا في الحواشي إلى أكثر تلك المصادر.

هذا ما قصدنا في هذه المقدمة. والآن نأخذ بيد القارئ الكريم لنسيح معه في هذا الكتاب سياحة طويلة.

---

[1] قال أناتول فرانس أحد أعظماء الأكاذمية الفرنسوية في خطبته أمام تمثال رنان في هذا العام عن لسان إلاهة الحكمة آثينا: «إن قريحة اليونان أنزلتني إلى الأرض. ولما قضتُ خرجتُ منها. فجاء بعدهم البرابرة واجتاحوا العالم. وكانوا يخافون 'الجمال' ويحسبونه شرّاً. فلما رأوني 'جميلة' شكوا فيَّ ولم يعلموا أنني الحكمة. فطردوني إلخ» (الجامعة السنة الرابعة الصفحة ٣١٠). قلنا وبذلك تتصل حلقة الارتقاء الإيطالي بحلقة الارتقاء اليوناني ولهذا قالوا إن هذا أصل ذاك كما ترى في الخطبة المذكورة وفي خطبة رنان التي تقدمتها.

Khalil Baydas
(1875–1949)

Introduced and translated by Spencer Scoville

Born in Nazareth, Khalil Baydas became one of the most important literary figures in Palestine in the years leading up to World War I. As one of the early graduates of the Russian Orthodox schools in Palestine, he embodies the great influence that Russian culture had on the Christian Orthodox communities of the Levant before the Bolshevik Revolution of 1917. Among the later graduates of these schools were Mikhail Naimy, Anton Ballan, Iskander al-Khuri al-Baytjali, and Kulthum ʿAwdah Vasilieva. Baydas was deeply concerned with making quality prose literature available to the Arabic reading public. He introduced a large amount of Russian literature into the Arabic literary arena through both his own literary translations and the work of other translators that he edited and published. The bulk of this literature was presented in the volumes of the literary journal that he owned and edited, *al-Nafaʾis* ("Treasures"), later *al-Nafaʾis al-ʿAsriyya* ("Contemporary Treasures"), which ran between 1908 and 1923. Baydas translated many works of fiction and history from Russian into Arabic, including Tolstoy's *Anna Karenina* and Pushkin's *The Captain's Daughter*.

Baydas's close connection to Russian culture informed his opinions on politics in Palestine, which at the time were markedly anti-British. An outstanding orator and passionate political activist, Baydas served on several committees for the Orthodox community in Jerusalem. A particularly enthusiastic speech delivered by him in Jerusalem in 1920, on the occasion of the annual Nabi Musa celebration, provoked the ire of the British Mandate administration and led to his arrest and imprisonment. After publication of *al-Nafa'is* ceased in 1923, Baydas continued to live in Jerusalem, teaching at St. George's School and translating literature. In 1948 he sought to remain in his home in Jerusalem but was forced by the violence to move to Amman and eventually to Beirut, where he died in 1949.

Baydas printed the following essay on the novel twice, first in the inaugural issue of his literary journal (1908) and later as the introduction to a collection of short stories (original as well as translated) entitled *Masarih al-Adhhan* (1924; "Stages for the Mind"). It shows how keenly he felt the need to defend both the morality and literary merit of the novel, common concerns for novelists and translators of the *Nahda*.

Recommended Reading

Hafez, Sabry. *The Genesis of Arabic Narrative Discourse*. Saqi Books, 1993.
Hopwood, Derek. *The Russian Presence in Syria and Palestine, 1843–1914: Church and Politics in the Near East*. Clarendon, 1969.
Scoville, Spencer. "The Agency of the Translator: Khalil Baydas' Literary Translations." UMI, 2012. PhD dissertation, U of Michigan.
———. "Reconsider Nahdawi Translation: Bringing Pushkin to Palestine." *The Translator*, vol. 22, no. 2, 2015, pp. 1–14.

Stages for the Mind

Introduction to the First Edition

No one can ignore the importance and high standing of novels among all literary works throughout the world, for they are some of the greatest pillars of civilization, and the most widely published and circulated of all printed works. Of all publications, novels take root most firmly in the heart and soul, have the most long-lasting influence on morals and customs, and are the most capable of both building and tearing down.

In novels we find a representation of all life's forms and images—of good and evil, virtue and vice, justice and oppression, truth and deception, faithfulness and treachery, sincerity and hypocrisy, comfort and suffering.

Novels describe the conditions of different nations and the lessons of history. They depict incidents of love and passion, of war and peace, along with the acts of integrity, loyalty, treachery, and betrayal that they encompass.

Novels stage the life of a man in all of his roles: in the springtime of his life and in its autumn, in his ascent and his decline, in times of pain and hope, pleasure and suffering, in poverty and in wealth, through his passions and tribulations; in short, in every possible state and condition.

Writers have dedicated themselves to writing novels, and readers have flocked to read them; some novels have done well, while others have floundered. The novel shifts and transforms, until it captures the interest of the majority in each nation and becomes a companion to readers both male and female. The novel has become one of the most beautiful expressions of the literary arts, taking as its subject the social, civil, and creative life of man.

Each nation has seen the appearance of a group of outstanding intellectuals who write nothing but novels—immortal novels—that have been widely translated. These novels set off a great reverberation, which is followed by tremendous explosions within the souls of the people and momentous upheavals in the state of nations.

These novelists—so skilled at portraying the inner workings of the soul—have penetrated into its depths, as they have plumbed the deepest reaches of the heart. They disseminate their representations of emotions and truths among the people in the garb of diversion and entertainment.

There have been giants in literature—Corneille, Racine, Molière, Balzac, Hugo, Tolstoy, Shakespeare, Walter Scott,

Turgenev, Dostoevsky, Goethe, Schiller, Dickens, Mark Twain, Ibsen, Dumas père and fils, Zola, Chateaubriand, Maupassant, Bourget, and many others. From their writings have emerged lessons and warnings, nourishment for the soul and live coals for the intellect, contemplation and knowledge, wisdom and philosophy.

The novelist writes for the masses, who are the majority of each nation. He writes for souls starving and confused, for hearts parched and in pain.

The masses favor the novel because it is their book, their companion, and their friend. It offers the most beautiful entertainment for their spare time and the best respite in their times of leisure. It is the most effective means of reforming their habits and refining their morals, the sweetest well from which the intellect can draw.

The novelist, if he does not associate with the masses and study their conditions and is not one of them, living among them, or if he lacks the power of imagination and the skill to illustrate and describe, and if he does not have a true literary eye for each event—and if he is not completely comfortable with his topic, nay, completely devoted to it, and does not constantly push his work forward toward the highest degrees of perfection, and no inspiration, revelation, nor prophecy is revealed to him—then as a novelist he is no genius.

And if he has not read hundreds of novels, and hundreds of histories, and has not pored over the events of the world, delved into every society, and understood the meaning of life and its secrets and ways, and if he does not derive the purpose of his novel from real-life events and human nature and make it accord with truth and reality—then as a novelist he is no master.

And if he is not a prophet who perceives what others do not, if he is not a poet soaring through the skies of imagination or an expert on social affairs intimately acquainted with the world around him—then as a novelist he is no skilled practitioner.

For the true genius, the truly skillful artist, is the novelist who has lived for art, written for art, and died for art.

The true novel, the artistic novel, is one that aims for wise meanings and literary purposes, for the extolment of virtue and the debasement of vice, for the cultivation of morals and the enlightenment of intellect, the purification of hearts and the reformation of actions.

The novel is that which is pure of every pollutant, free from any stain; it has a lasting effect on the reader's soul and leads him to contemplation, guides him toward literary refinement and pure love. This is the true novel, the artistic novel, the immortal novel. I do not mean the counterfeit, corrupted novel—a book not written by a belletrist or drawn by the pen of a novelist with imagination and skill.

Of course, there are hundreds or even thousands of novels that were not written for the most noble of purposes. They also circulate, and readers are drawn to them like a moth to a flame. They are displayed in every market and sold like any other product for the cheapest of prices. Indeed, the markets are filled with those things that sell best.

These novels, if it is even proper to call such frivolous works novels, are written and published with only commercial interests in mind. Neither their writers nor their readers—from the general masses, of course—care about their style. They are not put off by their many faults, the superficiality of their subject matter, or other things that concern only the belletrist. Our markets are all astir with the sale of this good, or this poison, which its publishers make available at all times and in all places, so that none can do without it.

For the publishers of such "novels" have muddied the spring of the true novel and debased it by their work, while harming readers by corrupting their morals and leading them into error. In doing so, these publishers have committed a crime against language, literature, morals, sentiments, and virtue. . . .

For a single novel, even a short one, that resounds with the beauty of art and merges with the elements of the soul is better than hundreds of the frivolous products sold by these swindlers, most of whom resort to this industry because they have few other means of earning a living. How evil are their deeds! . . .

There is no doubt that the value of the novel lies in the benefits that it contains and the lessons it aims to impart. The value of the novelist lies in the truths that he depicts for the reader and in the attractive, artistic style with which he depicts them.

The novel, in the form in which we now know it, appeared in the East only recently. Until then, most of what we had in this genre was translated from Western languages. Our literati took up translation with great enthusiasm and with very few exceptions also authored their own works, especially longer novels. Many were successful in choosing the best novels from the greatest European authors and translating them faithfully into Arabic, although it is true that others translated feeble, superficial novels of the kind that fling their reader into an abyss of wrongdoing, evil, and all manner of ills and shortcomings.

The more a nation's literary productivity improves and the more it roots itself in civilization, the more it will naturally become inclined toward those things that are more beneficial and virtuous and turn away from the ugly and the shallow, enabling more authors to rise up and rival their Western counterparts in composing literary and nationalistic novels.

It is no secret that the novel in the West has a surfeit of great qualities, for the West has preceded us in many things. The West has hundreds or even thousands of ingenious novelists, unrivaled masters of the craft. So if we translate their works or imitate their styles, then we will enrich our own literature and improve the style, clarity, and artistry of our authors. But let us be mindful of God in all that we translate and write. Let us take the novelistic art forward, toward perfection, and present to the nation only the finest things available from this bountiful spiritual storehouse.

This is what I wished to say by defining the novel in the intro-
duction to this book—*Stages for the Mind*—which I now present
to my esteemed audience. It is composed entirely of novelistic,
artistic chapters, each of which contains a moral, a lesson, or a
piece of instructive wisdom for the reader.

I have just presented this book to the esteemed professor,
my honored friend Elias Effendi Anton Elias, owner of the
al-'Asriyya ["The Contemporary"] Press in Egypt. He has pub-
lished recently, from his own pen and from the pens of other
writers and literati, many wonderful things that are not to be
missed. He has also announced his intention to continue print-
ing everything that contains benefit and good for the public.
This is indeed a wonderful step forward in the service of litera-
ture and art in the East. None could pull this off so successfully
and confidently except one blessed with a strong will and lofty
concerns, talent, and creativity, as Professor Elias is. He has
expended great efforts on behalf of learning and knowledge.

It is my hope that the professor, after reviewing this book,
will publish it in the most beautiful and artistic form, as he
does with all publications that are entrusted to him. For this he
is to be thanked greatly. It is also my wish that this book will
be beneficial and nurturing to the soul and worthy of interest.
God grant us success.

Khalil Baydas
Jerusalem, 1 May 1924

Source of Arabic Text on Which the Translation Is Based

Baydas, Khalil. مسارح الأذهان: مجموعة أدبية فنية روائية في حقيقة الحياة [masarih
al-adhhan: majmu'a adabiyya fanniyya riwa'iyya fi haqiqat al-hayah;
*Stages for the Mind: A Literary, Artistic, Novelistic Collection about the
Realities of Life*]. 2nd ed., al-Ittihad al-'Amm lil-Kuttab wal-Suhufiyyin
al-Filistiniyyin, 1924, pp. 9–16.

خليل بيدس
(١٨٧٥-١٩٤٩)

مسارح الأذهان

«مقدمة الطبعة الأولى»

لا يجهل أحد ما للروايات من الشأن الخطير والمقام الرفيع بين سائر كتب الأدب عند جميع الأمم.

فهي من أعظم أركان المدنيّة

وفي مقدمة المطبوعات انتشاراً وتداولاً

وأشدها رسوخاً في النفوس والقلوب

وأثبتُها أثراً في الأخلاق والعادات

وأعظمها عاملاً في البناء والهدم.

لأن فيها تمثيلاً لمظاهر الحياة وصورها—من خير وشر، وفضيلة ورذيلة، وعدل وجور، وصدق وكذب، ووفاء وغدر، وإخلاص ورياء، وهناء وشقاء.

وفيها وصف أحوال الأمم، وعِبَر الزمان، وحوادث الحب والغرام، والحرب والسلام؛ وما يتخلل ذلك كله في عفة وأمانة، وغدر وخيانة.

وفيها عرض حياة الإنسان في جميع أدواره، في ربيع حياته وخريفها، في صعوده وهبوطه، في آلامه وآماله، في سرّائه وضرّائه، وفقره وغناه، وأهوائه وأشواقه، وسائر أطواره وأحواله.

وقد أقبل الكتّاب على تأليف الروايات، وتهافت القراء على مطالعتها؛ وأجاد من كل فريق فئة، وضلّت فئات، والرواية تتقلب وتتحول، إلى أن أصبحت موضوع اهتمام السواد الأعظم من كل أمة، وسمير كل قارئ وقارئة على الإطلاق، وأصبحت فناً من أجمل فنون الأدب—موضوعه الإنسان في حياته الاجتماعية والعمرانية والخلقية.

وظهر في كل أمة جمهور من نوابغ المفكرين، لم يكتبوا إلا الروايات— الروايات الخالدة—التي تناقلتها اللغات، وكان لها دويّ عظيم، عقبته انفجارات هائلة في النفوس، وانقلابات خطيرة في أحوال الأمم.

وقام هؤلاء الروائيون—وهم مصوِّرو أحوال النفس البارعون—يَلِجون أعماق هذه النفس، كما يَلِجون أعماق القلب، ويصورون العواطف، ويمثلون الحقائق، وينشرونها على الناس في أثواب اللهو والفكاهة.

وظهر جبابرة الفن، أمثال كرنيل وراسين ومولير وبلزاك وهوغو وتولستوي وشكسبير وولتر سكوت وتورغينيف ودوستويفسكي وغوته وشلُّر وديكنس ومارك توين وايبسن ودوماس الكبير والصغير وزولا وشاتوبريان ودوريه وموباسان وبورجيه وغيرهم وغيرهم—فكان من ذلك العِبَر، وكانت المواعظ؛ وكان من ذلك غذاء النفوس، وقبس البصائر، وكان التأمل والعلم، وكانت الحكمة والفلسفة.

الروائي يكتب للعامة، وهم السواد الأعظم من كل أمة

يكتب للنفوس الحائرة، والقلوب المتألمة

يكتب للنفوس الجائعة، والقلوب الظمأى.

والعامة يميلون إلى الرواية، لأنها كتابهم ورفيقهم وعشيرهم، وهي أجمل ما يتلهّون به في ساعات فراغهم، وأفضل ما يرتاحون لمناجاته في خلوتهم، وأنجع ما يُتوسل به لإصلاح عاداتهم وتثقيف أخلاقهم، وأعذب مورد يستمدّون منه البصائر.

والروائي—إن لم يعاشر العامة ويدرس أحوالهم، أو لم يكن منهم ويعِش بينهم، أو لم تكن فيه قوة التصور ومهارة التصوير وبراعة الوصف، ولم يكن فيه النظرة الأدبية الصادقة إلى كل حادث، والارتياح التام بل الكلف التام ببحثه، وإن لم يسر بعمله على الدوام إلى الأمام، إلى أعلى درجات الكمال، ولم يكاشفه الإلهام والوحي والنبوّة—فليس بروائي عبقري.

وهو—إن لم يقرأ مئات الروايات، مئات التواريخ، ولم يطّلع على حوادث الكون، ويَلِج كلَّ مجتمع، ويدرك معنى الحياة وأسرارها وأساليبها، وينتزع غرض روايته من حوادث الحياة وطبيعة الإنسان، ويجعلها منطبقة على الحقيقة والواقع—فليس بروائي متفنن.

وهو—إن لم يكن نبياً، يرى ببصيرته ما لا يراه غيره؛ وإن لم يكن شاعراً يحلّق في سماء الخيال، ولم يكن عالماً اجتماعياً يعلم الأحوال ويطّلع على كل شأن من الشؤون—فليس بروائي ماهر.

فالروائي الحقيقي العبقري المتفنن الماهر—هو من عاش للفن، وكتب للفن، ومات في سبيل الفن.

والرواية الحقيقية، والفنية، هي التي ترمي إلى المغازي الحكمية أو الأغراض الأدبية؛ إلى تمجيد الفضائل أو التنديد بالرذائل؛ إلى تهذيب الأخلاق وتنوير العقول وتنقية القلوب وإصلاح السيرة.

وهي النقية من كل شائبة، الخالية من كل وصمة؛ التي تُبقي أثراً في نفس القارئ، وتحدوه على التأمل، وتقوده في سبيل الرقي الأدبي والحب النقي. هذه هي الرواية الحقيقية، الرواية الفنية، الرواية الخالدة.

لا الرواية المبتذلة المشوَّهة، التي لم يكتبها أديب، ولم يرسمها قلم روائي مصوّر بارع.

ولا جرم أن بين الروايات مئات وألوفاً لم تُكتب للغرض الأسمى؛ وقد انتشرت أيضاً، وتهافت القراء عليها كما تتهافت الفراشة على النار؛ وهي تُعرض في كل سوق وتُباع بيع السلع وبأبخس الأثمان،—وإنما يُجلب إلى كل سوق ما يُنفق فيها.

وهذه الروايات—إذا جاز تُسمّى أمثال هذه السخافات روايات—لم يكتبها أربابها وينشرها الناشرون إلا لأغراض تجارية محضة، فلا هم ولا القراء—من العامة طبعاً—يعبأون بعبارتها، وكثرة أغلاطها، وتفاهة موضوعها، وغير ذلك مما لا يتنبه له إلا الأديب، ومما لا أراني في حاجة معه إلى البيّنة والدليل، وهذه أسواقنا تعجّ عجيجاً بباعة هذه السلع، أو هذه السموم، التي ينفثها ناشروها في كل مكان وزمان، وقد عمّت بها البلوى.

إن ناشري هذه «الروايات» قد كدّروا بعملهم مشرب الرواية، وأسقطوا منزلتها، وعاثوا في القراء بفساد آدابهم وزيغ خطتهم، وجنَوا على اللغة، والأدب، والأخلاق، والعواطف، والفضيلة . . .

إن رواية، ولو صغيرة، تجلى فيها جمال الفن، فامتزجت بأجزاء النفس، لخير من المئات من أمثال تلك السلع التافهة، التي يتاجر بها بعض المشعوذين، ممن ضاقت بهم وسائل الكسب، فلجأوا إلى هذه الصناعة، وبئس ما عملوا . .

ولا شك أن قيمة الرواية، هي في ما تتضمنه من الفائدة، وتتوخّاه من العبرة. وقيمة الكاتب الروائي، هي في ما يمثله للقارئ من الحقائق، بالأسلوب الفني الشائق.

وقد ظهرت الرواية في الشرق بالصورة التي نعرفها الآن، منذ عهد غير طويل، وكان أكثر ما ظهر من هذا النوع منقولاً عن اللغات الغربية، وأقبل أدباؤنا على الترجمة إقبالاً عجيباً، ولم يتصدَّ للتأليف، وخصوصاً تأليف الروايات الكبيرة، إلا النفر القليل. وقد أحسن كثيرون باختيار أحاسن روايات نوابغ الإفرنج، ونقلها إلى العربية أحكم نقل. وقد أجادوا وأفادوا، بقدر ما أساء غيرهم بنقل الروايات الركيكة السخيفة، التي تقذف بقرائها في مهاوي الضلال والشر وسائر ضروب المعايب والنقائص.

غير أن الأمة كلما ارتفع شأنها الأدبي وتبسّطت في المدنيّة مالت بطبعها إلى الأنفع والأفضل، وأعرضت عن القبيح والسخيف، وكثر فيها من ينهض لمجاراة أهل الغرب في وضع الروايات الأدبية والوطنية.

ولا يخفى أن الفن الروائي في الغرب طافح بالحسنات، وقد سبقنا الغرب بذلك مراحل كثيرة، ففيه من الروائيين المتفننين مئات وألوف، وهم أساتذة الفن لا جدال. فإذا نقلنا عنهم، أو نزعنا إلى أسلوبهم، فإنما نزيد آدابنا ثروة وجمالاً، ونزيد كتّابنا أسلوباً وإطلاعاً وفناً. ولكن لنراقب الله في كل ما ننقل أو نؤلّف، ولنَسِر بالفن الروائي إلى الأمام، إلى الكمال، ولا نقدّم إلى الأمة إلا أفضل ما يقدّم من هذا الغذاء الروحي الطيب.

هذا ما أردت أن أقوله في تعريف «الرواية» توطئةً للإشارة إلى هذا الكتاب—«مسارح الأذهان»—الذي أقدّمه الآن إلى الجمهور الكريم، وكله فصول روائية فنية، ليس منها إلا ما يتضمن أدباً أو عبرة أو ضرباً من ضروب الحكمة والتثقيف.

وقد قدّمته إلى حضرة الأستاذ الفاضل والصديق الكريم إلياس أفندي أنطون إلياس صاحب المطبعة العصرية في مصر، وكان قد نشر هذه الأيام، وقلمه وأقلام غيره من الكتّاب والأدباء، طائفة صالحة من المطبوعات الجميلة التي لا تجارى، وأعلم عزمه على متابعة نشر كل ما يتوسم فيه الفائدة والنفع للجمهور. وهي لعمر الحق خطوة جميلة جداً في سبيل خدمة الأدب والفن في الشرق، لا يستطيع إتيانها وإتقانها، إلا من أوتي ما أوتيه الأستاذ إلياس، من قوة الإرادة والهمة العالية، وموهبة الإجادة والإبداع، والبذل الكثير في سبيل العلم والعرفان.

وفي مأمولي أن الأستاذ بعد أن يطّلع عليه، سيبرزه في أجمل شكل فني، شأنه في كل ما يتولى أمره من المطبوعات، التي يُشكر عليها أجمل شكر. كما أن في مأمولي كذلك أن يكون هذا الكتاب غذاء نافعاً للنفوس، حرياً بالإقبال عليه، وبالله التوفيق.

خليل بيدس
القدس في ١ مايو (أيار) سنة ١٩٢٤

Zin al-'Abdin al-Sanusi
(1899–1965)

Introduced and translated by William Granara

Zin al-'Abdin al-Sanusi was a prominent figure in the *Nahda* movement in Tunisia in the first half of the twentieth century. Like most Arab *Nahda* writers, he was a polymath, working primarily in journalism but writing on history, literature, and politics as well. He authored, in addition to hundreds of articles and essays, several historical biographies, a number of short stories, a play, and a novel. In tune with the spirit of the *Nahda*, al-Sanusi espoused the ideals of political (read: anticolonial), social, and cultural reform; secular modernity; and the creation of a socially committed national Arabic literature.

In Tunisia, unlike in Syria and Egypt, the question of secularism, particularly in binary opposition to religion, was less pronounced. First, Tunisia did not have the highly influential Christian intelligentsia that asserted itself at the forefront of the *Nahda* movement in the eastern Arab world, rendering the role of Islam in society a question of acute sensitivity in national debates. Second, Islam, as the bête noire of French colonial criticism of Arab backwardness, remained a formidable weapon for Tunisians' struggle against European imperial hegemony. Al-Sanusi, like other Tunisian and North African intellectuals of the time, saw Islam as a vital component of national identity but one they felt free to criticize in its more antiquated manifestations, such as the old-guard turbaned clerics who were often parodied as obstacles in the way of progress.

The following selections are part of the introduction that al-Sanusi wrote to the second volume of poetry published by Tunisia's national poet Muhammad al-Shadhili Khaznahdar. Al-Sanusi's comments barely address Khaznahdar and his

poetry, giving instead his own views of (secular) modernity
and the role of the artist-intellectual in society. What we see is
a view of the past with an eye on the present to explicate the
dynamic process of development in the history of Arabic lit-
erature, a hallmark of the modern Arab *Nahda*. More interest-
ingly, we see al-Sanusi staking a relatively conservative position,
unlike many of his Tunisian contemporaries, who were more
radical than he, on the ways and means of modernity. This con-
servatism is reflected especially in his snobbish and dismissive
view of jazz music. Nonetheless, he argues persuasively for
renovation (reform) of Arabic literature and the arts to keep
pace with social and political developments.

Recommended Reading

Granara, William. "Modern Tunisian Literature." *EI* (*Encyclopedia of
Islam*), vol. 10, Brill, 1999, pp. 660–62.
———. "Picaresque Narratives and Cultural Dissimulation in Colonial
North African Literature." *Arab Studies Journal*, vol. 11, no. 2–vol. 12,
no. 1, 2003–04, pp. 41–56.
Mosbahi, Hassouna. "Outstanding Figures in Twentieth-Century Tuni-
sian Culture." *Banipal*, vol. 39, 2010, pp. 40–43.
Omri, Mohamad-Salah. "History, Literature, and Settler Colonialism in
North Africa." *MLQ*, vol. 66, 2005, pp. 3273–98.
Perkins, Kenneth J. *A History of Modern Tunisia*. Cambridge UP, 2004.

Fashioning and Modernizing
Arabic Literature

Islam under the Arabs succeeded in fashioning a common lan-
guage and literature among all its adherents, and so the Arab
who travels to Egypt, Tunisia, Algeria, and even Morocco does
not find himself to be a stranger. Moreover, even a Muslim

who penetrates the furthest reaches of India is not deprived of brethren to speak with or pages to read in his own venerable language. However, nature has often combated this civilizational unity, especially in the case of literature. Classical Arabic has been kept at a distance from the theater and excluded from music and singing and has thus been replaced [in these arts] by vernacular Arabic. Undoubtedly, this is the result of the intensive restraints placed on Arabic literature that held the language back from keeping pace with the progress of the world, in literature and materially. It is not the place of language to keep pace with the times. What matters is that the development of rhetoric and belles lettres be in tune with current trends.

If we look more closely, we realize that literature rests on two pillars and is composed of two essential elements: verbal expression and meaning. The subject matter [in literature] is not an issue of great contention. Arab literary scholars, even in dividing poetic genres into praise and elegy, never said that literature should end with these [two] genres, nor did they say that it could not extend to prose fiction, for example, which incidentally has become one of the most important literary genres in other "awakening" nations such as ours. Be that as it may, we must create for ourselves what we lack in literary genres and engage more extensively in what is appropriate to the present circumstances.

Lyrical Rhetoric

Verbal expression is to meaning as the face is to the soul of a young woman. No matter how pure and noble she is, she must have [external] beauty and the proper cosmetics to attract people's attention to her inner beauty and true perfection.

The beauty of expression and its rhetorical eloquence depend upon several things:

(i) The musicality of expression: Dissonance among letters is abhorred, while its opposite, that is, harmony, is preferred.

On this point we should be aware that the musicality of expression, which is a vital element in the art of literary creation, together with the judgment of it, is a matter that cannot be determined with exactitude or subjected to firmly established rules. Many a hackneyed phrase, an unsteady word, or a disagreeable axiom was given prominent stature by those who knew how to use them and lift them from their common usage. The same thing happened for many words and phrases that the ancients considered a sign of rhetorical eloquence and purity, which occupied everyone's tongues and pens until this took away their splendor and wore out their novelty. Then good taste turned against them and men of letters refrained from using them.

(ii) The musicality of sentences: The most important manifestations of this are assonance in all its various kinds, and that the construction of the sentence reveals in its coherence and organization both emotion and thought. However, any appearance therein of artificiality reverses the result. He whose spirit is uncompliant and talent unready and so studies the rules laid down by the ancients to teach rhetoric is led astray by them because they [the ancients] reckoned that the arts could be grasped by an absolute mastery of rules alone. They led their disciples into error for centuries. By God, anyone who now reads the many volumes of prose and poetry penned by great writers from the time when the science of rhetoric was first established until the most recent decades of this century encounters an odd situation. Namely, he finds the existence of an inordinate number of verbal maneuvers intricately connected to the science of rhetoric that do not engender in the reader any emotion or present him with any exciting image, although these maneuvers do clearly demonstrate mastery of the lesson and an exerted effort to copy the models of it.

(iii) The musicality of composition: They [the ancients] liked rhymed prose, and they venerated poetry as the highest form of literature for the meter and harmony of its words as well as its rhyme scheme. To all this the Andalusians [the Muslims of medieval Spain] added new sections to the existing sixteen meters, and now contemporary poets have begun to change the rhyme structure altogether. There is nothing wrong with this as long as there is nothing in it that is incompatible with poetic unity, which has been the ultimate objective in establishing rules and compiling anthologies.

And what could possibly mar the unity of the following verses by Ibn Zuhr from his strophic poem [*muwashshaha*]:

What's with the infatuated lover
   who like a drunkard
      does not recuperate from his intoxication?
Our days and nights
   spent by the canal
      can they be recalled?
Since the musk of Darin
   takes great benefit
      from the fragrant breezes
And the beauty of the splendid place
   no sooner
      revitalizes us
A river, exquisitely elegant
   over which a graceful tree
      provides shade
Water flows
   [with] one floating and one drowned
      in the harvest of sweet basil

Ibn Zuhr depicts his longing for this gentle landscape and visualizes it most realistically, immortalizing it for future generations by way of a lively image of the gentility of the age and its refined sentiments toward an invigorating natural beauty. When we read him today, his meaning becomes clear in the fluidity of these lines—*and the beauty of the splendid place no sooner revitalizes us*—even though the passage of time has dulled the splendor of the image, for the taste of this generation has moved away from Andalusian music and singing. But this is inevitable for every society. It is in the very nature of art to transform tirelessly, since taste, by its own nature, seeks out novelty and is itself always inclined to change.

Take European music, for example. After having been cultivated by the refinement of Germanic classical music, European music has been abruptly turned upside down in the aftermath of the Great War [World War I], with Afro-Americans taking over the grand music halls with their jazz bands and raucous beats, which presently exhaust the dancers with their non-stop pounding rhythms. Many critics have called on society to resist this savage hubbub, which has taken the place of true art, to the detriment [of society]. Dancing has become nothing more than spastic convulsions that allow male and female bodies to come into contact!

We can also give examples of shifting tastes in the pictorial arts. Beauty in painting, photography, and fashion was once to be found in the harmony and similarity of shades and colors, so that even when these differed from each other, they changed in concert a little bit at a time so that they remained to the eye free of discord.

The situation is totally the reverse today. Drapery and furniture, which were formerly crafted in pale shades, have become no less colorful than the flag of the state of Sharif Hussein,[1] with its chalky white, blood red, chrysolite green, and charcoal black. The necktie, which for many years was either black or white, today adopts the seven different colors of the rainbow, which clash in a display of stunning foolishness. Indeed, women's cosmetics have also taken this bizarre turn; the young woman who doesn't paint her lips to look like a flaming triangle, who doesn't circle her eyes with greenish-blue halos, and who doesn't dress from head to toe in five discordant colors that make her look like a tropical bird decked out in every shade and hue found in nature will not be considered to have good taste, because she fails to conform to the new standards. Whether we are right or wrong in our judgment of this new wave, its current is so torrential that no nation, even one with a hundred million [citizens], can protect itself against it. For if taste is a species of emotion that has learned how to use reason, then we cannot make reason or logic sovereign over it.

As we stated above, we see no benefit in trying to suppress people's defiant love of development and change in poetic meters and in music, whether in pattern or in rhyme. But we take note that this development should happen naturally and not through the adopting of genres that are abnormal or idiosyncratic. Such development is inevitable, especially as the number of theaters increases and the use of Arabic becomes widespread in them. There is no stopping this development, whether a legal dictum were to decree its ban or conservatives were to announce its prohibition.

However, we can find hardly anyone who does not believe that the removal of excessive fetters helps talent flourish, whose current might otherwise be halted by the futile pressure of rules and laws. I've read much of the poetry of Safi al-Din al-Hilli and admired its subtlety and grace, but I've never seen a classical ode [qasida] of his that can compare with the strophic poem [muwashshaha] of his that begins:

The bosom of night splits from the throat of morning
    O cupbearers,
Soft raindrops falling on the petals of chamomile blossoms
    are hidden pearls,
Inviting us to the sweetness of waking up in the morning
    It is good fortune,
The spigot on the neck of the wine jug changes hue
    from the darkness of the vine-branch's blood,

The black-eyed beauties of the garden imbibe its blood-red wine,
　　from bowls of reddish brown,
Give me to drink a liquor that fills goblets to the brim
　　with the brilliance of light,
[So that] the mind is laid to rest and the soul is resuscitated
　　by the comfort of secrets,
A daughter of the vine ages with the Magi
　　in the temples of fire,
Cultivating its vine among the singing girls
　　was the hand of Plato himself!

Has the shift in rhyme scheme and the change in meter from the classical Arabic tradition disturbed the bewitching imagery and language here? In the new meters, there are poems that are no less powerful in spirit and language, most of which I cannot recall at the moment but are nonetheless in wide circulation and easy enough to review for those who wish to do so.

If development within this type of literature is happening today, and indeed happened even in the past, then this will be especially true in the future, when Arabic will circulate widely among the masses thanks to the modern media, compulsory education, and the increasing distribution of newspapers, things that were not available to our forefathers.

Semantic Rhetoric

This [semantic rhetoric] is the more important of the two fields of rhetoric because it is intimately tied to the spirit and ultimate goal of rhetoric and perhaps to rhetoric's most vital element, the ideal that governs the poet's intellect. Layla and her beloved madman, and Khawarnaq and Sadeer, the two palaces of the Lakhmid king Nu'man ibn Mundhir, represent [respectively] the ideal models of love and architectural grandeur in all of Arabic poetry, to which poets elevate their descriptions in praise and veneration. This is in spite of the fact that they [the poets] have not been affected by them except by way of inherited literary tradition. This inheritance is necessary, inasmuch as we find its influence in all languages. However, what is absurd in all this is to make the appearance of these models the condition for poetry being "proper Arabic" now in the fourteenth century [AH]. It would behoove us to unburden ourselves of the nightmare of the past and look toward the lofty examples that surround us today and that suffice to allow us to forget the camels and cooking stones of the ancient Arabs. It is strange that we cohabit with the ruins of Carthage and the amphitheater of El Djem, whose greatness has been left untouched by the hands of time, and yet you find hardly any mention of them, nor have they become the model for architecture among the Tunisians. There is therefore no doubt that the modern Renaissance [*Nahda*] has made significant progress in breaking new ground for contemporary themes that are in harmony with the spirit of the new century. The eminent poet whose anthology we introduce here, Muhammad al-Shadhili Khaznahdar, stands at the forefront of those who are guiding the way. A great deal of his poetry, especially that composed after World War I, is about social and literary subjects relevant to the ongoing developments we are beholding. With this poetry, he has rendered a great service to literature and helped with its diffusion by tapping into the spirit of the people and touching them emotionally, and because of him we aspire to greater freedom and to an intellectual independence that will in no way harm the unity of literature. Thus, the spirit of literature has a chance to keep pace with the times while remaining both free and uplifting.

Note

[1]Hussein bin Ali was the grand sharif of Mecca and king of the Hejaz region (r. 1916–24), who led the Arabs in revolt against the Ottoman Empire during World War I.

Source of Arabic Text on Which the Translation Is Based

Al-Sanusi, Zin al-'Abdin. Introduction to the first edition. ديوان محمد الشاذلي خزنه دار [diwan muhammad al-shadhili khaznahdar; Poetry Collection of Muhammad al-Shadhili Khaznahdar]. Al-Dar al-Tunisiyya lil-Nashr, 1972, pp. 15–19.

زين العابدين السنوسي
(١٨٩٩-١٩٦٥)

تكون الأدب العربي ووجوب تطوره

فالإسلام قد نجح على أيدي العرب في تكوين لغة وأدب عام بين عموم أتباعه فالعربي الذي يسافر إلى مصر أو تونس أو الجزائر وحتى المغرب لا يجد نفسه غريباً بل أن المتغلغل في أقصى الهند لا يكاد يعدم إخواناً وصحفاً يقرأها بلغته الكريمة إلا أن الطبيعة كانت تغالب تلك الوحدة المدنية خصوصاً في شخص الأدب فقد ابتعدت العربية الفصحى عن المسارح وأقصيت عن الموسيقى والغناء حيث حلت العامية مكانها. ولا شك أن ذلك نتيجة شدة القيود التي وضعت في الأدب العربي مع الوقوف باللغة عن مسايرة التطور العالمي مادياً وأدبياً. فأما مسايرة اللغة للتيار فهذا ليس محله وأما تطور البلاغة والآداب بما يناسب العصر ويماشي التيار العالمي فإننا إذا دققنا النظر عرفنا أن الأدب يقوم على دعامتين ويتألف من عنصرين هما: ١) اللفظ و٢) المعنى.

أما الموضوع فليس محل إشكال كبير لأن الأدباء العرب وإن قسموا أبواب الشعر إلى رثاء ومديح . . . إلا أنهم لم يقولوا بوقوف الأدب عند حد تلك الأبواب وعدم تعديه إلى القصة—مثلاً—التي أصبحت من أهم أقسام الأدب عند غيرنا من الأمم الناهضة. وعلى ذلك فما علينا إلا تجديد ما ينقصنا من أقسام الأدب وطرقها والتوسع في ما يناسب الحال من الموجودات.

«البلاغة اللفظية»

اللفظ بالنسبة للمعنى كالوجه بالنسبة لروح الفتاة فمهما كانت طاهرة شريفة لا بد لها من الجمال والتدمية (التجمل بما يحسن البشرة والوجه) لتستلفت الأنظار إلى جمالها النفسي وكمالها الحقيقي.

والجمال اللفظي أو بلاغته تعتمد على أشياء، من:

أ) موسيقية اللفظ. فبغضوا تنافر الحروف واستحسنوا عكسه—وهنا—لا بد أن نتنبه إلى أن موسيقى الألفاظ (التي هي العنصر المهم لفن البديع)

والحكم عليها أمر لا يطرد بدقة ولا ينعكس ولا يمكن أن يضبط بقواعد حقيقية. فرب تركيب مبتذل أو كلمة مقلقلة أو وضعية متنافرة اتيحت لها شخصية بارزة عرفت كيف تستعملها فرفعتها عن مستواها وأعطتها المقام الأسمى. كما أن كثيراً من الألفاظ والتراكيب التي عرفها الأقدمون بأنها مظهر البلاغة والجزالة قد لاكتها الألسن وثنتها الأقلام بما ذهب ببهجتها وأخلق جدتها. فأصبحت تنبو عنها الأذواق السلمية ويتنزه عنها الأديب.

ب) موسيقية الجمل. وأهم مظاهرها الجناس بأنواعها وأن يكون التركيب يشف بنسجه وتنظيمه عن العاطفة وخالجة الضمير. على أن ظهور التصنع في ذلك مما يعكس النتيجة فالذي لم تُلِن روحه ولم تستعد قريحته ثم درس القواعد التي وضعها الأقدمون لتعليم البلاغة ضلة منهم إذ حسبوا أن الفنون يمكن تحصيلها باتقان القواعد وشد ناصيتها فأضلوا اتباعهم حقبة طويلة ولعمرك فأن من يطالع أكثر دواوين الكتاب ورسائلهم منذ ما أحكم هذا العلم (البلاغة!) إلى حدود هذا القرن يجد حالاً غريبة فهي مجموعة هائلة من التمارين المتشابكة على علم البلاغة لا تولد في قارئها عاطفة ولا تصور له منظراً مستفزاً، وإن أبانت على اتقان للدرس وعمل مجهد للانطباع على تلك القوالب.

ج) موسيقية التركيب. فحببوا السجع لما فيه من ترنيمة القافية ثم اعتبروا الشعر المظهر الأسمى للأدب لما أختص به من اتّزان الكلمات وتناسقها وترجيعة القافية وعلى ذلك توسع الأندلسيون في زيادة أقسام جديدة لأبحر الشعر الستة عشر، وأخذ المعاصرون في تغيير نظام القافية. وهو عمل لا بأس به إذ لا منافاة فيه لمرمي الوحدة التي هي الغاية المعقولة لوضع القواعد وتدوين التأليف.

وماذا عسى يكدر هاته الوحدة من قول ابن زهر في موشحه:

ما للموله	من سكره لا يفيق	ياله سكران
هل تستعاد	أيامنا بالخليج	وليالينا
إذ يستفاد	من النسيم الأريج	مسك دارينا
وإذ يكاد	حسن المكان البهيج	أن يحيينا
نهر أظله	دوح عليه أنيق	مونق فينان
والماء يجري	وعائم وغريق	من جنى الريحان

فلقد صور لهفته على ذلك المناخ العليل وزوّقها أوقع تزويق بما خلد لجميع الأجيال صورة حية لرقة طباع عصره ومبلغ دقة شعورهم بجمال الطبيعة المنعشة حتى أننا إذا قرأناه اليوم هب عنا وتجلي في سلاسته

إذ يكاد   حسن المكان البهيج   أن يحيينا

نعم أن مرور الزمن أثر في بهجته من حيث ابتعاد ذوق هذا الجيل عن الموسيقى والأنغام الأندلسية إلا أن ذلك أمر ضروري لكل مجتمع والفن دائب التحول بطبيعته لأن الأذواق تستبدع الطريف بطبيعتها وتميل إلى التحول على أي حال.

خُذ لذلك مثلاً الموسيقى الأوروبية فإنها بعد أن تغلغلت في الرقة على المنهاج الألماني انقلبت بعد الحرب فجأة فإذا زنوج أمريكا يرأسون حفلات القصور الكبيرة ويضربون (الجزباند) بنغماتها الخشنة التي لا تلبث أن تنهك قوى الراقصين بهزاتها المتواترة المتتابعة وقد كتب الكتاب كثيراً لردع المجتمع عن هذا «الصخب الوحشي الذي حل مكان الفن الرقيق فجر معه فناً آخر للتدهور إذ أصبح الرقص أيضاً تشنجات عصبية يلتصق في أثنائها (الجنس الخشن) بجسوم الجنس اللطيف المتجرد!»

بل يمكننا أن نمثل أيضاً لتبدل الذوق بمناظر الدهان فقد كان جمال الرياش والتصوير واللبوس في تناسب الألوان وتماثلها حتى إذا قضى عنها بالتغاير تغايرت في انسجام شيئاً فشيئاً منظور فيها إلى عدم التنافر. فأصبحت اليوم على العكس من ذلك تماماً فالستائر والأثاث التي كانت في ألوان محتشمة أصبحت لا تقل تلوناً عن علم دولة الشريف حسين فيها الأبيض (اليقق) والأحمر (القاني) والأخضر (الزبرجدي) والأسود (الفاحم) وربطة الياقة التي كانت في السنين الفائتة أما سوداء أو بيضاء. أصبحت اليوم كقوس قزح فيها سبعة ألوان متضاربة في رقاعة (بهيجة) بل أن نفس تدمية الوجه وتحسينه قد سارت في هذا المهيع الغريب فالفتاة التي لا تصور من فمها مثلثاً ملتهباً قائم الإضلاع ولا تحيق بعينيها هالة من الزرقة المخضرة ولا تلبس من بين معقد زرها إلى ركبتيها خمسة ألوان متنافرة حتى تصبح أشبه بطيور المنطقة الحارة، فيها جميع ألوان الطبيعة وأشكالها، أن الفتاة التي لا تسلك هذا الطريق اليوم لا تعد من صاحبات الذوق.

وسواء حكمنا بصواب هذا الطور أو خطئه فإن تياره جارف لا يمكن وقاية أمة تعد المئة مليون منه. فإذا الذوق عنصر من عناصر العاطفة وهو عنصر تعلم استخدام العقل فلا يمكن لنا أن نجعل من العقل والمنطق سلطاناً عليه.

إننا كما أسلفنا لا نرى فائدة من محاولة كبح الجماح لعاطفة التطور في الأوزان والموسيقى لا وزناً ولا قافية. لكننا نلاحظ أن ذلك التطور يجب أن يكون طبيعياً لا من نوع التعليق بالشذوذ والتفرد. وهو لا بد واقع خصوصاً إذا كثرت المسارح وراجت فيها العربية فإذاك يصبح التطور ضربة لازب سواء صدرت فيه فتوى الإباحة أو أعلن حرمته المحافظون.

على أننا لا نكاد نجد من لا يعتقد أن إسقاط القيود الزائدة مساعد على استثمار مواهب قد يوقف تيارها ذلك الإرهاق الذي لا طائل تحته من القواعد والقوانين. ولقد قرأت كثيراً من أشعار صفي الدين الحلي فعجبت برقته وانسجامه إلا إني لم أرَ له قصيداً مدرسياً (Classique) يضارع موشحه الذي مطلعه.

أيها الساقون	شق جيب الليل عن نحر الصاح
لؤلؤ مكنون	وبدا للطل في جيد الإقاح
طائر ميمون	ودعانا للذيذ الاصطباح
بدم الجرزون	فأخضب المبزل في نحر الدنان
في صحاف جون	تتلقى دمها حور الجنان
بسناء النور	فاسقنيها قهوة تكسو الكؤوس
راحة الأسرار	وتميت العقل إذ تحيي النفوس
في بيوت النار	بنت كرم عتقت عند المجوس
يد أفلاطون!	غرست كرمتها بين القيان

فهل كدر خيالها ولغتها الجميلين تغاير القافية وخروج الوزن عن أنغام قحطان! وفي الأوزان الجديدة قصائد لا تقل عن هاته روحاً ولغة لم تحضرني الآن على أنها متداولة فلا يصعب مراجعتها على الراغبين.

فالتطور إذاً واقع الآن ومن قبل في هذا القسم من الأدب، وهو حيوي بالنسبة للمستقبل خصوصاً متى ازداد روجان العربية بين العموم بفضل الوسائل الحديثة من التعليم الإجباري وروجان الصحف ... مما لم يكن موفوراً للأوائل.

«البلاغة المعنوية»

هي أهم قسمي البلاغة لأنها تتعلق بروحها وغايتها ولعل عنصرها الأهم
المثل الأعلى المسيطر على عقلية الشاعر. فليلى ومجنونها. والخورنق والسدير
قصري النعمان بن المنذر أمثال عليا للحب والضخامة المعمارية في الأدب
العربي يرفع إليها الشعراء موصوفاتهم تعظيماً وتبجيلاً رغم عدم تأثرهم بها
تأثراً حقيقياً اللهم إلا تأثراً تقليدياً متوارثاً عن الكتب. نعم! هذا المتوارث لا
بد منه بحيث نجد أثره في جميع اللغات إلا إن الفاحش في المسألة هو أن
يشترط ورود أمثال تلك القوالب ليصبح الشعر «عربياً جزلاً» في القرن الرابع
عشر فحرى بنا أن نخفف من كابوس الماضي عنا ونلتفت لما يحيط بنا من
أمثال عليا فيها اليوم ما يكفي بل ما ينسينا قلصان العرب وأثافيهم. وأنه لمن
الغريب الفاحش أن نساكن أطلال «قرطاجنة» ومسرح «الجم» الذي لم تعمل
في عظمته أيدي السنين ومع ذلك لا تكاد تجد له ذكراً فضلاً عن أن يصبح مثلاً
للمعمار عند التونسيين ولا شك أن النهضة الحديثة قد سارت شوطاً حسناً
في طرق الموضوعات العصرية والملائمة لنفسية الجيل. وحضرة شاعرنا صاحب
الديوان الأستاذ محمد الشاذلي خزنه دار من أمة وهداة هذا الطريق فأكثر
أشعاره خصوصاً بعد الحرب في المواضيع الاجتماعية والأدبيات الملائمة للتطور
الحاضر وهو بمحاذاته تلك أيد نصراء الأدب فازداد الأدب انتشاراً إذ أصبح
ألصق بروح القوم وأقرب من نفوسهم الأمر الذي نؤمل معه زيادة التحرر مع
تنمي روح الاستقلال الفكري الذي لا يضر بالوحدة الأدبية وعندما يتاح لروح
الأدب أن تماشى العصر حرة رشيدة.

زين العابدين السنوسي

Part 5: Novels and Novellas

Starting with Butrus al-Bustani and his son Salim's journals *al-Jinan* ("Gardens") and *al-Zahra* ("The Flower"), this part both draws on and interrogates the theories of literature and culture presented in part 4. Short stories and novel excerpts present literature as an aesthetic model engaged in challenging and rethinking gender, political, and social norms rather than merely reflecting them. These texts illustrate an interaction between vice and morality that could not be explained through the civilizing task of literature that some theorists were discussing in the Arab world, Europe, and beyond during that time. They also illustrate many different interpretations about what literature is and how it affects the reading public.

In an editorial, Butrus tells what he deems publishable, from serialized novels to historical and scientific articles, and Salim calls for readers to renew their subscriptions.

The entry from *al-Zahra* is about a man believing a story he had heard performed (told) in a local café, which calls attention to the role of literature in shaping *Nahda* sensitivities.

The novella entitled *Henry and Amelia*, written by Butrus's daughter Adelaide and serialized in *al-Jinan*, depicts romantic love and expresses the ethical and aesthetic ideals that *Nahda* literature is meant to embody. Though good triumphs at the end, this selection unsettles gender categories through cross-dressing, casting reality and appearance as complementary structures in fiction.

In Zaynab Fawwaz's tragic story about a girl who loves a younger man and refuses to marry anyone but him, the power of attachment triumphs over social norms. But this comes at a great price for the individual who stays true to his or her desire.

In *Hasanat al-Hubb* ("The Virtues of Love"), Labiba Hashim presents a suspenseful story about a nun who has allegedly "lost her way" and seeks shelter with an affluent family. When night falls, the story takes a dramatic turn, exposing what is hidden under the cloak of darkness—and that of the nun.

Set in India, *Fi Sabil al-Zawaj* ("For the Sake of Marriage"), by Mahmud Ahmad al-Sayyid, an author from Iraq, picks up the theme of romantic love seeking to triumph against all odds. This excerpt includes a preface on the Iraqi literary *Nahda* and provides, along with the works of the al-Bustanis, Fawwaz, and Hashim, a clear exposé of the complex linguistic, cultural, and political relations that shaped modern Arabic literature at the end of the nineteenth and the beginning of the twentieth century.

al-Jinan and al-Zahra
(1870)

Introduced and translated by Elizabeth M. Holt

Residents of Beirut in the 1860s witnessed the beginning of what would become a burgeoning print industry. *Hadiqat al-Akhbar* ("The Garden of News"), the only locally produced newspaper, maintained close ties to the Ottoman government, relating political and mercantile updates from the region and abroad, while also serializing the fiction of its editor, Khalil al-Khuri. Later that decade, Yusuf al-Shalfun published the short-lived *al-Shiraka al-Shahriyya* ("The Monthly Company") and *Majmu'at al-'Ulum* ("The Collection of Knowledge"), a semi-regular publication of lectures and odes delivered at al-Jam'iyya al-'Ilmiyya al-Suriyya (Syrian Scientific Society, established in 1868). The year 1870 was pivotal for periodical production in Beirut, and this part of the volume presents selections from the al-Bustani family's new journal *al-Jinan* ("The Gardens") and al-Shalfun's short-lived literary project, the 1870 satirical journal *al-Zahra* ("The Flower").

Recommended Reading

Ayalon, Ami. *The Arabic Print Revolution: Cultural Production and Mass Readership*. Cambridge UP, 2016.
———. *The Press in the Arab Middle East: A History*. Oxford UP, 1995.
Hanssen, Jens. *Fin-de-Siècle Beirut*. Oxford UP, 2005.
Holt, Elizabeth M. *Fictitious Capital: Silk, Cotton, and the Rise of the Arabic Novel*. Fordham UP, 2017.
———. "From Gardens of Knowledge to Ezbekiyya after Midnight: The Novel and the Arabic Press from Beirut to Cairo, 1870–1892." *Authoring the Nahda: Writing the Arabic Nineteenth Century*, special issue of *Middle Eastern Literatures*, vol. 16, no. 3, 2013, pp. 232–48.

————. "Narrative and the Reading Public in 1870s Beirut." *Journal of Arabic Literature*, vol. 40, no. 1, 2009, pp. 37–70.

Sheehi, Stephen. *Foundations of Modern Arab Identity*. U of Florida P, 2004.

Announcements and Anecdotes

The following announcement was written by Butrus al-Bustani in Beirut toward the end of 1869 and reprinted in *al-Jinan*'s first issue. It informed readers of Arabic of a new variety journal entitled *The Gardens*, to be published beginning in January 1870 by Butrus and his son Salim. In the following years, al-Bustani and his son continued garden-themed newspapers, with *al-Janna* ("The Garden") and *al-Junayna* ("The Small Garden"), in which they reported on current events and listed commodity prices. This announcement was an augury of the early 1870s boom in Beirut periodicals printed on private presses, around which emerged a newly forming reading public of Arabic.

Al-Jinan: *Announcement 1*

The presence of several Arabic-language gazettes publishing news and local and foreign happenings has greatly facilitated the work of those overseeing important matters; our language, however, remains without its own great medium to disseminate general knowledge, whether scientific, literary, historical, industrial, commercial, or civil, in addition to literary pieces and anecdotes, as takes place in foreign countries. The benefits [this would bring] to all are evident in its being a means to encourage the spread of general knowledge and strengthen its foundations among the public [and to encourage] exchanges between peoples and the revitalization and improvement of the language, and through [that revitalization] the preservation of accord between the people and supporters of nationalist elements. Among those gates, a gate is [now] opened to the possessors of knowledge, and a space in which the pen of the skillful might circulate.

Given what we have seen in terms of the preparation and inclination of speakers of the noble Arabic language, both compatriots and foreigners, toward attaining such a means, while at the same time keeping in mind the needs of our language and our compatriots, we have decided to place our trust in the Almighty as we aim to reach the intended goal by establishing an Arabic-language newspaper entitled *al-Jinan* (the plural of *janna* ["gardens"]), which will encompass the stated benefits from our pen as well as the pens of those who wish to present us with valuable selections—original or translated—in the aforementioned fields.

Al-Jinan will be published in installments distributed to subscribers periodically, with twenty-four installments per year and an installment coming out at least every fifteen days. Installments will be sent directly to subscribers free of charge, and we will include at the end of the final installment of each year an index of what it contains and what materials the rest of the sections have contained, such that at the end of the year the installments together make up a single book.

We do not need to announce to subscribers that every beginning is difficult, but *al-Jinan* will strive to bring about improvement and success and to broaden the scope of its concerns with time. We should hardly need to urge writers to present us with what they have in the way of useful lessons.

———Butrus al-Bustani

The following anecdote was published in the short-lived weekly satirical journal *al-Zahra* in Beirut in the fall of 1870, in its thirty-fifth issue. *Al-Zahra* printed humorous stories, jokes, and each week an installment of the novel *al-Shabb al-Maghrur* ("The Conceited Youth"), by its editor, Yusuf al-Shalfun. This anecdote evokes the popular narrative heritage with which the serialized Arabic novels of this period both resonated and competed.

Al-Zahra: *Anecdote*

It is told that a man of the people of Homs became obsessed with 'Antar b. Shaddad, and so every night he would go to the storyteller's circle to hear a portion of his story. One night he stayed late in his shop, until after sunset, and so went without dinner. That night was the battle of 'Antar and Kasri, and the storyteller read up to the point where 'Antar falls captive to the Persians. They captured him and shackled his legs. And there [the storyteller] stopped talking, and the people dispersed. The man was totally overcome, and the world turned black before his eyes. He went home depressed and sad, and his wife offered him food. He kicked the table, and the dishes broke, and everything that was in them spilled all over the furnishings of the house, and he cursed the woman quite fiercely. She castigated him, so he beat her severely. He went out wandering in the markets not knowing what to do. The circumstances overwhelmed him, and he went to the home of the storyteller, where he found him asleep, and so he woke him and said to him, "You have put the man in prison and shackled his legs and [then] you come home to sleep with peace of mind. I beg you to finish this scene until you get him out of prison, for I am not able to sleep. My life will only get worse if this situation continues. What do you collect from the audience in a night? I will give that amount to you now." So the storyteller took the book and read the rest of the scene to him until 'Antar got out of prison. Then the man said to him, "May God make you glad and relax your mind now, for my spirit has recovered, so take this money because to you the credit is due." Then he happily left for home. [When he got there,] he asked for food and apologized to his wife, [saying that] the storyteller had put 'Antar in shackles when she was bringing him food to eat. So how could he eat while 'Antar was captured and in shackles? He said, "But now I have gone to the storyteller's home, and he read me the remainder of the tale so that I could get 'Antar out of prison. Praise be to God! My spirit has recovered, so forgive me for behaving rashly, and give me that food you have."

Next is an announcement from one of the last issues of *al-Jinan*'s first year. This variety journal proved to be one of the most successful Arabic periodicals in the city's early-1870s boom in Arabic journals and newspapers. Salim was *al-Jinan*'s most prolific author of serialized novels and short stories, and he wrote regular social and political commentary. The journal published the work of a number of other writers, featuring fiction, essays, histories, and updates on local and European news. *Al-Jinan* continued publication until the mid-1880s, when the journal proved unable to weather the death of Butrus in 1883 and a year later of Salim.

Al-Jinan: *Announcement 2*

It is by His great might and the protection of those overseeing important matters that *al-Jinan*'s first year nears its end. We have attained much more than we had foreseen in terms of achievement and success, and that is the greatest proof of the progress of the Arab nation under the protection of the [Ottoman] High State, ever advancing in the stages of civilization and knowledge. Many have entered the gardens [*jinan*] of literature and useful news by spending glittering gold and precious time in reading unbiased newspapers and writings based upon the foundations of truth and integrity. Because of that, and because it is evident that those seeking these gardens are many and that the majority of this year's subscribers will be renewing their subscriptions, we have decided to continue to send *al-Jinan* this coming year to all who do not request that we stop doing so. That is to say that we are not requiring those who wish to renew their subscriptions to request that in writing or orally, but rather we are asking those who do not wish to renew their subscriptions to be so kind as to let this be known so that we can stop sending them *al-Jinan*. And we request those who wish to subscribe for the coming year, and who did not subscribe this year, to be so kind as to let that be known before we begin our second year, so that we may be informed as to how many copies to print each time. And finally we ask God the Almighty to grant them health, success, and a long life of many years, for He sees and hears all, and His response is just.

The following coda appeared in the late fall of 1870, at the end of the last installment of al-Shalfun's novel serialized in *al-Zahra, al-Shabb al-Maghrur*. Editors and authors were at pains to please an audience of subscribers and win their ongoing support. While Salim al-Bustani's first novel, *al-Huyam fi Jinan al-Sham* ("Love in the Gardens of Damascus"), was serialized to apparent success that year in *al-Jinan*, al-Shalfun's attempts at penning an Arabic novel appear not to have been in line with the desires of a newly emerging reading public for Arabic narrative. *Al-Zahra*, despite the expressed hope that it might be otherwise, lasted just one year.

Al-Zahra: *Coda*

Given that *al-Shabb al-Maghrur* has come to an end, many have asked that we run next an edifying history in serialized form. So, from this point forward, we will run a history of the war

of the Tubbaʿ kings of Yemen before Islam, excerpted from
the book *Jamharat al-ʿArab* ("The Arab Populace"), as it is likely
to appeal to our esteemed subscribers. Likewise, we pledge to
alter the form of our newspaper at the beginning of the new
year to include useful foreign and local news that will appeal to
the reader, in accordance with what space will allow for, as we
seek to spread general benefits to the public.

The following announcement, appearing beneath the table
of contents in the Beirut-based Jesuit journal *al-Bashir*
("The Omen") in August 1871, was signed by Luwis Sabunji,
a Catholic priest and the former publisher, along with
al-Shalfun, of the weekly variety journal *al-Najah* ("Suc-
cess"). These were the early years of the private Arabic press
in Beirut, and the decisions that Sabunji details here give us
an idea of the many pressures felt by authors and editors as
they negotiated what precisely made for appropriate narra-
tive in the eyes of the newly forming reading public.

Al-Bashir: *Announcement*

We inform our respected audience that starting on the first day
of this present month of August, we completely quit work-
ing on the journal *al-Najah*. We are refraining entirely from
involvement in its publication in order to return to [work on
the journal] *al-Zahra*—claimed to be its mother—which is over-
due. From now on, we will not pen a line or write an article
in *al-Najah*. And we will never publish a political summary in
it as we did previously. And we will not translate the novel
[*The Count of*] *Monte Cristo*, which we had taken upon ourselves
the responsibility of translating from French to Arabic, while
correcting those blunders transgressing religion. In order to
lift all responsibility from ourselves for the journal *al-Najah*,
as well as responsibility for the blunders in the novel [*The Count*

of] *Monte Cristo*—the reading of which is forbidden to all Cath-
olics by Rome due to its excessive crudeness against religion—
we have taken the initiative to issue this announcement, written
the sixteenth of August in the year 1871.

—Father Luwis Sabunji,
former publisher of *al-Najah*, Beirut

Sources of Arabic Texts on Which the Translation Is Based

The text for the first الجنان [al-jinan; The Gardens] announcement is
at *HathiTrust Digital Library*, babel.hathitrust.org/cgi/pt?id=njp.32101
007751447;view=1up;seq=8.

The text for the anecdote about عنتر [ʿantar; "Antar"] is in *al-Zahra*, vol. 1,
no. 35, 1870, pp. 275–76.

The text for the second الجنان [al-jinan; The Gardens] announcement is
in *al-Jinan*, vol. 1, no. 22, 1870, pp. 686–87.

The text for the coda to الشاب المغرور [al-shabb al-maghrur; The Conceited
Youth] is in *al-Zahra*, vol. 1, no. 43, 1870, p. 314.

The text for the البشير [al-bashir; The Omen] announcement is in *al-Bashir*,
vol. 1, no. 51, 19 Aug. 1871, back page.

الجنان والزهرة
(۱۸۷۰)

إعلانات وطرائف

[إعلان من] الجنان

إنه قد تيسر بهمة أولياء الأمور العظام وجود عدة كازتات في اللغة العربية لأجل نشر الأخبار والمجريات الداخلية والخارجية ولم تزل لغتنا معدومة واسطة من الوسائط الكبرى لنشر المعارف العمومية من علمية وأدبية وتاريخية وصناعية وتجارية ومدنية وغير ذلك من النبذ والملح الأدبية مما هو جارٍ في البلدان الأجنبية وقد ظهرت فوائده للخاص والعام لأنه فضلاً عن أنه يكون وسيلة لتنشيط المعارف العمومية وتقوية أركانها بين الجمهور وتبادل ذلك بين قوم وقوم وإحياء اللغة وتحسينها والمحافظة على الاتفاق فيها بين أهلها ومعاضدة ما وُجد من العناصر الوطنية في هذه الأبواب يفتح باباً لأصحاب المعارف وميداناً يجول فيه قلم المهرة من أصحاب القلم.

وبناء على ما نراه من الاستعداد والميل في المتكلمين بلغتنا العربية الشريفة من أبناء وطن وأجانب إلى الحصول على واسطة كهذه طالما جال في خاطرنا شدّة اضطرار لغتنا وأبناء وطننا إليها قد عزمنا بالاتكال على عنايته تعالى على إبراز المقصد المذكور من القوة إلى الفعل بإنشاء جريدة في اللغة العربية تسمّى الجِنان (جمع جَنّة) تحتوي على الفوائد المذكورة من قلمنا وقلم مَن يرغب أن يتحفنا بقطع نفيسة من أصلية ومترجمة في الأبواب المار ذكرها.

ويكون طبع الجنان أجزاءً يصير توزيعها على المشتركين وقتاً فوقتاً بحيث يكون عدد الأجزاء في السنة أربعة وعشرين جزءا من قطع وحرف هذا الجزء بحساب جزء في كل خمسة عشر يوماً على الأقل وترسل الأجزاء رأساً إلى المشتركين خالصة الأجرة وسندرج في آخر الجزء الأخير من كل سنة فهرساً لما تضمه وتضمنته باقي الأجزاء من المواد والمسائل لكي تُجعل الأجزاء في آخر السنة كتاباً واحداً. . . . .

هذا ولا يلزم أن نعلن للمشتركين أن كل ابتداء صعب وأن الجنان سيسعى على قدم التحسين والنجاح وتوسيع دائرة مباحثه مع الوقت. ولا حاجة إلى تنشيط أصحاب القلم أن يتحفونا بما عندهم من الفوائد.

بطرس البستاني

[طرفة من] الزهرة

وحُكي أن رجلاً من أهل حمص كان يتعصب لعنتر بن شداد ويحضر كل ليلة إلى حلقة القصاص يسمع فصلاً من قصته ففي إحدى الليالي تأخّر في حانوته إلى بعد المغرب فحضر إلى هناك بدون عشاء وكان في تلك الليلة سياق حرب عنتر مع كسرى فقرأ القصاص إلى أن وقع عنتر في الأسر عند الفرس فحبسوه ووضعوا القيد في رجله وهناك قطع الكلام وانفضت الناس فدخل على الرجل أمرٌ عظيم واسودت الدنيا في عينيه وذهب كئيباً حزيناً إلى بيته فقدمت له زوجته الطعام فرفس المائدة برجله فتكسرت الصحون واندلق ما فيها على فرش البيت وشتم المرأة شتماً قبيحاً فصادمته في الكلام فضربها ضرباً شديداً. وخرج يدور في الأسواق وهو لا يقر له قرار ثم غلب عليه الحال فذهب إلى بيت القصاص فوجده ناماً فأيقظه وقال له قد وضعت الرجل في السجن مقيداً وأتيت تنام مستريح البال فأرجوك أن تكمل لي هذا السياق إلى أن تخرجه من السجن لأنني لا أقدر أن أنام ولا يطيب عيشي ما دام هذا الحال وأنظر ما تجمعه من الجمهور في ليلتك أنا أعطيك إياه الآن فأخذ القصاص الكتاب وقرأ له باقي السياق حتى خرج عنتر من السجن فقال له أقرّ الله عينك وأراح بالك الآن طابت نفسي فخُذ هذه الدراهم ولك الفضل ثم انصرف إلى بيته مسروراً وطلب الطعام واعتذر للمرأة بأن القصاص وضع له القيد في رجل عنتر وهي جاءته بالطعام ليأكل فكيف يمكنه أن يذوق طعاماً وعنتر محبوس مقيد. قال وأما الآن فقد ذهبت إلى بيت القصاص وقرأ لي باقي الحديث إليَّ أن أخرجه من السجن والحمد لله قد طابت نفسي فهاتي ما عندك من الطعام واعذريني عما فرط مني.

«إعلان» [من الجنان]

إنه بحوله تعالى وبأنظار أولياء الأمور العظام قد قاربت سنة الجنان الأولى النهاية. وقد أتى على أكثر مما كنا نترصد من التوفيق والنجاح وذلك أكبر دليل على ارتقاء الأمة العربية بظل الدولة العليا الأبدية الدوران إلى درجة حسنة من درجات عصر التمدن والمعرفة فإن كثيرين من الأهلين قد دخلوا جنان الأدب والأخبار المفيدة ببذل الذهب الوضاح وجوهر الوقت الثمين في سبيل مطالعة الجرائد والكتابات المبنية على أسس الصحة والاستقامة وخلق الغرض. فبناء على ذلك ومما أن الظاهر أن طلاب الجنان كثيرون وأن أكثر مشتركي هذه السنة يجددون اشتراكهم قد عزمنا على أن نداوم إرسال الجنان في السنة القادمة إلى جميع الذين لا يطلبون إلينا ان نقطع إرساله عنهم. أي أننا لا نكلف الذين يرغبون تجديد الاشتراك إلى طلب ذلك خطأً أو شفاهاً راجين الذين يرغبون أن لا يجددوا اشتراكهم أن يتكرموا بإفادة ذلك لنقطع عنهم الجنان. ونرجو الذين يرغبون الاشتراك عن السنة القادمة من الذين لم يشتركوا هذه السنة أن يتكرموا بإفادة ذلك قبل دخول السنة الثانية لكي نكون على بصيرة من جهة العدد الذي نطبعه كل مرة. هذا وأننا نسأل الله تعالى أن يمن عليهم بالصحة والتوفيق وطول البقاء مدة أعوام كثيرة وهو السميع البصير وبالإجابة جدير.

«إعلان» [من الزهرة]

بما أن رواية الشاب المغرور قد انتهت وكان كثيرون قد طلبوا منا إدراج تاريخ مفيد على التتابع فسنضع من الآن وصاعداً تاريخ حرب ملوك التبابعة في اليمن قبل الإسلام مأخوذاً عن كتاب جمهرة العرب عسى أنه يروق لدى حضرة المشتركين الكرام كما أننا نعدهم بأننا سنغير هيئة صحيفتنا هذه في بداية السنة الجديدة بوضعنا بها أخباراً أجنبية ومحلية مفيدة مما تروق للقارئ مطالعته وذلك بحسب ما يقتضيه المقام رغبة بإشهار الفوائد العمومية للجمهور.

«إعلان» [من البشير]

نُعلم حضرة الجمهور بأننا من تاريخ أول شهر آب الحاضر قد تركنا شغل جرنال النجاح بالكلية. وأحجمنا عن التداخل في إنشائه على الإطلاق لكي يرجع إلى ما كانت عليه الزهرة التي ادّعت بأنها أمّه. ومن الآن وصاعداً لا نخطُّ فيه خطأً ولا نكتب فيه فصلاً. ولا ننشئ فيه خلاصة سياسية أبداً كما كنا ننشئ سابقاً. ولا نترجم رواية مونتي كريستو التي كنا قد أخذنا على أنفسنا مسؤولية ترجمتها من الفرنساوي إلى العربي مع تنقيحها من الأغلاط المخالفة للدين. فلكي نرفع عنا كل مسؤولية جرنال النجاح ومسؤولية أغلاط رواية مونتي كريستو الممنوعة قرأتها من رومية على جميع الكاثوليك لما فيها من الغلطات الباهظة ضد الدين قد بادرنا إلى إشهار هذا الإعلان تحريراً في ١٦ آب غ سنة ١٨٧١.

كاتبه
القس لويس صابونجي
منشئ النجاح سابقاً
في بيروت

Adelaide al-Bustani
(1849–1933)

Introduced and translated by Elizabeth M. Holt

"Henry and Amelia," appearing in *al-Jinan* in 1870, is the only story Adelaide al-Bustani ever published, and it is one of the earliest Arabic short stories (or perhaps translations of a short story) written by a man or woman. Born in 1849 and received into the National Evangelical Church in 1872, Adelaide was one of Butrus al-Bustani's many daughters. Butrus, Salim, their cousin Suleiman, and later Adelaide's sister Alice played important roles in late-nineteenth-century Arabic literature, and the biography of Adelaide's mother, Rahil Ata al-Bustani, appeared in the Egyptian women's journal *Fatat al-Sharq* ("Young Woman of the East") in 1919.

The story's provenance remains a question; it may be an original work of Arabic fiction or a loose translation from an unlocatable source text. The names and customs that appear in the story all seem to come from elsewhere, yet such was nineteenth-century Beirut and its bourgeoisie, a point the story plays on from its opening lines.

Recommended Reading

Hayek, Ghenwa. "Experimental Female Fictions; or, The Brief Wondrous Life of the *Nahda* Sensation Story." *Authoring the* Nahda: *Writing the Arabic Nineteenth Century*, special issue of *Middle Eastern Literatures*, vol. 16, no. 3, 2013, pp. 249–65.

Holt, Elizabeth M. *Fictitious Capital: Silk, Cotton, and the Rise of the Arabic Novel*. Fordham UP, 2017.

———. "From Gardens of Knowledge to Ezbekiyya after Midnight: The Novel and the Arabic Press from Beirut to Cairo, 1870–1892." *Authoring the* Nahda: *Writing the Arabic Nineteenth Century*, special issue of *Middle Eastern Literatures*, vol. 16, no. 3, 2013, pp. 232–48.

———. "Narrative and the Reading Public in 1870s Beirut." *Journal of Arabic Literature*, vol. 40, no. 1, 2009, pp. 37–70.

Jessup, Henry Harris. *The Women of the Arabs*. Dodd and Mead, 1873.

Zachs, Fruma. "From *Difaʿ al-Nisaʾ* to *Masʾalat al-Nisaʾ* in Greater Syria: Readers and Writers Debate Women and Their Rights, 1858–1900." *International Journal of Middle Eastern Studies*, vol. 41, no. 4, 2009, pp. 633–65.

"Henry and Amelia"

From the pen of the lady Adelaide al-Bustani

Due to the severity of the heat in cities upon the arrival of summer, some people, fearing illness, go to the mountains. This custom exists not only in our country but in Europe as well. Some go to the mountains and some to places built along seashores for a change of air and a stroll. And so in a certain summerhouse three ladies and a gentleman met. The first woman's name was Martha, and she was a middle-aged widow who was not without beauty, and the second's name was Hannah. Hannah had an olive complexion and black eyes and was of medium height. The third's name was Amelia, and she was fair, with blue eyes, a face like the new moon, and a neck like a clear crystal, and she was tall with a thin waist. After fifteen days passed, the bonds of affection grew strong between [the four of] them, and it was a happy turn of events, for the kind young man was good to the ladies and treated them all with affection and tenderness. Upon examination, he found the tenderness, loyalty, kindness, and piety of Amelia's heart to surpass those of her two companions. And so his heart was inclined to her, and he was always around her, doing every deed for her happiness and comfort. If they were sitting at the table, he would present her with all the delicious foods, saying, "My dear lady

Amelia, would you permit me to offer you some of this food?"
She would take a little and thank him for his generosity. And if
she spoke, he would listen with all his attention to every word
she said. The assistance he would extend to the two ladies Mar-
tha and Hannah, by contrast, was no more than what was called
for by the duties of a man toward any women.

Only a few days passed before the fire of envy and jealousy
blazed in the hearts of those two ladies, so they took to busy-
ing themselves with plans to prevent any increase in affection
between that young man and the young woman. And so it hap-
pened that the gentleman Henry left one day for the nearby
forest in order to hunt, while the three ladies remained seated
in a hall decorated with beautiful flowers, and in one of whose
corners were musical instruments. After they tired of talking,
the lady Amelia was asked to play some lovely melodies to
chase away the troubling thoughts that were running through
their minds. So she sat down with kindness and simplicity upon
a chair in front of one of the musical instruments and started
playing with those elegant fingers of hers, joining her clear,
melodious voice with the sound of the instrument. At this, the
lady Martha turned to the lady Hannah and signaled for her
to follow, and the two left the hall together for the bedroom.
They entered and locked the door, saying, "This is the time for
planning what we need to do in order to get what we want."
The lady Martha said, "Don't fear, my dear, I've planned a ruse
with which I will outwit the gentleman Henry." Hannah said,
"What might your ruse be?" Martha responded, "Be patient
until this evening, and you will see what the ruse is, and you
will see that I will succeed in all of my plans." And Hannah said,
"My dear, I have no doubt in your cleverness or the perfection
of your planning."

As for the lady Amelia, when she tired of playing and saw
that her two companions had left her, she left the hall to search
for them. When she saw that the door of the bedroom was

closed, she did not ask to enter but rather told herself, "I'll go to the nearby spring and watch the sunset." So she put on her hat and shawl and headed for the spring. A few steps before she reached the spring, she heard the sound of someone breathing, so she looked and there was a man resting with a sunburned face. She got a little closer and looked and discovered that it was the gentleman Henry, so her heart took pity on him and she took off her shawl, spreading it in a tree above his head to keep the sun from his handsome face. Then she went to sit by the spring. Before long, Henry awoke from his sleep and looked, and there was the shawl spread out above his head. He gazed at it and realized that it was Amelia's. So he rose and, with the shawl over his arm, went to look for her. When he approached the spring, he found that kind lady sitting and listening to the running water, so he greeted her and asked, "Is this your shawl?" She smiled and nodded, and the signs of embarrassment were clear on her face as she answered, "Yes." Then she told him what had happened, and he thanked her for her kindness and said, "Would you allow me to sit here a little while?" She responded, "With the greatest pleasure." And so he sat down near her and started to speak to her . . .

To be continued . . .

. . . saying, "Look, my lady, what is more beautiful than these sights around us?" She said that they were truly very beautiful, and he said, "But there is a sight more beautiful and majestic than the others here," and he gestured toward her. She said to him, "How can you speak to me so boldly?" Upon hearing that, he asked her to allow him to put his ring on her hand as a sign of their engagement, and she did, saying, "Don't wonder at the speed of my answer, for your kindness, all your commendable qualities, and your intelligence drew my heart to yours." That pleased him greatly. A moment later they both arose to return to the inn. When they arrived, they found that Martha and

Hannah were waiting for them for dinner, so they all sat down together at the table and began to talk about different matters. When Martha saw the ring that was on Amelia's hand, she was shocked. She looked at Hannah and said in a low voice, "Look! That ring! It must be a token from the gentleman Henry, for I haven't seen it on her hand before now." And from that moment she was determined to carry out every part of her plan.

After they had finished dinner and gone to their rooms, Martha took advantage of the opportunity to go to the door of Henry's room. She knocked and asked, "Would you allow me to enter?" [Opening the door for her,] he said, "You are welcome to come in, but what did I do to earn the honor of a lady entering and bringing light to my dark room, deprived as it is of the fair sex?" She responded, "I come only to offer you advice that will bring you comfort in your future life, and were it not for the fact that I consider you to be like a brother to me, I would never dare to mention it." So he said, "What is your advice? What you say disturbs me, so tell me now." So she said to him, "It is difficult for me to see a person such as yourself being drawn to this evil, deceitful woman devoid of all feelings and being tricked by her deceptive speech." He answered her, trembling, "You mean the lady Amelia?" She said, "Yes." He responded in a shaking voice, his face turning pale, "No, no, I do not think what you are saying has any basis." She said, "If you do not believe what I am saying, then look with your own eyes, and the truth of it will be clear to you." He said, "I won't believe anything about the beautiful, kind lady Amelia, who is free from trickery and deception, until I see it for myself." She said to him, "You can, tonight. Three hours after sunset, sit beside the window looking out on the beach and see what happens." When she finished saying this, she left the gentleman in a sea of thought, awaiting that hour with great anxiety. When the time approached, he seated himself beside the window. From there he watched while two people strolled along the beach. He said to himself, "I wonder who these two are." After peering a moment longer, he saw a handsome young man putting his hand in the hand of the lady Amelia. He said, "Oh no, this is a catastrophe! Am I awake or in a dream? I do not believe my eyes. What am I going to do?" He looked out from the window again to verify that the lady was indeed Amelia. From that time the fire of envy and jealousy was lit in his heart toward that young man, and he regretted his love, faith, and reliance on her. He threw himself on his bed, saying, "What a catastrophe! How could you—oh my dear, who revealed to me your love, loyalty, and trust—do this to me?" He remained in that state all night, and in the morning he said to himself, "Parting is inevitable." Yet despite everything, his love for her remained in his heart. So he decided that he would go away. He sat down at his table and wrote her this letter: "Tonight a telegraph arrived from the city of London, informing me of the death of my father and requesting my immediate presence to receive his property and personal affairs. I beg you to forgive me, my dear, for my inability to say goodbye to you." After he made his preparations to travel, he went to the owner of the inn and gave her the letter, saying, "I beg of you to give this to the lady Amelia when she comes out of her room." Then he said goodbye and left. As for Amelia, she went, as was her custom now, to Henry's room to invite him to eat breakfast with her. When she arrived at his door, she knocked and stood awaiting a response. Yet there was none, so she said, "Perhaps he is deep in sleep," and she knocked a second time without receiving an answer. At that, she returned to find her two companions. On her way [to find them,] the owner of the inn met her and gave her the letter, which she quickly opened and read, before going to tell Martha and Hannah what had happened.

After several days passed, the ladies made their own preparations to travel, as loneliness had overcome them, and they went, each to her homeland. When Hannah realized that she had not benefited in the least from her ruse, she regretted it a great deal and said to herself, "What did we do? A deed like this incites the anger of the Creator upon us, for we have erred against that innocent lady, and this might cause her distress her entire life." She was determined to reveal everything, to beg the forgiveness of the gentleman Henry and the lady Amelia, so immediately she wrote three letters, one to him, the second to her, and the third to Martha, inviting them all to her home to spend the night in pleasure and relaxation. After responses arrived from all of them saying that they would come at the specified time, she began to prepare her house, especially the reception hall, which she decorated with green vines and beautiful flowers, such that if you entered it, you would think that you were in the most beautiful little garden. After she made all the necessary arrangements, she put on her fancy clothes and her precious jewels and sat to await her guests. At two in the afternoon, Henry arrived in the company of Martha, at which Hannah was surprised and exclaimed aloud, "What a wonder! How did this coincidence come about when I know the two of you do not live in the same country?" Henry replied, "Did word not reach you that I am pledged to marry the lady Martha in three weeks?" Just then, Amelia entered, and when Henry and Martha saw her, they were struck with surprise, as they had thought that only the two of them had been invited. As for Hannah, she greeted Amelia at the door welcomingly, and Amelia greeted all of them and sat in wonder at this coincidence.

After they spent a moment talking about different things, Hannah turned to Amelia and said to her, "Is there anything more beautiful than these white flowers that are on your head, and what is more elegant than this white velvet gown with no likeness save the purity of your heart, so free of deception and malice?" Then she turned to Martha and said to her, "How this black gown studded with precious stones suits you. But I saw you once in clothes that suited you even more." So Martha asked, "When was that?" Hannah said to her, "Do you not remember that night while we were at the inn when you wore the clothes of a man, and you and the lady Amelia went down to the beach and the two of you went walking, your hand in hers?" When Martha heard this, her body trembled and she became very afraid. When Henry heard this, he almost lost his senses, and the fire of anger was lit in his heart. He approached Martha and said, "How remarkable! This is what you would do to me? This is your love for me? How is it possible for the wicked demon of envy to drive you to do something like this?" Martha's fear was so great that she remained silent. Henry then turned to Amelia and said to her, "My forgiveness and apologies, oh my faithful dove clad in these pure white clothes that I do not doubt indicate the pureness of your heart." Then he knelt on both knees before her and asked for her forgiveness for everything that he had done.

Amelia, in her overwhelming confusion and surprise, turned from one to another and did not utter a single word. Overcome with emotion, Henry cried, "Answer me now or I'll die of grief!" She awoke from her stunned state and forgave him for what had happened. He arose and approached Martha and said, "Get up and leave this place, and do not let me see your face again." Then he turned to Hannah and thanked her for her generosity and let her know that he considered her to be like a sister to him, and he asked Amelia to prepare for a wedding in two weeks.

When the time came, Amelia was married to Henry, and they spent their life together in good fortune and happiness until the destroyer of all pleasures came between them. As for Martha, her cunning smote her heart, and she died angry and in grief. From this we may deduce that whoever digs a pit for his brother shall fall in it and that the thread of a lie is short. The End.

If some of the ladies have joined the gentlemen in reading al-Jinan, *then the gentlemen deserve to have something from the fine, fair pen of the ladies. Lo! The gate to the gardens* [al-jinan] *has opened for the ladies.*

Note

I thank Nora Boustany, Christine Boustany, and Kamran Rastegar for their generosity and help in my search for information about Adelaide, and special thanks to Christine Lindner for her careful work in the National Evangelical Church records that at last turned up Adelaide.

Source of Arabic Text on Which the Translation Is Based

الجنان [al-jinan; The Gardens], vol. 1, nos. 12 and 13, 1870, pp. 366–67, 391–428, 686–87.

أديليد البستاني
(١٨٤٩-١٩٣٣)

هنري وأميليا

من قلم الست أديليد البستاني

إنه لشدة الحر في المدن عند دخول الصيف يذهب البعض من الأهالي إلى الجبال خوفاً من الأمراض وهذه العادة ليست في بلادنا فقط بل في أوروبا أيضاً فالبعض يذهبون إلى الجبال والبعض إلى محلات مبنية على شطوط البحر لتغيير الهواء والتنزه ففي صيفية ما التقى ثلاث سيدات وخواجا فالسيدة الأولى اسمها مرثا وكانت أرملة في وسط عمرها ولم تكن خالية من الجمال والثانية اسمها حنة وكانت حنة سمراء اللون سوداء العينين ذات قدّ معتدل. والثالثة اسمها أميليا وكانت بيضاء اللون زرقاء العينين ووجهها كالبدر وعنقها كالبلور الصافي طويلة القامة رقيقة الخصر. فبعد مضي خمسة عشر يوماً قويت علائق الألفة بينهم جميعاً وسرّوا جداً بتلك المصادقة لأن ذلك الشاب اللطيف كان يلاطف تلك السيدات ويعاملهن بكل رقة ومحبة. فبعد الاختبار وجد أن رقة ووداعة ولطف ونقاوة قلب السيدة أميليا تفوق ما لرفيقتيها من ذلك فمال قلبه إليها وكان يلازمها ويقدم لها كل خدمة تأول إلى سرورها وراحتها وكان إذا جلسوا على المائدة يقدم لها من جميع الأطعمة اللذيذة قائلاً يا سيدة أميليا أتسمحي لي أن أقدم لك قليلاً من هذا الطعام. فتأخذ قليلاً وتشكر فضله. وكانت إذا تكلمت ينتبه بكل إصغاء إلى كل حرف من كلامها. وأما المساعدة التي كان يقدمها للسيدتين مرثا وحنة إنما كانت ناتجة فقط عن واجبات الرجال بمساعدة النساء. فلم يمضِ إلا أيام قليلة حتى اضطرمت في قلب تلك السيدتين نيران الحسد والبغض. فأخذتا تهتمان بتدابير ما يمنع ازدياد المحبة بين ذلك الشاب وتلك الصبية. فاتفق أن الخواجا هنري خرج ذات يوم إلى حرش مجاور لتلك اللوكاندة لأجل الصيد وأما السيدات الثلاث فبقينَ جالسات في قاعة مزينة بالزهور الجميلة وكانت في إحدى زواياها آلات موسيقية. وبعد ما مللنَ من التكلم عزمت السيدة أميليا على أن

تلعب بعض أنغام لطيفة لطرد الأفكار المزعجة التي كانت تجول في خاطرهن فجلست بلطف وبساطة على كرسي قدام آلة الموسيقى وابتدأت تلعب بتلك الأنامل الظريفة قارنة صوتها الرائق الرخيم بصوت الآلة. وعند ذلك التفتت السيدة مرثا إلى السيدة حنة وأومأت إليها أن تتبعها فخرجتا من القاعة إلى حجرة النوم ولما دخلتا إليها وقفلتا الباب قالت إن هذه هي ساعة التدبير ماذا يجب أن نفعل لننال المرام. فقالت السيدة مرثا لا تخافي يا عزيزتي أني قد دبّرت حيلة أحتال بها على الخواجا هنري فقالت السيدة وما عسى أن تكون حيلتك فأجابتها اصبري إلى المساء وستنظرين ما هي الحيلة وترين أني سأنجح في كل تدبيري. فأجابتها يا عزيزتي أني لا أشك بحذقك وحسن تدبيرك. وأما السيدة أميليا فبعد ما ملّت من الترتيل ورأت أن رفيقتيها قد تركتاها خرجت من القاعة لتفتش عليهما فلما رأت باب حجرة النوم مغلقاً لم تطلب الدخول بل قالت في نفسها أذهب إلى العين التي بالقرب منا وأنتظر غروب الشمس. فلبست برنيطتها وشالها وتوجهت نحو العين فقبل وصولها إلى العين ببعض خطوات سمعت صوت تنفُّس فنظرت وإذا رجل مضطجعاً وقد أصابت الشمس وجهه فتقدمت قليلاً ونظرت فوجدت أنه الخواجا هنري فرق له قلبها وخلعت شالها ونشرته على شجرة فوق رأسه ليمنع الشمس عن وجهه الجميل ومضت وجلست بجانب العين. ثم بعد قليل هبِّ هنري من نومه ونظر وإذا شال منشور فوق رأسه فترفس فيه فعلم أنه شال السيدة أميليا فنهض وحمل الشال على ذراعه ومضى ليفتش عليها. فلما وصل إلى العين وجد تلك السيدة اللطيفة جالسة بجانب العين تصغي إلى دوي الماء فحيّاها وقال أهذا الشال شالك فتبسمت وأحنت رأسها وكانت علامة الحياء تلوح على وجهها وقالت نعم. ثم أخبرته بما جرى فشكر معروفها وقال أتسمحين لي أن أجلس هنا قليلاً فقالت حباً وكرامةً فجلس بالقرب منها وأخذ يكلمها . . .

ستأتي بقيتها

. . . قائلاً انظري يا سيدتي ما أجمل هذه المناظر التي حولنا. فأجابته حقاً أنها جميلة جداً فقال ولكن يوجد هنا منظر أجمل وأظرف من كل هذه وأومأ إليها فقالت له من أين لك هذه الجسارة أن تقول لي هكذا فعند ذلك طلب منها أن تسمح له أن يضع خاتمه في يدها علامة الخطبة فسمحت له قائلة لا تتعجب من سرعة الجواب لأن لطفك وجميع خصالك الحميدة

وفطنتك جذبت قلبي إليك فسرّه ذلك جداً. وبعد ذلك ببرهة نهضا راجعين إلى اللوكاندة. فلما وصلا رأيا أن السيدة مرثا وحنة كانتا تنتظرانهما للعشاء فجلسوا جميعاً على المائدة وابتدأوا يتكلمون بأمور مختلفة. ولما رأت السيدة مرثا الخاتم الذي كان في يد السيدة أميليا اندهشت ونظرت إلى السيدة حنة وقالت بصوت منخفض انظري أن هذا الخاتم ليس هو إلا علامة من الخواجا هنري فإني ما نظرته في يدها إلا الآن. فمن تلك الساعة عزمت على إجراء حيلتها. فلما فرغوا من العشاء ذهب كلٌّ إلى حجرته واستغنمت السيدة مرثا الفرصة ومضت إلى الخواجا هنري وقرعت باب حجرته وقالت له أتأذن لي أن أدخل فقال أهلاً وسهلاً من أين حصل لي هذا الشرف أن أجد السيدات يدخلن ويزرن حجرتي هذه المظلمة الخالية من هذا الجنس اللطيف. فأجابته أن دخولي إلى هنا ليس إلا لأقدم لك نصيحة تؤول إلى راحة حياتك المستقبلة ولو لم أحسبك كأخ لي لما أتجاسر أن أذكرها. فقال ما عسى أن تكون نصيحتك فإنك أشغلت بالي بهذا الخبر فتكلمي حالاً. فقالت له يصعب عليّ أن أرى شخصاً فريداً مثلك ينقاد إلى هذه الخبيثة المحتالة الخالية من الحاسيات وينخدع بكلامها الباطل. فأجابها مرتعداً أتعنين السيدة أميليا فقالت نعم. فأجابها بصوت مرتعد وقد علا وجهه الاصفرار كلا كلا إني لا أظن أن كلامك هذا له أصل. فأجابته بما أنك لا تصدق كلامي فإن شئت فسترى بعينك. وعند ذلك يتضح لك حقيقة هذا الكلام. فقال إني لا أصدق شيئاً عن السيدة أميليا الجميلة اللطيفة الخالية من الغش والخداع حتى أنظر بعيني. فأجابته أنك في هذه الليلة بعد غروب الشمس بثلاث ساعات تجلس بجانب الطاقة المشرفة على شطوط البحر فترى ما يحدث. فلما فرغت من كلامها خرجت من عند الخواجا هنري وتركته غائصاً في بحار التفكر ينتظر تلك الساعة برغبة عظيمة. فلما قرب الوقت جلس بجانب تلك الطاقة وبينما هو على تلك الحالة نظر وإذا شخصان يتمشيان على شاطئ البحر. فقال في نفسه يا ترى من هما هذان وبعد أن تفرّس قليلاً رأى شاباً لطيفاً واضعاً يده في يد السيدة أميليا. فقال وآ أسفاه ما هذه المصيبة هل أنا في يقظة أو في حلم إني لا أصدق عينيّ. ماذا أفعل. ثم أشرف ثانية من الطاقة وتحقق أن تلك السيدة هي السيدة أميليا. فمن تلك الساعة اشتعلت في قلبه نيران الحسد والبغض نحو ذلك الشاب وتأسف على محبته وأمانته وأركانه إلى السيدة أميليا وطرح نفسه على سريره قائلاً ما هذه المصيبة أيمكنك أيتها العزيزة التي أظهرت لي محبتك وودادتك

وصدقك أن تفعلي بي هكذا. فبقي على تلك الحالة الليل كله. ولما أصبح الصباح قال في نفسه لا بد من الافتراق ولكن مع كل هذا بقيت محبتها في قلبه. فعزم على السفر فجلس قدام مائدته وكتب لها كتاباً قاصداً أن يحتال به عليها. وهذا ما كتبه الليلة ورد لي تلغراف من مدينة لندن. يخبرني بوفاة أبي ويطلب حضوري حالاً لأستلم الأموال وكل ما يخصه. فأرجوك يا عزيزتي أن تعذريني لعدم إمكاني أن أودعك. فبعد ما تهيّأ للسفر ذهب إلى صاحبة اللوكاندة وأعطاها المكتوب قائلاً لها أرجوك أن تعطيه للسيدة أميليا عند خروجها من حجرتها ثم ودعها وذهب. وأما السيدة أميليا فذهبت كجاري عادتها إلى حجرة الخواجا هنري لتدعوه للذهاب معها إلى الفطور فلما وصلت إلى الباب قرعت ووقفت تنتظر الجواب فلم يكن من مجيب فقالت لعله مستغرق في النوم فقرعت ثانية فلم يأتِها جواب. فعند ذلك رجعت تطلب رفيقتيها وبينما هي ذاهبة لقيتها صاحبة اللوكاندة وأعطتها المكتوب ففتحته بسرعة وقرأته ثم ذهبت وأخبرت مرثا وحنة بما جرى. فبعد مضي بضع أيام تجهزن للسفر لأن الوحدة غلبت عليهن وذهبت كل واحدة منهن إلى وطنها. أما السيدة حنة فلما رأت أنها لم تستفد شيئاً من حيلتها ندمت جداً. وقالت في نفسها ماذا جرى وماذا فعلنا إن فعلاً كهذا يجلب غضب الباري علينا لأننا قد أخطأنا ضد تلك السيدة البرية وربما يكون ذلك سبباً لتكدير عيشها كل حياتها. فعزمت على كشف الأمر وطلب السماح من الخواجا هنري والسيدة أميليا وكتبت في الحال ثلاثة مكاتيب أحدها للخواجا هنري والثاني للسيدة أميليا والثالث للسيدة مرثا تدعوهم إلى بيتها ليصرفوا ليلة في الحظ والانشراح. فبعد وصول الجواب من كل منهم بأنهم سيحضرون في الوقت المعين ابتدأت بإعداد بيتها وترتيبه ولا سيما قاعة الاستقبال فإنها زينتها بعروق خضر وزهور جميلة حتى كنت إذا دخلت إليها تظن أنك في أجمل جنينة. ثم بعد ما أكملت ما يلزمها لبست ملابسها الفاخرة وحلاها الثمينة وجلست تنتظر ضيوفها. ففي الساعة الثانية من الليل أتى الخواجا هنري برفقة السيدة مرثا فتعجبت السيدة حنة من ذلك الأمر فسألتها يا للعجب كيف هذه المصادفة أني أعلم أنكما لستما ساكنين في بلاد واحدة فأجابها الخواجا هنري أما بلغك أني مزمع أن أتزوج بالسيدة مرثا بعد ثلاثة أسابيع. وبينما هما في هذا الكلام وإذا السيدة أميليا داخلة في الباب فلما رآها الخواجا هنري والسيدة مرثا تعجبا لأنهما ظنا أنهما قد دعيا وحدهما. وأما السيدة حنة فلاقتها إلى الباب

واستقبلتها بالترحاب فحيتهم جميعاً بالسلام وجلست متعجبة من هذه المصادفة. فبعد ما صرفوا برهة يتكلمون عن أشياء مختلفة التفتت السيدة حنة إلى السيدة أميليا وقالت ما أجمل هذه الزهور البيضاء التي على رأسك وما أنقى هذا الثوب المخمل الأبيض الذي لا يشبهه إلا نقاوة قلبك الخالي من الغش والرداءة ثم التفتت إلى السيدة مرثا وقالت لها كم يليق لك هذا الثوب الأسود المرصع بالحجارة الكريمة إلا أنني قد نظرتك مرة في ثوب كان يليق لك أكثر من هذا فأجابتها متى كان ذلك فقالت لها أما تتذكرين تلك الليلة التي لبست فيها ونحن في اللوكاندة ثوب رجل ونزلت أنت والسيدة أميليا إلى شاطئ البحر وكنتما تتمشيان ويدك بيدها فلما سمعت ذلك ارتعدت فرائصها وخافت خوفاً شديداً. أما الخواجا هنري فلما سمع ذلك كاد يغيب عن الرشاد واشتعلت نيران الغضب في قلبه وتقدم نحو السيدة مرثا وقال يا للعجب أهذا فعلك نحوي ومحبتك لي كيف أمكن للشيطان الحسد الخبيث أن يقودك إلى فعل كهذا وأما هي فلشدة خوفها بقيت صامتة ولم تقدر أن تجاوبه بكلمة ثم التفت إلى السيدة أميليا وقال لها العفو والمعذرة أيتها الحمامة الوديعة المسربلة بهذا الثوب الأبيض النقي الذي لا أشك بأنه يدل على نقاوة قلبك ثم ركع على ركبتيه أمامها وطلب منها الصفح عن كل ما صدر منه. أما هي فكانت لشدة حيرتها وتعجبها تلتفت من الواحد للآخر ولم تجاوبه بكلمة وهو لشدة فرحه صرخ قائلاً جاوبيني حالاً وإلا أموت كمداً. فاستفاقت حينئذ من غفلتها وسامحته على ما مضى. فقام وتقدم نحو السيدة مرثا وقال لها قومي وأخرجي من هنا ولا تدعيني انظر وجهك بعد ثم التفت إلى السيدة حنة وشكر فضلها وطلب منها أن تحسب أنها كأخت له والتمس من السيدة أميليا أن تتهيأ للعرس بعد أسبوعين فلما حان الأوان زفت أميليا على هنري وقضيا حياتهما بالحظ والمسرات إلى أن فصل بينهما هادم اللذات وأما مرثا فذهب كيدها في نحرها فماتت غيظاً وكمداً. ومن هنا يستفاد أن من حفر لأخيه حفرة يسقط هو فيها وان حبل الكذب قصير انتهى.

إذ كان بعض السيدات يشاركن السادة في قراءة الجنان يحق للسادة أن يكون لهم شيء من قلم السيدات الرائق اللطيف وها قد انفتح باب الجنان للسيدات.

Zaynab Fawwaz
(c. 1850–1914)

Introduced and translated by Marilyn Booth

Zaynab Fawwaz was born in the largely Shi'i region—and center of Shi'i intellectual activity—of Jabal 'Amil in southern Lebanon, into a family of limited means. She received her earliest education from the wife of a local feudal ruler but at some point left Lebanon and ended up in Cairo. There she gradually inserted herself into the journalistic world of Cairo and published in the newspaper *al-Nil* ("The Nile") and other Arabic periodicals in the 1890s. She was one of a growing number of elite Arab women at the time who wrote on issues of gender rights, specifically the status of women with regard to education, marriage and the family, and labor.

Also in the 1890s, she published a biographical dictionary of famous women (as well as one novel and a play). In this work of over five hundred pages, Fawwaz draws on the tradition of Arabic biographic writing to offer brief accounts of the lives of famous women across the world—most centrally, women of Arab and Turkish provenance as well as those from Muslim communities elsewhere. The dictionary, titled *al-Durr al-Manthur fi Tabaqat Rabbat al-Khudur* ("Scattered Pearls in the Classes of Cloistered Ladies"), was published 1893–96 and seems to have inspired early editors of women's magazines to publish biographies of famous women as encouragement for young (and older) female readers and as evidence for those who doubted that women could combine—and had long combined—stellar public careers, intellectual production, and the domestic and child-rearing tasks that they were called upon to assume.

The translation below is drawn from this work. However, unlike almost all the other biographic sketches in *al-Durr al-Manthur*, this one treats a woman unknown beyond her immediate social circles. This life story enacts, through narrative, issues that were relevant in Fawwaz's day: the right of young people to choose marriage partners, the shifting socioeconomic patterns of urban Egypt and attendant issues of class versus lineage versus personal life choices, the plight of single women abandoned by their husbands (in this case, the mother of the young man in the story), and new educational norms and institutions and the questions these raised for social and economic status among those not of a recognized elite. It ends with a gesture to the practice of feminine seclusion among the middle and upper strata of Egyptian and Ottoman societies.

This text illustrates the fluidity of generic boundaries and source use at the turn into the twentieth century. Some years after Fawwaz's volume came out, when Labiba Hashim was writing short stories for her journal *Fatat al-Sharq* ("Young Woman of the East"), she adapted Fawwaz's biographical narrative, omitting the opening biographical framework (where Fawwaz names her source as someone in her female network, gives biographical veracity to the narrative by specifying Sharafiyya's birthdate, and tells readers she is still alive). Hashim summarizes and modernizes the language; her version—which she terms "a real-life story," somewhere between anecdote, biography, and fictional narrative—is much less emotive than Fawwaz's biographical one and less descriptive. Hashim also eschews the subject's name as title, taking her title instead from Fawwaz's final words: "The House of Griefs: A Real-Life Story" (bayt al-ahzan: qissa mashhuda).

Work Cited

Hashim, Labiba. بيت الأحزان: قصة مشهودة [bayt al-ahzan: qissa mashhuda; The House of Griefs: A Real-Life Story]. *Fatat al-Sharq*, vol. 4, no. 6, April 1910, pp. 239–40.

Recommended Reading

Booth, Marilyn. *Classes of Ladies of Cloistered Spaces: Writing Feminist History through Biography in Fin-de-siècle Egypt.* Edinburgh UP, 2015.

———. "Fiction's Imaginative Archive and the Newspaper's Local Scandals: The Case of Nineteenth-Century Egypt." *Archive Stories: Facts, Fictions, and the Writing of History,* edited by Antoinette M. Burton, Duke UP, 2006, pp. 274–95.

———. *May Her Likes Be Multiplied: Biography and Gender Politics in Egypt.* U of California P, 2001.

———. "Zaynab Fawwaz al-Amili." *Essays in Arabic Literary Biography, 1850–1950,* edited by Roger Allen, Harrassowitz Verlag, 2010, pp. 93–98.

Fawwaz, Zaynab. "Fair and Equal Treatment." Translated by Marilyn Booth. *Opening the Gates: A Century of Arab Feminist Writing,* edited by Margot Badran and miriam cooke, Indiana UP, 1990, pp. 221–26.

Zeidan, Joseph T. *Arab Women Novelists: The Formative Years and Beyond.* State U of New York P, 1995.

"Sharafiyya, Daughter of Sa'id Qabudan"

She was born in the year 1260 of the *Hijra* [1844] and is still living. This biographic subject has events to her name that testify to her fidelity and loyalty; she may be considered to have an odd and wondrous story. I was told of her by one of the ladies who are trustworthy in what they report. These events are so strange that I wanted to include her in this history so that remembrance of her would remain for all ages.

There lived in the Bulaq neighborhood of the city of Cairo a man who was a captain and whom people called Sa'id Qabudan [Sa'id the Captain]. He had married a young woman, Mistress Makhduma, sister of Ra'if Pasha, one of the high naval commanders in the government of Egypt. From her Sa'id Qabudan was blessed with a daughter, whom he named Sharafiyya [the

Honorable]. But she remained in her father's embrace only eight years, before he passed away in AH 1268 [1851–52], fighting in the recent Crimean War.[1]

This girl was of utmost delicacy and sweet grace. She was raised on fine principles, and her mother taught her reading, writing, handiwork, and all of women's particular occupations, embroidery and the like, to the point where she surpassed other girls of her time. She was obedient to her mother, and in her actions she was led by her mother's words. This mother was affectionate and caring toward her daughter, always compassionate and fond, and thus the girl flourished and reached the age of eighteen.

In the city of Izmir [in the Ottoman Empire] lived a woman of middle status whose husband had left her, abandoning his city. She did not know where he went. He left her with a son who, although still very young, rivaled the full moon in beauty and the sapling in his erect figure and steady temperament. She was still raising her son, with much yet to do, when all the money she had saved ran out and she could find nothing for them to eat. She got word that her husband was in Cairo, and so she took her son, aged thirteen, and went to Egypt to search for his father as she remembered him in her mind. As fate would have it, she stayed with Mistress Makhduma, who received her in welcome and with generosity, opening her heart as well as her home to the fullest. She spoke to her brother, Ra'if Pasha, about the situation. He mounted a search for her husband but turned up no word of him. Unable to find him, he took the boy and enrolled him in one of the government schools. Ra'if Pasha did not have children of his own because he had never married; indeed, he reached the age of eighty without marrying.

At that time Sharafiyya was still eighteen years of age, and [the boy] Muhammad Kamal was thirteen. Sharafiyya was of medium height, her body full and her face round, her eyes large and well spaced, her eyebrows curved and her complexion wheaten. She was appealing and amiable, with black hair and eyes that beguiled the heart of anyone who saw her. As for Muhammad Kamal, he was tall, slender, and light-complexioned, with blond hair and blue eyes, his face well-appointed and his disposition generally charming, though few of this description can acquire such a magnetic quality as he had.

When he entered the Saʿid Qabudan home, Sharafiyya began to look after all his requirements, from clothing to food to anything else of which he had need. Her mother viewed her with an astonished eye and pondered her daughter's situation and her preoccupation with this boy, but she restrained herself from having any suspicious thoughts, for she deemed the lad far too young to engage the affections of an eighteen-year-old. At this age, he was not someone with whom a woman would fall in love. When he entered school and consequently was no longer in Sharafiyya's presence, Sharafiyya's thoughts and musings were many. She began to much prefer withdrawing into solitude. She did not fritter away her time in idleness but filled it with occupations that would benefit the lad, such as sewing clothes and addressing his other needs. He would return to their home only on the weekends, on the eve of Friday, following the usual rules of boarding schools in Egypt. Sharafiyya always awaited expectantly the time of his arrival for holidays.

During this period, many suitors were coming around. Her mother wanted to marry her off,[2] since she was her only child, and to celebrate her wedding joyfully before her own death. Each time a suitor came, her mother would present him to her and show him favorably, but Sharafiyya did not accept this easily from her mother. She responded by weeping and wailing, to the point where she could not endure hearing anyone broach this subject with her. Her behavior upset her mother terribly. Her mother suspected that the person who was seducing her daughter away from marrying was the boy's mother. So she spoke to the woman about it and was so insistent and rude as to eject her from the household. After the departure of the boy's mother, Sharafiyya's emotional state grew worse. She feared that now she would be deprived of seeing her beloved. She became so stricken with grief that she could not eat or sleep. She remained full of bewilderment and confusion until Thursday evening came and Muhammad Kamal arrived as usual. Told that his mother had left the house and gone to the home of Ra'if Pasha, he was distressed and worried. For the lad too had imbibed Sharafiyya's love from his childhood. And the older he got, the more her love imprinted itself. But he regarded himself as paltry, poor, and contemptible whenever he compared himself with her. He had been working hard, striving to acquire enough learning that he would be deserving of her. It was not long before he graduated from the Mubtadiyan School and entered the College of Military Arts, through the intercession of Ra'if Pasha.

After a time, Sharafiyya's mother, Mistress Makhduma, was gathered into God's embrace. The girl passed into her uncle's care, as though she were his own daughter. Suitors began to ask him for her hand, and he presented these men to her, but she always refused. He was at his wits' end with her. He could not imagine what was keeping her from getting married.

Kamal was still in Ra'if Pasha's home with his mother, who from the time she had left Mistress Makhduma's house and entered the home of the pasha was still there when the girl joined the household, so once again they were all under one roof. The uncle did not suspect in the slightest that Sharafiyya's hesitation and reticence were due to this boy, for he regarded the two as enormously far apart in both wealth and age. The pasha did not know the boy's lineage, but in his nature and comportment the pasha saw indications of a sound family background and that the boy was of good stock and honorable.

As Sharafiyya's refusal to marry persevered, the pasha feared that God would take him before he could arrange a wedding for this orphan girl. He complained to a friend and asked him to get his wife to help, for she could question the girl as if she were her mother; she could probe [the girl's feelings], to understand why the girl continued to refuse marriage. The pasha's friend (also a pasha) did as his friend asked. When his wife questioned Sharafiyya, Sharafiyya made it very clear that she could not go against her nature, for she was utterly and completely inclined toward Muhammad Kamal. The motherly figure who spoke to her saw that Sharafiyya would not marry anyone other than this lad, that she would not go against the feelings of her heart, and this is what the woman told her husband. By that time Kamal had acquired the rank of lieutenant, which gave him the courage to ask for Sharafiyya in marriage. He went to the pasha's friend and begged him to speak to Ra'if Pasha about Sharafiyya, to ask him to bestow her upon him and accept him as his humble servant forever if he would only give him his blessing. So the friend approached Ra'if about the engagement and told him that he had learned well what Sharafiyya's situation was from the words of his wife, who had found her strongly inclined toward the youth. This was the reason, he said, why Sharafiyya would not consider marrying anyone else. When Ra'if Pasha heard this, his reaction was that this was an impossibility. "This can never be!" he said. "The boy is not her match. How can I marry him to the daughter of my sister, when I have raised him as a charity case? He is poor and cannot offer a dowry, nor can he even pay his own expenses, let alone establish a home. And in the end, his origins are unknown!"

Said his friend, "Well, he is poor, but he will advance little by little, rising through the ranks until he attains the level we have attained. We were poor in the beginning, weren't we? We had salaries of 150 dirhams, and we struggled and strove until we attained the highest positions appropriate for the likes of us. He's trying to do exactly the same thing. And as for his being of unknown origin, well, we don't know our origin either. None of us knows our family background! We don't know who is Circassian and who is from Morea and who is from Crete. We left our lands not knowing what would happen to us. And now here we are—God be praised!—among the men of the Egyptian governing elite."

The friend did not give up arguing until the pasha relented. But meanwhile, years had passed. The pasha allowed the lad's engagement to Sharafiyya, and they began working on the trousseau and all the necessary wedding arrangements. It was as though Sharafiyya had found her dead hopes brought back to life. She was newly alive to all that was astonishingly beautiful in life.

Alas, though, fate did not allow her to realize these joys, attacking her instead with its strongest phalanx. She was stricken with a shocking blow, the sort that would collapse high mountains and dissolve the bedrock of the earth. With a week to go before the wedding, the lad took to his bed, and in days he was gathered into God's embrace. The green trunk of his youth was severed, and his beauty withdrew inside the layers of the cosmos. Praise be to the Everlasting One who never dies.

Let the onlooker contemplate the state of Sharafiyya, for the pen is incapable of describing her state and the grief and despair she endured. She entered her room—which she called the house of sadness—and dropped the curtains upon it and upon herself and mourned her beloved, and she does so still. After these things came to pass, her uncle, Ra'if Pasha, died. To this very day she remains buried under layers of grief, begging to die, that she might join her beloved in the other world. But she cannot do so. She has been imprisoned in her house of grief for more than thirty years. Rare are those who would have the forbearance to endure this tragedy.

Notes

[1]This seems to be an error on the author's part, as the Crimean War began toward the end of 1853. Perhaps the error is in Sa'id Qabudan's death date.

[2]While this could be more felicitously translated as "wanted to see her married," I use the transitive to suggest her mother's active interest and role—a form of the verb used in this era more often with regard to fathers marrying off their daughters.

Source of Arabic Text on Which the Translation Is Based

Fawwaz, Zaynab. الدر المنثور في طبقات ربات الخدور [al-durr al-manthur fi tabaqat rabbat al-khudur; Scattered Pearls in the Classes of Cloistered Ladies]. Al-Matba'a al-Kubra al-Amiriyya, 1893–96, pp. 358–60.

زينب فوّاز
(نحو ١٨٥٠-١٩١٤)

شرفية ابنة سعيد قبودان

وُلدت في سنة ١٢٦٠ هجرية وهي لغاية الآن على قيد الحياة ولهذه المترجمة وقائع تشهد لها بالوفاء وتُعتبر من العجائب المستغربة قد أخبرتني عنها إحدى السيدات الموثوق بقولهن ولغرابة هذه الوقائع أحببت درجها في هذا التاريخ لكي تخلد لهذه المترجمة ذكراً مدى الأعصار وهو أنه كان في مدينة بولاق مصر رجل قبودان يقال له سعيد قبودان وكان قد اقترن بفتاة اسمها السيدة مخدومة شقيقة رائف باشا أحد رؤساء البحر في الحكومة المصرية فرزق منها سعيد قبودان بنتاً فسمّاها شرفية ولم تمكث في حجر والدها سوى ثمان سنوات حتى توفاه الله وكان ذلك سنة ١٢٦٨ هجرية وهو مجاهد في حرب القرم الأخيرة.

وكانت هذه البنت غاية في الرقة واللطف وقد رُبِّيت على مبادئ حسنة وقد علمتها والدتها القراءة والكتابة والأشغال اليدية جميع ما تختص به النساء من تطريز وغيره حتى فاقت بنات عصرها وهي مطيعة والدتها منقادة لكلامها وكانت تلك الوالدة تحني عليها ضلوع الرأفة والحنو إلى أن بلغت الثامنة عشرة من سنيها.

وكانت في مدينة إزمير إمرأة متوسطة المقام وكان قد تركها زوجها منسحباً من بلده ولم تعلم أين ذهب وترك لها ولداً صغيراً ولكنه يضاهي البدر جمالاً والغصن اعتدالاً وما زالت منتظرة تربي ولدها إلى أن فرغ منها المال المدّخر معها ولم تجد ما تفتات به هي وولدها وقد تواترت الأخبار عن وجود زوجها في مصر فأخذت ولدها وكان في سن الثالثة عشرة من سنيه وحضرت به إلى مصر لتبحث عن والده كما خلد في فكرها وقد نزلت بالأمر المقدور على السيدة مخدومة فتلقتها على الرحب والسعة وفتحت لها في قلبها فضلاً عن منزلها أعظم محل وكلمت شقيقها رائف باشا في أمرها فبحث عن زوجها فلم يعلم له خبراً ولما لم يجده أخذ الغلام وسلمه إلى إحدى المدارس الأميرية. وكان رائف باشا عديم الولد لأنه لم يتزوج أبداً إلى أن بلغ الثمانين من العمر.

وكانت شرفية في ذلك الوقت لم تتجاوز الثامنة عشرة وكان محمد كمال في سن الثالثة عشرة. وكانت شرفية ربعة القوام ممتلئة الجسم مستديرة الوجه واسعة العيون مقرونة الحواجب قمحية اللون جذابة خفيفة الروح سوداء الشعر والعيون تخلب لب من يراها. وأما محمد كمال فإنه كان طويل القوام نحيل الجسم أبيض اللون أشقر الشعر أزرق العيون مستدير الوجه يميل دمه إلى الخفة مع أنه قل من كان بهذا الشكل أن يستحصل على هذا الجاذب.

ولما دخل إلى منزل سعيد قبودان صارت شرفية تعتني بأمره كل الاعتناء من ملبس ومأكل وكل ما يلزم له وجميع سد احتياجاته وكانت والدتها تنظر إليها بعين الاستغراب وتفكر في أمرها وانشغالها بأمر هذا الغلام ولكنها تراجع نفسها عن الظنون في ابنتها لأنها ترى أن الغلام صغير جداً ليس أهلاً لأن تحبه بنت ثمانية عشرة سنة وليس هو ممن يحب وهو في هذا السن. ولما دخل المدرسة وبعد عن شرفية كثرت عليها الأفكار وصارت تحب الخلوة بنفسها ولكنها لم تضيع أوقاتها بدون أن تشتغل بشيء يعود نفعه على الغلام مثل خياطة ملبوس وغيره مما يلزم له وكان لا يأتي إلا في كل ليلة جمعة على حسب أصول المدارس الداخلية في القطر المصري وكانت شرفية تنتظر ميعاد مجيئه كلياً في الأعياد.

وفي تلك الفترة تكاثرت عليهما الخطاب وكانت والدتها تحب أن تزوجها لأنها وحيدتها وتفرح بها قبل وفاتها. وكلما جاءها خاطب تعرضه عليها والدتها وتحسنه في عيونها وهي لا تقبل منها ذلك ولا تجيبها إلا بالبكاء والنحيب حتى أنها صارت لا تقبل من يفاتحها بمثل هذا الكلام. فكدّر فعلها هذا والدتها وظنت أن الذي يغريها على هذا الفعل هي أم الغلام فكلمتها بهذا الخصوص وأغلظت لها القول حتى أخرجتها من منزلها ولما خرجت زاد وجد شرفية وخافت أنها تُحرم من رؤية حبيبها فحزنت الحزن الشديد حتى حُرمت النوم والطعام. وما زالت في أفكار الدهشة والحيرة إلى أن كانت ليلة الجمعة فحضر محمد كمال على حسب العادة ولما بلغه أن والدته خرجت من المنزل وتوجهت إلى منزل رائف باشا اغتمّ لذلك وكان الغلام أيضاً قد أشرب حب البنت من حين طفوليته وكلما نما سنه ينمو حبها معه ولكنه كان ينظر إلى نفسه فيجدها حقيرة بالنسبة إلى شرفية ولكنه صار يجتهد في الاستحصال على العلوم الكافية لأن تجعله أهلاً لها ولم يمض زمن يسير إلا وخرج من مدرسة المبتدئان ودخل المدرسة الحربية بواسطة رائف باشا.

وبعد مضى مدة توفى الله مدة والدتها السيدة مخدومة وبقيت البنت في حجر خالها كأنها ابنته وصارت تطلبها الخطّاب منه فيعرض عليها ذلك فلم تقبل فاحتار في أمرها ولم يدر ما الذي يمنعها عن الاقتران.

وكان كمال لم يزل في منزل رائف باشا مع والدته فإنها من حين ما خرجت من عند السيدة مخدومة دخلت إلى منزل الباشا المشار إليه ومكثت عنده إلى أن انضمت البنت إليه فصاروا كما كانوا جميعاً في بيت واحد وكان الباشا لا يظن أن هذا التوقف من شرفية حاصل بسبب هذا الغلام لأنه يرى أن بينه وبينها بوناً بعيداً من حيث الثروة والسن أيضاً. وأما النسب فهو وإن كان لا يعلم نسبه إلا أنه كان يرى في خلال طباع الغلام ما يدل على صحة نسبه وأنه من نسل طيب وأنه شريف النفس أبيها. ولما طال أمر شرفية بالامتناع عن الزواج خاف الباشا أن يتوفاه الله قبل أن يزوج هذه البنت اليتيمة فشكا ذلك إلى بعض أصدقائه وقال له بأن يكلف قرينته لأنها كوالدتها أن تسألها في ذلك وتفهم ما سبب امتناعها عن الزواج. ففعل الباشا المشار إليه ما كلفه به صديقه وقد سألتها قرينته لها وأظهرت لها أنها لا تقدر على مخالفة الطبيعة حيث أن لها ميلاً كلياً إلى جهة محمد كمال فاستنتجت منها تلك السيدة أنها يستحيل عليها الاقتران بغير هذا الغلام وأنها لا تقدر على مخالفة إحساساتها القلبية فأخبرت زوجها بذلك. وكان كمال في ذلك الوقت قد استحصل على رتبة ملازم وصار له جراءة على طلب شرفية فتقدم إلى الباشا المشار إليه والتمس منه أن يكلم رائف باشا في أمر شرفية وأن ينعم عليه بها وأن يقبله عبداً له ما دام في هذه الدنيا لأنه على كل حال هو غرس نعمته. فتقدم إليه صديقه بأمر الخطوبة وأخبره أنه اختير أمر شرفية بلسان زوجته فوجدها تميل إلى الغلام وهذا سبب امتناعها عن الاقتران بغيره. ولما سمع رائف باشا هذا الخبر استعظمه وقال هذا شيء لا يكون أبداً لأن الغلام لا يصلح لها فكيف أزوجه بنت أختي وأنا مربّيه بنوع الثواب وهو فقير ولا يقدر على أداء المهر ولا مصروف نفسه فضلاً عن فتح المحل ومصاريفه مع كونه مجهول الأصل.

فقال له فأما كونه فقيراً فسوف يتقدم شيئاً فشيئاً ويستحصل على الرتب حتى يصير بدرجتنا حيث أننا نحن كنا في ابتداء أمرنا فقراء وكان الواحد منا راتبه مئة وخمسين درهما فاجتهدنا إلى أن استحصلنا على أرفع الرتب اللائقة بمثلنا وها هو مجتهد أيضاً. وأما من جهة كونه مجهول الأصل فنحن أيضاً لا نعلم أصلنا لأن الواحد منا لا يعلم أصل نفسه ولا من هم أهله فمن هو

جركسي ومن هو مرلي ومن هو كريدلي وقد أُخرجنا من بلادنا ما نعلم ماذا يؤول أمرنا إليه وها نحن والحمد لله قد صرنا من خواص رجال الحكومة المصرية.

ولم يزل به حتى أنعم له رائف باشا بعد امتناعه جملة سنين وعقد للغلام على شرفية وشرعوا في أمر الجهاز وما يلزم للفرح وكانت شرفية في ذاك الوقت قد أُحيي ميت أمالها وأدهشها الفرح الشديد عن كل ما في الكون.

ولكنها وآ أسفاه لم يسمح لها الدهر بإتمام تلك الأفراح حتى هجم عليها بجيوشه الجبارة وصدمها صدمة تزول من هولها الجبال الراسية ويذوب لها الحجر الجلود. وذلك أنه لما بقى لإقامة الفرح أسبوع واحد حمّ الغلام ووقع رهين الفراش ولم يمكث بعد ذلك سوى أيام قلائل حتى توفاه الله وقصف غصن شبابه النضر وانزوى جماله تحت أطباق الثرى سبحان الحي الباقي الذي لا يموت.

فلينظر الرائي إلى حال شرفية التي يعجز القلم عن وصف حالها وما صارت إليه من الحزن والكدر حتى أنها دخلت إلى غرفتها التي سمتها بيت الأحزان وأسبلت عليها الستور وصارت تندب حبيبها وتبكيه إلى الآن. وتوفي بعد ذلك خالها رائف باشا ولم تزل إلى هذا الوقت مدفونة تحت أطباق الحزن تطلب الموت لعلها تجتمع بحبيبها في العالم الآخر فلم تجد لذلك من سبيل. ولها مسجونة في بيت حزنها ما يزيد على الثلاثين سنة وقل من يصبر على هذا المصاب.

Labiba Hashim
(1882–1952)

Introduced and translated by Ghenwa Hayek

A pioneer by any standards, Labiba Hashim had a prolific career that is even more astonishing when one considers the time, places, and circumstances of her life. Born in 1882 in Beirut, she was educated at French and English missionary schools. The female protagonist of *Hasanat al-Hubb* ("The Virtues of Love") claims to belong to the same French religious order, the Sisters of Love, as the nuns who ran the Beirut school that Hashim attended, which suggests that a certain tongue-in-cheek humor can be listed among Hashim's many other qualities. *Hasanat al-Hubb*, her first story to be published, appeared in 1899 in Ibrahim al-Yaziji's prestigious journal *al-Diya'* ("The Glow"). The story's clever plotting reveals Hashim's vivid imagination; and, as the dramatic irony of the story's title emerges from the embarrassed gatekeeper's attempt to explain his compromising yet fortunate situation to his astonished employer, we have further evidence of Hashim's mischievousness. Love's virtues are certainly not what the reader expected them to be!

Hashim and her family moved to Cairo in 1900. There she met and mingled with the intellectual elite. She published her first novel, *Qalb al-Rajul* ("The Heart of Man"), in 1904. In 1906 she founded her own journal, *Fatat al-Sharq* ("Young Woman of the East"), which continued to be published until 1935. Not content with being a publisher, she also became the first Arab woman to teach at a university, when the Egyptian University invited her to become a lecturer there in 1911, a role she reprised in 1912.

In 1919 she once more found herself at the forefront of history when she was invited by the newly formed government of

King Faisal I to serve as the general inspector of girls' schools in Damascus. However, once the Sykes-Picot agreement decreed that Syria was to fall under French mandate, Hashim returned to Egypt. A year later, in 1921, she moved to Chile, where she published the magazine *al-Sharq wal-Gharb* ("East and West"), only to return to Egypt in 1924. In addition to her fiction, Hashim compiled her university lectures into a book titled *Kitab al-Tarbiya* ("The Book of Education").

Recommended Reading

Abu-Lughod, Lila, editor. *Remaking Women: Feminism and Modernity in the Middle East.* Princeton UP, 1998.

Ashour, Radwa, et al., editors. *Arab Women Writers: A Critical Reference Guide, 1873–1999.* American U in Cairo P, 2008.

Baron, Beth. *The Women's Awakening in Egypt: Culture, Society, and the Press.* U of California P, 2005.

Booth, Marilyn. *May Her Likes Be Multiplied: Biography and Gender Politics in Egypt.* U of California P, 2001.

Hayek, Ghenwa. "Experimental Female Fictions; or, The Brief Wondrous Life of the *Nahda* Sensation Story." *Middle Eastern Literatures*, vol. 16, no. 3, 2013, pp. 249–65.

"The Virtues of Love"

My esteemed reader, permit me to tell you the story of an incident that truly happened. This story, in addition to its strange events and its humor, contains a moral, since it warns of similar things that could happen in any time or place.

It is told that in the city of Constantinople there was a majestic, broad-pillared castle, where a noble family, an elderly widow and her five married children and their children, twenty in all, lived together. The house was furnished with the finest cloth and the richest decorations.

On the evening of 15 June 1889, there came a soft knock at the gate. The gatekeeper peered out of the peephole. He saw standing there a staggeringly beautiful girl, with a breathtaking face and black eyes that could shoot arrows through a person's heart. From her appearance, she looked to be around twenty-four years old. She wore a simple flowing black dress with large sleeves and a white head covering that was crimped at the edges, indicating that she was a nun, a servant of religion. The man was taken aback by her beauty, and he could not take his eyes off her. He felt his heart beating powerfully in his chest, as though his soul were chanting, in the words of the Egyptian poet:

> I perceive a pain in my breast that does not cease.
> Is this what lovers have named passion?[1]

He opened the gate for her, and she walked in and looked at him kindly and modestly. In a voice whose sweetness and gentleness could make the heart flutter, she asked, "Is this Ya'qub Bey's dwelling place?" He replied, "Yes, my lady." She said, "And is the mistress of the castle here?" He said, "Yes." She took out a *carte de visite* that read, in French, *Sœur Augustine Maria*, and she handed it to him, asking, "Would you be so kind as to give this to the lady of the house and tell her that I need to see her?" He took her card and went inside, and then he returned as fast as he could, saying politely, "Would the lady please follow me inside; my mistress would like to see her." He led her to the reception hall, and then he bowed to her politely and left.

She stood there for a moment, taking in the grandeur of the castle and its decorations and contemplating its doorways and corridors, and then she walked into the foyer and sat down at one end, signs of worry and uncertainty appearing on her fair face. She distracted herself by looking around at the objects and ornaments in the foyer, admiring the beauty, care, and excellent taste that each item revealed. Shortly thereafter, the lady of the house walked in, a majestic woman impressive to behold, with her curtains of white hair and graced with great dignity. The nun rose and greeted her respectfully, and the older woman returned her greeting with a smile and sat down beside her.

The nun began the conversation by explaining to her hostess the reasons for her visit. She said, "I am a nun, a sister from the order of the Sisters of Love in Egypt. I was sent to these parts by the mother superior on some business, but as it happened I arrived here in the evening, and now it is too late for me to continue on to the convent that is my destination. As you can see, I am only a girl and a stranger here, and I do not know the way, and I am afraid to seek shelter in a place whose people I don't know. I was at a loss for what to do until some passersby recommended that I come here to your home, since your family is known for its kindness, generosity, and good reputation. So I mustered up the courage to knock at your gate, hoping that I would find hospitality and would be allowed to spend the night here, content and safe from all danger. If you grant my wish and are kind enough to let me into your home, then you will have all my gratitude and my blessings; if not, then please, I beg of you to ask one of your servants to accompany me to my destination, and I thank you in either case."

The lady of the house said, "You are welcome to stay here, blessed sister, for as long as you like."

The girl's face lit up in joy and gratitude, and she thanked her in the sweetest of words. Then they moved on to talk of other things, and the nun proved to be a charming conversationalist, in addition to being blessed with rare beauty and wonderful kindness. She won over her hostess's heart, and the latter thanked God for having led the young nun to her home. Then the lady of the house personally showed her guest to the best room in the castle, after introducing her to all the other members of her family, who were as taken with her beauty as they were with her manners.

Meanwhile, the gatekeeper spent a long while anxious and distracted, waiting for the nun to emerge. His impatient heart pined for another glance at her beautiful face, and the minutes of his wait began to feel like days, so he went to the house servants to inquire about her. From them he found out that she was spending the night in the castle and that the lady of the house had given her the north-facing room on the top floor. He retraced his steps, consoling himself with the thought of seeing her when her stay was over.

The family spent the evening with the nun, delighting in and admiring her virtues and pleasant speech. They sat around her and engaged her in conversation, basking in the enchantment of her perfect manners and delicate character. They remained like this until midnight, or thereabouts, when all rose to go to their bedrooms, and the nun retired to her room. Silence reigned over the house. As the clock chimed one in the morning, nothing could be heard in the castle except for the sound of leaves rustling in the trees that encircled the house on all sides. The wind rattled their branches frightfully, and in the darkness the sound was wild and strange.

The palace was surrounded by a vast garden spreading out in all directions, its grounds decorated with plants and flowers and overlooked by trees. A high fence stretched all around it; its two ends met in a towering iron gate. Nearby stood a small shack, furnished with a couple of chairs and a table; in one of the corners was a bed upon which a man lay. It was the same gatekeeper who had been so taken by the visitor's beauty. He lay awake, unable to sleep, his thoughts occupied by the nun, who had not left his mind since he first laid eyes on her.

Finally he got up wearily and went out to walk in the garden, casting his gaze toward his enchantress's bedroom, where the woman who had stolen his composure and his sleep lay. He saw that a light was glinting from her window, blinking on and off as if the person in the room was pacing back and forth. His heart soared at the thought that she was still awake, and he began to contemplate going upstairs and peeking at her through the keyhole. But his upbringing got the best of him before he gave in to that impulse; he had been brought up in this household since his early youth, and owing to his dependability and good service the family trusted him with their money, their storerooms, and everything in the house. But love can work wonders and meddle with minds, and there's no escaping its clutches; those under its spell follow its whims, even if it leads them astray. So he [went in the house and] climbed the staircase and turned down the long corridor that led to her door. And all this time he was imagining the girl's beauty, particularly now that she was in her nightgown instead of in the dark, heavy robes that hid her figure from sight. He imagined that she must be as graceful as a willow branch and as beautiful as the moon. He crept toward the door, his heart beating wildly, stopping briefly to wipe the cold sweat off his brow. He gathered his strength and carefully leaned toward the keyhole, afraid that she would hear a sound that would startle her. He peered in through the keyhole. . . .

It is hard to describe the shock and upset that hit him; in fact, had he been hit by lightning at that very moment, it wouldn't have stunned him as much as what he saw. That beautiful woman, that pious nun, that saintly sister and servant of the convent was standing in the middle of the room. She'd cast off her nun's robes and wimple, and they lay to one side, revealing a body covered in weapons belted on by a leather strap. At her waist hung a metal ring containing a number of keys of different shapes and sizes. Her kind glances had been replaced by an evil glare, and sin and evil radiated from her eyes; what made everything worse was the cigarette that she sucked at voraciously, its smoke billowing from her mouth and forming clouds around her, which the draft in the room blew away. [As he watched,] she picked up the oil lamp and brought it to the window, moving it in a way that indicated she had companions waiting out there in the darkness, and that she was communicating with them in code.

The blood froze in the gatekeeper's veins, and his eyes grew wide. At first he couldn't move, but then he realized that he had not a moment to spare, otherwise he could lose his life and inadvertently cause the ruin of the entire household. He rushed to his mistress's room and pounded on the door insistently. She woke up in a panic and asked, "Who's there?" He replied, "It's your servant Butrus, my lady; please hurry and get up." She got up and opened the door, and the gatekeeper threw himself at her feet, whispering in a voice trembling with fear, "Thieves, thieves!"

He had barely uttered the words when his mistress leaped back like a bird that has been splashed with water and shouted, "Where are these thieves, and how do you know?" He replied, "I'm so ashamed at my daring, my lady, but my heart was pierced by the arrow of that devil who walked into this house in the guise of a nun. I came up to see her, and I discovered her secrets—thank God, love has many advantages." She said, "I don't understand what you're talking about. Tell me right away where these thieves are!" So he took her by the hand and tried to lead her, but she halted in fear and cried again, "Where are the thieves?" He said, "My lady, don't waste any more time. Know that the woman you host here is not a nun, as her outward appearance suggests, but a thief whose accomplices are waiting outside. She used the nun's robes as a disguise so that she could sneak into your home and steal all the money and objects she could. Come to her door, and you'll see what I mean." She looked through the keyhole, and she almost fainted with fright. The servant held her up and walked her back to her room. She rang the bell for the house servants, who rushed in one after the other. She pretended to be ill and screamed in pain, asking them to wake her children. In a flash, the entire family was assembled in her room, where she let them in on the secret, and they began to discuss what to do.

At that moment, the nun, having heard the fuss, came in to see what was happening. She was back in her nun's robes, and she held a rosary in her hand. She looked at all of them as benevolently as before and kindly asked why they were all up. They told her that their mother had been taken ill and was racked with pains from one moment to the next. She consoled them with her sweet talk and then sat near the "sick" woman's bed, while the latter continued to pretend that she was in terrible pain. The nun knelt by the bed and began to pray fervently.

Meanwhile, some of the servants who were in on the secret left on orders to fetch the doctor. But in truth they headed to the police station and informed them of the true story. A few minutes later, the castle was surrounded by soldiers, and the thieves outside had been apprehended. Soon after that, the nun was brought down from the house in handcuffs, and they all met with their due punishment.

Note

¹The poem is "I perceive a pain in my breast that does not cease," by Mohammad Imam al-'Abd (1862–1911), who was actually Sudanese, not Egyptian.

Source of Arabic Text on Which the Translation Is Based

Hashim, Labiba. حسنات الحب [hasanat al-hubb; The Virtues of Love]. الضياء [al- diya'; The Glow], edited by Ibrahim al-Yaziji, Matba'at al-Ma'arif, 1898–99, pp. 634–40.

لبيبة هاشم
(١٨٨٢-١٩٥٢)

حسنات الحب

يأذن لي القارئ الكريم أن أقص على مسامعه حادثة جرت حقيقة وهي
مع ما فيها من غرابة الواقعة وفكاهة الحديث لا تخلو من فائدة للمطالع إذ
تنبه التحذر من مثلها مما يمكن حدوثه في كل زمان ومكان.

رُوي أن في مدينة القسطنطينية قصراً شاهق البنيان متسع الأركان تقطنه
أسرة شريفة مؤلفة من أرملة طاعنة في السن وخمسة بنين متزوجين ولهم
أولاد بحيث كان عدد أعضاء تلك الأسرة ما يزيد عن العشرين وكان القصر
مفروشاً بأحسن الرياش ومزداناً بأثمن التحف.

ففي مساء ١٥ يونيو من سنة ١٨٨٩ قُرع الباب قرعاً خفيفاً فأطل الحاجب
من كوّة صغيرة فرأى فتاة ذات جمال باهر يدهش الأبصار وعينين سوداوين
ترميان الفؤاد بنبال ويتبين من هيئتها أنها في الرابعة والعشرين من العمر
متدثرة برداء أسود بسيط الهيئة واسع الأكمام وعلى رأسها قبعة بيضاء مغضَّنة
(مكشكشة) الأطراف مما يدل على أنها راهبة من خدمة الدين. فبُهت الرجل
لذاك الجمال وجعل لا يرفع طرفه من النظر إليها وقد شعر في فؤاده بخفقان
شديد وكأن لسان حاله ينشد قول الشاعر المصري:

أرى لوعة بين الجوانح لا تهدأ
أهذا الذي سمَّاه أهل الهوا وجدا

ثم فتح لها الباب فدخلت ونظرت إليه بلطف واحتشام وقالت بصوت
يأخذ بمجامع الفؤاد رقة وحلاوة أليس هذا منزل يعقوب بك. فقال بلى يا
سيدتي. قالت وهل السيدة صاحبة القصر هنا. قال نعم. فتناولت بطاقة زيارة
قد كُتب عليها باللغة الفرنسوية «الأخت أوغستين ماريا» وأعطته إياها قائلة
تكرم بتسليم هذه إلى حضرة السيدة واخبرها أني بحاجة إلى مقابلتها. فأخذ
بطاقتها وانطلق بها ثم عاد بما أمكنه من السرعة قائلاً بتأدب لتتفضل السيدة

بالدخول فإن مولاتي بانتظارها. قال ذلك وسار أمامها حتى أوصلها إلى ردهة الاستقبال ثم انحنى أمامها باحترام وانصرف.

فلبثت واقفة هنيهة تتفرس في عظمة القصر وزخرفه وتنعم النظر في مداخله ومخارجه ثم دخلت الردهة وجلست في إحدى جوانبها وكانت تبدو على محياها الصبيح مظاهر القلق والارتباك فأخذت تتلاهى بالنظر إلى موجودات الردهة وزينتها معجبة بما فيها من جمال الرياش وحسن الترتيب وكمال الذوق. ولم يكن إلا القليل حتى أقبلت ربة المنزل وكانت سيدة جليلة والمنظر عظيمة الشأن بكللها المشيب ويزينها الوقار فنهضت الراهبة وحيتها باحترام فأجابت السيدة تحيتها بابتسام ثم جلست بإزائها.

فابتدرت الراهبة مضيفتها بحديث أوضحت لها فيه أسباب زيارتها قالت إني راهبة من أخوات المحبة في بلاد مصر أرسلتني رئيسة الدير إلى هذه الديار في بعض المهام فاتفق وصولي مساء بحيث تعذّر عليّ استئناف المسير وحدي لبلوغ الدير الذي أقصده. وأنا كما ترينني فتاة غريبة أجهل الطريق المؤدي إليه وأخشى خطر الالتجاء إلى مكان لا أعرف صفات أهله فحرت في أمري وأخيراً نصح لي بعض المارّة ممن سألتهم بأن أقصد هذا المنزل لما امتاز به أهله من طيب العنصر ومكارم الأخلاق وحسن السمعة وعليه تجرأت على طرق منزلك آملة أن أجد فيه من كرم الضيافة ما يجعلني أبيت هذه الليلة قريرة العين آمنة من كل خطر. فإن شئت تحقيق آمالي وتكرمت بقبولي في منزلك أوليتني نعمة وطوقت جيدي بفضلك وإلا فأرجو أن تأمري أحد خدمك بمرافقتي ليرشدني إلى الدير ولك مني الشكر الجزيل في كل حال.

فقالت ربة المنزل بل مرحباً بك وأهلاً بمقدمك أيتها الأخت المباركة ومهما طال زمن إقامتك عندنا فإنك مقبولة على الرحب والسعة.

وأشرق وجه الفتاة فرحاً واستبشاراً وشكرتها بأعذب الألفاظ. وبعد ذلك انتقلتا في الحديث إلى أمور شتى كانت تُظهر ما للراهبة من طول الباع في حسن المعاشرة ولطف المحاضرة فوق ما وهبها الله من الجمال النادر واللطف الساحر بحيث أخذت بمجامع قلب المضيفة التي جعلت تمجد الخالق العظيم. ثم سارت بها بعد ذلك إلى أحسن غرفة من القصر فأنزلتها بها بعد أن عرّفتها بسائر أعضاء أسرتها فلم يكن يعجبهم ببديع طلعتها أعظم منه بباهر آدابها.

أما البواب فلبث مدة طويلة قلق البال مشتت الأفكار وهو ينتظر خروج الراهبة بقلب قد فارقه الصبر ليتمتع بنظرة أخرى من محياها الفتان ولما طال

انتظاره وهو يحسب الدقائق أياماً طوالاً ذهب فاستخبر عنها بعض الخدم فعلم أنها ستقيم تلك الليلة في القصر وقد أنزلتها ربة المنزل بالغرفة الشمالية من الطبقة العلوية. فعاد أدراجه معللاً النفس بمشاهدتها عند انتهاء مدة الضيافة.

وقضى أهل المنزل تلك الليلة مع الراهبة وهم في أتم السرور والأعجاب بمحاسنها ولطف حديثها وقد اجتمعوا حولها وجلسوا يؤانسونها ويحادثونها وهم يرون من كمال آدابها ورقة أخلاقها ما سحرهم جملة. وما زالوا على ذلك إلى أن انتصف الليل أو كاد فنهض كل منهم إلى مضجعه ودخلت الراهبة غرفتها وساد السكوت في المنزل فلم تُسمع رنة الساعة الأولى بعد نصف الليل حتى كان السكون مخيماً حول القصر لا يُسمع هناك سوى حفيف الأشجار التي تكتنفه من كل جهاته والرياح تهب متخللة أغصانها فتحدث في المكان رهبة يزيدها ظلام الليل استيحاشاً.

وكان بالقصر حديقة غناء واسعة الأرجاء ممتدة الأطراف قد كسيت أرضها بالنبات والأزهار وخيمت فوقها الأشجار وامتد حولها سور مرتفع ينتهي طرفاه بباب كبير مصفح بالحديد وعلى مقربة منه غرفة صغيرة فيها من الأثاث كرسيان ومائدة وفي إحدى زواياها سرير ملقى عليه رجل هو الحاجب بعينه الذي هام بجمال زائرة القصر وكان حتى تلك الساعة يتململ على سريره وقد هجره الرقاد وناب مكانه خيال الراهبة فلم يبرح من أمام ذهنه منذ وقع نظره عليها.

وأخيراً نهض متثاقلاً وخرج يتنقل في الحديقة ونظره متجه دائماً نحو مخدع فاتنته التي سلبت لبه وأسهرت جفنيه. وإنه لكذلك إذ لمح من نافذتها نوراً يظهر تارة ويحتجب أخرى كما لو كان شخص يمشي بإزائه ذهاباً وإياباً فخفق فؤاده لتحققه أنها لا تزال مستيقظة وأخذت عواطفه تجذبه لصعود السلم واستراق النظر إليها من خرق الباب ولكن آدابه كانت تحول دون إتمام قصده ولا سيما وأنه قد رُبّي في ذلك المنزل منذ حداثته فشب على الأمانة وحسن الخدمة بحيث كانوا يأتمنونه على أموالهم وخزائنهم وكل ما في منزلهم. ولكن الحب أبو العجائب يلعب بالأفكار وليس من قضائه فرار فصمم على اتباع هواه ولو كان في ذلك تلفه فاجتاز السلم ثم عطف في رواق طويل انتهى به إلى باب غرفتها وكان في أثناء ذلك يتصور مقدار جمال فاتنته وهي بلباس النوم بدلا من ذلك الثوب القاتم الذي كان يحجب غصن قوامها عن النظر.

فيتجلى له منظرها مما يفضح قدّ البان ويزري بجمال القمر. ثم اقترب من الباب بقلب خافق ولكنه توقف لحظة يمسح العرق البارد المتحلب من جبينه وعاد فاستجمع ما بقي لديه من القوة وانحنى بكل تأنٍّ وحذر خوف أن تُسمع له حركة ترتاع لها تلك الظبية الآنسية ونظر إلى الداخل من ثقب الباب . . .

وهنا يصعب وصف ما فاجأه من الدهشة والانقلاب فإنه لو انقضت عليه صاعقة حينئذ لم يكن تأثيرها بأعظم مما ناله من ذلك المشهد. فإنه رأى تلك المخلوقة الجميلة والراهبة الورعة بل أخت الملائكة وخادمة الدير منتصبة على قدميها في وسط الغرفة وقد خلعت عنها الرداء الخارجي والقته جانباً فظهر من تحته جسمها مدججاً بالسلاح وممنطقا بحزام من الجلد وإلى الجهة اليسرى من خصرها حلقة من حديد تضم عدداً وافراً من المفاتيح المختلفة الحجم والشكل. وقد تبدلت منها تلك النظرات اللطيفة بشرر كان يتطاير من مقلتيها كأنها بعض الأئمة الأشرار ويزيد في انقلاب سحنتها ما كانت تمتصه بشره من التبغ في ذلك الحين فيخرج دخانه من فيها كغيوم تتكاثف من حولها فيبددها النسيم. ثم اقتربت من المصباح فأخذته بيدها وأدنته من النافذة وجعلت تحركه بإشارة تدل على وجود رفاق لها متربصين بالخارج فتكلمهم برموز وإشارات متفق عليها قبلاً.

أما الرجل فجمد الدم في عروقه وجحظت مقلتاه فلبث هنيهة لا يبدي حراكاً وأخيراً تنبه من غفلته فعلم أن الحال لا تسمح له بضياع دقيقة واحدة ربما كانت سبباً لفقدان حياته وخراب المنزل. فهرول مسرعاً نحو مخدع مولاته وقرع الباب بإلحاح فاستيقظت تلك مذعورة وقالت مَن الطارق. فقال خادمها بطرس يا سيدتي فعجلي بالنهوض. فقامت وفتحت وإذا بالبواب قد ترامى على قدميها هاتفاً بصوت قد أرجفه الخوف «لصوص لصوص.»

ولم يأتِ على هذه الكلمة حتى انتفضت مولاته كعصفور بلله القطر وصاحت به أين اللصوص وكيف عرفت ذلك. فقال الصفح يا مولاتي عن جرأتي فقد نفذ في فؤادي سهم حب تلك الشيطانة التي دخلت المنزل بهيئة راهبة فأتيت لأراها وكان من ذلك أني اطّلعت على سرائرها والحمد لله وللحب كم له من حسنات. قالت ويحك لم أفهم مغزى كلامك اخبرني حالاً أين اللصوص. فأخذها بيدها وأراد المسير فتوقفت جزعاً وصاحت مكررة أين اللصوص. فقال يا سيدتي لا تضيعي الوقت واعلمي أن التي أضفتها في منزلك ليست براهبة

كما تدل ظواهرها بل هي شريكة لصوص ينتظرونها خارجاً وقد استعانت بذلك الثوب على دخول منزلك خدعة لاختلاس ما فيه من المال والمتاع فاقتربي من باب غرفتها يتضح لك الأمر. فاقتربت لما نظرت كاد يغشى عليها من شدة الهلع فبادر الخادم لمساعدتها وإرجاعها إلى غرفتها وللحال قرعت الجرس فانتبه الخدم وأخذوا يفدون الواحد بعد الآخر فتمارضت أمامهم وجعلت تصرخ متألمة ثم أشارت إليهم بأن يوقظوا أولادها فلم يكن إلا كطرفة عين حتى كان أفراد الأسرة كلهم مجتمعين في غرفتها فبلغتهم الأمر سراً فأخذوا يتشاورون فيما يفعلون.

وعند ذلك أقبلت الراهبة لترى ما الخبر لأنها سمعت جلبة القوم وكانت مرتدية بثوبها الخارجي وبيدها سبحة فنظرت إليها ببشاشتها المعهودة وتلطفت بالسؤال عن سبب انزعاجهم فأخبروها أن والدتهم مريضة وقد تنتابها الآلام من حين إلى آخر. فأخذت تهون عليهم الأمر وتخفف عنهم بعض الارتباك بحديثها العذب ثم جلست إزاء سرير المتمارضة وكانت لا تزال تستغيث متظاهرة بشدة الألم فركعت بجانبها وجعلت تصلي صلاة حارة.

وفي تلك الفترة كان بعض الخدم ممن عرفوا سر الحادثة قد توجه بأمر مولاه لاستدعاء الطبيب والحقيقة أنه ذهب توّاً إلى مركز رئيس الشحنة (البوليس) وأطلعه على حقيقة الأمر فلم تمضِ على ذلك إلا دقائق قليلة حتى كان القصر محاطاً بحلقة من الجنود وألقي القبض بغتة على اللصوص الذين في الخارج وكانوا عديدين وأنزلت الراهبة مكتوفة اليدين لينالوا جميعهم مر العقاب.

Mahmud Ahmad al-Sayyid
(1904–37)

*Introduced by Muhsin al-Musawi and
translated by Anna Ziajka Stanton*

Widely recognized as the first significant Iraqi novelist, Mahmud Ahmad al-Sayyid was also a champion of new ideas, especially women's liberation, democracy, secularism, and socialism. A Baghdadi by birth and residence, he was well known among the rising educated class, especially as he went to the Baghdad Engineering School, where a number of the future Iraqi elite were also educated. He entered government service in 1920 and soon after became secretary of the Labor Bureau at the Ministry of the Interior. He later served as secretary of the Chamber of Deputies. Through his strong ties to Hussein al-Rahhal, the "pioneer Marxist ideologue in Iraq" (al-Musawi 103) and editor of the Marxist newspaper *al-Sahifa* ("The Journal") until 1927, al-Sayyid showed early signs of committed writing. Both al-Sayyid and al-Rahhal became central to the Solidarity Club, which counted among its members the lawyer, writer, and critic Mustafa 'Ali, the biographer of the great Iraqi poet Ma'ruf al-Rusafi, and the minister of justice under the government of 'Abd al-Karim Qasim.

The protagonist in al-Sayyid's novel *Jalal Khalid* (1928; "Jalal Khalid") is partly modeled on Hussein al-Rahhal and his socialist thought, and the work also takes up the topic of Arab and Indian education and reflects al-Sayyid's travels to India and Germany. The novel excerpted below, *Fi Sabil al-Zawaj* (1921; "For the Sake of Marriage"), is set in India and steeped in emancipatory discourse; another novel, *Masir al-Du'afa'* (1922; "The Fate of the Weak"), treats similar themes. Al-Sayyid fits therefore into an early trend in Iraqi fictional writing that prioritizes the emancipation of women, social justice, independence, and political freedom.

Work Cited

Al-Musawi, Muhsin. *Reading Iraq: Culture and Power in Conflict*. I. B. Tauris, 2006.

Recommended Reading

Al-Musawi, Muhsin. *The Postcolonial Arabic Novel: Debating Ambivalence.* Brill, 2003.
———. *Reading Iraq: Culture and Power in Conflict*. I. B. Tauris, 2006.
Bashkin, Orit. "'Out of Place': Home and Empire in the Works of Mahmud Ahmad al-Sayyid and Dhu Nun Ayyub." *Comparative Studies of South Asia, Africa, and the Middle East*, vol. 28, no. 3, 2008, pp. 428–42.
Walther, Wiebke. "The Beginnings of the Realistic School of Narrative Prose in Iraq." *Quaderni di studi arabi*, vol. 18, 2000, pp. 175–98.

FROM *For the Sake of Marriage*

Publisher's Introduction

In the venerable country of Iraq, in days past, the towers of literary glory once rose high and lofty. But fate let this glory decline until it nearly disappeared.

In this new age—this age of progress and learning—we find a great spirit beginning to course along the banks of the Tigris and Euphrates. Throughout Mesopotamia today, it is again possible for writers, circumstances permitting, to raise aloft the banners of literature and writing—although much of what they have produced remains concealed, needing industrious hands to unearth it from its hiding places.

I have seen fit to encourage the author of this novel, the esteemed young writer Mahmud Effendi al-Mudarris [Mahmud

Ahmad al-Sayyid], to publish it. I hope I have done well in taking upon myself this duty toward literature and toward its sons. I beg the esteemed readers to help me in this task by showing an interest in this novel, so that I find the motivation to print many works by our exemplary scholars and writers, both old and contemporary. May we trust in God.

—Nu'man al-A'zami, owner
of the Arabic Bookshop in Baghdad

Introduction

He who pursues a higher purpose is a model for us all, and there is no greater and better purpose for a young man than his pursuit of literature. We hope very much that Iraqis will continue to apply themselves to what matters for both them and their nation and in particular to writing. For writing is one of the most important means of advancing the nation and bringing culture and learning to the minds of its citizens.

Surely this is a truth known by anyone who has the least familiarity with the conditions of people in civilized countries. These people understood the secret of writing from the outset and saw its true value. They made it their sole means of advancing the intellect, enlightening the mind, and educating the self, and they depended on it to disperse knowledge throughout the nation.

In these civilized countries, a great many writers have appeared whose versatile skills allow them to treat every topic in which they recognize a public benefit: philosophy, politics, history, morality, literature, and much more. I single out for particular mention those novelists who incorporate the ideas and knowledge that they wish to disseminate into their stories, where they can be easily grasped by readers. Without doubt this is the best means of transmitting truths to the people, by bringing them within reach of their minds and intellects.

It is regrettable that our country takes no part in any of this. Our educated people content themselves with reading what they like of European and Arabic—Egyptian and Syrian—books and novels, yet not one of them has considered imitating the Europeans, or the Egyptians or Syrians, in this crucially important matter [of writing books]. It has not occurred to any among them to try his hand at the [novelistic] pursuit, as far as he has the means to do so. All we have is the novel *The Awakening*, recently composed by the illustrious writer Suleiman Faidhi Effendi al-Mosuli. And that was a solitary work, which our compatriots have not followed with another.

Thus it has delighted me to see my friend al-Sayyid Mahmud al-Mudarris, despite being young, inexperienced, and new to the art of writing, persevering to the extent of his abilities and girding himself to take up this pursuit—the novelistic pursuit. Only one with great literary talent could successfully discharge such a responsibility. Here he offers readers this small preliminary novel, the outcome of his efforts; and the hope is that the esteemed readers will give encouragement to the writer and impel him to continue with his work. The hope as well is that they will not judge or scrutinize the style and content of the novel too closely or compare it with more refined novels, and so on, but rather consider only the purpose for whose sake it was composed.

We hope that our most distinguished Iraqi men of letters—especially the younger ones—will also fulfill their duty in doing this, for this is an essential part of stimulating people's interest in literature. And for this we thank them.

—(Baghdad) 1 March 1921, Hussein al-Rahhal

The Meeting of the Two Lovers

We leave Jinnaram as he is about to depart for his appointment at the temple, and we return to Kastur, whom we left during the second half of the night, her thoughts having long succumbed to apprehensions and frightful fantasies before she finally lost herself in sleep.

Once the night had dissipated and morning shone, she began preparing to go out, taking pains to fix herself up so as to appear before her beloved in her most attractive guise. She donned a gown of red silk and gathered her hair into a single braid at the back of her head, and she adorned her throat with a necklace of costly pearls. Then she placed on her head a filmy veil, letting its two ends hang down her back. After she completed her toilette and the time for the appointment had arrived, she mounted her carriage and departed.

As soon as she arrived at the temple, she entered its densely wooded garden, where they were to meet. Meeting there was neither difficult nor forbidden, for men often came here with their wives and womenfolk to worship together free of supervision. She spied her beloved from a distance, sitting on a protruding stone behind a large tree.

No sooner had she spotted him than her heart fluttered and her knees shook, but she steadied herself and went forward. When their eyes met, Jinnaram was the first to utter a greeting, and he smiled and extended his hand to her in welcome. He too was overtaken with the shyness of love, and he trembled. As they clasped hands, that electric current flowed to his beloved, and she felt the same emotion.

Then they both sat down, and Kastur began by saying, "Perhaps you were astonished, my lord, at my summoning you to this place to speak to you alone, after several months passed during which we did not meet at all."

"Indeed, I was most surprised," said Jinnaram, "for I had nearly despaired of meeting you again. After seeing your father's opposition when I asked him for your hand in marriage. . . . But despite this"—he regarded her beseechingly—"I remain as much in love with you as I was before, and I will be patient, for patience is beautiful, O my heart's desire, and may God unite us forever when the time comes."

"Ah, you only add to my worries! Until when must we be patient? What use is patience, and what hope have I left in our eternal union, and. . . ." (She stopped, and her tongue faltered, and her expression changed.)

Jinnaram saw her anxiety, and while he soothed her and inquired about its cause, she withdrew from the folds of her gown the two letters from the Hero of the Mountain.[1]

He took them at once, and hardly had he finished reading them when he almost burst with fury and rage (because he was brave and passionate, and moreover jealousy, which blinds and deafens, had intensified his zeal and agitation), but then he returned to his senses and said, "Now I understand, Kastur, the reason why your father forbid you to marry me. Who could have thought that men who seem honorable would patronize the vilest thieves and give in to their demands?"

"Honorable? Which attributes do such men possess that make them worthy of this title? A man is not honorable except when he performs what honor and humanity require of him. What honor is there in a man who would take as a son-in-law a thief who is an enemy of God and the people? He is no better than the worst criminals whose hands are sullied with the blood of the oppressed and the innocent. And what humanity is there in a father who does not think of his daughter's future or care whether she is destined for happiness or misery, 'that happiness resulting from harmony between the spouses, and that misery that comes from its lack.' He is a terrible, wicked person."

"His actions are an insult to both truth and humanity," agreed Jinnaram. "But since he is your father, what can be done? A father can behave however he wishes when it comes to his daughter. No one has the power to oppose him—not even his daughter."

"Who allows a father to act in this manner?"

"Our religion."

"A religion is not a true religion (in every sense of the word) unless it accords with the requirements of reason, satisfies the desires of a pure heart and an unblemished conscience, and suits the needs of humanity, justice, and equality by prescribing fairness, forbidding wrongdoing, and calling upon all human beings to treat each other with compassion and mercy. And when it's possible for human beings to do many things that contravene justice and equality—as when fathers usurp the rights of their daughters, for example—how then could religion grant fathers such broad power? This power that makes a daughter, who has a mind and feelings and sentiments of her own, like an object that her father owns and can play with however he wishes and however his purposes demand. He gives her away to whomever he wants, without considering what will harm her and what will benefit her. This is surely a remarkable thing."

"What you say is true; yet I do not believe that there is any religion on the face of the earth that deprives a woman of her rights and debases and humiliates her to this degree. It is rather that the text articulating the rightful obedience that religion does obligate her to perform toward her guardian has been interpreted in this repugnant manner, and thus we see our countrymen acting as they do."

"Who interpreted the text?"

"The religious leaders interpreted it."

"Then it is clear that they are in error."

"You speak truly, but should you or I oppose the religious leaders in this matter, we would do so alone, for public opinion is with them and obeys their will, and moreover it has been their custom since ancient times to act like this. When custom governs a nation, it becomes a religion. You know what happens to those who oppose religion and criticize ancient national traditions."

"How could I not know? Were this not the case, I would not be prohibited from talking about my situation and speaking openly in defense of my rights. I would not be compelled to remain silent as my heart dissolves in pain and agony."

Here Jinnaram sensed danger and wanted to change the topic
of their conversation and to calm Kastur, so he said, "And yet,
Kastur, I do not think that this thief, who dares to make these
feeble threats against us, will be able to do either of us any harm."

"How is that?"

"You will understand by my actions, not my words." (He said
this with enthusiasm and confidence.)

"I knew you would say this, and indeed I trust in your famous
courage and audacity. But despite this, how can my heart be at
ease about this murderous thief who receives no rebuke for
shedding blood? The people have been unable to catch him and
his gang, and he remains as safe as an eagle in the sky. What is
the means by which we may rid ourselves of this criminal?"

"I told you, my darling, he will not be able to harm us in any
way, although I cannot deny the danger of the situation. I will
look into the matter and tell you what I decide to do. So do not
worry. I advise you to conceal this from everyone, especially
your father, and wait for my signal in three days."

After that he took the two letters and placed them in his
pocket, and they rose and bid each other farewell and went their
separate ways.

Note

¹The Hero of the Mountain is a local thief and brigand, to whom Kas-
tur has secretly been promised in marriage by her father; she learns this
unhappy news by chance in a previous chapter after coming upon several
letters from him to her father.

Source of Arabic Text on Which the Translation Is Based

Al-Sayyid, Mahmud Ahmad. الأعمال الكاملة لمحمود أحمد السيّد [al-aʿmal
al-kamila li-mahmud ahmad al-sayyid; Complete Works of Mahmud
Ahmad al-Sayyid]. Edited by ʿAli Jawad al-Tahir, Dar al-Hurriya lil-Tibaʿa,
1978, pp. 19, 21–22, 43–47.

محمود أحمد السيّد
(١٩٠٤–١٩٣٧)

في سبيل الزواج

«مقدمة الناشر»

لقد كان لقطر العراق العزيز في خوالي الأيام مجد أدبي عالي الصروح، ثم قضت الأقدار أن يتضاءل ذلك المجد حتى غاب أو كاد.

وفي هذا العصر الجديد—عصر التجدد والعلم—صرنا نجد روحاً عالية أخذت تنسرب من ضفاف دجلة والفرات، ففي جوانب وادي الرافدين اليوم أدباء وحملة أقلام لو سمحت لهم الظروف المناسبة لتسنى لهم أن يرفعوا للأدب والكتابة بنوداً معلمة. غير أن نفثات أقلامهم ما زالت مطوية مخفية تحتاج إلى الأيدي العاملة التي تخرجها من مدافنها.

وقد رأيت أن أشجع مؤلف هذه الرواية حضرة الشاب الأديب محمود أفندي آل المدرّس على طبعها. عسى أن أكون قد قمت بالواجب نحو الأدب وأبنائه. والمرجو من القراء الكرام أن يساعدوني بهذا الواجب فيقبلون على هذه الرواية كي يكون لي بذلك دافع قوي إلى طبع آثار كثيرة لعلمائنا وأدبائنا الأماثل من قدماء ومعاصرين وعلى الله الاتكال.

نعمان الأعظمي
صاحب المكتبة العربية في بغداد

«مقدمة»

من طلب الغاية صار آية، ولا غاية أسمى وأحسن للشاب من طلبه للأدب. كم نتمنى لأبناء العراق أن يواصلوا سعيهم بالاشتغال في ما يهمهم ويهم أمتهم، سيما في الكتابة التي هي من جملة العوامل والأسباب المهمة في ترقية شؤون الأمة وتثقيف عقول أفرادها وتعليمهم.

أجل، إن هذه حقيقة يعرفها كل من له أدنى إطلاع على أحوال أهل البلاد الراقية الذين عرفوا سر الكتابة في بادئ الأمر فقدروها حق قدرها، وجعلوها الواسطة الوحيدة لترقية الأفكار، وتنوير العقول وتهذيب النفوس واستعانوا بها على نشر العلم بين سواد الأمة.

وقد ظهر فيهم عدد كثير من الكتّاب فتفننوا بالكتابة تفنناً تطرقوا به لكل موضوع عرفوا من ورائه الفائدة للجمهور. كالفلسفة والسياسة والتاريخ والأخلاق والأدب وغير ذلك. وأخص منهم بالذكر أصحاب الروايات الذين أدمجوا بقصصهم كلما أرادوا نشره من الأفكار والعلوم على اختلاف ضروبها. حتى كادت تكون كأنها تلمس باليد. ولا ريب في أن هذه أحسن الوسائل لبثّ الحقائق وتقريبها من الأذهان والعقول.

ومما يؤسف له أن قطرنا (قطر العراق) ليس له نصيب مما ذكرناه أبداً. فالمهذبون عندنا يكتفون بقراءة ما يردهم من التأليف والروايات الإفرنجية أو العربية—المصرية والسورية—ولم يلتفت أحد منهم إلى تقليد الإفرنج أو المصريين أو السوريين في هذه المسألة الجديرة بالأهمية ولا خطر لأحد منهم أن يتطرق لهذا الموضوع فيكتب أو يؤلف فيه ما استطاع إلى ذلك سبيلاً. اللهم إلا الرواية «الإيقاظية» التي ألفها في الأيام الأخيرة الكاتب المجيد سليمان فيضي أفندي الموصلي. وتلك واحدة لم يتبعها أبناء وطننا بأخرى.

وقد سرني وأيم الحق أن رأيت صديقي السيد محمود آل المدرّس مع صغر سنه وحداثة عهده وابتدائه بفن الكتابة، مثابراً في الاشتغال حسب طاقته والاستعداد لتطرق هذا الموضوع—الموضوع الروائي—الذي لا يستطيع الخروج من عهدته إلا من كان له في الأدب حظ عظيم. وها هو يبرز للقراء هذه الرواية الصغيرة التمهيدية التي هي نتيجة عمله ومسعاه والأمل وطيد بأن القراء الكرام يشجعون الكاتب ويحثونه على أن ينحو نحو العمل. وأن يغضوا الطرف ولا يلتفتون إلى أسلوب الرواية ووضعها ونسبتها إلى الروايات الراقية وغير ذلك. بل إلى الغاية التي وُضعت من أجلها فقط.

كما أننا نأمل أيضاً من أدبائنا العراقيين الأفاضل—سيما الشبان—أن يقوموا بواجبهم نحو هذا الأمر الذي هو من جملة العوامل الأساسية لتنشيط الناس على الأدب. وما ذلك عليهم بعزيز.

(بغداد) أول مارس سنة ١٩٢١
حسين الرحال

«التقاء الحبيبين»

نترك جينارام وهو على وشك الذهاب إلى المعبد في الوقت المعين ونرجع إلى كستور التي تركناها في النصف الأخير من الليلة الماضية وهي سابحة في نومها، بعد أن خارت قواها الدماغية لما انتابها من الهواجس والتصورات المخيفة.

فإنها بعد أن ولى الليل وأسفر الصباح قامت تتأهب للذهاب وأخذت تبذل طاقتها في إصلاح شأنها لتظهر بين يدَي حبيبها بأجمل حالاتها. لبست ثوباً حريرياً أحمراً، وجمعت شعرها فجعلته عقيصة واحدة في مؤخر رأسها، وتقلدت في عنقها قلادة لؤلؤ ثمينة، ثم طرحت على رأسها برقع خفيف وأرسلت طرفيه على ظهرها. وبعد أن تمت زينتها وصار الوقت المعين ركبت عربتها وخرجت من هناك.

ولما أن وصلت المعبد دخلت حديقته الكثة الأشجار التي كان فيها موعد اللقاء—ولم يكن اللقاء هناك صعباً أو ممنوعاً لأن الرجال في أغلب الأوقات يصحبون نساءهم وأزواجهم ويأتون للعبادة هناك بلا مراقبة ولا ممنوعية. فلمحت حبيبها عن بعد جالساً على صخرة ناتئة وراء شجرة كبيرة.

ولم تكد تلمحه إلا وخفق قلبها، واصطكت ركبتاها ولكنها تجلدت وتقدمت حتى إذا وقعت العين على العين ابتدرها جينارام بالتحية مبتسماً ومد إليها يده يصافحها وقد بدا عليه خجل الحب، وأخذته القشعريرة. ولما أن تصافحا واتصلت اليد باليد جرى ذلك التيار الكهربائي إلى حبيبته فشاركته بالانفعال.

وبعد ذلك جلسا وأخذت كستور تخاطبه قائلة: «ربما تعجب يا سيدي لاستدعائي أباك إلى هذا المحل ومخاطبتك على انفراد، بعد أن صار لنا عدة أشهر لم نتلاقَ في خلالها أبداً.»

«نعم قد أخذني العجب لأنني كنت أكاد أيأس من الالتقاء بك مرة أخرى. بعد أن رأيت ما من ممانعة أبيك عندما طلبت منه الاقتران . . . ولكن مع ذلك»—ثم رمقها رمقة الاستعطاف—«فأني لا أزال على ما كنت عليه باق على ودك وسأصبر الصبر الجميل، يا منية القلب، عسى أن ينعم الله علينا باللقاء الدائم ولو بعد حين.»

«آه لقد زدت في شجوني . . . فإلى متى يكون الصبر. وهل ينفع الصبر أو يبقى لي أمل باللقاء الدائم وقد . . . . » (فقطعت الحديث وتلعثم لسانها وتغيرت سحنتها.)

فأحس جينارام باضطرابها وبينما هو يخفف عنها ويسئلها عن السبب إذ أخرجت له من ثنايا ثوبها الكتابين الذين لبطل الجبل.

فتناولهما حالاً، ولم يكد يتم قراءتهما حتى كاد يتميز من الغيظ والحنق (لأنه كان شجاعاً غيوراً، ومع ذلك فغيرة الحب التي تعمي وتصم زادته حماسةً وهياجاً) ولكنه رجع إلى صوابه ودهائه فقال: «ها قد علمت يا كستور السبب الذي يسوق والدك إلى الامتناع من زواجك . . . ولكن من كان يظن أن الذين عليهم صبغة الأشراف يوالون أو يلبون دعوة أناس لصوص أنذال؟»

«أشراف؟ أي صفات حازها هؤلاء حتى يجدر أن يطلق عليهم هذا الاسم . . . لا يكون الرجل شريفاً إلا بعد أن يؤدي ما يقتضيه واجب الشرف والإنسانية. وأي شرف عند رجل أجاز لنفسه مصاهرة لص من أعداء الله والناس جميعاً. وهو من أعاظم الجناة الملوثة أيديهم بدماء الأبرياء المظلومين. ثم وأي إنسانية عند أب لم يفكر في مستقبل ابنته ولم ينظر في مصيرها من سعادة أو شقاء 'تلك السعادة الحاصلة من الوفاق بين الزوجين، وذلك الشقاء المتأتي من ضد ذلك.' إن هو إلا سافل لئيم.»

«أما عمله هذا فهو في الحقيقة مغاير للحق والإنسانية ولكن ما الحيلة وهو أب. والأب له أن يتصرف بشؤون ابنته كيفما شاء. فهو لا يتمكن على معارضته أحد—حتى ابنته نفسها.»

«من أجاز للأب ذلك؟»

«ديننا.»

«إن الدين لا يكون ديناً صحيحاً (بكل معنى الكلمة) ما لم يكن مطابقاً لما يقتضيه العقل، موافقاً لما يرتضيه الوجدان النقي والضمير الطاهر وملائماً للإنسانية والعدل والأنصاف، آمراً بالمعروف، ناهياً عن المنكر، داعياً لاستعمال الرأفة والرحمة بين البشر. ولما كان احتمال وقوع أشياء مغايرة للعدل والأنصاف بين أفراد البشر، كغصب الآباء حقوق بناتهم مثلاً، فكيف أعطى الدين للأباء هذه السلطة الواسعة. تلك السلطة التي جعلت البنت وهي ذات عقل وشعور وإحساس كمتاع تحت ملك أبيها، يلعب بها كيفما شاء وشاءت أهوائه واقتضت أغراضه. ويعطيها لمن يريده ويختاره بدون التفات لما يضر الابنة وما ينفعها. إن هذا إلا أمر عجيب.»

«حق ما تقولين، ولكنني مع ذلك لا أعتقد بوجود دين على وجه البسيطة أسقط حق المرأة وجعلها مهانة ذليلة إلى هذه الدرجة. بيد أن النص الناطق

بالإطاعة المشروعة التي فرض الدين أداءها لوليها. قد فسر بهذه الصورة الشنيعة التي نرى بني قومنا يعملون بها.»

«من فسر ذلك النص؟»

«فسره رؤساء الدين.»

«إذاً اتضح أنهم على ضلال مبين.»

«صدقتِ ولكن أنا يتاح لي أو لك معارضة رؤساء الدين بهذا الشأن، سيما وإن الرأي العام طوع إرادتهم ومع إرادتهم، ومع ذلك فالعادة جرت منذ القدم على هذا المنوال. ومتى تحكمت العادة في أمة صارت ديناً. وأنت تعلمين كيف تكون عاقبة الذين هم للدين معارضين وللتقاليد القومية القديمة منتقدين.»

«كيف لا أعلم . . . ولولا ذلك لما أرغمت على عدم المصارحة بأمري والمجاهرة مدافعة عن حقوقي. ولما أُجبرت على السكوت وقلبي يذوب توجعاً وتفجعاً.»

وهنا أحس جينارام بخطورة المبحث وأراد تغيير الكلام والتهوين على كستور فقال: «بيد أنني يا كستور لا أظن أن ذلك اللص الذي حاول أمراً بتجرأه على ذلك التهديد البارد يستطيع أن ينال منك أو مني منالاً.»

«كيف ذلك؟»

«ستعلمين بالفعل لا بالكلام.» (قال ذلك بحماس وشدة.)

«أنني أعلم ذلك قبل أن تقول لي وأنا واثقة من شهامتك وإقدامك المشهور. ولكن مع هذا فهل يطمئن قلبي من هذا اللص الفتاك الذي لا تأخذه في سفك الدماء لومة لائم سيما وقد عجزت أن تناله هو وعصابته الناس، وهو في محل يكاد يكون أمنع من عقاب الجو. وما عسى أن تكون الحيلة التي نتخلص بها من ذلك الغدار.»

«قلت لك يا حبيبتي أنه لن يستطيع أن ينال منا شيئاً ولما كنت لا أقدر أن أنكر خطورة هذا الأمر فسأنظر في مسألة وأخبرك بما سأعزم عليه فكوني باطمئنان. وأوصيك أيضاً أن تخفي هذا الأمر خصوصاً عن والدك وانظري إشعاري النهائي بعد ثلاثة أيام.»

وبعد ذلك أخذ الكتابين ووضعهما في جيبه وقاما من هناك فودعا بعضهما وذهب كل منهم إلى حال سبيله.

Part 6: Poetic Expressions

This part introduces the poets Hafez Ibrahim, Mahmud Sami al-Barudi, and 'Aisha Taymur. Aligning the well-known works of Ibrahim and al-Barudi with Taymur's less-studied poetry allows us to rethink the question of the literary canon and its relation to national narratives of cultural and political development. The ideal citizen—man, woman, and child—is a central theme in these poems, which show how heroism and bravery, truth and fidelity intersect with less normative models of power and communication that shape literary genres.

Ibrahim presents the poem as a space for expressing views on education and ethics. His didactic use of poetry, which takes the shape of a question-and-answer session between an adult and a child, calls attention to the role of literature in inculcating *Nahda* values. The education he espouses is activated in al-Barudi's poems about politics, pride, and exile following the 'Urabi revolution in late-nineteenth-century Cairo. In his criticism of the tyranny embodied in neoclassical poetry, al-Barudi extols the traditional values of the Arab warrior-poet in order to express a modern struggle and sensitivity. Taymur's poem reminds us that female power, though silent, is no less powerful than male power. Power takes shape in various ways and at various levels in this part, thereby complicating our understanding and assessment of the *Nahda* poetic tradition and its relation to the Arabic classical tradition.

Hafez Ibrahim
(1872–1932)

Introduced and translated by Kamran Rastegar

Hafez Ibrahim is considered one of the premier poets of the
Nahda period, identified along with Mahmud al-Barudi and
Ahmad Shawqi with what came to be known as the neoclassi-
cal movement, which revived classical forms such as the qasida
(ode) to address contemporary social and often political themes.
Celebrated as a composer of patriotic and anticolonial poems
and given the populist title Poet of the Nile, Ibrahim is some-
what less well appreciated for his prose, despite its importance.
His prose works include the didactic work *Su'al . . . wa-Jawab*
("Questions . . . and Answers") excerpted here, which takes the
form of a meandering dialogue concerning matters of social
mores, ethics, and education, among other themes. In works
such as these, we are presented with a distilled sense of how
deeply concerned *Nahda* thinkers were with questions of per-
sonal improvement and education and the responsibility of the
individual to society—even if the legitimacy for these views
was no longer derived from a religiously based conception of
morality. Ibrahim's *Questions . . . and Answers*, for example,
gives little emphasis to religious morality, using instead the con-
cept of social responsibility as the framework for establishing
the qualities of virtue.

In Ibrahim's case, these concerns may also have had a per-
sonal element: born in modest circumstances, Ibrahim moved
through the ranks of the Egyptian army and the government
bureaucracy before gaining fame for his poetry. Many of his
generation found that the emergence of new social institutions
such as the modern state administration, national schools, and
the reformed military required a revisiting of ethical and social

questions—finding affirmation in certain traditional conceptions of virtue while also forging new stances on other matters.

Recommended Reading

Arberry, A. J. "Hafiz Ibrahim and Shauqi." *Journal of the Royal Asiatic Society of Great Britain and Ireland*, vol. 1, 1937, pp. 41–58.

Badawi, M. M. *A Critical Introduction to Modern Arabic Poetry.* Cambridge UP, 1975.

Hartman, Michelle. "Hafiz Ibrahim." *Essays in Arabic Literary Biography, 1850–1950*, edited by Roger Allen, Harrassowitz Verlag, 2010, pp. 149–59.

Jayyusi, Salma Khadra. *Trends and Movements in Modern Arabic Poetry, Volume 1*. E. G. Brill, 1977.

Khouri, Mounah Abdallah. *Poetry and the Making of Modern Egypt, 1882–1922*. E. G. Brill, 1971.

FROM *Questions . . . and Answers*

Chapter 2: Duty to the Self

Q. How do you know you have a self?

A. I know that I have a self, for I understand, I feel, and I desire.

Q. How do you know that you comprehend, and what is the sign of your intellect or your intelligence?

A. My intelligence is evident to me whenever I memorize a lesson or solve a problem, and when the best of the explanations that my teachers and relatives offer me guide me toward what is right, just, and laudable.

Q. What is the sign of your feelings or your sentiments?

A. My having feelings is evident to me whenever I see myself drawn to love and comfort those like me. So if I behold a beautiful sight or I hear of a good deed, my self is moved and my emotions roused.

Q. What is the sign of your will?

A. My will is evident to me whenever I see my self showing an inclination to distraction and amusement but oppose it by engaging in work. And whenever I have a penchant to carry out a blameworthy act but resist it until I cast it away. And whenever I face two choices, I set [my will] on making the more noble choice, even if it is a bitter one while the other [choice] is sweet.

Q. And what allows you to recognize these signs—signs of the intellect, feeling, and will?

A. My inner self and conscience.

Q. What is the inner self or conscience?

A. It is that inner voice that allows me to differentiate between good and evil. It is the guide that leads me through life and the judge that holds me accountable when I do wrong and puts me at ease when I submit to it and do good.

Q. And must a person heed the call of conscience?

A. Yes, a person must heed this call and carry out what it inspires him to do, and never waver in the face of difficulties or be confounded in the face of hardship.

Chapter 3: Duty to the Body

Q. Why should you preserve the health of the body?

A. I should preserve the body's health because of that firm bond between the body and the soul, because if the body falls ill, the soul is unsettled.

Q. Are you then absolutely certain that the condition of the body affects that of the soul?

A. Yes, for I remember that when I fell ill last year, I was unable to work and [afterward] I was no longer the same child I knew before illness struck.

Q. How do you feel when you are in good health?
A. I feel I am in good health whenever I find myself happy and energetic, bursting with desire to fulfill my duties.

Q. How do you preserve the health of your body?
A. I preserve the health of my body by committing each day to its good hygiene, to exercising it in the open air, and to avoiding excess in all things, especially what is [religiously] forbidden. In short, I preserve my body by following the rules of good health.

Q. Does the body require this much care?
A. Yes, for it is a machine of extraordinary composition, precise construction, and delicate temperament.

Chapter 4: How to Be a Virtuous Man

Q. You have said that you would like to be a virtuous man—how can you achieve that?
A. I can achieve that by:
First: developing and nourishing my powers of the self, by which I mean that I would endeavor to expand my intellectual capability as well as my sensitivity and will.
Second: strengthening in my self the characteristics that [already] beautify it, and seeking out what is lacking from it in order to bring it closer to perfection.
Third: healing and correcting all that I see as a malformation in my self and taming it to oppose its whims.
Fourth: training my self to love virtues and developing self-control.

Q. How do you develop your intelligence?
A. I develop my intelligence first by working hard at school; second by befriending my teachers and conversing with them; and third by reading useful books, so that I feel each day that I am a better person than I was the day before.

Q. How do you develop your feelings?
A. I develop my feelings by being concerned with all that happens around me rather than by focusing on what happens to me only. So I engage all that happens to my friends by being happy for their happiness and sad for their sadness and by offering them advice and compassion and everything else that I am able to. I also develop my feelings by allowing my self to freely appreciate all that is beautiful in nature and great in mankind.

Q. How do you develop your will?
A. I develop my will by setting for my self, every morning, a path from which I will not deviate. And by always reminding my self: I want to be a hard-working student, a devoted son, a committed patriot, and a complete man.

Chapter 9: Faults That Must Be Avoided

Q. How do you view the drunkard?
A. I believe that I abhor him because he is trying, unknowingly, to poison himself and ruin his life. I believe that he is hurting his self and condemning it by casting off its cloak of honor. And I believe that he is condemning his family because he is depriving them of life's bare necessities in order to feed his desires.

Q. How do you view a man who is controlled by his anger?
A. I believe that he is a man who lacks control over his self and is unable to rein in his anger, thus exposing himself to making mistakes. Even when he returns to his senses, his anger is only replaced by remorse.

Q. How do you view a man who beats his wife?
A. I believe that he is committing a cowardly act because he is attacking someone who is physically weaker than him. His action is loathsome because he is shirking his duty toward his partner in life, the mother of his children.

Q. How do you view a man who mistreats his children?

A. I believe that he is failing in his duties to educate them and that he is stripping away the respect and affection that his children have for him. Instead, he is planting fear in them, so that should they obey him, which they will do fearfully rather than willingly.

Q. How do you view a driver who is cruel to his horses?

A. I believe that he is committing a cowardly act, because he is beating an animal that is unable to defend itself. I believe that he is acting in an extremely ungrateful manner by ignoring the solemn tasks that his horses perform each day. He who is cruel and hard-hearted toward animals is likely to be the same toward people.

Q. What would you do if hateful thoughts were to overtake your mind and resentment were to settle in your heart?

A. I would sit alone and I would address my self, saying that since people are created to be brothers to one another then they should love one another. I would also tell [my self] that as you are not free from sin, you should become accustomed to forgiving others. May bad deeds be written in the sand and may good deeds be etched in stone.

Q. How may one gain tolerance of others?

A. One may gain tolerance of others if he endures his opponents' shortcomings when arguing with them, especially if the crux of the argument revolves around politics or religion. For if we demand freedom [of belief] for ourselves, why would we deny it to others?

Q. What would you do if you were stricken by feelings of jealousy or envy?

A. I would say to my self: Jealousy and envy are flaws that stem from narcissism and insensitivity. For if I ever sense the impulse of envy, I look around me and say to my self: Thank God I find my self in a condition that many others would wish to have.

Q. How does one suffer from narcissism or egoism?

A. A narcissist is one who is unaffected and unmoved by the problems of others. So you find him indulging in seclusion and removing himself from societies with noble aims, such as cooperative associations and charitable organizations.

Q. When is one ungrateful and a denier of blessings?

A. One is ungrateful if he forgets or pretends to forget the origin of kindness. A child is ungrateful if he scoffs at the care of his relatives or the advice of his teachers. The ungrateful person is he who would never reciprocate kindness, for what else can we call one who answers good deeds with bad ones?

Q. How do you view lying?

A. I believe that lying is the pinnacle of the shortcomings from which we should turn away. He who lies deceives. He who lies acts in a cowardly manner. He who lies degrades human dignity.

Q. What would you do if you found that you had lied?

A. If I had done this, I would meet with the person whom I had deceived with my lying and I would tell him the full truth about the matter, regardless of the consequences.

Q. How do you view duplicity?

A. I believe it to be the ugliest form of lying, because the duplicitous person is able to harm people in ways unrivaled by the liar. He conceals beneath a veil of virtue his ill intent until he is able to fool those who engage with him.

Q. When is a man considered a coward?

A. He is a coward if he attacks those who are weaker than him and retreats in the face of danger when duty calls. He also shirks responsibility, and when his desire or fear is stirred up, he betrays those who have trusted him.

Q. When is a person conceited?

A. A person is conceited when he overvalues his own worth, his wealth, and his social rank, seeing in himself what others do not see in him, which leads him to disdain them. . . . Conceited people forget that only virtue determines men's fortunes, and they are ignorant of the fact that humility is one of virtue's pillars.

Source of Arabic Text on Which the Translation Is Based

Ibrahim, Hafez. الأعمال النثرية [al-a'mal al-nathriyya; Prose Works]. Al-Majlis al-A'la lil-thaqafa, 2007, pp. 467–92.

حافظ إبراهيم
(١٨٧٢-١٩٣٢)

سؤال . . . وجواب

الفصل الثاني: «واجب النفس»

س: كيف تعرف أن لك نفساً؟

ج: أعرف أن لي نفساً لأني أفهم، وأحس، وأريد.

س: كيف تعلم أنك تفهم وما هو مظهر فهمك أو ذكائك؟

ج: إن مظهر ذكائي يتجلى لي كلما حفظت درساً أو حللت مسألة، والفضل كل الفضل في ذلك للإيضاحات التي أتلقاها عن أستاذي وأقاربي فهي التي ترشدني إلى كل ما هو حق وعدل ومحمود.

س: ما هو مظهر شعورك أو إحساسك؟

ج: إن مظهر إحساسي يتجلى لي كلما رأيت نفسي محمولاً على حب أشباهي ومواساتهم، فإذا تراءى لي منظر جميل أو قص علي نبأ عمل جليل تحركت نفسي وتنبهت عواطفي.

س: ما هو مظهر إرادتك؟

ج: إن مظهر إرادتي يتجلى لي كلما رأيت في نفسي ميلاً إلى اللهو واللعب فخالفتها ونزعت إلى العمل، وكلما هممت بارتكاب أمر ملوم فقاومتها حتى أصرفها عنه، وكلما وقفت موقف الخيار بين شيئين فوطنتها على اختيار أشرفهما وإن كان مراً وصرفتها عن أجملهما وإن كان حلواً.

س: ما الذي يأذن لك بتحقيق تلك المظاهر—مظاهر الفهم، والإحساس، والإرادة؟

ج: سريرتي أو ضميري.

س: ما هي السريرة أو الضمير؟

ج: هي ذلك الصوت الداخلي الذي يلهمني التفريق بين الخير والشر؛ هي الدليل الذي يقودني في الحياة، والقاضي الذي يقاضيني على عمل الشر، والذي أرتاح لوقوفي بين يديه عند صنع الخير.

س: أيجب على المرء أن يطيع نداء السريرة؟

ج: نعم يجب على المرء أن يطيع ذلك النداء وأن يعمل بما يوحيه إليه، فلا يحجم في سبيله أمام الصعوبات ولا يجمد أمام المشاق.

الفصل الثالث: «واجب الجسم»

س: لماذا يجب عليك أن تحافظ على صحة الجسم؟

ج: يجب عليّ أن أحافظ على صحة الجسم لأجل تلك الصلة المتينة التي بينه وبين الروح، فإذا مرض الجسم اضطربت الروح.

س: ألنت إذا على يقين تام من أن حالة الجسم تؤثر في حالة الروح؟

ج: نعم لأني أذكر عندما مرضت في العام الماضي أنني كنت غير قادر على العمل ولم أكن ذلك الطفل الذي كنت أعهده قبل المرض.

س: كيف تشعر أنك في صحة جيدة؟

ج: أشعر أنني في صحة جيدة كلما وجدت نفسي مسروراً، نشطاً تنبعث فيّ قابلية القيام بالواجب.

س: كيف تحافظ على صحة جسمك؟

ج: أحافظ على صحة جسمي بتعهده كل يوم بالنظافة والاعتناء ومعالجة تمرينه في الهواء الطلق، وباجتناب الإفراط في كل شيء، وخصوصاً اجتناب المحرمات، والاختصار أحافظ على جسمي باتباع قانون الصحة.

س: أيحتاج الجسم إلى كل هذه العناية؟

ج: نعم فإنه آلة عجيبة التركيب، دقيقة الصنع، لطيفة المزاج.

الفصل الرابع: «كيف تكون رجلاً فاضلاً»

س: لقد قلت إنك تود أن تكون رجلاً فاضلاً، فكيف تستطيع ذلك؟

ج: أستطيع ذلك:

أولاً: أنمّي وأغذّي قوى النفس، أعني أنني أجاهد في توسيع مدارك الذكاء، والإحساس والإرادة.

ثانياً: أقوي في نفسي صفاتها التي تتجمل بها وأسعى وراء ما أجده فيها من النقص حتى تشرف على الكمال.

ثالثاً: أعالج وأداوي كل ما أراه في نفسي من العيوب وأروض نفسي على مخالفة الهوى.

رابعاً: أعود نفسي حب الفضائل وتنمية قوى النفس.

س: كيف تنمّي ذكاءك؟

ج: أمّي ذكائي أولاً بالاجتهاد في المدرسة. ثانياً بصحبة المتعلمين والتحدث إليهم. ثالثاً بقراءة الكتب النافعة، حتى أشعر أنني في يومي خير مني في أمْسي.

س: كيف تنمّي شعورك؟

ج: أمّي شعوري بأن أهتم بكل ما يقع حولي لا أقتصر في ذلك على ما يقع لي، بل أتناول كل ما يقع لأصحابي؛ فأفرح لفرحهم وأحزن لحزنهم وأعينهم بالنصيحة والعطف وكل ما تصل إليه طاقتي. وأمّي أيضاً شعوري بإرسال نفسي على سجيتها تستحسن كل ما هو جميل من صنع الطبيعة وعظيم من صنع الإنسان.

س: كيف تنمّي إرادتك؟

ج: أمّي إرادتي بأن أضع لي في كل صباح خطةً لا أنحرف عن صراطها. وأقول لنفسي دائماً: إني أريد أن أكون تلميذاً مجتهداً وولداً باراً، ووطنياً نافعاً، ورجلاً كاملاً.

الفصل التاسع: «النقائص التي يجب اجتنابها»

س: ماذا ترى في الرجل السكير؟

ج: أرى أني أمقته لأنه يعمل على تسميم نفسه، وسوء مصيره، وهو يجهل ماذا يعمل.

وأرى أنه مسيء إلى نفسه، جان عليها لأنه يطرح عنها رداء الشرف.

وأراه جانياً على أسرته لأنه يحرمها من ضروريات القوت ليرضي شهواته.

س: ماذا ترى في الرجل الذي يملك الغضب عنانه؟

ج: إني أرى الرجل الذي لا يملك أمر نفسه ويكبح جماح غضبه يتعرض لركوب الزلل؛ حتى إذا ثاب إلى رشده حل منه الندم محل الغضب.

س: ماذا ترى في الرجل الذي يضرب زوجته؟

ج: أرى أنه يفعل فعل الجبان لأنه يهاجم من هو أضعف منه حولاً. إن عمله ممقوت لأنه يقصر في واجب الاحترام لرفيقة حياته، وأم أولاده.

س: ماذا ترى في الرجل الذي لا يحسن معاملة أولاده؟

ج: أرى أنه يقصّر في واجب الإصلاح، وينزع من نفوس أولاده احترامهم لذاته وميلهم إليه، ويغرس فيها مكان ذلك خوفهم منه فإذا أطاعوه: أطاعوه رهبة لا رغبة.

س: ماذا ترى في السائق الذي لا يرفق بخيوله؟

ج: أرى أنه يفعل فعل الجبان لأنه يضرب حيواناً لا يملك أمر الدفاع عن نفسه وأرى أنه فوق ذلك يبالغ في نكران الجميل لأنه يتناسى الأعمال الجليلة التي تقوم بها خيوله في كل يوم: إن الذي يكون فظاً غليظ القلب مع الحيوانات لا يبعد أن يكون كذلك مع الناس.

س: ماذا تصنع إذا نزلت برأسك فكرة البغض أو زار صدرك ضيف الحقد؟

ج: أجلس إلى نفسي وأناديها أيتها النفس، إن الناس قد خلقوا إخواناً فيجب عليهم أن يتحابوا؛ وأقول لها إن لك من الذنوب ما تحتاجين معه إلى طلب الصفح عنه فيجب عليك أن تتعودي الصفح عن غيرك. فلتخط السيئات على الرمال، ولتنقش الحسنات على الصخور.

س: كيف يكون المرء متسامحاً؟

ج: يكون متسامحاً إذا تحمل في الجدال غضاضة المعارضة، وخصوصاً إذا كان محور الجدال يدور على السياسة والدين. فإنا ننشد الحرية لأنفسنا فلماذا لا نترك لغيرنا حق التمتع بها؟

س: ماذا تصنع إذا خطر بك خاطر الغيرة أو الحسد؟

ج: أقول بيني وبين نفسي: إن الغيرة أو الحسد خلقان ذميمان يصدران عن حب الأثرة وغلظ القلب. على أني كلما أحسست بنزوة من نزوات الحسد تلفت حولي وقلت لنفسي إني أراني بحمد الله في حالة يتمناها الكثير.

س: كيف يكون المرء محباً لذاته (أو صاحب أثرة)؟

ج: إن المحبّ لذاته هو الذي لا تتأثر نفسه ولا تتحرك عواطفه لمصاب غيره، فتراه يبالغ في العزلة والهروب من المجتمعات النبيلة المقصد كجمعيات التعاون والجمعيات الخيرية.

س: متى يكون المرء ناكراً للجميل كافراً بالنعمة؟

ج: يكون المرء ناكراً للجميل إذا نسي أو تناسى مصادر المعروف. ويكون الطفل ناكراً للجميل إذا لسوء سلوكه من عناية أقاربه ونصائح معلميه. فناكر الجميل

على كل حال هو ذلك الذي لا يقابل الإحسان بمثله، فما عسى أن تسمّي من يقابل الإحسان بالسيئة؟

س: ماذا ترى في الكذب؟

ج: أرى أنه رأس النقائص التي يجب أن نفر منها. من كذب فقد غش. من كذب فقد جبن. من كذب فقد انتقص كرامة النفس البشرية.

س: ماذا تصنع إذا اتفق لك أنك كذبت مرة؟

ج: إذا اتفق لي ذلك أبادر إلى لقاء من غششته بالكذب وأنفض إليه جملة الأمر على حقيقتها مهماً كانت المغبة.

س: ماذا ترى في النفاق؟

ج: أرى أنه أقبح ضروب الكذب: لأن المنافق المداجي يبلغ الكيد للناس ما لا يبلغه الكذوب، ويخفي خلف ستار الفضيلة ما يخفي من سوء المقصد حتى ينخدع به من يحدثه.

س: متى يكون المرء جباناً؟

ج: يكون المرء جباناً إذا هاجم من هو أضعف منه حولاً، وتقهقر أمام الأخطار عند تأدية الواجب، وفر من المسؤولية وصاح به صائح الرغبة أو الرهبة فتخون من كان له مؤتمنا.

س: متى يكون المرء متكبراً؟

ج: يكون المرء متكبراً إذا بالغ في تقدير قيمة نفسه، وثروته، ومركزه فرأى في نفسه ما لا يراه غيره فيها حتى يسوقه ذلك إلى احتقار الناس . . . فالمتكبرون ينسون أن الفضيلة وحدها هي التي تقوم بأقدار الرجال، ويجهلون أن التواضع أحد أركان الفضيلة.

Mahmud Sami al-Barudi
(1839–1904)

Introduced and translated by Yaseen Noorani

Mahmud Sami al-Barudi is widely regarded as the founder of modern Arabic poetry and was a leader of the so-called 'Urabi Revolt in Egypt (1881–82), which was suppressed by the British, who then occupied the country.

At the time al-Barudi was born, Egyptian society was divided into a ruling elite, whose members were of Ottoman and Circassian origin or affiliation, and those regarded as native Egyptians, who composed most of the remainder of the population. Al-Barudi was the scion of a Circassian family of means and status. Like his father, a brigadier general, he took up a military career. In 1863, he joined the retinue of Khedive Isma'il, the ruler of Egypt, and served in Ottoman campaigns in Crete and during the Russian War. During the 1870s, al-Barudi began to feel discontented with the extravagant and oppressive rule of Isma'il, whose expenditures created a fiscal crisis and led to British and French intervention. Al-Barudi took part in the political and intellectual ferment of the time, forging links with intellectuals of the so-called native Egyptian classes, as well as with the leading military officer, Ahmad 'Urabi, and his associates. This culminated in al-Barudi's participation in the 'Urabi Revolt, during which al-Barudi served briefly as Egypt's prime minister. He was exiled by the British to Ceylon in 1882, and he was not allowed to return to Egypt until 1899.

Titles have been provided for the selected poems. "Heroic Manifesto," published in 1875 when al-Barudi was a high-ranking military officer, helped establish his reputation as the leading poet of his time. It displays the heroic poetic persona that is his trademark. The next two poems of political denunciation, evidently composed in the 1870s, were not published at the time but probably circulated clandestinely. The final poem, composed during al-Barudi's exile, is an apologia justifying his actions during the 'Urabi Revolt.

Recommended Reading

Badawi, M. M. *A Critical Introduction to Modern Arabic Poetry*. Cambridge UP, 1975.

De Young, Terri. *Mahmud Sami al-Barudi: Reconfiguring Society and the Self*. Syracuse UP, 2015.

Jayyusi, Salma Khadra. *Trends and Movements in Modern Arabic Poetry*. Vol. 1, Brill, 1977.

Noorani, Yaseen. *Culture and Hegemony in the Colonial Middle East*. Palgrave Macmillan, 2010.

FROM *Diwan*

Ode 1: "Heroic Manifesto"

I was heedless of all but what the conscience encloses,
    and I concealed all but what is betrayed by a sigh.
Is a man able to keep his condition hidden
    when hot winds and flames rage within his chest?
May God curse passion, so forceful is it
    upon a man when it finds him alone and overpowers him.
The soul yields to it, though the soul is proud;
    the heart quails before it though the heart is steadfast.
I cast away my lance and sheathed my sword
    and held back my colt though the plunder was plenty,
And stood clipped of my claws after having
    pounced with a roar that resounded on the horizons.
I call upon the chiefs of my people, seeking aid—
    is there no one among you who hears and gives refuge?

The night has stretched long for me, I'm weary of it,
    for in the past my nights were always too short.
May God keep that time of love, so fine was it,
    and may he preserve the time of youth that passed, resplendent,
When life was the dappled shade of boughs
    upon us and the fresh waters of loyalty were plenty,
And when we, a band of pleasure seekers,
    were possessed of virtues none to be despised;
The cup circling among us, in playgrounds,
    where amusement is a friend and youth a companion;
Our glances messengers between souls,
    and sprigs of basil ambassadors between our cups.
We linked together the wings of night with day,
    and we flew with our pleasures wherever they took us.
We said to our cupbearer, "Send it over,
    for life does not last long after youth."
He brought it around, a fiery sun-wine
    that riles up the minds of men.
When we drank it, we stayed where we were,
    while the room around us began revolving.
So many nights whose darkness I outlasted,
    until the first gleam of dawn appeared;
I filled my mind and delighted my sight,
    I gratified my hearing, but my hands stayed pure—
I did with them as the generous do for their kin
    and neighbors; though those who do wrong are many.
We were transfixed then by the fluttering of doves
    that, among the foliage of boughs, were warbling,
In answer to their companions in thickets,
    whom they missed and serenaded;
Soft ones, they know not the misery of life,
    or how the wheel of fortune turns around;
They rest upon their own heads as their pillows,
    plush with long feathers and down;
It is as if they wore, woven upon themselves,
    necklaces not fastened by any string;

Leaving one grove and entering another,
    enraptured by full shade and a brook;
When the sun caresses them they glitter as if
    they were clothed in brocade and silk.
When I made out the glimmer of the morning's throat,
    and that not a strand of the weave of darkness remained,
I set out with a proud stride, for indeed,
    he swaggers who is chaste despite his power of action.
I am of a character that refuses any shameful thing and of a resolve
    that knocks off balance a swarming horde.
When I set out, the whole earth
    is my ambit, and my resting places are fortresses.
There is no wonder that no home can detain me,
    for eagles of the air have no nests.
A glory-seeking soul whose mount is not wearied
    by journeys of day and night that never cease,
Accustomed never to pull up short
    from its solemn purpose until matters are settled.
It has an ear that hears the unknown,
    and an eye that sees what the seer does not see.
I have been faithful to what the noble discerned
    in me and one like me is bound to keep faith.
I am envied of my grandeur as if
    I were the lord of every soul in this age.
When I attack, fate leaves off its aggression
    and when I speak, men's hearts fill their chests.
I hold the keys to speech and a wisdom
    that is a brilliant star of resplendent light.
Had I lived in the age of poetry of long ago,
    Farazdaq and Jarir would have acknowledged my excellence.
Had I lived in the time of Abu Nuwas he would never have said,
    "O girl next door, your father is too jealous."[1]
It is no loss to me that I came after them,
    for my excellence is famed the world over:
It may happen that the first out loses the race
    and it may happen that the leaders are overtaken by latecomers.

Ode 2: "A Political Prophecy"

I bid farewell to an age of unrestrained passion,
  an age whose features were still soft and fresh;
What I loved of its beauty had scarcely passed,
  before its thorn found the recess of my heart.
How to reach a state in which we can manage to survive,
  in which we are immune to the shocks of fate,
When there is no friend who does not slander you absent,
  no companion at whose presence the eye is gladdened.
We hoped for a revolution that would give us peace,
  until it took place and its outcome appalled us.
The heart is disturbed in all that it endeavors,
  and the mind is confounded by what it fears.
What was beneficial among those of the past,
  has become harmful among those who remain.

. . . .

Once familiar, Egypt has become a stranger;
  sovereignty has been shaken, its foundations disturbed.
Because of tyranny the tiller has left his land;
  fearing penury, the merchant has forsaken commerce;
The reign of fear is so complete
  that men lie sleepless under the blanket of night.
A bitter abode—were it not for its buried treasure
  of past virtue, we would not abide in it;
Yet I would be content in it, unblessed by its bounty,
  seeing my hopes lie elsewhere, were it not for its inhabitants.
O my soul, don't panic, for good is still awaited,
  and he who is patient, his resolve does not falter;
There may well be a dawning of light
  after the darkness whose gloom is engulfing.
I see souls overburdened by what they carry;
  he who can draw his sword shall draw it.
Two months, or even less, if things worsen;
  In their passing is that which enriches the poor.
If I see true, it is with insight by which I possess
  knowledge of the hidden, for a man's insight oversees him.[2]

Ode 3: "A Political Manifesto"

I have sucked out the marrow of this age in experience,
  and I have tasted what it has, bitter and sweet,
And I have found nothing that keeps better over the passage of time,
  more delightful to the soul, than freedom of action.
But we are the quarry of evil in a time
  in which those with sense must obey those with none.
An age ruled by a base company,
  more painful to the soul than the misery of bereavement;
Scoundrels fit to be spat out of office
  and barred from responsibility out of contempt.
After glory, Egypt has been by them abased,
  and the pillars of rule damaged and disturbed.
The government of Cairo brought low
  after nobility was once the flower of governments.
A band of men who, when they see me approaching,
  fall silent in anger, their gall boiling in hatred.
If my virtue galls them, it is no wonder,
  for the shining sun is blinding to the eye.
I am above all that they soil themselves in;
  the honey bee scorns the depravity of the dung beetle.
How wretched a company and how wretched a land Egypt,
  become a playground for every swindler and prattler;
A land entrenched in tyranny, crisscrossed
  from mountain to sea by bolts of treachery;
Its people enveloped in a black blindness,
  in which none can move without stumbling

. . . .

They do not push away a hand though it
  sullies their honor, out of cowardice and weakness;
They fear death and plot against it, knowing not
  that death cannot be stayed by plotting;
How can one accuse his creator,
  when every soul is destined to die?
Never can a man find peace and comfort
  without having plunged into a sea of adversity.

Why then do your souls not scorn to be wronged,
  and why do you not cease to be afflicted for your indolence?
While before you is Egypt, in which war made perish
  the noblest of your forbears in ancient times;
A race of men who planted the pillars of truth and held
  reign over mankind, rich as well as poor;
They harvested the fruits of greatness with gleaming swords
  and plucked the mountain flower of hope from among thorns;
Egypt came to flower after lying fallow,
  drenched by showers of fresh dew.
The earth did not sprout until it was leavened
  with blood shed from necks put to the sword;
They waged a campaign so frightful, it made
  a peace that encompassed even wolf and lamb;
Until Egypt became an impregnable fortress
  able to fend off the hand of any foreign enemy.
Time brought low her champions, and she became,
  after being unassailable, trampled upon by every wayfarer.
What ignominy do you now bring through failure
  upon that glory raised to heaven by the sword—
For if a man has no intellect by which to live
  let him then be counted among cows and sheep.
So take the matter into your hands, before it escapes you,
  and be not chained by tardiness—the world is with haste

. . . .

This is the counsel of one who wishes no substitute
  for you—is there any substitute for a man's own people?
For you I have forsaken sleep, fashioning verses
  without parallel in ancient poetry;
Like lightening in speed, like thunder in rhythm,
  pouring down like rain, an untrammeled torrent;
A brilliant poem, met by the hearing with ecstasy,
  and uplifting the senses in joy,
A full year in the making, wrought by thought
  whose miracles are attested by the races of men and spirits.

. . . .

The souls of men perish, yet it shall abide new
over the passage of ages, like the seven long odes.[3]

Ode 4: "The 'Urabi Revolt: The True Story"

Though time has muddied the waters from which I drink,
and blunted my blade with continuous calamity,
Persecution has not changed my character,
nor treachery affected my conduct.

. . . .

O you who despise me in ignorance,
and know not that I am a crown pearl,
Console yourself with ignominy in place of glory and away with
you,
for glory is not attained by senseless raving.

. . . .

Some say that I engaged in unlawful rebellion—
that is a vice that is not of my character.
I called for justice, pursuing
God's approval, and I called up the men of virtue.
I commanded the good and forbade the evil,
and that is a law to which all men are bound;
If my stand was truly rebellion,
then I sought in my rebellion obedience to my creator.
What sin is there in calling for consultative rule,
which supplies the criterion for all who seek guidance?
Indeed, it is a divine prescription, incumbent
upon every being, ruler and ruled.
How can a man be free and civilized
yet suffer every reprobate to do what he pleases?

. . . .

Yet I gave my utmost in counseling a group
who refused in their treachery to accept sincere advice.
They chose to rule the people by force and hastened
to destroy what had been built by trustworthy hands.

As injustice persisted, a body of men rose up
    from the army, striving beneath banners,
And their countrymen supported them and flocked
    to them quickly, following and joining,
Seeking from the lord of the land his fulfillment
    of the sincere promises he had made to the people.
But when the rulers refused but to persist
    and the demand for right was thwarted,
Certain persons traded guidance for error
    in duplicity and sold their religion for a farthing:
So came those who helped them in error
    with the deceit of an assassin and the ruse of a thief.
When they had their way in the country and were assured
    of the defeat of its sworn defenders,
They stayed and said, "This, O people, is now our land,
    and none of us is going to leave it."
They rampaged there, expelling those whose might
    they feared, and that was but one of the calamities;
And the Nile Valley became plunder,
    its once-proud kingdom a rogue's venture.
This is the manifest truth, so ask not
    but me concerning it, for I am cognizant of truth.
O Egypt, may God increase your shade and water,
    your earth with the sweet floods of the Nile,
And may the hand of your morning breeze forever nourish
    with fragrant breaths that heal all who breathe them;
For you are the sanctuary of my people, the home of my family,
    the playground of my friends, the track of my horses;
The land in which I wore the amulets of childhood,
    and where my sword strap was hung on my shoulder.
. . . .
Though the vagaries of time have worked ill,
    I am, by the grace of God, ever trusting:
Things may return to their course after going awry,
    and to his homeland may return each who has left it.[4]

Notes

[1]Human b. Ghalib al-Farazdaq (died c. 730) and Jarir b. 'Atiyya al-Kalbi (died c. 728) were celebrated rival poets of the Umayyad period. Abu Nuwas, al-Hasan b. Hani' (756–814), was one of the foremost poets of the Abbasid period, known as the greatest wine poet of Arabic literature. The quoted verse is the first verse of a famous poem of Abu Nuwas that al-Barudi challenges with the current poem, which has been composed in the same rhyme and meter.

[2]These lines are from a poem that denounces the state of Egypt and predicts a battle that will cleanse it of political corruption. It is possible that the hoped-for revolution in which the poet expresses his disappointment is the replacement of the Khedive Isma'il by his son Tawfiq in 1879.

[3]These lines are from a long poem calling on Egyptians to revolt against tyranny during the reign of Isma'il.

[4]In these lines, which were composed in exile, al-Barudi proudly vindicates his political actions and condemns Egypt's ruling class and the British invasion.

Source of Arabic Texts on Which the Translation Is Based

Al-Barudi, Mahmud Sami. ديوان البارودي [diwan al-barudi; Poetry Collection of al-Barudi]. Edited by 'Ali Jarim and Muhammad Shafiq Maruf, Dar al-Ma'arif, 1971. "Heroic Manifesto," pp. 209–12; "A Political Prophecy," pp. 268–70; "A Political Manifesto," pp. 396–415; "The 'Urabi Revolt," pp. 385–91.

محمود سامي البارودي
(١٨٣٩-١٩٠٤)

ديوان

«القصيدة الأولى»

وَدَارَيْتُ إِلَّا مَا يَنِمُّ زَفِيرُ	تَلَاهَيْتُ إِلَّا مَا يُجِنُّ ضَمِيرُ
وَفِي الصَّدْرِ مِنْهُ بَارِحٌ وَسَعِيرُ؟	وَهَلْ يَسْتَطِيعُ الْمَرْءُ كِتْمَانَ أَمْرِهِ
عَلَى الْمَرْءِ إِذْ يَخْلُو بِهِ فَيُغِيرُ!	فَيَا قَاتَلَ اللهُ الْهَوَى مَا أَشَدَّهُ
وَيَجْزَعُ مِنْهُ الْقَلْبُ وَهْوَ صَبُورُ	تَلِينُ إِلَيْهِ النَّفْسُ وَهْيَ أَبِيَّةٌ
وَنَهْنَهْتُ مُهْرِي والْمُرَادُ غَزِيرُ	نَبَذْتُ لَهُ رُمْحِي وَأَغْمَدْتُ صَارِمِي
سَطَوْتُ وَلِي فِي الْخَافِقَيْنِ زَئِيرُ	وَأَصْبَحْتُ مَفْلُولَ الْمَخَالِبِ بَعْدَمَا
أَمَا مِنْ سَمِيعٍ فِيكُمُ فَيُجِيرُ؟	فَيَا لَسَرَاةِ الْقَوْمِ دَعْوَةُ عَائِذٍ
وَعَهْدِي بِهِ فِي مَا عَلِمْتُ قَصِيرُ	لَطَالَ عَلَيَّ اللَّيْلُ حَتَّى مَلِلْتُهُ
وَحَيَّا شَبَاباً مَرَّ وَهْوَ نَضِيرُ	أَلَا فَرَعَى اللهُ الصَّبَا مَا أَبَرَّهُ
عَلَيْنَا وَسَلْسَالُ الْوَفَاءِ نَمِيرُ	إِذِ الْعَيْشُ أَفْوَافٌ تَرِفُّ ظِلَالُهُ
عَلَى شِيَمٍ مَا إِنْ بِهِنَّ نَكِيرُ	وَإِذْ نَحْنُ فِيمَا بَيْنَ إِخْوَانِ لَذَّةٍ
بِهَا اللَّهْوُ خِدْنٌ والشَّبَابُ سَمِيرُ	تَدُورُ عَلَيْنَا الْكَأْسُ بَيْنَ مَلَاعِبٍ
وَرَيْحَانُنَا بَيْنَ الْكُؤُوسِ سَفِيرُ	فَأَلْحَاظُنَا بَيْنَ النُّفُوسِ رَسَائِلٌ
وَطِرْنَا مَعَ اللَّذَّاتِ حَيْثُ تَطِيرُ	عَقَدْنَا جَنَاحَيْ لَيْلِنَا بِنَهَارِنَا
بَقَاءُ الْفَتَى بَعْدَ الشَّبَابِ يَسِيرُ	وَقُلْنَا لِسَاقِينَا أَدِرْهَا فَإِنَّمَا
لَهَا عِنْدَ أَلْبَابِ الرِّجَالِ ثُؤُورُ	فَطَافَ بِهَا شَمْسِيَّةً لَهَبِيَّةً
وَظَلَّتْ بِنَا الْأَرْضُ الْفَضَاءُ تَدُورُ	إِذَا مَا شَرِبْنَاهَا أَقَمْنَا مَكَانَنَا
إِلَى أَنْ بَدَا لِلصُّبْحِ فِيهِ قَتِيرُ	وَكَمْ لَيْلَةٍ أَفْنَيْتُ عُمْرَ ظَلَامِهَا
وَنَعَّمْتُ سَمْعِي والْبَنَانُ طَهُورُ	شَغَلْتُ بِهَا قَلْبِي وَمَتَّعْتُ نَاظِرِي
وَجِيرَتِهِ والْغَادِرُونَ كَثِيرُ	صَنَعْتُ بِهَا صُنْعَ الْكَرِيمِ بِأَهْلِهِ
لَهَا بَيْنَ أَطْرَافِ الْغُصُونِ هَدِيرُ	فَمَا رَاعَنَا إِلَّا حَفِيفُ حَمَائِمٍ
لَهُنَّ بِهَا بَعْدَ الْحَنِينِ صَفِيرُ	تُجَاوِبُ أَتْرَاباً لَهَا فِي خَمَائِلٍ
وَلَا دَائِرَاتِ الدَّهْرِ كَيْفَ تَدُورُ	نَوَاعِمُ لَا يَعْرِفْنَ بُؤْسَ مَعِيشَةٍ
مِنَ الرِّيشِ فِيهِ طَائِلٌ وَشَكِيرُ	تَوَسَّدُ هَامَاتٍ لَهُنَّ وَسَائِداً

كَأَنَّ عَلَى أَعْطَافِهَا مِنْ حَبِيكِهَا   تَمَائِمَ لَمْ تُعْقَدْ لَهُنَّ سُيُورُ

خَوَارِجُ مِنْ أَيْكٍ دَوَاخِلُ غَيْرِهِ   زَهَاهُنَّ ظِلٌّ سَابِغٌ وَغَدِيرُ

إِذَا غَازَلَتْهَا الشَّمْسُ رَفَّتْ كَأَنَّمَا   عَلَى صَفْحَتَيْهَا سُنْدُسٌ وَحَرِيرُ

فَلَمَّا رَأَيْتُ الصُّبْحَ قَدْ رَفَّ جِيدُهُ   وَلَمْ يَبْقَ مِنْ نَسْجِ الظَّلَامِ سُتُورُ

خَرَجْتُ أَجُرُّ الذَّيْلَ تِيهًا وَإِنَّمَا   يَتِيهُ الْفَتَى إِنْ عَفَّ وَهْوَ قَدِيرُ

وَلِي شِيمَةٌ تَأْبَى الدَّنَايَا وَعَزْمَةٌ   تَرُدُّ لُهَامَ الْجَيْشِ وَهْوَ يَمُورُ

إِذَا سِرْتُ فَالْأَرْضُ الَّتِي نَحْنُ فَوْقَهَا   مَرَادٌ لِمُهْرِي وَالْمَعَاقِلُ دُورُ

فَلَا عَجَبَ إِنْ لَمْ يَصُرْنِي مَنْزِلٌ   فَلَيْسَ لِعِقْبَانِ الْهَوَاءِ وُكُورُ

هَمَامَةُ نَفْسٍ لَيْسَ يَنْقِي رِكَابَهَا   رَوَاحٌ عَلَى طُولِ الْمَدَى وَبُكُورُ

مُعَوَّدَةً أَلَّا تَكُفَّ عِنَانَهَا   عَنِ الْجِدِّ إِلَّا أَنْ تَتِمَّ أُمُورُ

لَهَا مِنْ وَرَاءِ الْغَيْبِ أُذْنٌ سَمِيعَةٌ   وَعَيْنٌ تَرَى مَا لَا يَرَاهُ بَصِيرُ

وَفَيْتُ بِمَا ظَنَّ الْكِرَامُ فِرَاسَةً   بِأَمْرِي وَمِثْلِي بِالْوَفَاءِ جَدِيرُ

وَأَصْبَحْتُ مَحْسُودَ الْجَلَالِ كَأَنَّنِي   عَلَى كُلِّ نَفْسٍ فِي الزَّمَانِ أَمِيرُ

إِذَا صُلْتُ كَفَّ الدَّهْرُ مِنْ غُلَوَائِهِ   وَإِنْ قُلْتُ غَصَّتْ بِالْقُلُوبِ صُدُورُ

مَلَكْتُ مَقَالِيدَ الْكَلَامِ وَحِكْمَةً   لَهَا كَوْكَبٌ فَخْمُ الضِّيَاءِ مُنِيرُ

فَلَوْ كُنْتُ فِي عَصْرِ الْكَلَامِ الَّذِي انْقَضَى   لَبَاءَ بِفَضْلِي «جَرْوَلٌ» وَ«جَرِيرُ»

وَلَوْ كُنْتُ أَدْرَكْتُ «النُّوَاسِيَّ» لَمْ يَقُلْ   «أَجَارَةَ بَيْتَيْنَا أَبُوكِ غَيُورُ»

وَمَا ضَرَّنِي أَنِّي تَأَخَّرْتُ عَنْهُمُ   وَفَضْلِي بَيْنَ الْعَالَمِينَ شَهِيرُ

فَيَا رُبَّمَا أَخْلَى مِنَ السَّبْقِ أَوَّلُ   وَبَرَّ الْجِيَادَ السَّابِقَاتِ أَخِيرُ

«القصيدة الثانية»

أَسْتَوْدِعُ اللهَ عَصْرًا قَدْ خَلَعْتُ بِهِ   عُذْرَ الْهَوَى وَهْوَ غَضَّاتٌ مَكَاسِرُهُ

لَمْ يَمْضِ مِنْ حُسْنِهِ مَا كُنْتُ أَعْهَدُهُ   حَتَّى أَصَابَ سَوَادَ الْقَلْبِ نَاقِرُهُ

كَيْفَ الْوُصُولُ إِلَى حَالٍ نَعِيشُ بِهَا   وَالدَّهْرُ مَأْمُونَةٌ فِينَا بَوَادِرُهُ

إِذْ لَا صَدِيقَ يَسُرُّ السَّمْعَ غَائِبُهُ   وَلَا رَفِيقٌ يَرُوقُ الْعَيْنَ حَاضِرُهُ

كُنَّا نَوَدُّ انْقِلَابًا نَسْتَرِيحُ بِهِ   حَتَّى إِذَا تَمَّ سَاءَتْنَا مَصَائِرُهُ

فَالْقَلْبُ مُضْطَرِبٌ فِي مَا يُحَاوِلُهُ   وَالْعَقْلُ مُخْتَبَلٌ مِمَّا يُحَاذِرُهُ

قَدْ كَانَ فِي السَّلَفِ الْمَاضِينَ نَافِعُهُ   فَصَارَ فِي الْخَلَفِ الْبَاقِينَ ضَائِرُهُ

. . .

تَنَكَّرَتْ مِصْرُ بَعْدَ الْعُرْفِ وَاضْطَرَبَتْ   قَوَاعِدُ الْمُلْكِ حَتَّى رِيعَ طَائِرُهُ

فَأَهْمَلَ الْأَرْضَ جَرًّا الظُّلْمِ حَارِثُهَا   وَاسْتَرْجَعَ الْمَالَ خَوْفَ الْعُدْمِ تَاجِرُهُ

وَاسْتَحْكَمَ الْهَوْلُ حَتَّى مَا يَبِيتُ فَتًى   فِي جَوْشَنِ اللَّيْلِ إِلَّا وَهْوَ سَاهِرُهُ

وَيَلُمُّهُ سَكَنًا لَوْلَا الدَّفِينُ بِهِ   مِنَ الْمَآثِرِ مَا كُنَّا نُجَاوِرُهُ

أَرْضًى بِهِ غَيْرَ مَغْبُوطٍ بِنِعْمَتِهِ   وَفِي سِوَاهُ الْمُنَى لَوْلَا عَشَائِرُهُ

يَا نَفْسُ لَا تَجْزَعِي فَالْخَيْرُ مُنْتَظَرٌ   وَصَاحِبُ الصَّبْرِ لَا تَبْلَى مَرَائِرُهُ

لَعَلَّ بُلْجَةَ نُورٍ يُسْتَضَاءُ بِهَا   بَعْدَ الظَّلَامِ الَّذِي عَمَّتْ دَيَاجِرُهُ

إِنِّي أَرَى أَنْفُسًا ضَاقَتْ بِمَا حَمَلَتْ   وَسَوْفَ يَشْهَرُ حَدَّ السَّيْفِ شَاهِرُهُ

شَهْرَانِ أَوْ بَعْضُ شَهْرٍ إِنْ هِيَ احْتَدَمَتْ   وَفِي الْجَدِيدَيْنِ مَا تُغْنِي فَوَاقِرُهُ

فَإِنْ أَصَبْتِ فَعَنْ رَأْيٍ مَلَكْتُ بِهِ   عِلْمَ الْغُيُوبِ وَرَأْيُ الْمَرْءِ نَاظِرُهُ

«القصيدة الثالثة»

حَلَبْتُ أَشْطُرَ هَذَا الدَّهْرِ تَجْرِبَةً   وَذُقْتُ مَا فِيهِ مِنْ صَابٍ وَمِنْ عَسَلِ

فَمَا وَجَدْتُ عَلَى الْأَيَّامِ بَاقِيَةً   أَشْهَى إِلَى النَّفْسِ مِنْ حُرِّيَّةِ الْعَمَلِ

لَكِنَّنَا غَرَضٌ لِلشَّرِّ فِي زَمَنٍ   أَهْلُ الْعُقُولِ بِهِ فِي طَاعَةِ الْخَمَلِ

قَامَتْ بِهِ مِنْ رِجَالِ السَّوْءِ طَائِفَةٌ   أَدْهَى عَلَى النَّفْسِ مِنْ بُؤْسٍ عَلَى ثَكَلِ

مِنْ كُلِّ وَغْدٍ يَكَادُ الدَّسْتُ يَدْفَعُهُ   بُغْضًا وَيَلْفِظُهُ الدِّيوَانُ مِنْ مَلَلِ

ذَلَّتْ بِهِمْ مِصْرُ بَعْدَ الْعِزِّ وَاضْطَرَبَتْ   قَوَاعِدُ الْمُلْكِ حَتَّى ظَلَّ فِي خَلَلِ

وَأَصْبَحَتْ دَوْلَةُ «الْفُسْطَاطِ» خَاضِعَةً   بَعْدَ الْإِبَاءِ وَكَانَتْ زَهْرَةَ الدُّوَلِ

قَوْمٌ إِذَا أَبْصَرُونِي مُقْبِلًا وَجَمُوا   غَيْظًا وَأَكْبَادُهُمْ تَنْقَدُّ مِنْ دَغَلِ

فَإِنْ يَكُنْ سَاءَهُمْ فَضْلِي فَلَا عَجَبٌ   فَالشَّمْسُ وَهِيَ ضِيَاءٌ آفَةُ الْمُقَلِ

نَزَّهْتُ نَفْسِي عَمَّا يَدْنُسُونَ بِهِ   وَنَخْلَةُ الرَّوْضِ تَأْبَى شِيمَةَ الْجُعَلِ

بِئْسَ الْعَشِيرُ وَبِئْسَتْ مِصْرُ مِنْ بَلَدٍ   أَضْحَتْ مَنَاخًا لِأَهْلِ الزُّورِ وَالْخَطَلِ

أَرْضٌ تَأَثَّلَ فِيهَا الظُّلْمُ وَانْقَذَفَتْ   صَوَاعِقُ الْغَدْرِ بَيْنَ السَّهْلِ وَالْجَبَلِ

وَأَصْبَحَ النَّاسُ فِي عَمْيَاءَ مُظْلِمَةٍ   لَمْ يَخْطُ فِيهَا امْرُؤٌ إِلَّا عَلَى زَلَلِ

. . .

لَا يَدْفَعُونَ يَدًا عَنْهُمْ وَلَوْ بَلَغَتْ   مَسَّ الْعَفَافَةِ مِنْ جُبْنٍ وَمِنْ خَزَلِ

خَافُوا الْمَنِيَّةَ فَاحْتَالُوا وَمَا عَلِمُوا   أَنَّ الْمَنِيَّةَ لَا تَرْتَدُّ بِالْحِيَلِ

فَفِيمَ يَتَّهِمُ الْإِنْسَانُ خَالِقَهُ   وَكُلُّ نَفْسٍ لَهَا قَيْدٌ مِنَ الْأَجَلِ

هَيْهَاتَ يَلْقَى الْفَتَى أَمْنًا يَلَذُّ بِهِ   مَا لَمْ يَخُضْ نَحْوَهُ بَحْرًا مِنَ الْوَهَلِ

فَمَا لَكُمْ لَا تَعَافُ الضَّيْمَ أَنْفُسُكُمْ   وَلَا تَزُولُ غَوَاشِيكُمُ مِنَ الْكَسَلِ؟

وَتِلْكَ مِصْرُ الَّتِي أَفْنَى الْجِلَادُ بِهَا لَفِيفٌ أَسْلَافِكُمْ فِي الْأَعْصُرِ الْأُوَلِ

قَوْمٌ أَقَرُّوا عِمَادَ الْحَقِّ وَامْتَلَكُوا أَزِمَّةَ الْخَلْقِ مِنْ حَافٍ وَمُنْتَعِلِ

جَنَوْا ثِمَارَ الْعُلَا بِالْبِيضِ وَاقْتَطَفُوا مِنْ بَيْنَ شَوْكِ الْعَوَالِي زَهْرَةَ الْأَمَلِ

فَأَصْبَحَتْ مِصْرُ تَزْهُو بَعْدَ كُدْرَتِهَا فِي يَانِعٍ مِنْ أَسَاكِيبِ النَّدَى خَضِلِ

لَمْ تَنْبُتِ الْأَرْضُ إِلَّا بَعْدَمَا اخْتَمَرَتْ أَقْطَارُهَا بِدَمِ الْأَعْنَاقِ وَالْقُلَلِ

شَنُّوا بِهَا غَارَةً أَلْقَتْ بِرَوْعَتِهَا أَمْناً يُؤَلِّفُ بَيْنَ الذِّئْبِ وَالْحَمَلِ

حَتَّى إِذَا أَصْبَحَتْ فِي مَعْقِلٍ أَشِبٍ يَرُدُّ عَنْهَا يَدَ الْعَادِي مِنَ الْمِلَلِ

أَخْنَى الزَّمَانُ عَلَى فُرْسَانِهَا فَغَدَتْ مِنْ بَعْدِ مَنَعَتِهَا مَطْرُوقَةَ السُّبُلِ

فَأَيُّ عَارٍ جَلَبْتُمْ بِالْخُمُولِ عَلَى مَا شَادَهُ السَّيْفُ مِنْ فَخْرٍ عَلَى زُحَلِ

إِنْ لَمْ يَكُنْ لِلْفَتَى عَقْلٌ يَعِيشُ بِهِ فَإِنَّمَا هُوَ مَعْدُودٌ مِنَ الْهَمَلِ

فَبَادِرُوا الْأَمْرَ قَبْلَ الْفَوْتِ وَانْتَزِعُوا شِكَالَةَ الرَّيْثِ فَالدُّنْيَا مَعَ الْعَجَلِ

. . .

هٰذِي نَصِيحَةُ مَنْ لَا يَبْتَغِي بَدَلاً بِكُمْ وَهَلْ بَعْدَ قَوْمِ الْمَرْءِ مِنْ بَدَلِ؟

أَسْهَرْتُ جَفْنِي لَكُمْ فِي نَظْمِ قَافِيَةٍ مَا إِنْ لَهَا فِي قَدِيمِ الشِّعْرِ مِنْ مَثَلِ

كَالْبَرْقِ فِي عَجَلٍ وَالرَّعْدِ فِي زَجَلٍ وَالْغَيْثِ فِي هَلَلٍ وَالسَّيْلِ فِي هَمَلِ

غَرَّاءُ تَعْلَقُهَا الْأَسْمَاعُ مِنْ طَرَبٍ وَتَسْتَطِيرُ بِهَا الْأَلْبَابُ مِنْ جَذَلِ

حَوْلِيَّةٌ صَاغَهَا فِكْرٌ أَقَرَّ لَهُ بِالْمُعْجِزَاتِ قَبِيلُ الْإِنْسِ وَالْخَبَلِ

. . .

تَفْنَى النُّفُوسُ وَتَبْقَى وَهْيَ نَاضِرَةٌ عَلَى الدُّهُورِ بَقَاءَ السَّبْعَةِ الطُّوَلِ

«القصيدة الرابعة»

فَإِنْ تَكُنِ الْأَيَّامُ رَقَّقْنَ مَشْرَبِي وَتَلَّمْنَ حَدِّي بِالْخُطُوبِ الطَّوَارِقِ

فَمَا غَيَّرَتْنِي مِحْنَةٌ عَنْ خَلِيقَتِي وَلَا حَوَّلَتْنِي خُدْعَةٌ عَنْ طَرَائِقِي

. . .

أَلَا أَيُّهَا الزَّارِي عَلَيَّ بِجَهْلِهِ وَلَمْ يَدْرِ أَنِّي دُرَّةٌ فِي الْمَفَارِقِ

تَعَزَّ عَنِ الْعَلْيَاءِ بِاللُّؤْمِ وَاعْتَزِلْ فَإِنَّ الْعُلَا لَيْسَتْ بِلَغْوِ الْمَنَاطِقِ

. . .

يَقُولُ أُنَاسٌ إِنَّنِي ثُرْتُ خَالِعاً وَتِلْكَ هَنَاتٌ لَمْ تَكُنْ مِنْ خَلَائِقِي

وَلَكِنَّنِي نَادَيْتُ بِالْعَدْلِ طَالِباً رِضَا اللهِ وَاسْتَنْهَضْتُ أَهْلَ الْحَقَائِقِ

أَمَرْتُ بِمَعْرُوفٍ وَأَنْكَرْتُ مُنْكَراً وَذٰلِكَ حُكْمٌ فِي رِقَابِ الْخَلَائِقِ

فَإِنْ كَانَ عِصْيَاناً قِيَامِي فَإِنَّنِي
وَهَلْ دَعْوَةُ الشُّورَى عَلَيَّ غَضَاضَةٌ
بَلَى إِنَّهَا فَرْضٌ مِنَ الله وَاجِبٌ
وَكَيْفَ يَكُونُ الْمَرْءُ حُرَّاً مُهَذَّباً

. . .

عَلَى أَنَّنِي لَمْ آلُ نُصْحاً لِمَعْشَرٍ
رَأَوْا أَنْ يَسُوسُوا النَّاسَ قَهْراً فَأَسْرَعُوا
فَلَمَّا اسْتَمَرَّ الظُّلْمُ قَامَتْ عِصَابَةٌ
وَشَايَعَهُمْ أَهْلُ الْبِلَادِ فَأَقْبَلُوا
يَرُومُونَ مِنْ مَوْلَى الْبِلَادِ نَفَاذَ مَا
فَلَمَّا أَبَى الْحُكَّامُ إِلَّا تَمَادِياً
أُنَاسٌ شَرَوْا خِزْيَ الضَّلَالَةِ بِالْهُدَى
فَجَاؤُوا إِلَيْهِمْ يَنْصُرُونَ ضَلَالَهُمْ
فَلَمَّا اطْمَأَنُّوا فِي الْبِلَادِ وَأَيْقَنُوا
أَقَامُوا وَقَالُوا تِلْكَ يَا قَوْمُ أَرْضُنَا
وَعَاثُوا بِهَا يَنْفُونَ مِنْ خِيفَ بِئْسُهُ
وَأَصْبَحَ وَادِي النِّيلِ نَهْباً وَأَصْبَحَتْ
فَهَذَا هُوَ الْحَقُّ الْمُبِينُ فَلَا تَسَلْ
فَيَا «مِصْرُ» مَدَّ اللهُ ظِلَّكِ وَارْتَوَى
وَلَا بَرِحَتْ تَمْتَارُ مِنْكِ يَدُ الصَّبَا
فَأَنْتِ حِمَى قَوْمِي وَمَشْعَبُ أُسْرَتِي
بِلَادٌ بِهَا حَلَّ الشَّبَابُ تَمَامِي

. . .

فَإِنْ تَكُنِ الْأَيَّامُ سَاءَتْ صُرُوفُهَا
فَقَدْ يَسْتَقِيمُ الْأَمْرُ بَعْدَ اعْوِجَاجِهِ

أَرَدْتُ بِعِصْيَانِي إِطَاعَةَ خَالِقِي
وَفِيهَا لِمَنْ يَبْغِي الْهُدَى كُلُّ فَارِقِ؟
عَلَى كُلِّ حَيٍّ مِنْ مَسُوقٍ وَسَائِقِ
وَيَرْضَى بِمَا يَأْتِي بِهِ كُلُّ فَاسِقِ؟

أَبَى غَدْرُهُمْ أَنْ يَقْبَلُوا قَوْلَ صَادِقِ
إِلَى نَقْضِ مَا شَادَتْهُ أَيْدِي الْوَثَائِقِ
مِنَ الْجُنْدِ تَسْعَى تَحْتَ ظِلِّ الْخَوَافِقِ
إِلَيْهِمْ سِرَاعاً بَيْنَ آتٍ وَلَاحِقِ
تَأَلَّهُ مِنْ وَعْدٍ إِلَى النَّاسِ صَادِقِ
وَحَالَ طِلَابُ الْحَقِّ دُونَ التَّوَافُقِ
نِفَاقاً وَبَاعُوا الدِّينَ مِنْهُمْ بِدَانِقِ
بِخُدْعَةِ مُغْتَالٍ وَحِيلَةِ سَارِقِ
بِعَجْزِ الْمُحَامِي دُونَهَا وَالْمُوَاثِقِ
وَمَا أَحَدٌ مِنَّا لَهَا بِمُفَارِقِ
عَلَيْهِمْ وَكَانَتْ تِلْكَ إِحْدَى الْبَوَائِقِ
إِمَارَتُهُ الْقَعْسَاءُ نُهْزَةَ مَارِقِ
سِوَايَ فَإِنِّي عَالِمٌ بِالْحَقَائِقِ
ثَرَاكِ بِسَلْسَالٍ مِنَ النِّيلِ دَافِقِ
أَرِيجاً يُدَاوِي عَرْفُهُ كُلَّ نَاشِقِ
وَمَلْعَبُ أَتْرَابِي وَمَجْرَى سَوَابِقِي
وَنَاطَ نِجَادَ الْمَشْرِفِيِّ بِعَاتِقِي

فَإِنِّي بِفَضْلِ اللهِ أَوَّلُ وَاثِقِ
وَيَرْجِعُ لِلْأَوْطَانِ كُلُّ مُفَارِقِ

'Aisha Taymur
(1840–1902)

Introduced and translated by Marilyn Booth

Also known as al-Taymuriyya ("the female Taymur"), 'Aisha Taymur was an Egyptian poet and prose writer born into an elite and intellectual Ottoman Turkish family of Kurdish origins. She was among the earliest women writing in Arabic in the modern period of print media to publish works and gain renown during her lifetime. Her legacy includes poetry in Persian, Turkish, and Arabic as well as an allegorical novel and essays on the politics of gender in Egypt.

Famously, Taymur tells of the early support she received for her intellectual pursuits from her father, Isma'il Taymur Pasha, a career bureaucrat for the Egyptian state. He brought tutors into the household, and from them 'Aisha learned the Qur'an and studied Islamic legal science as well as the grammar and poetic heritage of the Arabic, Turkish, and Persian languages. She also writes about her mother (a Circassian concubine) as a forceful personality, and it may have been from her mother that 'Aisha got some of her force, which shines through in the poem "With Pure Virtue's Hand."

Taymur's education and emerging poetic bent were curtailed by her marriage at age fifteen (standard practice for her class and era). After the deaths of her husband and father, Taymur went back to her linguistic and literary interests. Her *diwan* ("collection") of Arabic poetry is probably the earliest book by a female author to be published in Egypt (*Hilyat al-Tiraz* ["Brocade Decoration"])—and "With Pure Virtue's Hand" was the first in that volume.

Composed as a traditional monorhyme ode, the poem plays with levels of rhetoric and meaning: that almost every line offers at least double possibilities cannot be conveyed fully in a translation. The connecting thread is a strong statement of women's abilities and persistence in intellectual pursuits despite their formal invisibility. Indeed, Taymur exploits the tropes of veiling and gender-based sequestration (both of which can be conveyed in the Arabic word *hijab*) to assert women's preeminence as intellectual and artistic heavyweights. She also uses masculine (and masculinist) discourse on manly chivalry to debunk the notion of "stallion poets," whose masculinity is essential to their poetic prowess. She marshals the stellar poetry of premodern women—al-Khansa', 'Aliya bint al-Mahdi, Layla al-Akhyaliyya—as beacons for her own artistic presence.

Recommended Reading

Badran, Margot, and miriam cooke, editors. *Opening the Gates: A Century of Arab Feminist Writing*. Virago/Indiana UP, 1990.

Booth, Marilyn. "'A'ishah 'Ismat bint Isma'il Taymur." *Essays in Arabic Literary Biography, 1850–1950*, edited by Roger Allen, Harrassowitz Verlag, 2010, pp. 366–76.

———. "Biography and Feminist Rhetoric in Early-Twentieth-Century Egypt: Mayy Ziyadah's Studies of Three Women's Lives." *Journal of Women's History*, vol. 3, 1991, pp. 38–64.

Hatem, Mervat. "'A'isha Taymur's Tears and the Critique of the Modernist and the Feminist Discourses on Nineteenth-Century Egypt." *Remaking Women: Feminism and Modernity in the Middle East*, edited by Lila Abu-Lughod, Princeton UP, 1998, pp. 73–87.

Taymur, 'A'isha. "Family Reform Comes Only through the Education of Girls." Translated by Marilyn Booth. Badran and cooke, pp. 129–33.

———. Introduction to *The Results of Circumstances in Words and Deeds*. Translated by Marilyn Booth. Badran and cooke, pp. 126–28.

"With Pure Virtue's Hand"

With pure virtue's hand I guard the might of my *hijab*
and, with faultless self-shielding, among my peers I rise.

With my thoughts taking fire and my gift for sharp critique
    I have brought my poet's skills to new and perfect highs.
I composed poetry expressing an assemblage:
    before me, women sheltered, most noble, esteemed, wise.
I uttered my verse but as a lover's playful words
    loving bookish eloquence and logic much to prize.
Mahdi's daughter, Layla—these are my choice models
    as with innate acuity my best thoughts I poetize.
How superb these ladies are! A noble weave indeed
    in women and in maidens the men do recognize.
Given precious pearls of mind, a poet like Khansa'
    wanders rocky paths and for a brother, frantic, cries.
From the brow of my notebooks I fashioned my mirror
    and of ink's jet-black traces I created my dyes.
How often my fingertip adorns my paper's cheeks
    with script's downy touch or the skin of my youth's sighs.
The candles of my intellect sent their brilliance far,
    as the scent of my words perfumed dear ones' garden skies.
Women of great splendor wrapped in shawls of logic fine:
    and their envy my presence or my absence defies.
In sentiment's assembly my tresses I undid:
    those of goodly lineage their symbols will surmise.
The arts of my eloquence, my mind I protected:
    talisman dear, *hijab*'s amulet: danger denies.
My literature and my learning did me no harm
    save in making me the finest flower of minds wise.
Solitary bower, scarf's knot, are no affliction
    nor my gown's cut nor proud strong guarded paradise.
My bashfulness, no blockade to keep me from the heights
    nor could the veil's lowering o'er my ringlets disguise.
The wager's arena though the horsemen's ambitions
    from the hardships of the race suffered demise.
No! my might is my repose, my knightly prowess lies
    in the beauty of my striving: finest goals I prize.
Not to mention a secret whose essence is sheltered
    though word spread far to strangers of its rarity and size.
Like musk it is sealed in the drawers of treasuries:

but the fragrance of its sweetness spreads in saffron sighs.
Or like the seas as they embraced hidden gemlike pearls:
　　when the hands of seekers touch, the touch will paralyze.
Desiring to obtain and to have those lovely pearls,
　　what troubling trials these divers brave, deeds that sense defies!
World-renowned amber agreed to give pearls protection:
　　its nature is recited in every book one buys.
So I touch my fire to the wick in the lamp of skills
　　granted me by holy God, gifts of the Giver Wise.

Source of Arabic Text on Which the Translation Is Based

الديوان المحيي رفات الأدب البالغ من فنون البلاغة غاية الأرب المحتوى من حسن البراعة
على ما به امتاز المسمى طبقا لمعناه بحلية الطراز [al-diwan al-muhyi rufat al-adab
al-baligh min funun al-balagha ghayat al-arab al-muhtawi min husn
al-bara'a 'ala ma bi-hi imtaza al-musamma tibqan li-ma'nahu bi-hilyat
al-tiraz; The Diwan, Comprising the Mortal Remains of Literary
Refinement, Arising Profoundly from the Arts of Rhetoric Aimed at
What Is Most Soundly, Enfolding Wondrous Skill That Sets It Apart,
and Given a Title in Accord with the Meanings It Imparts: Embroidered
Ornaments]. Al-Matba'a al-'Amira al-Sharafiyya, AH 1303 (1885–86),
AH 1327 (1909–10). Also reproduced in Zaynab Fawwaz al-'Amili, الدر
المنثور في طبقات ربات الخدور [al-durr al-manthur fi tabaqat rabbat al-khudur;
Scattered Pearls in the Classes of Cloistered Ladies], al-Matba'a al-Kubra
al-Amiriyya, AH 1312 (1894–95), pp. 309–10.

عائشة التيمورية
(١٨٤٠-١٩٠٢)

بيد العفاف أصون عز حجابي

وبعصمتي أسمو على أترابي	*	بيد العفاف أصون عز حجابي
نقادة قد كملت آدابي	*	وبفكرة وقادة وقريحة
قبلي ذوات الخدر والأحساب	*	ولقد نظمت الشعر سيمة معشر
يهوى بلاغة منطق وكتاب	*	ما قلته إلا فكاهة ناطق
وبفطنتي أعطيت فضل خطابي	*	فبنية المهدي وليلى قدوتي
نسج العلا لعوانس وكعاب	*	لله درّ كواعب نسبوا لها
خنساء في صخر وجوب صعاب	*	وخصصن بالدرّ الثمين وهامت الـ
وجعلت من نقش المداد خضابي	*	فجعلت مرآتي جبين دفاتر
بعذار خط أو إهاب شبابي	*	كم زخرفت وجنات طرسي أملي
بعبير قولي روضة الأحباب	*	ولكم أضاء شمع الذكاء وتضوّعت
يغبطنها في حضرتي وغيابي	*	منطقت ربّات البهاء بمناطق
عرفت شعائرها ذوو الأنساب	*	وحللت في نادي الشعور ذوائبا
بتميمة غرّاء وحرز حجاب	*	عوّذت من فكري فنون بلاغتي
إلا بكوني زهرة الألباب	*	ما ضرّني أدبي وحسن تعلمي
وطراز ثوبي واعتزاز رحابي	*	ما ساءني خدري وعقد عصابتي
سدل الخمار بلمّتي ونقابي	*	ما عاقني خجلي عن العليا ولا
صعب السباق مطائح الركاب	*	عن طيّ مضمار الرهان إذا اشتكت
في حسن ما أسعى لخير ما آب	*	بل صواني في راحتي وتفرّسي
شاعت غرابته لدى الأغراب	*	ناهيك من سرّ مصون كنهه
ويضوع طيب طيبه بملاب	*	كالمسك مختوم بدرج خزائن
عن مسها شلت يد الطلاب	*	أو كالبحار حوت جواهر لؤلؤ
كم كابد الغواص فعل عذاب	*	درّ لشوق نوالها ومنالها
وشؤونه تتلى بكل كتاب	*	والعنبر المشهور وافق صونها
منح الإله مواهب الوهاب	*	فأثرت مصباح البراعة وهي لي

Part 7: Political Modernity

This part of the anthology focuses on notions of freedom in the context of civil society work, censorship, and personal expression. The selected texts portray a negotiation with and a contestation of the political, from emancipation from an authoritarian regime to coexistence with it. The texts offer a variety of strategies in the *Nahda* that allowed authors and thinkers to express their views, contest, and devise new models of social organization that are tied to political and gender representation.

'Abd al-Qadir al-Qabbani, who studied at Butrus al-Bustani's national school in Beirut, presents the freedoms of enterprise, expression, and speech as political components in a new age. These freedoms were soon to be threatened by an Ottoman censorship imposed on newspapers and journals. Depicting the press censor in turn-of-the-century Beirut, Salim Sarkis mocks in his satirical text the structure of Ottoman authority. He describes how this Ottoman-appointed official, tasked with examining all publishable material before it goes to press, is in fact unfit to do his job. In a style reminiscent of a modern-day *Onion* spoof, Sarkis criticizes censorship by recounting fabricated and completely nonsensical stories that this censor allowed to be published. Sarkis's parody is complemented by 'Abd al-Rahman al-Kawakibi's denunciation of tyranny in both democratic and dictatorial regimes. Al-Kawakibi describes wild capitalism as a structure of progress, cautioning against its simple incorporation into an Arab-Ottoman context. He undertakes a socialist reading of Islam by highlighting specific teachings that are intrinsically opposed to models of despotic rule.

While al-Kawakibi's critique of despotism allows us to consider individual rights, Nazira Zeineddine's emphasis on the body and opposition to veiling connect the question of rights to structures of dependency in patriarchal societies. Zeineddine discusses freedom by incorporating definitions from John Stuart Mill's *On Liberty* or the French Revolution's *Declaration of the Rights of Man and the Citizen* into Islamic legal definitions of rights and duties. Advocating free will, she calls for the adoption of reason in order to achieve an equality guaranteed by religion and natural law. It is by defending individual freedom that she contests the suppression of women, which relies on a false definition of gender. Echoing her call for the freedom to debate, Mayy Ziyadah, the famous *salonière* from the early twentieth century who transformed her parlor into one of the most coveted forums of the *Nahda*, discusses in her letters excerpted here how Voltaire and Diderot worked tirelessly against an ignorant censorship in eighteenth-century France. Responding to a fellow intellectual who had criticized her views on language, she presents a powerful defense of bilingualism, critiquing the binaries of linguistic purity and exclusivity, and asserts her right to think and write freely.

'Abd al-Qadir al-Qabbani
(1848–1935)

Introduced and translated by Tarek El-Ariss

'Abd al-Qadir al-Qabbani (or Kabbani) was a philanthropist, jurist, politician, and editor born in Beirut in 1848 to a family of Sunni notables with high-ranking positions in the Ottoman administration. He attended Butrus al-Bustani's al-Madrasa al-Wataniyya—the nonsectarian *Nahda* school par excellence—whose motto was, "Love for one's homeland is an item of faith." Al-Qabbani distinguished himself as a pioneering reformer in turn-of-the-century Beirut. He advocated educational and political reform in the framework of Ottoman rule. He founded and contributed to a number of civic associations promoting arts and culture and Arab-Ottoman cooperation. His enduring legacy is al-Maqasid [Al-Makassed] Philanthropic Islamic Association, which he founded with other Beirut notables and served as its first president in 1878 to address the needs of the community and bring it into the *Nahda*. From al-Maqasid emerged a network of schools (including schools for girls) and a hospital, which continue to operate in Lebanon to this day. He held other administrative positions as well—he was the director of education and the president of the city council—and oversaw a number of important infrastructural projects in the city.

"Freedom" is an editorial that al-Qabbani wrote in June 1880 to commemorate the five-year anniversary of the weekly newspaper he published, *Thamarat al-Funun* (1875–1910; "Fruits of the Arts"). The piece provides a vision of how a community leader in Beirut at the time conceived of political reform and gives a specific definition of freedom that draws on religious and philosophical concepts that are both classical and modern. It captures the fine line that people like al-Qabbani had to walk to effect change yet remain within the boundaries of Ottoman authority.

Recommended Reading

Elshakry, Marwa. *Reading Darwin in Arabic, 1860–1950.* U of Chicago P, 2013.
Hanssen, Jens. *Fin de Siècle Beirut: The Making of an Ottoman Provincial Capital.* Oxford UP, 2005.
Hanssen, Jens, and Max Weiss, editors. *Arabic Thought beyond the Liberal Age: Towards an Intellectual History of the Nahda.* Cambrdidge UP, 2016.
Nashabi, Hisham. "Shaykh 'Abd al-Qadir al-Qabbani and *Thamarat al-Funun.*" *Intellectual Life in the Arab East, 1890–1939*, edited by Marwan Buheiry, American U of Beirut P, 1981, pp. 84–91.

"Freedom"

Freedom consists in equal rights, in people's active participation to obtain benefits for their nation, and in their solidarity to protect the public welfare. True freedom is achieved when every citizen is allowed to speak and act in ways that do not contradict the law of the land and the public good or undermine religion and faith. The various parts that make up the [national] realm should work in tandem to ensure that all respect each other's rights, so that every citizen can be a guarantor for others by working tirelessly for their rights without going against what we have previously mentioned. Citizens should denounce anyone who opposes the fulfillment of freedom in its stated boundaries. Freedom grants a person the right not to be exiled from his homeland, or punished except in accordance with the law of the realm, or forced to suppress his opinion in deeds and words, or held accountable outside what the law of the state and religion permit. Freedom gives citizens the right to serve their country in accordance with their potential and what they see as fit and just, so that their love for their homeland can grow because they share in the tasks required for upholding the rule of law and ensuring the legitimacy of political authority. If this were to be achieved, then the members of the nation would truly anchor their love for it in the wise administration that joins them together as one body united by their love for their nation. This is not difficult to achieve, provided that good governance and good intentions prevail. And here I remember the saying of those who have gained wisdom through the years and from various experiences: "If you allow me to reform education, I will commit to reform the affairs of the entire world." For once human minds are imbued with national duty from childhood, and once they have acquired the necessary education, they can overcome all adversity. And as the saying goes, "What is acquired in childhood is retained through old age."

The greatest freedom of all is the freedom to own property and to work in agriculture, trade, and manufacturing. This freedom is the basis of proper administration. It has been proven without the shadow of a doubt that this freedom is best for the public good, and it is very hard to limit its scope. It is known that individuals are naturally predisposed to desire freedom, and this is the only path to felicity in government, especially when the latter is built upon just, solid, and beneficial foundations that will guarantee people's satisfaction and comfort. Unjustly preventing people from exercising their freedom amounts to depriving them of equal rights that do not distinguish between ruler and ruled, lord and vassal. There can be no misgivings about implementing equality in rights and responsibilities among different types of people, for this was mentioned and required by all Holy Scriptures. Despite the fact that destiny has blessed some with psychological qualities such as generosity, benevolence, wealth, intelligence, and the like, as well as with natural characteristics such as strength as opposed to weakness, all people are equal in the eyes of the law.

A state that makes equality the basis of its [rule and] operation solidifies its foundations, gains high repute, and avoids instability and corruption. This equality will breed good words and deeds and make people treat one another and themselves justly. All virtues arise from and are guaranteed by this supreme form of justice.

We have lived through dark ages where freedom was tarnished by despotism and equality did not prevail. But conditions have changed in our land since the reign of the late Sultan 'Abd al-Majid. The principles of freedom and equality occupy the utmost importance in the reign of our current glorious sultan ['Abd al-Hamid]. All we have to do is to demand our rights that were usurped by those despots whose practices are at the root of all backwardness and harm to the public good upon which the felicity of government and subjects depends. The nation depends on its people, and their glory depends on their unity and determination to work for its greater good. May God show us the way and inspire us to act wisely.

Source of Arabic Text on Which the Translation Is Based

Al-Qabbani, 'Abd al-Qadir. ثمرات الفنون [thamarat al-funun; Fruits of the Arts], no. 284, 7 June 1880, p. 1.

عبد القادر القبّاني
(١٨٤٨-١٩٣٥)

الحرية

إن الحرية هي المساواة في الحقوق واشترك الأهالي بالمثابرة على توفير فوائد الوطن وكثرة منافعه وتعاضدهم على قيام مصالحه ونجاحها وحقيقتها أن يباح لكل فرد من أبناء الوطن أن يكون حر القول والعمل ما لم يخالف شريعة البلاد ومصلحتها العمومية ويخل بشيء من المذهب والدين. ويجب تكافل الأجزاء المؤلفة منها المملكة على إلزام حقوق بعضهم لبعض بحيث يكون كل فرد من أفرادهم كفل للباقين المساعدة على فعل كل شيء لا يخالف ما ذكرناه وأن ينكروا جميعاً على من يعارض في إجراء الحرية التي لا تتعدى الحدود التي بيناها ومن حقوقها أن لا ينفى الإنسان من وطنه أو يعاقب فيه إلا بحكم مطابق لأصول المملكة وأن لا يكتم الإنسان رأيه في ما يفوه به أو يكتبه ولا يؤاخذ بشيء من ذلك ما لم يخرج عن دائرة الشريعة والقانون وأن تشترك أجزاء الوطن بخدمته بحسب الطاقة واللياقة العادلة لتعظم محبتهم له باشتراكهم بالتكاليف التي عليها قيام الملك. وإذا توفر ذلك صار الذبّ عنه مشتركاً فعلاً لرسوخ محبة الوطن الذي أحكم بحسن انتظامه ربط جميع الأجزاء وجعلهم جزءاً واحداً تجمعه محبة الوطن ولا يصعب ذلك إذا تحسنت الإدارة وأحسن كل قصده بصفاء نية. وهنا يورد بعض الحكماء الذين حنكتهم الأيام والتجارب فإنه قال إن سمحتم لي بتحسين التربية ألزمت نفسي لكم بإصلاح أحوال العالم بأسره فإن العقول البشرية متى رسخت بها الواجبات الوطنية من نعومة الأظفار وبلغت ما يناسبها من المعارف تغلبت على كل شيء يقاوم ما رسخ وقد قيل من شبّ على شيء شاب عليه.

وأعظم الحرية حرية التملك والفلاحة والتجارة والصناعة لأن إجراءها من أصول الإدارة وفنونها حيث ثبت بالبراهين القاطعة أن هذه الحرية من أعظم المنافع العمومية ومن أصعب الأمور تضييق دوائرها. ومن المعلوم أن النفوس تميل إلى الحرية من أصل فطرتها وأنها الوسيلة الوحيدة لسعادة الملك لا

سيما إذا كانت مبنية على قواعد عادلة ثابتة مفيدة فإنها توجب راحة الأهالي وإسعادهم والتوسعة عليهم في ما يرومون من الأعمال التي نفعها عام لأن التضييق في ما يجوز فعله بدون وجه عادل يعدّ حرماناً للحقوق المتساوية بين الرئيس والمرؤوس والشريف والمشروف عليه. ولا شبهة في مساواة الحقوق والأحكام مطلقاً بين جميع الأصناف كما دلت عليه وأمرت به الكتب السماوية غير أن الأقدار الإلهية ميزت بعضهم على بعض من الأزل بصفات معنوية كالكرم والسماحة والغنى والذكاء وما شاكلها وعكسها وطبيعة كقوة البدن وضعفه إلا أنهم متساوون بالأحكام الوضعية. فكل دولة جعلت التسوية مدار أعمالها الدائمة رسخت قواعدها وعلت كلمتها وسلمت من تطرق الخلل والفساد ومن ذلك تتولد الاستقامة في الأقوال والأفعال فينتصف كل فرد لغيره كما ينتصف لنفسه وهذا غاية منتهى العدل وجميع الفضائل مدرجة فيه ومتفرعة منه.

وقد مضت علينا عصور مظلمة كانت الحرية فيها مشوبة بالاستبداد والتسوية غير سائدة لكن الأحوال تغيرت فنتجت بلادنا منذ أيام المرحوم السلطان عبد المجيد مبادئ الحرية والمساواة وكمل لها أعظم نصيب في عهد حضرة سلطاننا الحالي المعظم فلم يبقَ علينا إلا أن نطالب بحقوقنا التي ضبن بها علينا بغو المستبدين الذين يفضلون المحبة الذاتية التي هي أساس كل تأخر وسبب كل ضرر على المنفعة العمومية المنوط بها سعادة الملك والرعية. فالوطن بأهله وعزمهم باتفاق كلمتهم على جر المنفعة إليه يبصرنا الله بما يجب علينا ولنا وألهمنا بفضله رشدنا.

Salim Sarkis
(1867–1926)

Introduced by Yoav Di-Capua and
translated by Lior Sternfeld

Salim Sarkis was a legendary news entrepreneur who came from a family of publishers in Beirut. Working both as a journalist and a publisher, he launched some of the most creative news platforms in the Arab world. This was during a time in which news in the Arabic language became both a business and a dominant cultural phenomenon. Yet because of the heavy hand of the Ottoman administration and better opportunities elsewhere, Sarkis left Beirut to contribute to the emergence of the Arabic international press in places like Paris, London, and the United States. In 1905, he settled in Egypt, where he started yet another newspaper and served as an editor and an influential journalist until his death.

Written in 1896, this selection describes the daily business of Beirut's Ottoman censor (*maktubji*). Censorship had been lax before the 1870s, but the decades after that saw more aggressive state intervention. Though news flowing from the Reuters-Havas telegraphic agency in Alexandria constantly subverted this intervention, the practice of censorship did not cease. Sarkis tells us of censors who did not actually know Arabic and were so culturally provincial that they could not comprehend any international news. Interestingly, censorship was aimed not only at specific sensitive events and news items but also at the very foundation of Arab political modernity. Thus, for instance, regardless of their specific context, the Ottoman censors categorically prohibited the usage of words such as *unity, oppression, independence, reform, revolution, political assassination, rights, constitution,* and *elections.*

Recommended Reading

Ayalon, Ami. *The Arabic Print Revolution: Cultural Production and Mass Readership.* Cambridge UP, 2016.

———. *The Press in the Arab Middle East: A History.* Oxford UP, 1995.

Cioeta, Donald J. "Ottoman Censorship in Lebanon and Syria, 1876–1908." *International Journal of Middle East Studies,* vol. 10, no. 2, 1979, pp. 167–86.

Strauss, Johann. "Who Read What in the Ottoman Empire (Nineteenth and Twentieth Centuries)?" *Middle Eastern Literatures,* vol. 6, no. 1, 2003, pp. 39–76.

The Censor's Oddities

Who Is the Maktubji?

The *maktubji* of the province of Beirut is His Excellency 'Abdullah Effendi Najib, although he is not the only [censor] that this book has in mind. I have decided to use the title *maktubji* since it has become associated with the newspaper censor in modern times. Historically, *maktubji* referred to the governor's secretary in each Ottoman province and was in no way associated with newspapers. However, when the Ottoman government decided to delegate newspaper censorship responsibilities to the *maktubji* of Beirut, this title became more closely associated with newspaper censorship than with keeping state secrets.

How Are Newspapers Monitored?

Once the editor of the Ottoman newspaper has written his articles, edited them, typeset them, and prepared them for publishing and distribution, the newspaper administration sends two copies to the censor. The publisher, editor, and staff have to wait for the draft to be returned before they can begin publishing.

The draft is usually sent out at 10 a.m. and might not be returned until 3 or 4 p.m., during which time the entire newspaper operation must come to a complete halt. When the draft arrives at the government headquarters, the officer attached to the censor takes it from the delivery boy and places it on his master's desk. The boy remains waiting until the officer takes pity on him and relents and sends the draft for review to a former censor named ʿAbd al-Rahman Effendi al-Hout, because the current censor, ʿAbdallah Najib, knows as much Arabic as I know of the language of Adam.

Carnot Did Not Die

A few days after [the periodical] *Lisan al-Hal* ["Current Affairs"] was published,[1] we received a telegram from a Parisian friend informing us of the death of Monsieur Carnot, the president of the [French] Republic, who was stabbed in Lyon by the wretched Caserio. The telegram was published, but only after the censor crossed out the news of his "killing" and ordered us to refer to his death by saying "he returned to God's graces," because mentioning the murder of a king worried the Turks, as it could challenge their authority. Though reluctant, I was forced to do their bidding.

The Death of the Persian Shah

In the month of May 1896, someone attacked the late Persian shah, taking him down with a bullet that also finished off the hopes of the Persians. Newspapers around the world published the news of this terrible murder, except those in Beirut, which wrote as follows:

> It was reported early afternoon yesterday in an official telegram that the great champion of the faith, the magnificent Shah of Iran,

has died. Embassies the world over have lowered their flags, and the world mourns this terrible tragedy. We had reported in a previous issue that the people of Persia were preparing to celebrate the Shah's fiftieth year on the throne on the sixth of this month, and the hands of fate suddenly took him away only a few days before the celebration. May God have mercy on his soul in heaven.

Meaningless Words

When I saw that he [the censor] was crossing out every meaningful article, I wanted to test the limits of his understanding and censorship. So I wrote a political article under the title "Current Events" and put it in the center of the newspaper. It read as follows:

> Peace has spread throughout the world. Kings and ministers have announced their peaceful intentions. His Majesty the Emperor Carnot the Third, Czar of Russia, went to America and gave a speech whose tone was no less peaceable than the speech given by the English Prime Minister Mr. Bismarck in Chile, who confirmed the alliance with Her Majesty Empress Eugénie, the Queen of France, and Archduke Rudolph, the Emperor of Brazil, in merging the Kingdom of Switzerland with the Republic of Germany. They also agreed on the construction of a railroad line under the Baltic Sea in order to facilitate trade between Africa and the Caucuses. Thus, today, the political world is in complete harmony.

In spite of the mix-ups and exaggeration of this news item, the censor approved it and furnished it with his seal of approval with the word "görülmisdir" ["it was observed"]. When it was published in *Lisan al-Hal*, it spread among the people, as all the men of letters who read it at the time recall.

It is well known that Carnot was president of the French Republic and that he never left France. Prince Bismarck was in Germany and had no relation with the English government, nor had he been to Chile. As for the Empress Eugénie, she lives in exile, and the French Empire no longer exists. Likewise, Archduke Rudolph had already committed suicide, and Brazil had become a republic. Switzerland is a republic, and Germany is an empire. The Baltic Sea is as far from Africa as the honorable censor's mind is from his head. Yet this was allowed to be published.

Notes

The translator would like to thank Eric Eyges for his help in the translation.

[1]*Lisan al-Hal* was established and operated in 1877, by Khalil Khattar Sarkis, a close relative of Salim's.

Source of Arabic Text on Which the Translation Is Based

Sarkis, Salim. غرائب المكتوبجي [ghara'ib al-maktubji; The Censor's Anecdotes]. Dar al-Hamra' lil-Tiba'a wal-Nashr, 1990, pp. 20–25.

سليم سركيس
(١٨٦٧–١٩٣٦)

غرائب المكتوبجي

«ما هو المكتوبجي؟»

إن مكتوبجي ولاية بيروت هو سعادتلو عبد الله أفندي نجيب ولكنه ليس وحده المقصود في هذا الكتاب وإنما استعملت اسم المكتوبجي لأنه أصبح من الأوضاع العصرية لمراقب الجرائد مع أن المكتوبجي في حقيقة معناه وطبيعته الأصلية لا علاقة له بالجرائد وإنما هو سكرتير الوالي ولكل ولاية من الممالك العثمانية مكتوبجي خاص. لكن الحكومة العثمانية اختارت أن تعهد إلى مكتوبجي ولاية بيروت أمر مراقبة الجرائد فأصبح اسم الرجل معروفاً بمراقبته للجرائد أكثر من كونه كاتم أسرار الولاية.

«كيف تراقب الجرائد»

بعد أن يكتب محرر الجريدة العثمانية مقالات جريدته وترتب حروفها وتصلح أغلاطها حتى تصير جاهزة للطبع والتوزيع تبعث الإدارة بنسختين منها إلى المكتوبجي وعلى المطبعة والمحرر والعملة أن ينتظروا رجوع المسودة المذكورة قبل أن يبدأوا بالطبع. وترسل المسودة عادة الساعة العاشرة إفرنجية صباحاً وقد تبقى عند المكتوبجي إلى الساعة الثالثة أو الرابعة بعد الظهر والتعطيل شامل الإدارة والمطبعة والعملة والمحرر.

فعندما تصل المسودة إلى سراي الحكومة يأخذها العسكري الملازم في خدمة سعادته من صبي الإدارة ويضعها على طاولة مولاه ويبقى الغلام في انتظاره إلى أن يرحم ويشفق وعند ذلك يتنازل فيرسل المسودة المذكورة إلى أحد خلفاء قلم المكتوبجي المسمّى عبد الرحمن أفندي الحوت ليطالعها قبله وذلك لأن المكتوبجي الحالي عبد الله نجيب يعرف من اللغة العربية قدر ما أعرف أنا من لغة آدم.

«لم يمت كارنو»

بعد أن صدر لسان الحال يومياً بأيام قليلة جاءتنا برقية رسالة من صديق باريزي تنبئ بمقتل الموسيو كارنو رئيس الجمهورية في ليون من خنجر كازاريو الشقي فنشرت التلغراف إلا أن المكتوبجي حذف خبر قتله وأمرنا أن نقتصر على ذكر موته بقوله (انتقل إلى رحمة ربه) لأن ذكر قتل الملوك يخيف الأتراك لأنه يخيف سلطانهم فاضطررت إلى أن أفعل ذلك مكرها.

«موت شاه العجم»

في شهر مايو من سنة ١٨٩٦ هجم أحدهم على المغفور له شاه العجم ففتك به برصاصة أصابته فذهب بآمال الأعجام ونشرت جميع جرائد العالم خبر هذا المقتل الفظيع إلا جرائد بيروت فإنها نشرت الخبر كما يأتي.

ورد قبيل عصر أمس نبأ برقي رسمي ينعي المرحوم المغفور له ناصر الدين خان شاه إيران المعظم فنكست قناصل الدول أعلامها وأسف القوم على هذا المصاب الجلل.

وقد ذكرنا في عدد سابق أنهم كانوا في بلاد فارس يستعدون استعداداً عظيماً للاحتفال بعيد جلوسه للسنة الخمسين في السادس من هذا الشهر فوافاه القدر والمحتوم فجأة في وسط ذلك الاستعداد قبيل حلول العيد بيومين أو ثلاثة. رحمه الله وجعل الجنة مثواه.

«كلام بدون معنى»

فلما رأيت أنه يحذف كل مقالة مفيدة ذات معنى أردت أن أمتحن درجة فهمه ومبلغ التضييق، فكتبت مقالة سياسية تحت عنوان (الأحوال الحاضرة) في صدر الجريدة قلت فيها ما يأتي:

«قد عمّ السلم الأرض قاطبة وقام الملوك والوزراء يعلنون مقاصدهم السلمية فذهب حشمتلو الإمبراطور كارنو الثالث قيصر روسيا إلى أمريكا وألقى هناك خطبة لا تختلف في لهجتها السلمية عن الخطبة التي ألقاها المستر بسمارك رئيس وزارة إنجلترا في شيلي قال فيها أنه تم عقد التحالف

مع حضرة الإمبراطورة أوجيني ملكة فرنسا والأرشيدوق رودلف إمبراطور البرازيل على ضم إمبراطورية سويسرا إلى جمهورية ألمانيا والاتفاق على مد خط حديدي تحت بحر البلطيق يساعد على تسهيل التجارة بين أفريقيا والقوقاس. وهكذا فالعالم السياسي اليوم في راحة تامة» إلى آخر ما هناك من الخلط والمبالغة فصادق المكتوبجي عليها وذيلها باسمه الكريم مع كلمة «كورلكشدر» وطبعت في لسان الحال وانتشرت بين الناس كما يذكر كل من قرأها من الأدباء.

ومعلوم أن كارنو كان رئيساً لجمهورية فرنسا ولم يخرج من فرنسا مطلقاً والبرنس بسمارك كان في ألمانيا ولا علاقة له بوزارة إنجلترا ولم يرَ بعينه بلاد شيلي والإمبراطورة أوجيني منفية من بلادها والإمبراطورية ملغاة من فرنسا كما أن الأرشيدوق رودلف كان قد مات منتحراً والبرازيل صارت جمهورية وسويسرا جمهورية وألمانيا إمبراطورية وبحر البلطيق يبعد عن أفريقيا قدر ما يبعد العقل عن رأس حضرة المكتوبجي. ومع ذلك سمح بنشرها.

'Abd al-Rahman al-Kawakibi
(1855–1902)

Introduced and translated by Yaseen Noorani

'Abd al-Rahman al-Kawakibi was an intellectual and political activist who played a leading role in the formation of Islamic political liberalism and anti-Ottoman Arab nationalism. He was born in Aleppo to a prominent family of religious scholars and notables. He studied in his family's school and later earned a degree in law. He supplemented his formal education with readings of European works translated into Turkish and Arabic. He began his career in journalism as an editor of the government newspaper in Aleppo, before helping found the first Arabic newspaper in Aleppo, which was quickly shut down because of its criticisms of government policies. A second newspaper met the same fate. Al-Kawakibi then took up a succession of official posts offered to him by the authorities, and he opened a legal practice, which became known for assisting the poor. However, he continued to experience tension with the Ottoman governor of Aleppo, culminating in his being prosecuted on the charge of treason and sentenced to death. Although al-Kawakibi succeeded in overturning the conviction, he decided to flee Ottoman jurisdiction and secretly moved to Cairo in 1899. There he published the two works on which his reputation rests.

The first of these works is *Umm al-Qura* ("The Mother of Towns"), framed as the minutes of a fictional secret conference in Mecca at which delegates from all parts of the Muslim world have convened to discuss the political and social reformation of the Muslim community. The second work, from which the excerpts here are taken, is entitled *Taba'i' al-Istibdad wa-Masari' al-Isti'bad* ("The Characteristics of Despotism and

the Fatalities of Enslavement"). This work, a treatise on the
nature of political despotism and the social and psychic cor-
ruption that it causes, draws heavily on an Italian work by Vit-
torio Alfieri entitled *Of Tyranny* (*Della tirannide*) as well as on
traditional Arabic literary themes and language of tyranny and
enslavement. In this work, al-Kawakibi develops the idea that
despotism operates by stripping the individuals it enslaves of
their will and agency. Moreover, he sets forth an account of
a democratic and quasi-socialist Islamic order that establishes
individual freedom and social cohesion through its institutions
and the virtues it inculcates in all citizens. This order is based
on the universal human moral and social principle that he calls
"communality."

Recommended Reading

Dawn, C. Ernest. "From Ottomanism to Arabism: The Origin of an Ide-
ology." *The Review of Politics*, vol. 23, no. 3, 1961, pp. 378–400.
Haim, Sylvia G. "Alfieri and al-Kawakibi." *Oriente moderno*, 1954, pp. 321–34.
Noorani, Yaseen. *Culture and Hegemony in the Colonial Middle East*. Palgrave
Macmillan, 2010.
Rahme, Joseph G. "'Abd al-Rahman al-Kawakibi's Reformist Ideology,
Arab Pan-Islamism, and the Internal Other." *Journal of Islamic Studies*,
vol. 10, no. 2, 1999, pp. 159–77.
Tauber, Eliezer. "Three Approaches, One Idea: Religion and State in the
Thought of 'Abd al-Rahman al-Kawakibi, Najib 'Azuri, and Rashid Rida."
British Journal of Middle Eastern Studies, vol. 21, no. 2, 1994, pp. 190–98.

FROM *The Characteristics of Despotism and the Fatalities of Enslavement*

What Is Despotism?

Despotism, in a word: self-satisfaction with one's own opinion and the refusal to accept counsel, or the imposing of one's own opinion in matters of common interest.

When the word *despotism* is used, it denotes the despotism of governments in particular, because they manifest most clearly its harms, which have made the human being the most miserable among living creatures. The domination of the soul [and its passions] over the intellect, that of the father, the teacher, and the husband, and that of the heads of some religions, associations, and social classes—such domination can be described as despotism, metaphorically or with qualification.

Despotism, in the terminology of political thinkers, is the willful action of an individual or a group with regard to the rights of others, without fear of consequence. This terminological meaning may be denoted by other terms used in place of *despotism*: "enslavement," "coercion," "domination." In opposition to these terms are the words "equality," "common feeling," "communion," "public authority." Used in place of the adjective *despotic* are the words "strong man," "tyrant," "autocrat," "absolute ruler." In opposition to *despotic government* are the words "just," "accountable," "limited," "constitutional." Used in place of the description of subjects "ruled by despotism" are the terms "captives," "abased," "wretched," "vegetative."[1] In opposition: "free," "proud," "alive," "honorable."

This is the definition of *despotism* by way of synonyms and antonyms. The definition by way of description is that despotism is the characteristic of a government that is unrestrained in action or in authority and that intervenes in the affairs of its subjects as it wills without fear of being held accountable or punished by overseers. The explanation for this is the government's not being bound to act in accordance with the law, with traditional models, or with the will of the nation; such is the case with absolute governments. Or the government may be bound by one of these but through its power and influence is able to nullify this bond as it wishes. This is the case with most governments that call themselves limited or republican.

The forms of despotic government are many, and this treatise cannot detail them all. It suffices here to indicate that the characteristic of despotism, just as it applies to the absolute rule of an individual who came to power through force or inheritance, may also apply to an elected ruler of limited powers whenever this ruler is not held accountable. It also applies to collective governments, even if elected, because group participation does not prevent despotism, though difference of opinion may correct it somewhat. The despotism of rule by consensus may be more harmful than the despotism of an individual. Despotism also applies to constitutional governments in which the legislative, executive, and oversight powers are completely separated. This is because despotism is not eliminated so long as there is no mutual accountability such that the executive branch is accountable to the legislative and the legislative is accountable to the nation—for the nation knows that it is sovereign and knows how to provide oversight and demand accountability.

The severest degree of despotism, may God protect us from it, is the absolute government of an individual who has inherited the throne, is commander of the army, and holds religious authority. We may say that the fewer of these attributes are in place, the lower is the degree of despotism, until the point where we reach an elected ruler with a fixed term limit who is truly held accountable. Likewise, despotism lessens as the number of subjects ruled, the ownership of fixed property, and the disparity between rich and poor decreases, and as the people's level of knowledge rises.

Any government, no matter what its form, will not be free of despotism so long as it is not subject to intensive oversight and accounting, as took place during the early days of Islam in the reaction against [the caliphs] 'Uthman and 'Ali, may God be pleased with them, and as has taken place in the present French Republic in the affairs of the military decorations, Panama, and Dreyfus.[2]

Nature and history tell us that a government, when exempt from accountability and criticism because of the manipulation of the people or because of their negligence, quickly dons the cloak of despotism. Once despotism becomes entrenched, it persists and comes to rely on at least one of two powerful mechanisms: ignorant people and a standing professional army. These two [things] are the greatest misfortunes that can befall nations and the worst blights upon humanity. Though civilized nations have made great strides in eliminating ignorance, they are plagued by general military conscription, which makes life in them more wretched than in backward nations. Military conscription is more shameful for humanity than the ugliest forms of despotism. So much so that it is perhaps fair to say that if Satan invented conscription, then he has taken revenge upon Adam through his progeny in the worst possible manner! Indeed, if this type of military service, which has existed for two centuries, persists for another century, it will exhaust the patience of nations and bring them down all at once. Who can say how astonished the men of the future will be that this age's advancements in science were coupled with the worsening of this calamity, which leaves [us] no room to wonder at the ancient Egyptians' obedience to the pharaohs in building the pyramids as forced laborers. [They suffered from this] nothing more than fatigue and lost time. Military service, however, corrupts the morals of the nation by teaching it ferocity, blind obedience, and dependency. It kills motivation and the idea of independence and imposes on the nation intolerable expenditures. All of this exacerbates the misfortune of despotism: the despotism of governments over their people, on the one hand, and the despotism of nations over each other, on the other.

Let us return to the original topic and say this: Examining the history of civil governments reveals that an accountable government has never lasted longer than a half century to a century and a half at most. The only exception is the current government of England, due to the wakefulness of the English, who are not intoxicated by victories or disheartened by adversities. They are not distracted for even a moment from the supervising of their kings, to the extent that the ministry selects the king's aides and courtiers, not to mention his wife and in-laws. The English kings, having been bereft of everything but the crown for centuries, would jump at any opportunity for despotic rule, but there is little chance of negligence on the part of the people that would allow one of them to seize control of the army.

Bedouin governments are rarely despotic. Their subjects are mainly tribal people living in the desert, who can pack up and disperse easily whenever their personal freedom is violated or injustice is inflicted upon them by their government and they have no means of redress. Such governments are rarely led to despotism. The best example of this is the inhabitants of the Arabian Peninsula, who have hardly known despotism since before the age of the kings of Tubba', Himyar, and Ghassan to the present day, except for a few instances. Wisdom has it that the Bedouin condition is far from falling under the yoke of despotism, because the Bedouin way of life is fundamentally independent. Each tribesman relies only upon himself for his livelihood, in contrast to the model of the urban dweller. This model has become the object of sarcasm among modern sociologists, who say that human beings are animals of the type that naturally live in flocks inside caves and in certain pastures but have now become animals that, after reaching maturity, must live independently on their own, not fully bound to their relatives and community or to home and country. Thus is the lifestyle of most English and Americans, among whom each individual regards his connection with his nation and government as nothing more than the tie of a participant in a voluntary association, in contrast to nations that follow their governments even in matters of religion.

One who examines the conditions of nations sees prisoners living crowded and pressed together, preserving each other from the aggression of despotism like sheep pressing in upon each other when terrified by a wolf. Whereas among tribes and free nations, individuals possess complete independence and live apart. . . .

Despotism and Wealth

If despotism were a man recounting his lineage and relations, it would say, "I am evil, and my father is tyranny, my mother is abuse, my brother is treachery, my sister is misery, my paternal uncle is harm, my maternal uncle is humiliation, my son is poverty, my daughter is idleness, my clan is ignorance, my homeland is a wasteland, and my religion, honor, and life are money, money, money!"

It can be rightly said of money that power is money, time is money, intellect is money, knowledge is money, religion is money, stability is money, social rank is money, beauty is money, organization is money, economy is money, and fame is money. The upshot of this is that whatever can be profited from in life is money.

All these things can be bought and sold, that is, they can be exchanged for each other, and the measurements of equivalence are need, prestige, time, and labor, as well as the preservation of power, silver, gold, and dignity. Societies are their marketplace, and the chief of the market is the ruler. Look at a market that is controlled by a despot: he commands Zayd to sell and forbids 'Amr from buying, and plunders Bakr of his money while entertaining Khalid with the money of the people.

Money is subject to regulations. Some money is good, and some is bad; the difference is clear, and the best judge between them is the human conscience. Good money is that which is obtained for property, or as wages for work, or as compensation for time, or as collateral. Bad money is that which is obtained by selling one's honor, or is plundered, stolen, seized unfairly, or swindled.

The natural order among all animals, even fish and insects, with the exception of the female spider, is that members of the same species do not eat each other. But the human being does. The instinct of all animals is to seek sustenance from God, that is, from natural sources. But the human being, who wrongs himself, would rather snatch it from the hands of his brother, or even from his mouth. Indeed, how often does the human being eat up his fellow human being! . . .

Accumulating wealth, as in saving money, is a natural characteristic of some lower animals, such as ants and bees. There is no trace of this practice among higher animals aside from human beings. Human beings have taken on this characteristic because of need, real or imagined. This need is real only among the inhabitants of lands that are either infertile or subject to drought. The need is exacerbated among those who are physically unable to pursue their livelihoods in countries afflicted by the tyranny of nature or the tyranny of despotism. It is also worse in ill-administered countries with high charitable and public expenditures. . . .

Absolute equality requires that a portion of the money of the rich be distributed among the poor, such that equity is achieved without extinguishing motivation to work. Something along the lines of this principle is desired by most in the civilized European world. In the present time, groups that include organizations with millions of members are striving to attain such equality. These groups seek to attain equality or near equality in the rights and standards of living among all human beings. They struggle against economic tyranny, and they demand that land, fixed property, and large industrial manufacturing plants be communally owned by the general population of the nation; that labor and the products of labor be distributed evenly among all; and that the government pass clear laws on these matters and undertake to enforce them.

These principles, with some modifications, Islam established as a religion.

Despotism and Progress

Movement is the driving principle of creation, movement that persistently goes both up and down. Progress is the movement of life, that is, the movement of going up, in opposition to going down, which is movement toward death, decline, extinction, or backwardness.

This principle, just as it is the driving principle of the material world and its manifestations, is the driving principle as well in the properties of things and their elements. This is explained in the Qur'anic verse, "We bring the living from the dead and the dead from the living" (30.19), and the saying of the Prophet, "As soon as a thing reaches completion, its incompleteness becomes manifest," as well as in the saying, "History repeats itself," and the generally held principle that life and death are laws of nature.

This physical, psychic, and intellectual movement doesn't necessarily progress in a linear fashion either toward ascent or decline, but it is like a thermometer that goes back and forth between different states. Assessing its outcome depends on the direction that ends up prevailing: if we see the effects of the movement of progress prevail over the people in a given nation, then we judge that this nation will survive. If we see the opposite, then we conclude that this nation will die.

A nation is a collection of individuals bound together by lineage, homeland, language, or religion, just as a building is a collection of building blocks. As the blocks are in type, beauty, and strength, so is the building. As the members of a nation progress or decline, so progresses or declines its social body. If a single chamber of a fortress is defective, the fortress as a whole is defective, even if it is not perceived to be so. Likewise, if a mite alights on the edge of a ship, it weighs it down and causes it to tilt, if imperceptibly. Some politicians have asserted, on the basis of this premise, that for a nation to progress it is sufficient that each individual within it strive to improve himself, without thinking about the progress of the nation as a whole. . . .

Despotism can affect a nation in such a way as to turn its natural inclination toward progress into an inclination toward abasement, such that were it to be pushed toward the heights, it would waver and suffer pain like one who is blinded by light. And if it were forced to be free, it would feel misery and perhaps perish like domesticated animals that have been turned loose. At this point despotism becomes like a leech, content to suck the blood of the nation, not letting go until it dies with the death of the nation. . . .

Some Western sociologists hold the view that religion benumbs individual progress, and thus social progress, as opium benumbs the senses, or blocks access to it as clouds block sunlight. The extremists among them say that religion and reason are opponents vying for people's minds and that progress begins where religion ends. Thus the most accurate indication of progress among individuals and nations past and present is the strength or weakness of their attachment to religion.

These views are correct and irrefutable, but only in regard to religions based on superstition or those that exceed the limits of reason, such as a religion that requires the mind to imagine that one is three and three is one. Any submission to irrationality is proof of the corruption of some parts of the mind. Therefore the civilized world has come to regard the acceptance of any such doctrine as shameful, for it is a sign of stupidity.

This is not so for religions based upon pure rationality, such as Islam, which is described as one of the natural religions. By Islam I do not mean the religion followed by most Muslims at present, I mean the religion of the Qur'an, that is, the religion that any human being whose thoughts are not shackled by the machinations of others is capable of understanding from the Qur'an.

There is no doubt that religion founded upon reason is the best conveyer of thought away from the snares of the fabulists; the most useful restrainer of the self from excess; the most powerful influence for the cultivation of morals; the greatest aid in withstanding the travails of life; the most effective motivator of great deeds; the grandest proof of noble principles; and, as a result, the soundest criterion for gauging the spiritual condition of nations and individuals in regard to progress and decline.

Notes

[1] Al-Kawakibi's footnote: "*Vegetative* is a term used by Europeans to refer to a life resembling the life of a plant."

[2] In 1887 the president of the republic, Jules Grévy, was forced to resign from office after it was publicized that his son-in-law was trafficking in the awarding of decorations of the Légion d'Honneur. In 1892 the Panama scandals (Panama Affair), in which the large Panama Canal Company went bankrupt and government ministers were accused of taking bribes, led to political turmoil and instability. From 1894 to 1906 French society was rent into opposing camps by the Dreyfus affair, in which a Jewish military officer was accused of treason only to be finally exonerated of all wrongdoing.

364   'Abd al-Rahman al-Kawakibi

Source of Arabic Text on Which the Translation Is Based

al-Kawakibi, 'Abd al-Rahman. الأعمال الكاملة للكواكبي [al-a'mal al-kamila lil-kawakibi; Complete Works of al-Kawakibi]. Edited by Muhammad Jamal Tahhan, Markaz Dirasat al-Wahda al-'Arabiyya, 1995, pp. 437–39, 473–77, 505–08.

عبد الرحمن الكواكبي
(١٩٠٢-١٨٥٥)

طبائع الاستبداد ومصارع الاستعباد

ما هو الاستبداد؟؟

الاستبداد، لغة: هو غرور المرء برأيه والأنفة عن قبول النصيحة، أو الاستقلال في الرأي وفي الحقوق المشتركة.

و يراد بالاستبداد، عند إطلاقه: استبداد الحكومات خاصة، لأنها أعظم مظاهر أضراره التي جعلت الإنسان أشقى ذوي الحياة. وأما تحكم النفس على العقل، وتحكم الأب والأستاذ والزوج، ورؤساء بعض الأديان، وبعض الشركات، وبعض الطبقات، فيوصف بالاستبداد مجازاً أو مع الإضافة.

الاستبداد، في اصطلاح السياسيين: هو تصرف فرد أو جمع في حقوق قوم بالمشيئة وبلا خوف تبعة، وقد تطرق مزيدات على هذا المعنى الاصطلاحي فيستعملون في مقام كلمة «استبداد» كلمات: «استعباد،» و«اعتساف،» و«تحكم.» وفي مقابلتها كلمات: «مساواة،» و«حس مشترك،» و«تكافؤ،» و«سلطة عامة.» ويستعملون في مقام صفة «مستبد» كلمات: «جبار،» و«طاغية،» و«حاكم بأمره،» و«حاكم مطلق.» وفي مقابلة «حكومة مستبدة» كلمات: «عادلة،» و«مسؤولة،» و«مقيدة،» و«دستورية.» ويستعملون في مقام وصف الرعية «المستبَد عليهم» كلمات: «أسرى،» و«مستصغرين،» و«بؤساء،» و«مستنبتين،»[١] وفي مقابلتها: «أحرار،» و«أباة،» و«أحياء،» و«أعزاء.»

هذا تعريف الاستبداد بأسلوب ذكر المرادفات والمقابلات، وأما تعريفه بالوصف: فهو أن الاستبداد صفة للحكومة المطلقة العنان، فعلاً أو حكماً، التي تتصرف في شؤون الرعية كما تشاء بلا خشية حساب ولا عقاب محققين. وتفسير ذلك هو كون الحكومة أما هي غير مكلفة بتطبيق تصرفها على شريعة، أو على أمثلة تقليدية، أو على إرادة الأمة، وهذه حالة الحكومات المطلقة. أو هي مقيدة بنوع من ذلك ولكنها تملك بنفوذها إبطال قوة القيد بما تهوي، وهذه حالة أكثر الحكومات التي تسمّي نفسها بالمقيدة أو بالجمهورية.

وأشكال الحكومة المستبدة كثيرة، ليس هذا البحث محل تفصيلها. ويكفي
هنا الإشارة إلى أن صفة الاستبداد، كما تشمل حكومة الحاكم الفرد المطلق
الذي تولى الحكم بالغلبة أو الوراثة، تشمل أيضاً الحاكم الفرد المقيد المنتخب
متى كان غير مسؤول، وتشمل حكومة الجمع ولو منتخباً، لأن الاشتراك في
الرأي لا يدفع الاستبداد وإنما قد يعدله الاختلاف نوعاً، وقد يكون عند الاتفاق
أضر من استبداد الفرد. ويشمل أيضاً الحكومة الدستورية المفرقة فيها بالكلية
قوة التشريع عن قوة التنفيذ وعن القوة المراقبة، لأن الاستبداد لا يرتفع ما
لم يكن هناك ارتباط في المسؤولية فيكون المنفذون مسؤولين لدى المشرعين،
وهؤلاء مسؤولون لدى الأمة، تلك الأمة التي تعرف أنها صاحبة الشأن كله،
وتعرف أن تراقب، وأن تتقاضى الحساب.

وأشد مراتب الاستبداد التي يتعوذ بها من الشيطان هي حكومة الفرد
المطلق، الوارث للعرش، القائد للجيش، الحائز على سلطة دينية. ولنا أن نقول
كلما قل وصف من هذه الأوصاف خف الاستبداد إلى أن ينتهي بالحاكم
المنتخب الموقت المسؤول فعلاً. وكذلك يخف الاستبداد طبعاً كلما قل عدد
نفوس الرعية وقل الارتباط بالأملاك الثابتة وقل التفاوت في الثروة وكلما ترقِّي
الشعب في المعارف.

إن الحكومة من أي نوع كانت لا تخرج عن وصف الاستبداد ما لم تكن
تحت المراقبة الشديدة والاحتساب الذي لا تسامح فيه، كما جرى في صدر
الإسلام في ما نقم على عثمان ثم على علي رضي الله عنهما، وكما جرى في عهد
هذه الجمهورية الحاضرة في فرنسا في مسائل النياشين وبناما ودريفوس.

ومن الأمور المقررة، طبيعةً وتاريخياً، أنه ما من حكومة عادلة تأمن
المسؤولية والمؤاخذة بسبب غفلة الأمة أو التمكن من إغفالها إلا وتسارع
إلى التلبس بصفة الاستبداد، وبعد أن تتمكن فيه لا تتركه وفي خدمتها إحدى
الوسيلتين العظيمتين: جهالة الأمة، والجنود المنظمة، وهما أكبر مصائب الأمم
وأهم معائب الانسانية، وقد تخلصت الأمم المتمدنة نوعاً من الجهالة، ولكن
بليت بشدة الجندية الجبرية العمومية، تلك الشدة التي جعلتها أشقى حياة
من الأمم الجاهلة، وألصق عاراً بالإنسانية من أقبح أشكال الاستبداد، حتى رما
يصح أن يقال: إن مخترع هذه الجندية إذا كان هو الشيطان فقد انتقم من
آدم في أولاده أعظم ما مكنه أن ينتقم! نعم إذا ما دامت هذه الجندية التي
مضى عليها نحو قرنين إلى قرن آخر أيضاً تنهك تجلد الأمم وتجعلها تسقط

دفعة واحدة. ومن يدري كم يتعجب رجال الاستقبال من ترقي العلوم في هذا العصر ترقياً مقروناً باشتداد هذه المصيبة التي لا تترك محلاً لاستغراب اطاعة المصريين للفراعنة في بناء الأهرامات سخرة، لأن تلك لا تتجاوز التعب وضياع الأوقات، وأما الجندية فتفسد أخلاق الأمة حيث تعلمها الشراسة والطاعة العمياء والاتكال، وتميت النشاط وفكرة الاستقلال، وتكلف الأمة الإنفاق الذي لا يطاق، وكل ذلك منصرف لتأييد الاستبداد المشؤوم: استبداد الحكومات القائدة لتلك القوة من جهة، واستبداد الأمم بعضها على بعض من جهة أخرى.

ولنرجع لأصل البحث فأقول: لا يعهد في تاريخ الحكومات المدنية استمرار حكومة مسؤولة مدة أكثر من نصف قرن إلى غاية قرن ونصف، وما شذ من ذلك سوى الحكومة الحاضرة في إنكلترة، والسبب يقظة الإنكليز الذين لا يسكرهم انتصار، ولا يخملهم انكسار، فلا يغفلون لحظة عن مراقبة ملوكهم، حتى أن الوزارة هي تنتخب للملك خدمه وحشمه، فضلًا عن الزوجة والصهر، وملوك الإنكليز الذين فقدوا منذ قرون كل شيء ما عدا التاج، لو تسنى الآن لأحدهم الاستبداد لغنمه حالًا، ولكن هيهات أن يظفر بغرة من قومه يستلم فيها زمام الجيش.

أما الحكومات البدوية التي تتألف رعيتها كلها أو أكثر من عشائر يقطنون البادية يسهل عليهم الرحيل والتفرق متى مست حكومتهم حريتهم الشخصية وسامتهم ضيماً ولم يقووا على الاستنصاف، فهذه الحكومات قلما اندفعت إلى الاستبداد، وأقرب مثال لذلك أهل جزيرة العرب فأنهم لا يكادون يعرفون الاستبداد من قبل عهد ملوك تبع وحمير وغسان إلى الآن إلا فترات قليلة. وأصل الحكمة في أن الحالة البدوية بعيدة بالجملة عن الوقوع تحت نير الاستبداد وهو أن نشأة البدوي نشأة استقلالية، بحيث كل فرد يمكنه أن يعتمد في معيشته على نفسه فقط، خلافاً لقاعدة الإنسان المدني الطبع، تلك القاعدة التي أصبحت سخرية عند علماء الاجتماع المتأخرين، القائلين بأن الإنسان من الحيوانات التي تعيش أسراباً في كهوف ومسارح مخصوصة، وأما الآن فقد صار من الحيوان الذي متى انتهت حضانته عليه أن يعيش مستقلاً بذاته، غير متعلق بأقاربه وقومه كل التعلق، ولا مرتبط ببيته وبلده كل الارتباط، كما هي معيشة أكثر الإنكليز والأمير والذين كان الذين يفتكر الفرد منهم أن تعلقه بقومه وحكومته ليس بأكثر من رابطة شريك في شركة اختيارية، خلافاً للأمم التي تتبع حكوماتها حتى فيما تدين.

الناظر في أحوال الأمم يرى أن الأسراء يعيشون متلاصقين متراكمين، يتحفظ بعضهم ببعض من سطوة الاستبداد، كالغنم تلتف على بعضها إذا ذعرها الذئب، أما العشائر، والأمم الحرة، المالك أفرادها الاستقلال الناجز، فيعيشون متفرقين.

الاستبداد والمال

الاستبداد لو كان رجلاً وأراد أن يحتسب وينتسب لقال: «أنا الشر، وأبي الظلم، وأمي الإساءة، وأخي الغدر، وأختي المسكنة، وعمّي الضر، وخالي الذل، وابني الفقر، وبنتي البطالة، وعشيرتي الجهالة، ووطني الخراب، أما ديني وشرفي وحياتي فالمال، المال، المال!»

المال يصح في وصفه أن يقال: القوة مال، والوقت مال، والعقل مال، والعلم مال، والدين مال، والثبات مال، والجاه مال، والجمال مال، والترتيب مال، والاقتصاد مال، والشهرة مال، والحاصل: كل ما ينتفع به في الحياة هو المال.

وكل ذلك يباع ويُشترى، أي يستبدل بعضه ببعض، وموازين المعادلة هي: الحاجة والعزة والوقت والتعب، ومحافظة اليد والفضة والذهب والذمة، وسوقه: المجتمعات، وشيخ السوق: السلطان . . . فانظر في سوق يتحكم فيه مستبد، يأمر زيداً بالبيع، وينهي عمرواً عن الشراء، ويغصب بكراً ماله، ويحابي خالداً من مال الناس.

المال تعتوره الأحكام، فمنه الحلال ومنه الحرام، وهما بينان، ولنعم الحاكم فيهما الوجدان، فالحلال الطيب ما كان عوض أعيان، أو أجرة أعمال، أو بدل وقت أو مقابل ضمان. والمال الخبيث الحرام هو ثمن الشرف، ثم المغصوب، ثم المسروق، ثم المأخوذ إلجاءً، ثم المحتال فيه.

إن النظام الطبيعي في كل الحيوانات، حتى في السمك والهوام، إلا أنثى العنكبوت، أن النوع الواحد منها لا يأكل بعضه بعضاً، والإنسان يأكل الإنسان. ومن غريزة سائر الحيوان أن يلتمس الرزق من الله، أي من مورده الطبيعي، وهذا الإنسان الظالم نفسه حريص على اختطافه من يد أخيه، بل من فيه، بل كم أكل الإنسان الإنسان! . . .

التموّل، أي إدخار المال، طبيعة في بعض أنواع الحيوانات الدنيئة كالنمل والنحل، ولا أثر له في الحيوانات المرتقية غير الإنسان. الإنسان تطبّع على التموّل لدواعي الحاجة المحققة أو الموهومة، ولا تحقق للحاجة إلا عند سكان

الأراضي الضيقة الثمرات على أهلها، أو الأراضي المعرضة للقحط في بعض السنين، ويلتحق بالحاجة المحققة حاجة العاجزين جسماً عن الارتزاق في البلاد المبتلاة بجور الطبيعة أو جور الاستبداد، وربما يلتحق بها أيضاً الصرف على المضطرين وعلى المصارف العمومية في البلاد التي ينقصها الانتظام العام. . . .

فالعدالة المطلقة تقتضي أن يؤخذ قسم من مال الأغنياء ويرد على الفقراء، بحيث يحصل التعديل ولا يموت النشاط للعمل. وهذه القاعدة يتمنى ما هو من نوعها أغلب العالم المتمدن الإفرنجي، وتسعى وراءها الآن جمعيات منهم منتظمة مكونة من ملايين كثيرة، وهذه الجمعيات تقصد حصول التساوي أو التقارب في الحقوق والحالة المعاشية بين البشر، وتسعى ضد الاستبداد المالي، فتطلب أن تكون الأراضي والأملاك الثابتة وآلات المعامل الصناعية الكبيرة مشتركة الشيوع بين عامة الأمة، وأن الأعمال والثمرات تكون موزعة بوجوه متقاربة بين الجميع، وأن الحكومة تضع قوانين لكافة الشؤون حتى الجزئيات وتقوم بتنفيذها.

وهذه الأصول، مع بعض التعديل، قررتها الإسلامية ديناً. . . .

الاستبداد والترقي

الحركة سنّة عاملة في الخليقة، دائمة بين شخوص وهبوط. فالترقّي هو الحركة الحيوية، أي حركة الشخوص، ويقابله الهبوط، وهو الحركة إلى الموت أو الانحلال أو الاستحالة أو الانقلاب.

وهذه السنة كما هي عاملة في المادة وأعراضها، عاملة أيضاً في الكيفيات ومركباتها، والقول الشارح لذلك آية: «وَيُخْرِجُ الْحَيَّ مِنَ الْمَيِّتِ وَمُخْرِجُ الْمَيِّتِ مِنَ الْحَيِّ،»[٢] وحديث: «ما تم أمر إلا وبدا نقصه» وقولهم: «التاريخ يعيد نفسه.» وحكمهم بأن الحياة والموت حقان طبيعيان.

وهذه الحركة الجسمية والنفسية والعقلية لا تقتضي السير إلى النهاية شخوصاً أو هبوط، بل هي أشبه بميزان الحرارة كل ساعة في شأن، والعبرة في الحكم للوجهة الغالبة، فإذا رأينا في أمة آثار حركة الترقّي هي الغالبة على أفرادها، حكمنا لها بالحياة، ومتى رأينا عكس ذلك قضينا عليها بالموت.

الأمة هي مجموعة أفراد يجمعها نسب أو وطن أو لغة أو دين، كما أن البناء مجموع أنقاض، فحسبما تكون الأنقاض جنساً وجمالاً وقوة يكون

البناء، فإذا ترقت أو انحطت أفراد الأمة ترقت أو انحطت هيئتها الاجتماعية، حتى أن حالة الفرد الواحد من الأمة تؤثر في مجموع تلك الأمة. كما إذا لو اختلت حجرة من حصن يختل مجموعه وإن كان لا يشعر بذلك، كما لو وقفت بعوضة على طرف سفينة عظيمة أثقلتها وأمالتها حقيقة وإن لم يدرك ذلك بالمشاعر. وبعض السياسيين بنى على هذه القاعدة أنه يكفي الأمة رقياً أن يجتهد كل فرد منها في ترقية نفسه بدون أن يفتكر في ترقي مجموع الأمة. . . . .

وقد يبلغ فعل الاستبداد بالأمة ان يحول ميلها الطبيعي من طلب الترقّي إلى طلب التسفل، بحيث لو دفعت إلى الرفعة لابت وتألمت كما يتألم الأجهر من النور، وإذا ألزمت بالحرية تشقى وربما تفنى كالبهائم الأهلية إذا أطلق سراحها. وعندئذ يصير الاستبداد كالعلق يطيب له المقام على امتصاص دم الأمة، فلا ينفك عنها حتى تموت وموت هو بموتها. . . . .

بعض الاجتماعيين في الغرب يرون أن الدين يؤثر على الترقّي الإفرادي ثم الاجتماعي تأثيراً معطلاً كفعل الأفيون في الحس، أو حاجباً كالغيم يغشي نور الشمس. وهناك بعض الغلاة يقولون: الدين والعقل ضدان متزاحمان في الرؤوس، وإن أول نقطة من الترقّي تبتدئ عند آخر نقطة من الدين، وإن أصدق ما يُستدل به على مرتبة الرقي والانحطاط في الأفراد أو في الأمم الغابرة والحاضرة، هو مقياس الارتباط بالدين قوةً وضعفاً.

هذه الآراء كلها صحيحة لا مجال للرد عليها، ولكن بالنظر إلى الأديان الخرافية أساساً، أو التي لم تقف عند حد الحكمة، كالدين المبني على تكليف العقل بتصور أن الواحد ثلاثة والثلاثة واحد، لأن مجرد الإذعان لما لا يعقل برهان على فساد بعض مراكز العقل، ولهذا أصبح العالم المتمدن يعد الانتساب إلى هذه العقيدة من العار، لأنه شعار الحمق.

أما الأديان المبنية على العقل المحض كالإسلام الموصوف بدين الفطرة—ولا أعني بالإسلام ما يدين به أكثر المسلمين الآن، إنما أريد بالإسلام: دين القرآن، أي الدين الذي يقوى على فهمه من القرآن كل إنسان غير مقيد الفكر بتفصح زيد أو تحكم عمرو—فلا شك أن الدين إذا كان مبنياً على العقل، يكون أفضل صارف للفكر عن الوقوع في مصائد المخرفين، وأنفع وازع يضبط النفس من الشطط، وأقوى مؤثر لتهذيب الأخلاق، وأكبر معين على تحمل مشاق الحياة،

وأعظم منشط على الأعمال المهمة الخطرة، وأجل مثبت على المبادئ الشريفة،
وفي النتيجة يكون أصح مقياس يستدل به على الأحوال النفسية في الأمم
والأفراد رقياً وانحطاطاً.

---

¹ الاستنبات أو التنبت من اصطلاحات الفرنج، يريدون به الحياة الشبيهة بحياة النبات.
(الكواكبي)
² سورة الروم: ١٩.

Nazira Zeineddine
(1908–76)

*Introduced by miriam cooke and
translated by Zeina G. Halabi*

Nazira Zeineddine was a Druze Lebanese woman who was born in 1908 in Istanbul to Said Zeineddine, a judge in the Ottoman judicial system. When she was six, the family moved back to Lebanon, where Nazira attended Catholic schools. She learned Turkish, Arabic, French, and English, and she studied Islam with her father. Everything she had learned by the time she was eighteen reinforced her belief in women's rights to freedom and equality.

In 1927, some Syrian shaykhs announced that women had to veil when out in the streets. Nazira was shocked, since the veil at that point was no longer commonly worn. She was determined to prove these men wrong. In several public lectures, she contended that the Qur'an and the Sunna—rightly understood and interpreted—supported the claim of women's equality. She attacked the tradition, popular among male authorities, that women were lacking in faith and reason. Her argument for women's freedom centered on the question of the veil. Since nowhere in the Qur'an could be found a statement about covering the face, there could be no mandate for it.

In a few short months she collected these lectures and finished the four-hundred-page book from which the following excerpt is taken. *Al-Sufur wal-Hijab* (1928; "Unveiling and Veiling") propelled her to prominence overnight. Her most virulent opponent was Shaykh Mustafa al-Ghalayini, whom she had accused of hypocrisy. In his attempt to prove the superiority of Islam to the British and the French, his 1908 *al-Islam: Ruh al-Madaniyya* ("Islam: Spirit of Civilization") had touted the rights that Muslim women enjoyed. But he had, paradoxically, also denigrated women, as though afraid that they might actually believe in such rights. His 1928 *Nazarat fi-Kitab al-Sufur wal-Hijab* ("Views on the Book *Unveiling and Veiling*") even suggested that women who looked like Zeineddine should be grateful for the veil. In a few months she completed yet another tome, this one entitled *al-Fatah wal-Shuyukh* (1929; "The Girl and the Shaykhs"). It was a full attack on the shaykhs who had criticized her first book, and it devoted a large part to a refutation of Shaykh al-Ghalayini.

Recommended Reading

Amin, Qasim. *The Liberation of Women and The New Woman: Two Documents in the History of Egyptian Feminism.* American U in Cairo P, 2000.
Badran, Margot. *Feminism in Islam: Secular and Religious Convergences.* Oneworld Publications, 2013.
cooke, miriam. *Nazira Zeineddine: A Pioneer of Islamic Feminism.* Oneworld Publications, 2010.
Gabriel, Theodore, and Rabiha Hannan, editors. *Islam and the Veil: Theoretical and Regional Contexts.* Continuum, 2011.

FROM *Unveiling and Veiling*

Freedom Is the Foundation of Human Progress: Freedom of Thought and Freedom of Will

Ladies and Gentlemen:

The wise writer [Mustafa Lutfi] al-Manfaluti said, "One cannot achieve happiness in life without absolute freedom. Nothing should govern one's body, mind, soul, emotions, and thoughts except self-*discipline*. . . . Freedom is a sun that must shine within every soul. Anyone who is deprived of it shall live in deepest darkness, unbroken from the womb to the tomb. Freedom is life. Without freedom, our lives would be like those of puppets moving unnaturally in the hands of children."

Shaykh Muhammad ʿAbduh, God rest his soul, stated, "Islam has liberated the mind from prejudice and from the ties that had kept it bound to the will of others. . . . The soul was freed from enslavement to crooks and charlatans, and through faith in the one God the human being became the servant of God alone, free from bondage to all but Him. The human being had the right of all free men to freedom, a right that recognizes none as superior or base, lowly or elevated, and knows no difference among men except the difference of their actions, no disparity except that of their intellects and knowledge. Nothing brings them closer to God except the cleanliness of their minds from the stain of false illusion and the purity of their actions from deviance and duplicity."

Welcome, sacred freedom, freedom of thought and freedom of will, for you are the essence of faith, the foundation of all Renaissance [*Nahda*], and the deliverer of truth through inquiry. Welcome, freedom that grants us the right to preserve our honor and to rise in ways that strengthen our honor and bring us closer to the true faith and that benefit us and our children and our nation. . . .

I have mentioned freedom of will and freedom of thought, both of which remain ambiguous to many. Ignorance has demeaned their value, mutilated their beauty, and equated them to animal instincts, which ignorant people have called freedom. Freedom lies in reason. Its brilliant light shines in human beings only according to their reason. Animals, however, are without reason and thus without freedom of will and freedom of thought. Their dispositions are purely animalistic, harmful and without a trace of freedom.

Freedom of will—as sociologists have identified it—is the freedom of individuals to determine their actions according to ideal moral standards. Freedom of thought is the right of individuals to implement their beliefs regarding their wellbeing and that of others without fear or coercion, unobstructed by the interventions of the authorities or by the hatred and visceral reactions of the masses. We need to consider these two freedoms as the standard for the freedom of speech and all other freedoms, for they all aim at achieving individual and social wellbeing.

My Position and Vision

Ladies and Gentlemen:

It has become clear to you that my position is that of defending the freedom of women and that I am among those women who have favored unveiling over the wearing of the veil. In accordance with freedom of thought and under the banner of sovereign scientific authority, I hereby present to you my views and reflections in favor of unveiling and the liberation of women.

While I admit my shortcomings, I believe that my creed, which is that of many men and women, is closer to the essence of society and a better safeguard of the honor that we all cherish and strive to protect and respect. As some wise men have said, "Free thought is the foundation of all Renaissance. We ought to pave the way for it to flourish. It shall challenge and be challenged within the confines of *adab*.[1] Free thought may clash with other freedoms in a reasonable, healthy, and honest fashion, until the soundest argument prevails, for only the clash of ideas reveals truth."

Therefore I beg him who disagrees with me to examine and benefit from my thoughts and observations and proceed, according to the principle of the freedom of thought, to make his own in accordance with reason and religion. If he convinces me of his reasoning and I realize that his creed is a better safeguard of honor, closer to religion, and more beneficial to my family and to the nation, I shall immediately put on the veil and gladly adhere to it, even though it is the cruelest form of enslavement. It shall not matter if I sacrifice light, air, and all that grants us happiness in life for the sake of religion and the honor of my family and the nation.

If, however, my opponent is content in his reply with searching for apostasy and atheism in ways that defy the rules of debate, then I shall abstain from listening to his words and ask God to guide him and enlighten him with the rays of freedom. For when a soul sees the light, it shall abound with reason, *adab*, and respect for others. This enlightened soul thus favors reasoning over harmful argumentation, which people with bad faith deploy without proofs. To criticize my views without discussing them and without proper arguments demonstrates the weakness of the person's reasoning and argument.

In a lecture entitled "Why Should Girls Get an Education?," which I gave some time ago at the Lycée Laïque Français, I stated that I do not call for women to act like men, nor do I approve of new trends that transform women into seductive playthings that social scientists mock and that cause their children's faces to drown in tears. I do not want women to renounce their high position for one in which the meanings of motherhood and the family are lost. On the contrary, I am among those women and men who say that education overthrows ignorance by calling for virtue, dignity, and chastity. In fact, education is the guarantor of women's distinguished and honorable status.

In my present lectures, I repeat what I have previously stated: I believe that unveiling, education, and freedom are more conducive to honor and chastity and the preservation of the meaning of motherhood, the family, and the interest of society than veiling, ignorance, and enslavement. For *adab* is inscribed in the soul of the educated differently than in that of the ignorant, and in the soul of the free person differently than in that of the slave. Thus, society and the family shall become sound and happy only when justice and virtue reign and when the light of freedom—which is a given right, like sunlight—prevails. There will be no happiness, probity, or order as long as despotism and injustice prevail and half of the family and half of the society are deprived of that light. Unjustly fettered by their veils and denied freedom and progress, mothers will be unable to ensure their children's progress and happiness.

The great reformer Qasim Amin stated, "Any reform within our social institutions that does not begin with the reform of the family is sterile. It is impossible to improve the state of our families unless we advance the condition of women and prepare them to become complete human beings." . . . Such is the new and beautiful garment that women are entitled to wear instead of the antiquated one. I appeal to you to make use of my words should you deem them wise. For the Prophet said, "Wisdom is the believer's cherished objective: wherever he finds it, he shall keep it."

In any event, I demand of men not to accuse me of breaking the rules and escaping the prison of the veil. It was not I who did this, sirs, but your brother—my father—whom God created utterly free, fearing neither reproach nor criticism in the pursuit of truth. It was he who deemed my prison incompatible with God's justice and human justice, and with the welfare of the family and society. He was certain of the honor of my soul and its *adab*, and so he sent me into life and into the light unveiled. When I applied my reason, I understood his actions and did what I did. . . .

Gentlemen:

A man of letters once visited my father, seeking his opinion about a lecture I had given. The man complimented my writing and told my father, . . . "I hope the proponents of the veil will not dismiss these lectures and will judge them according to what they hear and understand."

I said, "If so, then I shall publish my lectures so that learned men will read them carefully. If they see light in them, then they will light the lamps of their knowledge and brighten the darkness around them. . . ." The man of letters examined the titles of my lectures and declared, "All that you demand for women in your arguments is rightfully theirs. However, I believe that making all these demands at once intimidates men, who have been so accustomed to subjugating and excluding women that they believe that their actions are righteous and just. If you work toward achieving only one goal at a time, I believe that the result will be guaranteed." I replied, "I am not accustomed to employing such stratagems in my work. All the rights I demand are either explicit in the Qur'an and the Hadith or could be inferred from them through reason. Men must concede to acknowledge all these rights at once, even if they must grant them to women one by one. People's minds are undoubtedly diverse, and there are those who will be quick to concede and others who will delay, although the sooner they concede, the better. I have no doubt that in the present age men's solidarity in oppressing women has been exposed as shameful and replaced by their collaboration in treating women justly. The majority of our people have become supporters of women and not their opponents." "God is the ally of those who believe: He brings them out of the depths of darkness and into the light" [Qur'an 2.257; 44].[2]

My Message to My Brothers Who Support the Veil

To those dear sirs who seek to hold on to the veil, subjugate women, and preserve traditions, you have your beliefs on this matter. We, who call for unveiling, the liberation of women, and the rejection of traditions, have our own. We respect your beliefs and your opinion, so we demand that you respect ours, for only God knows who among us is right. God said, "If God so willed, He would have made you all one people" [Qur'an 16.93; 172].

That which God desires is good itself. If God had seen evil in the difference of beliefs among the people, He would not have allowed it. Do you know better than Him about what is harmful and what is beneficial? . . .

Valuable Dicta of the Philosopher [John] Stuart [Mill]

Dear sir, as you consider your woman lacking in faith and reason while you have neglected her spirit and have rendered her body a pretty plaything at the service of your passions and leisure, please allow me to read to you some dicta of the prominent philosopher [John] Stuart Mill. In the introduction of a treatise entitled *On Liberty*, which he published following the death of his wife, Mill said:

"To the beloved and deplored memory of her who was the inspirer, and in part the author, of all that is best in my writings—the friend and wife whose exalted sense of truth and right was my strongest incitement, and whose approbation was my chief reward—I dedicate this volume. Like all that I have written for many years, it belongs as much to her as to me; but the work as it stands has had, in a very insufficient degree, the inestimable advantage of her revision; some of the most important portions having been reserved for a more careful examination, which they are now destined never to receive. Were I but capable of interpreting to the world one-half the great thoughts and noble feelings which are buried in her grave, I should be the medium of a greater benefit to it, than is ever likely to arise from anything that I can write, unprompted and unassisted by her all but unrivaled wisdom."

God bless Stuart and his wife. May there be more like them among us, for it is as though they have grasped the essence of Islam and proceeded according to it. Dear sir, have Stuart's words not moved you? Has their spirit not found its way to your heart and shown you the righteous path so that you can restore to your wife her stolen rights, the least of which is acknowledging her reason and her faith?

Dear sir, you have favored your reason over that of the woman on the basis of innate disposition. To do so is neither your right nor within your capacity, because such things are not revealed to you. You have thereby disobeyed your God. "They ask you about the Spirit. Say, 'The Spirit is part of my Lord's domain. You have only been given a little knowledge'" (Qur'an 17.85; 180). . . .

As for me, I confess that to favor men's reason over that of women, or to favor women's reason over that of men, on the basis of innate disposition, is neither my right nor within my capacity, for this matter is concealed from me. But since you have made such claims, I believe that I must defend my sex and myself. I maintain that human beings should not neglect scientific research about nature's secrets by considering only surface appearances. I caution you against considering my evidence for women's sound reason to be a call for elevating the status of women over that of men. I shall not do what men have done in the past, but I shall ask them to admit that women are their equals in reason and status. I shall thereby avoid negligence and exaggeration, adhering instead to justice, moderation, and equity.

Innate disposition, ladies and gentlemen, indeed defines the spirit of every human being at birth. The human spirit, as scientists and interpreters have understood it, is constitutively composed of two spirits: a physical spirit, which animals and humans share, and a rational spirit, which characterizes human beings alone. The rational spirit changes with time and becomes either refined or debased. The shared physical spirit, however, does not change. It can be neither refined nor debased.

Deliberating with men about the rational spirit, or reason, whether it is more dominant among men or women, does not reveal truth, for men's passions prevent them from conceding to truth. In order to convince men, we should first prove our point with a case that is analogous to mine yet toward which they exhibit no passion and then consider this indisputable case the premise for reaching a conclusion. This way the resulting outcome will be one to which they must necessarily concede. In order to understand innate disposition, we have to examine the shared spirit that one finds alone only among animals and then compare it with the innate disposition of the rational spirit.

Observe the males and females of any type of animal, and you will notice that males are physically stronger than females and females are superior to males in their instincts, as if God Almighty manifested His justice by giving females superior instincts and compelled males and females to join efforts and complement each other's capacities. Males benefit from the wisdom of females, who in turn benefit from the strength of males.

God Almighty created female animals with instincts superior to males. If this were not the case, then God would not have entrusted the female bird with the responsibility of nesting. The nest's undeniable precision is proof of a superior sense of wisdom. Furthermore, God entrusted female birds with the care and protection of hatchlings, a task that requires a refined sense of judgment and attentiveness. Such is the animal spirit known for its instinct that commands its physical actions. . . .

This is a given in the spirit of each animal and an unchanging law of nature that allows no exceptions. It is a given from which we conclude that women are innately disposed to the rational spirit or reason as much as men are predisposed to physical strength. If this were not the case, then God Almighty would not have chosen men to wage Lesser *Jihad* [i.e., war], which requires more physical strength than reason. Nor would He have entrusted women with raising the young, which requires strength of spirit and wisdom rather than physical strength. For all other responsibilities, God has entrusted both men and women with similar tasks. There is no doubt that God endowed women with the power of the spirit and the power of reason, both of which are equivalent to His intended gift to men.

Girls Are More Righteous than Boys

Gentlemen, we have said that innate disposition defines the spirit of every living thing from the moment of birth, before it changes and evolves, becoming refined or debased with time. Much can be inferred about human disposition from people's actions and states at a young age. Observe boys and girls: what do you notice before girls become cloistered and boys are set free?

You will notice that generally boys rip and girls mend. The former scatter, the latter tidy. The former are harsh, the latter merciful. The former upset, the latter please. The former exhaust, the latter soothe. The former spoil, the latter fix. The former rebel, the latter obey. The former harm, the latter help. The former play, the latter strive. The former soil, the latter clean. The former are rude, and the latter timid, so that unfortunately it has become a proverb among the Arabs to say, "Rudeness is the boy's weapon." On the other hand, parents say, "We love girls for what they are now and love boys for what they will become." Observe the deeds of the two sexes and decide who exhibits more signs of goodness in disposition and reason.

The Prophet said, "Love your male children." They asked, "What about female children, O Prophet?" He replied, "God need not remind you to love them, for they are endearing in their righteousness and affection."

Men are therefore better than women neither in innate disposition nor in reason, for reason is intrinsic to the rational spirit. Men would not have surpassed women in life and the workforce if it were not for the obstacles that men have created. Empowered by their physical might, men have oppressively and forcibly bound women and limited their movements without engaging reason in their actions. This is a disgrace that the pen would have been embarrassed to express had not love of truth forced it to do so.

Human beings are strange creatures indeed! When the soul that commands evil overcomes them, they are no different from animals, the furthest from tenderness and the most susceptible to cruelty, anger, impulse, oppression, aggression, and harm. However, when human beings are dominated by the rational righteous soul, which emanates from the divine spirit, the heavenly angels kneel before them, for none is kinder or wiser, more honest or just.

The sex whose members exhibit in their actions the rational soul is superior in reason. Rational minds are weighed in the scales of justice, wisdom, honesty, and goodness, not in those of injustice, evil, tyranny, and harm. Otherwise, reason would have been the share of the strong, the demonic, and the tyrannically oppressive.

Notes

[1]*Adab* is untranslatable. Depending on the context, it might mean "manners," "good taste," "respectability," or "propriety," but also "literature" or "culture." I leave it as is to capture this polysemy.

[2]English translations of the Qur'an used in this translation are by Haleem.

Works Cited

Haleem, M. A. S. Abdel. *The Qur'an: English Translation and Parallel Arabic Text.* Oxford UP, 2010.

Mill, John Stuart. *On Liberty.* 1896. *Bartleby.com*, July 1999, www.bartleby.com/130/101.html.

Source of Arabic Text on Which the Translation Is Based

Zeineddine, Nazira. السفور والحجاب [al-sufur wal-hijab; Unveiling and Veiling]. Edited by Buthaina Sha'ban, Dar al-Mada, 1998, pp. 45–53, 92–98.

نظيرة زين الدين
(١٩٠٨–١٩٧٦)

السفور والحجاب

الحرية أساس الحياة الإنسانية الراقية:
حرية الفكر وحرية الإرادة

سادتي وسيداتي:

قال الكاتب الحكيم المنفلوطي: لا سبيل إلى السعادة في الحياة إلا إذا عاش الإنسان فيها حراً مطلقاً، لا يسيطر على جسمه وعقله ونفسه ووجدانه وفكره مسيطر إلا أدب النفس . . . الحرية شمس يجب أن تشرق في كل نفس، فمن حُرمها عاش في ظلمة حالكة يتصل أولها بظلمة الرحم وآخرها بظلمة القبر. الحرية هي الحياة ولولاها لكانت حياة الإنسان أشبه شيء بحياة اللعب المتحركة في أيدي الأطفال بحركات صناعية.

وقال الشيخ محمد عبده رحمه الله تعالى:

«تجلَّت بالإسلام للإنسان نفسه حرة كريمة، وأطلقت إرادته من القيود التي كانت تقيدها بإرادة غيره. . . . وبالجملة فقد أُعتقت روحه من العبودية للمحتالين والدجَّالين وصار الإنسان بالتوحيد عبد الله خاصة حراً من العبودية لكل ما سواه. فكان له من الحق ما للحر على الحر، لا عليَّ في الحق، ولا وضيع، ولا سافل، ولا رفيع، ولا تفاوت بين الناس إلا بتفاوت أعمالهم، ولا تفاضل إلا بتفاضلهم في عقولهم ومعارفهم، ولا يقربهم من الله إلا طهارة العقل من دنس الوهم، وخلوص العمل من العوج والرياء.»

مرحباً بك أيتها الحرية القدسية، حرية الفكر وحرية الإرادة، فأنتِ أنتِ روح الدين، أنتِ أنتِ أساس كل نهضة، وأنتِ أنتِ مولدة الحقائق بالبحث. مرحباً بك أيتها الحرية التي تخوّلنا حقّ حفظ شرفنا وحقّ نهوضنا بالصور التي نعتقد أنها له وللدين أقرب، ولنا ولعيالنا ولأمتنا أنفع . . .

ذكرتُ حرية الإرادة وحرية الفكر، وقد يلتبس على البعض معنياهما، إذ طالما بخس الجهل قدرهما، وأراد أن يمسح جمالهما، وخلطهما بالنزعات الحيوانية التي سمّاها الجهلة حرية. إن الحرية محلها العقل، فلا تتجلّى بنورها الساطع إلا في الإنسان على قدر عقله. أما الحيوان فلا يملك عقلاً ليملك حرية إرادة أو حرية فكر، فنزعاته إذاً حيوانية محضة مضرة لا أثر للحرية فيها.

إن حرية الإرادة—كما عرّفها علماء الاجتماع—هي حرية الفرد في تحديد أفعاله على مقتضى ما تحتمل نفسيته من تصور لغايات الآداب المثلى. وحرية الفكر هي حق الفرد في أن يتبع بلا خوف ولا وجل موحيات عقله لخيره وخير الناس، لا يعوقه عن ذلك تدخل السلطات، أو كراهية الجماهير ونزعاتها. ولنا أن نقيس على هاتين الحريتين حرية القول والحريات جميعها، فكلها ترمي إلى خير الإنسان وتشييد المجتمع.

موقفي وخطتي

أيها السيدات والسادة:

اتضح لكم من موقفي أنه موقف دفاع عن حرية المرأة، وأني من اللواتي رجّحنَ السفور مع الذين رجّحوه على الحجاب. وعملاً بحرية التفكير وتحت راية السيادة العلمية المستقلة، أطرح لديكم كل خواطري وتأملاتي التي جعلتني أرجّح السفور، وأطلب تحرير المرأة.

وإني—وأنا معترفة بقصوري—أرى أن مذهبي، وهو مذهب كثير من السادة والسيدات، أكثر انطباقاً على روح الاجتماع وأضمن حافظ للشرف الذي نقدسه جميعاً، ونتلمّس أصلح الأسباب لصونه منزّهاً محترماً.

قال بعض الحكماء: «إن التفكير الحر أساس كل نهضة، فيجب علينا أن نفسح له المجال ليسير، فيقاوِم ويقاوَم ضمن دائرة الأدب. وتصطدم حريته بحريات أخرى اصطداماً معقولاً سلمياً شريفاً وهكذا إلى أن يتم النصر للفكر الصحيح فلا يتألق برق الحقيقة إلا إذا تصادمت الآراء.»

ولهذا أرجو ممن يرى غير ما رأيت أن ينظر في ملحوظاتي وتأملاتي ويُنعم فيها، ثم يتفضل عملاً بحرية التفكير، ببيان ملحوظاته وتأملاته التي يوحيها له العقل والدين في وقفة آتية، حتى إذا أقنعني بمنطقه، ورأيت نتائج مذهبه

أحفظ للشرف، وأطبق للدين، وأنفع لعائلتي وللأمة، سدلت النقاب حالاً على وجهي، وتمسكت راضية كل الرضا بالحجاب، ولو كان أشد أشكال الاستعباد، وما همني أن يكون النور والهواء، وكل دواعي السعادة في الحياة، فداءً للدين وللشرف ولعائلتي وللأمة.

أما إذا اكتفى مناظري في جوابه بالبحث عن المروق والإلحاد وما ينافي آداب المناظرة، فسأترفع عن سماع كلامه مكتفية بالرجاء من الله سبحانه وتعالى أن يصلحه ويرسل إلى نفسه شعاعاً من نور الحرية والهدى؛ إذ أن ذلك النور لا يطلع على نفس إلا زينها بالعقل والأدب واحترام الناس، وبدَّل فيها حجة المجادلة بالتي هي أحسن من حجة المجادلة بالإساءة التي يعتصم بها المرائي العاجز عن بيان الدليل والبرهان. وكذلك إن الاكتفاء بالقول إن نظراتي غير صحيحة دون مجادلة ودون إثبات بالبرهان، لدليلٌ على عجز قائله، وعلى عدم صحة ما يقول.

ذكرت في محاضرة ألقيتها منذ مدة في الكلية العلمانية تحت عنوان «لماذا تتعلم الفتاة» أني لست من القائلات بالترجل ولست من مستحسنات الطفرة التي تجعل المرأة مسخاً يتلاعب به الغواة، وتسخر منه فلاسفة الاجتماع وتغرق لديه أسرّة الأطفال بالدموع، وأني لا أريد أن تتنزل المرأة عن مقامها الرفيع إلى منزلة يضيع فيها معنى الأمومة والعيلة البشرية، ولكني من القائلات مع القائلين: أن العلم أدعى من الجهل إلى الصيانة والكرامة والعفاف، بل إنما هو الحافظ للمرأة مقامها السامي الشريف.

وإني الآن في محاضراتي هذه أعيد قبل كل شيء كلامي الذي ذكرت. وأعتقد أن السفور والعلم والحرية أدعى من الحجاب والجهل والعبودية إلى الصيانة والكرامة والعفاف وإدراك معنى الأمومة والعيلة البشرية وصلاح المجتمع، لأن الأدب لا يثبت في نفس الجاهل ثبوته في نفس العالم، ولا يثبت في نفس العبد ثبوته في نفس الحر. ولأن العيلة والمجتمع إنما ينتظمان ويسعدان متى سادهما العدل والحق. ومتى كان نور الحرية—(وهو حق مثل نور الشمس)—شاملاً. فلا سعادة ولا صلاح ولا انتظام مع الاستبداد والظلم وبقاء نصف العيلة والمجتمع محروماً ذلك النور، وبقاء الأم مظلومة ترسف بل ترزح تحت قيود حجابها محرومة حريتها وكل أنواع رقيها، الأمر الذي يحرمها القدرة على ترقية أولادها وإسعاد بنيها.

قال المصلح الكبير قاسم أمين: «كل إصلاح في هيئتنا الاجتماعية لا يبدأ فيه بإصلاح العائلة فهو عقيم. وليس من الممكن تحسين حالتنا العائلية إلا بترقية

شأن المرأة، وإعدادها إلى أن تكون إنساناً تاماً. «. . . إنها لحلّة جديدة للمرأة جميلة، يحق أن تتخذ بدلاً من الثوب العتيق.

ولي الرجاء منكم أن لا يثقل عليكم أن تأخذوا حكمة من كلامي إذا وجدتم فيه حكمة. فقد قال رسول الله (ص) «الحِكْمَةُ ضَالَّةُ المُؤْمِنِ أَنّى وَجَدَهَا أَخَذَهَا.»

وعلى كل حال أرجو من سادتي الرجال أن لا يتهموني بخرق النظام، والفرار من سجن الحجاب. فإني لم أفعل ذلك يا سادتي. إنما أخوكم أبي الذي خلقه الله حراً مطلقاً (وهو لا يخشى في سبيل الحق لومة اللائمين) هو الذي عدّ سجني منافياً عدل الله، وعدل الإنسان، ومصلحة العيلة والمجتمع، ووثق بشرف نفسي وأدبها، فأرسلني سافرةً إلى الحياة والنور. ولدى تحكيمي العقل رجّحت ما رأى ففعلت . . .

أيها السادة:

زار أحد الأدباء يوماً أبي، فأراه شيئاً مما أكتب ليرى رأيه، فأطرى ما كتبت وحكى حكاية، قال: «. . . عسى الحجابيون لا يتأثرون ولا يحكمون إلا بما يسمعون من هذه المحاضرات ويعون.»

قلت إذاً أجعل محاضراتي مطبوعة، يقرأها أولو الألباب على مهل. فإذا آنسوا فيها نوراً أشعلوا مصابيح علمهم وأنار كل منهم ما حوله من الظلام . . . قال الأديب وقد رأى فهرست محاضراتي وألقى نظرة على نظراتي: إن كل ما تطلبينه للمرأة في دفاعك حق لها. ولكني أرى أن طلبك ذلك كله دفعة واحدة يهول الرجل الذي قد تعوّد ظلم المرأة واستعباده إياها حتى أضحى يرى ذلك حقاً له وعدلاً. فلو طلبتِ الحق الثاني بعد الأول، ثم الثالث بعد الثاني وهلم جراً، لكان نيل النتيجة على ما أرى أضمن.

قلت: لم أتعود الحيل في العمل. فكل حق رأيته في كتاب الله وسنّة رسوله، أو أراني إياه العقل موافقاً للكتاب والسنّة، سأطلبه. وللرجل أن يسلم دفعة واحدة لكل ما يراه حقا إن شاء، وله أن يتدرّج إن شاء في إعطاء الحقوق واحداً فواحداً. ولا ريب أن عقول الناس متفاوتة، فمنهم من يتعجل العطاء ومنهم من يؤجله، ولكن خير البر عاجله. ولا أشك في أن تضامن الرجال في ظلم المرأة قد تفككت عراه في هذا العصر وحل محله التعاون على إنصافها، وأضحى

السواد الأعظم من الأمة مع المرأة لا عليها. ﴿ٱللَّهُ وَلِيُّ ٱلَّذِينَ ءَامَنُواْ يُخْرِجُهُم مِّنَ ٱلظُّلُمَـٰتِ إِلَى ٱلنُّورِ﴾ [البقرة/٢٥٧].

خطابي إلى إخواني الحجابيين

يا سادتي القائلين بإبقاء الحجاب وإسارة المرأة وإبقاء التقاليد، لكم مذهبكم في ذلك. ونحن القائلين بالسفور وتحرير المرأة ونبذ التقاليد، لنا في ذلك مذهبنا. إننا نحترم مذهبكم ورأيكم فاحترموا مذهبنا ورأينا والله أعلم بمن هو أهدى سبيلاً. قال الله سبحانه وتعالى: ﴿وَلَوْ شَاءَ رَبُّكَ لَجَعَلَ ٱلنَّاسَ أُمَّةً وَٰحِدَةً﴾ [هود/١١٨].

وإن ما يشاؤه الله سبحانه هو الخير عينه، فلو رأى الله جل جلاله اختلاف الناس في المذاهب مضراً، لما شاءه. أَوَأنتم أعلم منه تعالى بما يضر وينفع . . .

وفيه عبارات للفيلسوف استوارت فيها لنا عبرة

—واسمح لي يا سيدي الرجل، وأنت تحسب إمرأتك ناقصة العقل والدين، وقد أهملت روحها، وجعلت جسمها لعبة مزينة للهوك وهواك، اسمح لي بأن أقرأ لك العبارة التي وضعها الفيلسوف الكبير استوارت ميل في صدر كتابه المسمّى «الحرية،» وقد طبعه بعد وفاة زوجته، قال:

«إني أهدي هذا الكتاب إلى الروح التي ألهمتني أحسن ما وضعته فيه من الأفكار، إلى صديقتي وزوجتي التي كان غرامها بالحق والعدل أعظم ناصر لي، والتي كان استحسانها من أكبر المكافآت التي أرجو نيلها على عملي. كان لها في جميع ما كتبته إلى الآن، ولها في هذا الكتاب حصة من العمل لا تنقص عن حصتي فيه، وأكبر أسفي أن هذا الكتاب طبع بالحالة التي هو عليها الآن قبل أن تعيد النظر فيه. ولو كان في استطاعة قلمي أن يعبر عن نصف ما دفن معها من الأفكار العالية والوجدان السامي، لا ننفع العالم به أكثر مما ينتفع بجميع ما أكتبه، صادراً عن فكري ووجداني، بدون مشورة عقلها الفريد.»

لله استوارت، ولله زوجته، وأكثر من أمثالهما بيننا، كأنهما هما اللذان أدركا، مع من أدركوا، لب دين الإسلام فتمشيا عليه. ألم يؤثر في قلبك يا سيدي

الرجل ما قاله استوارت؟ ألم يسرِ منه لقلبك سيال روحيّ يردّك إلى الحق، فترد إلى زوجتك حقوقها المسلوبة، أقلها التسليم لها بالعقل والدين؟

يا سيدي الرجل، رجّحتَ عقلك من حيث الفطرة على عقل المرأة، وذلك ليس من أمرك، وليس في استطاعتك، لأنه أخفى الأشياء عليك. فخالفت بذلك أمر ربك ﴿وَيَسْأَلُونَكَ عَنِ ٱلرُّوحِ قُلِ ٱلرُّوحُ مِنْ أَمْرِ رَبِّي وَمَا أُوتِيتُمْ مِّنَ ٱلْعِلْمِ إِلَّا قَلِيلًا﴾ [الإسراء/٨٥]. ....

أما أنا فأقرّ وأعترف بأن ترجيح عقل الرجل من حيث الفطرة على عقل المرأة أو ترجيح عقل هذه على عقل هذا، ليس من أمري، ولا في استطاعتي، لأنه أخفى الأشياء عليّ. ولكن بما أنك ادّعيت، ما ادّعيت، رأيت أنه لا بد لي من الدفاع عن نفسي، وعن بنات جنسي، ورأيت أنه لا ينبغي للإنسان أن يهمل البحث العلمي في ما يلوح له من أسرار الطبيعة، آخذاً بالظواهر. ولا تظنن إثباتي أن المرأة أصلح من الرجل عقلاً، يسوقني إلى طلب ترجيح المرأة على الرجل منزلة.

إني لن أفعل كما فعل الرجل، ولكني أطلب منه أن يعترف بأن المرأة مثله عقلاً ومنزلة. بذلك أبتعد عن التفريط والإفراط، لازمة حد العدل والاعتدال والمساواة.

إن الفطرة، يا سادتي وسيداتي، هي ما تتصف به روح كل حيّ في أول خلقه، والروح في الإنسان، من حيث الخاصة، كما يُفهم من قول العلماء والمفسّرين، روحان: روح جسمانية مشتركة بين الإنسان والحيوان، وروح ناطقة يمتاز بها الإنسان على الحيوان. أما الروح الناطقة فهي تتغير بالاكتساب، فترقّى أو تتدنّى، وأما الروح الجسمانية المشتركة، فهي لا تتغير، فلا ترقى ولا تتدنّى.

إن مباحثة الرجل مباشرة في الروح الناطقة أو العقل، أهو أرجح من حيث الفطرة فيه منه في المرأة، أم هو أرجح فيها منه فيه، لا توصل إلى نتيجة تجلو الحقيقة. إذ أن هوى الرجل يثنيه عن الإذعان للحق، فوجب لحمله على الإذعان للحق أن أثبت قضية تشبه قضيتي لا هوى له فيها يثنيه، ثم أتخذ تلك القضية المسلّمة، مقدمة للقياس، فتظهر النتيجة التي لا مندوحة له عن الإقرار بها. إذن وجب لكي نعرف الفطرة أن ندرس الروح المشتركة، وهي لا تظهر منفردة إلا في الحيوان، ثم نقيس عليها الفطرة في الروح الناطقة.

انظروا إلى ذكر وأنثى من أي نوع كان في الحيوان. تروا أن الذكر أقوى جسماً من الأنثى، وأن الأنثى أصلح غريزة من الذكر. كأن الله سبحان وتعالى أراد أن يظهر عدله فأعطى الذكر الحظ الأوفر من قوة الجسم، وأعطى الأنثى الحظ الأوفر من صلاح الغريزة. وأراد أيضاً أن يظهر حكمته باضطراره كلاً من الأنثى والذكر للشركة، فيكمل كل منهما ما نقص في صِنْوه. فهذا يستفيد من تلك حكمة، وتلك تستفيد من هذا قوة.

أجل، إن الله تعالى جعل الأنثى في الحيوان، أصلح من الذكر، وأحكم منه غريزة، ولولا ذلك لما كلَّف الله أنثى الطير بناءَ العش، ولا يخفى ما في بناء العش من دقة لا يمكن أن تكون إلا بنت حكمة، ولما كلَّف تلك الأنثى تربية صغار النسل وحفظه، وهذا ما يستوجب من الحكمة والعناية قسطاً أوفر من ذاك، وما ذاك كله إلا من خصائص العقل الحيواني المعروف بالغريزة التي هي قائدة الحركات الجسدية. . . .

تلك حالة ثابتة في روح كل حيوان، وقاعدة طبيعية عامة لا تتغير، ولا استثناء فيها. وهي مقدمة صحيحة في القياس نستنتج منها أن الروح الناطقة أو العقل يَرجح فطرة في المرأة كما ترجح قوة الجسم في الرجل. ولولا ذلك لما خص الله تعالى الرجل بالجهاد الأصغر وهو يقتضي قوة من الجسم أكثر مما يقتضي من العقل، ولما خص المرأة بالعناية في تربية الصغار وهي تقتضي قوة من الروح والعقل أكثر مما تقتضي من الجسم، مع أنه سبحانه وتعالى كلَّف الإثنين في غير ذلك تكاليف لا فرق بينهما فيها. . . . فلا ريب أنه جلَّ عدله أسبغ على المرأة من قوة الروح والعقل ما يعادل نعمته المنظورة على الرجل.

وفيه البنات أصلح من البنين

قلنا يا سادتي: إن الفطرة هي ما تتصف به روح كل حيّ في أول خلقه قبل أن تتحول وتتغير، قبل أن تَرْقى أو تتدنّى بالاكتساب. إذن يُستدل على فطرة الإنسان من أحواله وأفعاله في صغره، فانظروا إلى البنين والبنات، حتى السن التي يحجر فيها عندنا على هؤلاء، ويطلق أولئك. فماذا ترون على الغالب؟

إنكم ترون على الغالب أولئك يفتقون وهؤلاء يرتقن، أولئك يبعزقون وهؤلاء يرتبن، أولئك يقسون وهؤلاء يرأفن، أولئك يكدّرون وهؤلاء يسررن،

أولئك يُتعبون وهؤلاء يُريحن، أولئك يفسدون وهؤلاء يصلحن، أولئك يتمردون وهؤلاء يطعن، أولئك يُضرّون وهؤلاء ينفعن أولئك يلعبون وهؤلاء يجددن، أولئك يوسخون وهؤلاء ينظفن، أولئك يَقِحون وهؤلاء يستحيين، حتى أمسى ويا للأسف من أمثال العرب «وقاحة الوجه سلاح الفتى» ومن أقوال الوالدين «نحب البنات لما هنّ عليه الآن، ونحب الصبيان لما يكونونه في المستقبل.» فتأملوا في أعمال الجنسين واحكموا في أيهما الأَدَلّ على الصلاح في الفطرة والعقل.

قال رسول الله (ص) «حِبُّوا أَوْلَادَكُمُ الذُّكُور» قالوا والإناث يا رَسولَ الله قال: «لَا حاجةَ أن يوصيَكُمُ اللهُ بالحبُ لَهُنَّ فَهُنَّ يُحَبّْنَ أَنْفُسَهُنَّ إِلَيْكُمْ بِصَلاحِهِنَّ وَحَنَانِهِنَّ.»

إذن ليس الرجل أصلح من المرأة عقلاً في الفطرة، وما العقل الصالح إلا شيمة النفس الناطقة المرضية، وما كان سبق الرجل المرأة في ميدان الحياة والعمل، إلا للسبب العارض الذي أحدثه الرجل، وهو تقييده قواها، وغلّه حركاتها بما شاء من القيود والأغلال، ظلماً وعدواناً، مستنداً في ذلك إلى قواه الجسدية، دون أن يشرك العقل أو الروح في أفعاله، فكانت شائنة يخجل القلم من أن يكتبها، لولا أن إظهار الحقيقة يحمله على ذلك.

أجل، إن الإنسان لمخلوق عجيب! متى غلبت فيه النفس الأمّارة بالسوء فليس في الحيوان أبعد منه عن رقة الشعور، وأكثر منه غضباً، وهوىً، وشراً، وظلماً وأذىً وضراً. وإذا غلبت فيه النفس الناطقة المرضية، وهي نفخة فيه من الروح الإلهية أوقع الله الملائكة له ساجدين، وليس فيهم ألطف منه شعوراً، وأوفر حكمة ونزاهة وعدلاً.

ومَن مِن الجنسين كثرت في أفراده انتصارات النفس الناطقة المرضية فهو الأصلح عقلاً. إن العقول الصالحة توزن بقسطاس العدل والحكمة والنزاهة والخير لا بميزان الظلم، والشر، والاستبداد، والضير. وإلا كان أوفر نصيب من العقل للأبالسة والشياطين، وللأشقياء الأقوياء، والظلمة المستبدين المضرين.

Mayy Ziyadah
(1886–1941)

Introduced and translated by Boutheina Khaldi

Mayy Ziyadah was a prolific Lebanese Palestinian writer, essay-
ist, poet, public speaker, and critic. She was born in Nazareth to
a Lebanese Maronite father and a Palestinian Greek Orthodox
mother. At an early age she cultivated a love for French liter-
ature, especially Romantic poetry. The influence of Romantic
poets such as Alphonse de Lamartine is reflected in her first col-
lection of poems written in French, *Fleurs du rêve* (1911; "Flowers
of the Dream"), which she published under the pseudonym Isis
Copia. It was published in Cairo after her parents had left with
her for Egypt in 1908 in search of a better life. Her work was
acclaimed by some critics who knew French, but it did not gain
wide recognition. In addition, she began to write in Arabic for
the newspaper *al-Mahrusa* ("The Protected One," i.e., Egypt),
which her father owned.

The Egyptian editor of *al-Jarida* ("The Gazette"), Ahmad
Lutfi al-Sayyid, advised Ziyadah to read the Qur'an to improve
her Arabic and offered her a copy as a gift. This encouraged her
to pursue her education in literature and Islamic philosophy at
the Egyptian University. Through her extensive contributions
to newspapers, she became a well-known figure in Egypt, and
she presided over an important salon for more than twenty
years (1913–36). Her salon was a microcosm of the Arab *Nahda*
itself, with intellectuals of different cultural and ideological
backgrounds participating in a weekly dialogue that spilled over
into the media.

The translations below are of two letters addressed by
Ziyadah to two prominent *Nahda* intellectuals: Ya'qub Sarruf
and Malak Hifni Nasif. Her correspondence functioned as a

rigorous exercise in disseminating knowledge, rejuvenating reason, and activating a critical sense that ran counter to systems of coercion and control.

Recommended Reading

Khaldi, Boutheina. *Egypt Awakening in the Early Twentieth Century: Mayy Ziyadah's Intellectual Circles.* Palgrave Macmillan, 2012.

———. "Epistolarity in a Nahdah Climate: The Role of Mayy Ziyadah's Letter Writing." *Journal of Arabic Literature*, vol. 40, no. 1, 2009, pp. 1–34.

———. "Microcosming the Nahdah: Mayy Ziyadah's Salon as a Hybrid Space." *Journal of Arabic Literature*, vol. 41, no. 3, 2011, pp. 1–41.

Letter to Yaʿqub Sarruf (1920)

Dear Sir,

When I received your letter last Monday, I was engrossed in reading the most interesting correspondence between two great philosophers, Voltaire and d'Alembert, about the greatest literary work that modern history has ever known: the *Encyclopédie*.

At that time, our friend Voltaire was exiled in Switzerland, and d'Alembert was in Paris assisting Diderot and the other encyclopedists in publishing the *Encyclopédie*, section by section, under the patronage of "Solomon of the North"—as Voltaire used to call Frederick the Great in a reference to his spiritual presence—who used to pay some of the French philosophers monthly salaries, which guaranteed them food, clothes, and housing. The French monarchy, meanwhile, at the peak of its glory, was concerned only with hunting them down, exiling them, and burning their works! After the French monarchy agreed to sponsor their literary project, they came under pressure from the clergy, which harassed them and put multiple obstacles in their way. So the monarchy censored them, and they reluctantly accepted it. The monarchy appointed the most ignorant censors for this task, who excised from the *Encyclopédie* everything they did not understand; and they did not understand a single thing!

Under these gloomy circumstances these two great men began a correspondence, and from a distance Voltaire helped d'Alembert compose the *Encyclopédie*. The two were alike in their intellectual might, in their desire to serve the public interest, and in their hatred of ignorance, pretension, and despotism. Likewise, their letters resemble each other in grievance and complaint, in the knowledge of human nature they demonstrate, and in the tolerance they show toward the foolishness of stupid people. How few are the words of bitterness that emanate from their broken hearts. How sweet are the words of consolation from their mighty yet restrained pens. How far into the distant future before them have their thoughts reached!

The *Encyclopédie* is their primary topic. The thoughts of the two collaborators revolve around it, for they are concerned with producing a work that will immortalize them for future generations. However, they are not confined solely to this topic; around this central point, flocks of other subjects flutter, social, philosophical, scientific, religious, and psychological. When they come across a funny story, joke, or anecdote, they pause upon it and laugh as though they were children, as though the government were not harassing them and they were not threatened with punishments—punishments no less cruel and appalling than those of the Inquisition itself, which is indeed what this was.

I read with admiration, laughing, sad, in sympathy with them, praising God as a believer does when faced with an extraordinary scene from nature. I praised God because He created these great minds, elevated souls, and luminous intellects.

I envy each of them for having a genius for a friend, contrasting their minds with the mind of one of my Jewish neighbors, who one morning caused turmoil by assembling all the cooks and servants of her house, to arrive at the solution to the formidable mathematical question: "What is one-quarter of fifty?"

At just that moment, your letter came, with its magisterial introduction. I closed my eyes and said, "What is with me and these two philosophers, that I envy one of them his friendship with the other? Life has blessed me with a friend just like them with whom I can converse and correspond and whose higher intellectual influence I receive!" Then I ripped open the letter, which you must pardon me for calling "Russian" twice over: once because it is like a Russian salad in its mix of dates, scripts, and colors of ink and again because the fire of the Red Revolution burns through it from the first word to the last.

You express frankly that you are angry with me and that you desire to reprimand and punish me. What are my sins? It is not necessary for me in reality to have done something wrong. As long as you wish to accuse me, you will create my sins out of nothing. Even your magnificent introduction is not free from stings, jabs, and pokes here and there.

You said, for instance, that I think in a European language before I express myself in Arabic. You said that, and you did not allow me to to argue. Would it help in my defense if I swore in all sincerity that whenever I write in Arabic I think in it, and that I think in a foreign language only incidentally, as all people do when they visualize someone or something and simultaneously conjure up the language that was used when they saw or heard that person or thing for the first time?

I admit that my knowledge of other languages [before I learned Arabic] has made me liken our society to a woman who in her entire life has never left her village of seven houses yet who says that it is the most beautiful city in the world and that it is the center of the universe. This knowledge of mine has made me ask myself, whenever I read an article by one of our so-called greatest writers or most outstanding poets, "What of their own personalities do these leading figures put into what they write? Where is that subjectivity of which I find no trace?" Why do I have to explain my tendencies and justify my linguistic preferences? If there is anyone who deserves blame, it is you, who renounced rhymed prose, commentaries, and appendices when they were the spirit of the age. If I had wanted to imitate someone, I would have imitated you. But I hate imitation, which distorts what is imitated and defaces the imitator. I like to be myself in my writing. "Oh my God! What is this arrogance and pretension?" you will say. To this I reply, "Oh my God! What is this injustice and despotism?"

Here is another accusation. You say in your letter that I am waiting for the least sign to dispense you from the introduction. How malicious you are when you say what you do not believe! But I do not want to argue with you, so I will forgive you for everything else you wrote in the letter in honor of the introduction.

I am writing to you as the sun sets over the horizon and the evening clouds swim in lakes of gold, amber, emerald, and ruby. In all corners of the earth, the heat of spring is rising and nature is awakening. How beautiful are the saplings that the municipality most kindly planted! They are in full bloom on both sides of our street. Did you go to the Sham al-Nassim celebrations today,[1] or were you content to walk along 'Imad al-Din Street? Perhaps you are walking outside right now and looking at this enchanting sunset and thinking about . . . ? As for me, I have not left the house in recent days, having recently faced a number of adversities. My mother complains about her arm, my father suffers from a toothache, and the phone is malfunctioning, possessed by a devilish spirit, as uncivilized people say. This is a real disaster. As for me, a thick needle pierced my thumb under the nail, and to console me with her affection and cure me with her special medicine, [my cat] Mademoiselle Tutu bit the ailing digit and ripped it up with her claws. So I said, laughing, "How similar cats are to philosophers sometimes!"

Letter to Malak Hifni Nasif (1913)

To the scholar in the wilderness:

Nothing is dearer to us than your kindness, except your firmness and your sincerity. Nothing is more beautiful than the echo of your voice, except the impact of your ideas. I clasp my hands and confess—though I ask God's forgiveness and yours—that I love how you suffer great spiritual pains at the misery and error of humanity. I hope from the depths of my soul that these pains will always find an open way to your heart and that your heart will remain generous and gentle, wounded with the injuries of the stranger and crying with the tears of the oppressed, sympathizing with the sufferer wherever he is. In short—forgive me! forgive me!—I wish you moral torment because it is sacred fire. Yes, it is the fire that purifies, the fire that softens, and the fire that lifts the soul on the wings of the flames to the heaven of higher meanings, lofty inclinations, noble desires, and enthusiasm for carrying out necessary reforms, implementing good principles, and raising up society in a Renaissance [*Nahda*] at which hearts tremble in joy and delight.

I wish this upon you, because were it not for your suffering, we would not find in your writings that deep lamentation that awakens the mind and touches the emotions at the same time. I do not deny that it is my selfishness speaking right now, although I said what I said hurriedly and in a whisper. So smile at my words if you wish; otherwise, my lady, listen not and pay me no heed. Ask me what I am whispering, and I will reply that

I am thanking God for your recovery and asking Him to protect you, because your well-being is the most precious thing to us.

I want to confide to you something that I noticed when I saw the impression that your article made on readers. Listen, my lady scholar, and keep my secret! I saw all of them receiving your words with looks of pride and smiles of admiration. But I saw our masters, the men—I say "masters" to quell their anger—delighted by our statement that they are unjust and despotic. Yes, I observed this in the expressions of every man I saw reading your article. I remembered then that there is no happiness in the world equal to the happiness of mutual understanding. If a person feels that there is someone who understands him, he is happy whether he learns from him his merits or his shortcomings, because knowledge of one's shortcomings is followed inevitably by knowledge of one's merits, even if good is less widespread than evil. For what are our failings but virtues magnified and enlarged, which expand and overflow without refinement from a conscience. They transgress the moral limits prescribed for them by social conventions—if these are really social—or drawn for them by psychology and ethics—if these are really ethical.

Pursuant to the desire for mutual understanding, in accordance with the ways of pridefulness, and aiming to enjoy the products of both, the thief is forever boasting about people's awareness of his skill in choosing new methods and devising more cunning tricks. The murderer is forever happy to disclose his crimes to men, hoping that they will find in them the deeds of a hero. The politician is forever serious about convincing others that his guile is strength and his distrust and evasion are signs of intelligence and sagacity. Likewise, man is joyful, and desires, and wants a woman to feel his despotism. He thinks that despotism is sovereignty and that it is the measure of his personality, which he wants strong. Whether a woman accepts his sovereignty or rebels against it makes no difference to him.

I think, and may God forgive me if I am wrong, that he prefers her rebellion to her submissiveness, because the more rebellious she is, the more his feeling of authority increases. Kings become happier when they shake their scepters, and those whose thrones are threatened with falling raise their heads higher with arrogance and pride beneath the weight of their crowns. Man is a king whose throne is ready to fall, because the winds of chaos are blowing on all sides, while women's advancement gains progressively more ground as time goes by.

But he is a dear king! He is a father, a brother, a friend, a fiancé, and a husband. If he falls, we fall with him, and if he rises, we grow great with his ascent. This is why we wish him the best, and we work hard in support of his nation, provided that he erects our throne next to his and that we stand at his side as an equal. We want to be equal in our duties and responsibilities. Indeed, our duties and responsibilities already exceed his! I wonder when man will consent to this fact?

How fine are your words, my dear lady scholar! You pity those who deserve pity and those who do not. Man deserves pity because he does not know that he deserves it, that by enslaving us he is committing suicide. If we turned our eyes from the future of our children and searched his personal life, we would find that no one but us can help him rid himself of his disgraceful shortcomings and urge him to develop a rich and fertile personality. Likewise, no one but him shows us our duties and gives strength to our weakness.

The veil? What is the veil? We welcome it as long as we are in an environment that does not know how to treat women and is unable to respect them. But how can we blame man for his words and his views, when the man of today was raised by the woman of yesterday? This is how his mother taught him to be, and if she did not teach him this, then she did not instruct him in anything better. She bears no guilt in this either, because her ignorance was the result of the agreement between her father and her husband to make her a slave. We do not blame the sons of those mothers. Yet our future is bright because our present is full of great hopes. The youth are torn between inherited customs, the influences of the [new] age, and the storms of chaos that are attacking outworn traditions from every side. However, the youth seek the right path and heed the voice of reform. So raise your voice, my lady, and do not despair! Speak with all your sincerity and write with all your courage! Speak up and do not be silent! For the seed that the farmer plants today will sprout to create the life of tomorrow and all days to come. And when the fields turn green with hope and the breezes of life stir waves within the crops, then the future will listen to the echo of a generation reciting the verses of the Prince of Poets, [Ahmad] Shawqi:

> O singer, king of canarie
> and prince of nightingales.
> Be patient with what distresses you
> otherwise do what pleases you.
> These new echoes reply, "I did! I did!"

—"Mayy"

Note

[1]Egyptian popular holiday on the Monday following the Greek Coptic Easter at the end of March, in April, or in early May.

Sources of Arabic Texts on Which the Translation Is Based

Letter to Yaʻqub Sarruf:

Al-Tannahi, Tahir. أطياف من حياة مي [atyaf min hayat mayy; Specters of Mayy's Life]. Dar al-Hilal, 1974, pp. 68–72.

Letter to Malak Hifni Nasif:

Nasif, Malak Hifni. النسائيات [al-nisaʼiyyat; Feminist Pieces]. 3rd ed., Multaqa al-Marʼa wal-Dhakira, 1998, pp. 203–05.

مي زيادة
(١٨٨٦-١٩٤١)

رسالة إلى يعقوب صرّوف (١٩٢٠)

أستاذي العزيز،

لما جاءتني رسالتك يوم الإثنين الماضي كنت غارقة في مطالعة مراسلة شائقة بين فيلسوفين عظيمين: فولتير ودالمبر، مراسلة دائرة حول أعظم أثر أدبي رأته القرون الحديثة: دائرة المعارف الفرنسية.

يومئذ كان صاحبنا فولتير منفياً في سويسرا وكان دالمبر في باريس يتعاون ويديرون والإنسيكلوبيديين الآخرين في إصدار دائرة المعارف جزءاً بعد جزء في ظل سليمان الشمال—كما كان فولتير يسمّي فريدريك الكبير في ظله المعنوي فقط—وهو الذي كان ينقد بعض فلاسفة فرنسا وعلمائها رواتب شهرية تكفل لهم الغذاء، والكساء، والسكن، في حين أن الملكية الفرنسية التي كانت يومذاك في أعلى أعالي مجدها لم تكن تفكر فيهم إلا لتطاردهم وتنفيهم وتحرق مؤلفاتهم!! وبعد أن وعدتهم هذه بالمساعدة الأدبية، قامت مدفوعة من الإكليروس تصادرهم وتكثر العقبات في سبيلهم . . . فرضت عليهم الرقابة، فقبلوها مرغمين، وعينت من الرقباء أجهلهم، فصار هؤلاء يحذفون كل ما لا يفهمون، ولم يكونوا يفهمون شيئاً!

في هذه الحالة المدلهمة أخذ الرجلان الكبيران يتراسلان، وكان فولتير يساعد دالمبر عن بعد في تأليف الإنسيكلوبيديا. وكلاهما يشبه رفيقه بما لديه من عظمة فكرية ورغبة في خدمة المصلحة العامة وكره للجهل والدعوى والاستبداد. كذلك تشابهت منهما الرسائل في التظلم وبث الشكوى، وفي معرفة الطبيعة البشرية والتساهل لغباوة الأغبياء. وما أقل كلمات المرارة الخارجة من قلبيهما المصدوعين. وما أعذب كلمات المؤاساة من قلميهما القادرين الملجمين. وما أبعد نقطة يدركها فكراهما في مدى المستقبل المنبسط أمامهما!

دائرة المعارف موضوعهما الأول، يحومان حوله باهتمام كما يهتم الشريكان في عمل يخلدهما أمام وجه الأجيال، إلا أنهما لا يقتصران عليه، بل ترفرف حول هذه النقطة الجوهرية أسراب المواضيع الاجتماعية والفلسفية والعلمية والدينية والسيكولوجية، حتى إذا عثرا على معنى ظريف أو نكتة أو ملحة،

وقفاعندها يضحكان كأنهما طفلان لم تصادرهما حكومة، ولم يهددا بعقوبات إن لم تكن عقوبات محكمة التفتيش بالاسم، فهي هي بالذات، ولا تقل عنها قسوة وهولاً.

كنت أقرأ معجبة ضاحكة مكتئبة متعزية معهما، ومسبحة الله كما يفعل المؤمن إزاء مشهد طبيعي رائع. أسبحه لأنه أبدع هذه العقول الكبيرة والنفوس السامية والأذهان المتوقدة، وأغبط كلاً منهما على صديقه العبقري مقابلة بين هذه العقول، وبين عقل إحدى جاراتنا الإسرائيليات التي كانت في ذلك الصباح قد أقامت القيامة بين برابرة الدار وطهاتها وخدمها أجمعين لتصل إلى حل هذه المسألة الرياضية الهائلة: «ربع الخمسين كام؟»

في تلك الدقيقة جاء كتابك ترافقه المقدمة الهمايونية، فأغمضت عينيّ قائلة: «مالي وللفيلسوفين أغبط الواحد منهما على الآخر، وأنا قد أسعدتني الحياة بصديق مثلهما أحدثه وأراسله، وأتلقى تأثيره الفكري العالي!» ثم فضضت الرسالة التي أستأذنك بتسميتها روسية «ثورية» مرتين: روسية من حيث أنها كالسلطة الروسية مخلوطة تواريخ وخطوطاً وألوان حبر—وروسية من حيث أن نار الثورة الحمراء تشتعل فيها اشتعالاً من أول كلمة إلى آخر سطر.

تجاهر بأنك ناقم ساخط راغب في معاقبتي وتعنيفي. وما هي ذنوبي؟ ليس من الضروري أن يكون لي ذنوب في عالم الوجود. ما دمت راغباً في إيقافي موقف المتهم، فإنك تخلقها من العدم. حتى المقدمة العظيمة لا تخلو من وخزة هنا، ونغزة هناك، ولطمة هنالك.

لقد قلت مثلاً إني أفكر بلغة أوروبية قبلما أعبر عن رأيي بالعربية— قلت ذلك، ولم تسمح لي بالاحتجاج. وهل دفاعي يجدي نفعاً إذا استشهدت الإخلاص أني ساعة أكتب العربية أفكر بها، ولا أفكر بلغة أجنبية إلا عرضاً كما يفعل جميع الناس الذين إذا ما استحضروا شخصاً أو شيئاً استحضروا معه اللغة التي كانت مستعملة ساعة رأوه أو سمعوه لأول مرة.

أعترف بأن معرفتي اللغات الأخرى قبل العربية جعلتني أشبّه جماعتنا بتلك المرأة التي لم تخرج في حياتها من قرية لا تزيد منازلها على السبعة عداً. وكانت تقول فيها إنها أجمل مدينة في العالم، وإنها أم الدنيا. وتلك المعرفة جعلتني أسائل نفسي كلما قرأت مقالاً لبعض من يدعون أعاظم الكتاب وفطاحل الشعراء قائلة: «وماذا وضع هؤلاء الأقطاب من ذاتيتهم

فيما كتبوا، بل أين تلك الذاتية التي لا أجد لها أثراً؟» ثم مالي أنا أشرح ميولي وأبرر سروري اللغوي. إذا كان هناك من يستحق الملام، فأنت هو. أنت الذي تنصلت من الأسجاع والحواشي والزوائد يوم كانت هذه روح العصر. لو أردت أن أقلد أحداً لقلدتك، لكني أكره التقليد الذي يسوّه المقلّد ويمسخ المقلّد وأنا أحب أن أكون أنا في كتابتي.«يا لطيف، ما هذه الكبرياء والدعوى!» هكذا ستقول أنت. «يا لطيف ما هذا الظلم والاستبداد!» وهكذا أجيبك أنا.

وهاك تهمة أخرى. تقول في رسالتك إني أنتظر أول إشارة لأعفيك من المقدمة، كم أنت شرير ساعة تقول ما لا تعتقد. ولكني لا أريد أن أخاصمك، وأغفر لك كل ما جاء في الرسالة إكراماً للمقدمة.

أكتب إليك والشمس تنزل درجات الأفق، وقد سبحت غيوم المساء كما في بحيرات من العسجد والعنبر والزبرجد والياقوت. في جميع أطراف الأفق تتوهج حرارة الربيع وتبدو يقظة الطبيعة. وعلى البسيطة مثل هذه اليقظة وتلك الحرارة. ما أجمل الشجيرات التي أنبتها لنا كرماً مصلحة التنظيم، تبسم بأزهارها الكليلة على جانبي شارعنا. هل ذهبت اليوم لشم النسيم، أم اكتفيت بالسير في شارع عماد الدين؟ ربما كنت الآن سائراً في الخلاء تنظر إلى هذا الغروب الساحر وتفكر في. . . . أما أنا فلم أخرج من البيت في هذه الأيام التي كثرت فيها علي المعاكسات. فأمي تشكو ذراعها، وأبي يشكو ألماً في ضرسه، والتليفون ملخبط زي عقل العفريت كما يقول البربري. وهذه من الدواهي الصماء حقيقة . . . وأنا شكتني إبرة غليظة تحت ظفر إبهامي. ثم رأت حضرة مدموازيل توتو أن تتحفني بصداقتها، وتعالجني بطبها الخاص، فعضت على الأصبع المريضة ومزقتها بمخالبها، فقلت ضاحكة: «ما أشبه القطط بالفلاسفة أحياناً!»

رسالة إلى ملك حفني ناصف (١٩١٣)

إلى باحثة البادية:

ليس أعز لدينا من لطفك إلا حزمك وصراحتك، وليس أجمل من صدى صوتك إلا فعل معناك. وإني لأقبض بيدي لأعترف بأني أحب—أستغفر الله وأستغفرك يا سيدتي—آلامك النفسية الشديدة من جراء شقاء الإنسانية

وضلالها، وأتمنى من أعماق فؤادي أن تجد دواماً تلك الآلام منفذاً رحباً إلى
قلبك، وأن يبقى ذلك القلب كريماً ليناً ينجرح لجرح الغريب ويبكي لبكاء
المظلوم، ويشفق على المتوجع أياً كان. بالاختصار—عفوك! عفوك!—أتمنى لك
العذاب المعنوي لأنه النار المقدسة. أجل، هو النار التي تطهر النار التي تلين
النار التي ترفع النفس على أجنحة اللهيب إلى سماء المعاني السامية والميول
الرفيعة والرغبات الكريمة، والتحمس لإجراء الإصلاحات اللازمة وتنفيذ المبادئ
الطيبة، والنهوض بالاجتماع بنهضة تهتز لها القلوب حمية وطرباً.

أتمنى لك ذلك، ولولاه لما وجدنا في كتابتك تلك الأنّة العميقة التي تنبه
الفكر وتلمس العاطفة في آن واحد. لا أنكر أن أنانيتي تتكلم الآن. غير أني
قلت ما قلت مسرعة هامسة. فابتسمي له إن شئت، وإلا فلا تصغي يا سيدتي
ولا تسمعي، بل اسأليني عما أهمس به لأجيب أني أحمد الله على إبلالك وأني
أسأله أن يديمك سالمة. وما أغلى سلامتك لدينا.

جئت أسر إليك أمراً وقفت عليه عندما شهدت صدى مقالتك لدى
جمهور القراء. اسمعي يا سيدتي الباحثة، وصوني سري! رأيت جميعهم يتقبل
أقوالك بنظرة الفخر وابتسامة الإعجاب، ولكني رأيت أسيادنا الرجال—أقول
«أسيادنا» تخمد نار غضبهم—قلت إني رأيتهم يطربون لتصريحنا بأنهم ظلمة
مستبدون. نعم آنست ذلك في ملامح كل من قرأ مقالك أمامي من أسيادنا
الرجال. فذكرت إذ ذاك ألا سرور في العالم يضاهي سرور التفاهم. فإذا شعر
المرء بأن من يفهمه كان سعيداً، سواء لديه إن تعرف منه على صفاته أو علاته،
لأن معرفة العلات تتبعها حتماً معرفة الصفات، وإن كان الخير أقل انتشاراً
من الشر وما النقائص إلا فضائل مضخمة مكبرة تتسع وتستفيض دون أن
تجد لها من الضمير مهذباً فتتجاوز الحدود المعنوية التي عينتها اصطلاحات
الاجتماع—إذا كانت اجتماعية—أو رسمتها علوم النفس والأخلاق، إذا كانت
أخلاقية.

فعملاً برغبة التفاهم، وطبقاً لنظام المباهاة، وتوصلاً للاستمتاع بنتيجة
هذه المباهاة وذلك التفاهم كان وسيكون السارق دائم المفاخرة بوقوف
الناس على براعته في اختيار الطرق الجديدة واستنباط الحيل الغريبة. وكان
وسيكون القاتل مسروراً بإعلان آثامه للورى آملاً أن يجدوا فيها أعمال بطل—
من نوعه! وكان وسيكون السياسي جاداً في إقناع الآخرين أن دهاءه اقتدار
وسوء ظنه وروغانه فطنة وحكمة. كذلك الرجل يسر، ويرجو، ويريد أن تشعر

المرأة باستبداده ظناً منه أن الاستبداد هو السيادة وأن هذه مقياس ذاتيته التي يريدها كبيرة. رضيت المرأة عن تلك السيادة أم تمردت عليها في نظره سيان، بل أظنه—سامحني الله إن كنت مخطئة—مؤثراً تمردها على إذعانها لأنها كلما زاد تمردها زاد شعوره بالسيطرة. وأشد الملوك فرحاً بهز الصولجان، وأرفعهم للرأس كبراً وتيهاً تحت ثقل التيجان، هم ذوو العروش المتداعية للهبوط. والرجل ملك متداع عرشه، لأن ريح الفوضى تهب عليه من كل جانب، وخطوات الارتقاء النسائي تتوالى متمكنة مع مرور الأيام.

لكنه ملك عزيز! هو الأب والأخ والصديق والخطيب والزوج فإذا سقط سقطنا معه، وإذا ارتفع كنا بارتفاعه عظيمات. لذلك نريد له خيراً ونجتهد في تأييد دولته، بشرط أن ينصب عرشنا بقرب عرشه، وأن نقف إلى جنبه وقفة المثيل بجوار المثيل. نريد أن نكون متساويين في الواجبات والمسؤولية. بل إن واجباتنا ومسؤوليتنا يفوقان ما عليه من مسؤولية وواجب! فيا ترى متى يرضى الرجل بتقرير هذه الحقيقة؟

ما أطيب قولك، يا سيدتي الباحثة، إنك تشفقين على من يستحق الشفقة ومن لا يستحقها. الرجل من الذين يستحقون الشفقة لأنه لا يعرف أنه يستحقها، إنه باستعبادنا لمنتحر. ولو صرفنا النظر عن مستقبل الذرية وبحثنا في حياته الفردية لوجدنا أن ما من أحد يساعده على التخلص من الشوائب الشائنة، ويحثه على إنماء شخصيته الغنية المخصبة إلا نحن. كما أنه لا يهدينا إلى واجباتنا ويضع في ضعفنا قوة إلاه.

الحجاب؟ وما الحجاب؟ مرحباً به ما دمنا في وسط لا يعرف كيفية معاملة المرأة ولا يستطيع احترامها، ولكن كيف نلوم الرجل على كلامه ونظراته ما دام رجل اليوم صنع امرأة الأمس؟ هكذا علمته أمه وإن لم تعلمه ذلك فإنها لم ترشده إلى ما يفضله، ولا ذنب لها لأن قصورها في جهلها لم يكن إلا نتيجة اتفاق أبيها وزوجها على جعلها عبدة. لا لوم على أبناء تلك الأمهات. إلا أن مستقبلنا صالح لأن حاضرنا مملوء بالآمال الطيبات. النشء تتنازعه طبائع الوراثة ومؤثرات العصر وعواصف الفوضى المهاجمة قديم التقاليد من كل ناحية. ولكنه ينشد الصراط السوي ويصغي إلى صوت الإصلاح. فارفعي صوتك، يا سيدي، ولا تيأسي! قولي بصراحتك، واكتبي بشجاعتك! جاهري ولا تصمتي! إن البذرة التي تزرعها اليوم يد زارع تنبت سنبلة في كيانها حياة

الغد، وما يتبعه من الأيام. وعندما تخضرّ المروج بنصرة الرجاء، فتتماوج فوق غلتها نسمات الحياة، إذ ذاك سيسمع المستقبل صدى جيل يردد أبيات الأمير شوقي:

صداح يا ملك الكنا   رويا أمير البلبل
صبراً لما تشقى به   أو ما بدا لك فافعل

فتجيب الأصداء الجديدة: لقد فعلت! لقد فعلت!

«مي»

NOTES ON CONTRIBUTORS

Muhsin al-Musawi is professor of Arabic literature at Columbia University. He is the author of *The Postcolonial Arabic Novel: Debating Ambivalence* (2003), *Arabic Poetry: Trajectories of Modernity and Tradition* (2006), *Islam in the Street: The Dynamics of Arabic Literary Production* (2009), and *The Medieval Islamic Republic of Letters: Arabic Knowledge Construction* (2015).

John Baskerville received his PhD in Arabic studies from the University of Texas, Austin. His research interest is Arabic sociolingusitics, with a focus on the role of colloquial Arabic in *Nahda*-era projects aimed at modernizing the Egyptian nation and civilizing the Egyptian masses.

Marilyn Booth holds the Khalid bin Abdallah Al Saud Chair in the Study of the Contemporary Arab World, Oriental Institute and Magdalen College, Oxford University. She is the author of *Classes of Ladies of Cloistered Spaces: Writing Feminist History in Fin-de-Siècle Egypt* (2015), the editor of *Harem Histories: Envisioning Places and Living Spaces* (2010), and the coeditor of *The Long 1890s in Egypt: Colonial Quiescence, Subterranean Resistance* (2014).

Kristen Brustad is associate professor of Arabic studies at the University of Texas, Austin. Her research interests are Arabic dialects, syntax, language ideology, and Arabic literary and linguistic history. She is the author of *The Syntax of Spoken Arabic* (2000) and coauthor of the *Al-Kitaab* Arabic-language book series.

miriam cooke is Braxton Craven Professor of Arab Cultures at Duke University. She is the author of *Anatomy of an Egyptian Intellectual: Yahya Haqqi* (1984), *Women Claim Islam: Creating Islamic Feminism through Literature* (2001), *Nazira Zeineddine: A Pioneer of Islamic Feminism* (2010), and *Dancing in Damascus: Creativity, Resilience, and the Syrian Revolution* (2017).

Yoav Di-Capua is associate professor of history at the University of Texas, Austin. His research interest is modern Arab intellectual history. He is the author of *Gatekeepers of the Arab Past: Historians and History Writing in Twentieth-Century Egypt* (2009) and *No Exit: Arab Existentialism, Jean-Paul Sartre, and Decolonization* (2017).

Anthony Edwards is assistant professor of Arabic at Washington and Lee University. He is currently finishing a book that investigates the role of Beiruti learned societies in crafting Modern Standard Arabic in the early *Nahda*.

Tarek El-Ariss is associate professor of Middle Eastern studies at Dartmouth College. He is the author of *Trials of Arab Modernity: Literary Affects and the New Political* (2013) and *Hacks, Leaks, and Scandals: Arab Culture in the Digital Age* (2018).

Ziad Fahmy is associate professor of modern Middle East history at Cornell University. He is the author of *Ordinary Egyptians: Creating the Modern Nation through Popular Culture* (2011) and is writing a book tentatively titled "Listening to the Street: Sound, Noise, and Soundscapes in Twentieth-Century Egypt, 1900–1950."

Angela Giordani is a PhD candidate in the History Department and Institute for Comparative Literature and Society at Columbia University. She is currently writing a dissertation on the production of Islamic philosophy as a textual tradition and scholarly field in twentieth-century Egypt. She is also the translator of the essay collection *Mehdi Amel: Theorizing Marxism from the Periphery: Selected Works* (forthcoming).

William Granara is Professor of the Practice of Arabic on the Gordon Gray Endowment at Harvard University. He is the author of "Ibn Hamdis and the Poetics of Exile" (1998) and the translator of *The Earthquake*, by Tahir Watter (2000).

Zeina G. Halabi is assistant professor in the Department of Arabic and Near Eastern Languages at the American University of Beirut. She is the author of *The Unmaking of the Arab Intellectual: Prophecy, Exile, and the Nation* (2017) and is working on a book provisionally entitled "Excavating the Present: History, Power, and the Arab Archive."

Ghenwa Hayek is assistant professor of modern Arabic literature at the University of Chicago. She is the author of *Beirut, Imagining the City: Space and Place in Lebanese Literature* (2014) and a translator from Arabic.

Elizabeth M. Holt is associate professor of Arabic at Bard College. She is the author of *Fictitious Capital: Silk, Cotton, and the Rise of the Arabic Novel* (2017) and is writing a new book on Arabic literature in the Cold War.

Boutheina Khaldi is associate professor of Arabic and comparative literature at the American University of Sharjah. She is the author of *Egypt Awakening in the Early Twentieth Century: Mayy Ziyadah's Intellectual Circles* (2012) and *Al-Mudmar fil-Tarassul al-Niswi al-'Arabi* (2015) and the coeditor of three textbooks: *Al-Adab al-'Arabi al-Hadith: Mukhtarat* (2010), *Al-Wafi fi Turath al-'Arab al-Thaqafi* (2010), and *Turath al-'Arab al-Ma'rifi* (2010).

Benjamin Koerber is assistant professor in the Department of African, Middle Eastern, and South Asian Languages and Literatures at Rutgers University. He is the author of *Conspiracy in*

Modern Egyptian Literature (2018) and the translator of Ahmed Naje and Ayman Zorkany's novel *Using Life* (2017).

Lital Levy is associate professor of Arabic literature at Princeton University. She is the author of *Poetic Trespass: Writing between Hebrew and Arabic in Israel/Palestine* (2014) and is working on a book provisionally titled "Partitioned Pasts: Jewish Writers in the Arab East."

Margaret Litvin is associate professor of Arabic and comparative literature at Boston University. She is the author of *Hamlet's Arab Journey: Shakespeare's Prince and Nasser's Ghost* (2011) and has translated Sonallah Ibrahim's 2011 novel *al-Jalid* ("Ice," forthcoming).

Yaseen Noorani is associate professor of Arabic-Persian language and literature at the University of Arizona. He is the author of *Culture and Hegemony in the Colonial Middle East* (2010) and the coeditor of *Counterhegemony in the Colony and Postcolony* (2007).

Kamran Rastegar is associate professor of Arabic and comparative literature at Tufts University. He is the author of *Literary Modernity between Europe and the Middle East: Transactions in Nineteenth-Century Arabic, Persian, and English Literatures* (2007) and *Surviving Images: Cinema, War, and Cultural Memory in the Middle East* (2015).

Spencer Scoville is assistant professor of Arabic at Brigham Young University. His research interests include translation in modern Arabic literature and the roles that graduates of the Russian schools played in Palestinian culture and politics. He has published a number of literary and scholarly translations from Russian and Arabic.

Stephen Sheehi is the Sultan Qaboos bin Said Professor of Middle East Studies at William and Mary. He is the author of *Foundations of Modern Arab Identity* (2004), *The Arab Imago:*

A Social History of Indigenous Photography, 1860-1910 (2016), and *Islamophobia: The Ideological Campaign against Muslims* (2011).

Lior Sternfeld is assistant professor of history and Jewish studies at the Pennsylvania State University. His research interests are histories of modern Iran and the Middle East, Jewish histories of the Middle East, and social movements in the Middle East. He is working on a book tentatively titled "Integrated after All: Iranian Jews in the Twentieth Century."

Shaden M. Tageldin is associate professor of cultural studies and comparative literature and director of the African Studies Initiative at the University of Minnesota. She is the author of *Disarming Words: Empire and the Seductions of Translation in Egypt* (2011). She is completing a book provisionally titled "Toward a Transcontinental Theory of Modern Comparative Literature."

Anna Ziajka Stanton is assistant professor of comparative literature at the Pennsylvania State University. She is the author of "A Whole Imaginary World: The Incomparable Fiction of Waguih Ghali" in the *Journal of Arabic Literature* (2015) and the translator of the novel *Limbo Beirut*, by Hilal Chouman (2016). She is working on a book about translation in the Arabic-English context since the nineteenth century.